Winner of the Historical Mystery Appreciation Society's Herodotus
Award for Best First U.S. Historical Mystery of the Year

A *Booklist* Top Ten Crime Novel of the Year

A *Jewish World Review* Top Ten Book of the Year

#1 Kabbalah title—Amazon.com

Named by Rome's *La Republica* newspaper
"The Literary Highlight of the Year"

A *St. Louis Post-Dispatch* Notable Book of the Year

A Barnes & Noble Top 100 Book

# Praise for The Last Kabbalist of Lisbon

"An ingenious debut. . . in its authentic evocation of Lisbon's clandestine Jewish community, its aura of constant menace and its startling, beautiful imagery steeped in Jewish mysticism, this exotic story is memorable and haunting.." —*Publishers Weekly*

"One of the more unusual and interesting first novels of recent vintage."
—*Kirkus Reviews*

"The novel's suspenseful twists are full of both shadow and luminosity—and are as intricate as the miniature paintings and designs of manuscript illumination."
—*New York Jewish Week*

"*The Last Kabbalist of Lisbon* is a period novel and a captivating mystery, a story of Jewish struggle and a crash course in the nuances and details blurred by words that can't encompass the persecution, forced conversion, clandestine worship, expulsion, flight and renewal that marked the Sephardic passage." —*Haddassah Magazine*

"Those who understand and appreciate the history of Kabbalah can revel in the mysticism; the uninitiated will gain perspective while enjoying a literary and historical treat."
—*Library Journal*

"Richard Zimler is a present-day scholar and writer of remarkable erudition and compelling imagination, an American Umberto Eco." —*Francis King, The Spectator*

"A riveting literary murder mystery, his novel is also a harrowing picture of the persecution of 16th-century Jews and, in passing, an atmospheric introduction to the hermetic Jewish tradition of the Kabbalah." —*The Independent*

"Historical accuracy, the structure of a mystery, the pace of a thriller...A fascinating novel with a spellbinding subject matter." —*Portuguese Elle*

"An intense and passionate account, an intricate novel with an undeniable touch of *The Name of the Rose*." —*O Independente*, Lisbon

"A tapestry of unforgettable images...absolutely unique." —*Jornal de Notícias*, Porto

"A superbly structured book...which can be read on different levels like a true kabbalistic text. Light-years from the usual bestselling novel with an esoteric theme."
—*A Tribuna*, Brazil

"A unique mixture of historical novel and thriller, telling a tale of intolerance and of the deeper significance of death, crime and violence." —*Diário de Notícias*, Lisbon

# The
# Last Kabbalist
# of Lisbon

## RICHARD ZIMLER

THE OVERLOOK PRESS
WOODSTOCK & NEW YORK

First published in paperback in the United States in 2000 by
The Overlook Press, Peter Mayer Publishers, Inc.
Woodstock & New York

WOODSTOCK:
One Overlook Drive
Woodstock, NY 12498
www.overlookpress.com
[for individual orders, bulk and special sales, contact our Woodstock office]

NEW YORK:
141 Wooster Street
New York, NY 10012

Library of Congress Cataloging-in-Publication Data

Zimler, Richard.
The last kabbalist of Lisbon : Richard Zimler.
p. cm.
1. Jews—Persecutions—Portugal—Lisbon—History—18th century—Fiction.
2. Lisbon (Portugal)—History—Fiction. I. Title.
PS3576.I464L37 1998 813'.54dc21 97-46184

BOOK DESIGN AND TYPE FORMATTING BY BERNARD SCHLEIFER

Manufactured in the United States of America
7 9 8 6
ISBN 1-58567-022-7 pbk

*For Alexandre Quintanilha*


*Thanks to Ruth Zimler,
Tracy Carns, Cynthia Cannell,
Joanne Gruber
and Quetzal Editores of Lisbon*

# Historical Note

In December of 1496, four years after Ferdinand and Isabella of Spain expelled all the Jews from their kingdom, King Manuel of Portugal was convinced to do the same. In exchange, he was to receive from the Spanish monarchs the hand of their daughter in marriage. Just before the expulsion order was to take effect, however, King Manuel decided to convert the Portuguese Jews rather than lose such valuable citizens. In March of 1497, he closed all ports of disembarkation and ordered the Jews rounded up and dragged to the baptism font. Although accounts have reached us of some Jews who committed suicide and murdered their children rather than become Christians, most did indeed agree under coercion to accept Jesus as the Messiah. Called New Christians, they were given twenty years to lose their traditional Jewish customs, a promise which proved hollow over the next two decades of prejudice and imprisonment. Even so, many of the New Christians persisted in their beliefs. In secret and at great risk, they said their Hebrew prayers and practiced their rituals, in particular those related to the observance of the Sabbath and the celebration of Jewish holidays. One such secret Jew was Berekiah Zarco, the narrator of *The Last Kabbalist of Lisbon*.

# The
# Last Kabbalist
# of Lisbon

# Author's Note
# The Discovery of Berekiah
# Zarco's Manuscript

Abraham Vital, a lawyer in private practice in Istanbul, makes a living petitioning the Turkish government to win benefits for persons who, because of injury or illness, can no longer work. In 1981, he waged a successful legal battle on behalf of a fifty-nine year old carpenter named Ayaz Lugo whose right arm and hand were paralyzed in a car crash.

Lugo died in June of 1988. His wife had already passed away six years earlier. They were childless. In his will, a grateful Lugo left Abraham Vital his home.

I was to stay in Lugo's house during the seven-month sojourn I spent in Istanbul in 1990 researching Sephardic poetry, in particular, the ballad form. It was graciously offered to me rent-free by Abraham Vital; he and I became acquainted through a mutual friend, my thesis advisor Dr. Isaac Silva Rosa, formerly of U.C. Berkeley and now of the University of Porto in Portugal.

Both Vital and Lugo are Sephardim, descendents of the waves of Jews who fled persecution in Spain and Portugal in the 15th, 16th, 17th and 18th centuries. Their ancestors had been offered exile in Istanbul—then known by Christians and Jews as Constantinople—as early as 1492. In that year, Turkish Sultan Bejazet II welcomed to his kingdom thousands of Sephardic Jews who were complying with an expulsion order issued by King Ferdinand and Queen Isabella of Spain.

On a stifling day in early May, Vital drove me to Ayaz Lugo's ancient home at the fringes of Istanbul's medieval Jewish Quarter, the Balat. Two stories of stone and flaking stucco rose up like an abandoned watchtower between a bakery and record store.

I moved in on May 9, 1990. Inside, everything appeared gray-brown, as if in a sepia photograph, until I started removing the dust.

I could touch the sagging ceilings of both floors of the house without standing on my toes. Cones of light filtered in to my bedroom through oval, platter-size windows. The furniture was of heavy, time-worn wood, pieces evidently purchased when Lugo was a boy; now all antiques.

In my bedroom closet I found thousands of sugar cubes neatly stacked in leather suitcases. Apparently, it had been scarce during World War II. Were the cubes already packed away in case Lugo had to make a quick exit? *Maybe Jews should always have at least one suitcase prepared,* I thought.

In a worm-eaten dresser, under cotton underwear, I found rancid Turkish chocolate bars. I was pleased; Lugo and I undoubtedly shared a sweet tooth.

My bed was an iron frame with a squashed mattress manufactured in Konya. The script of the tag was in Arabic, making it about seventy years old; in the 1920s, the Latin alphabet replaced the Arabic one throughout Turkey.

The house had no shower. One sink gave a thin stream of cold brown water that smelled of chlorine and rust. Lugo and his wife must have gone to the baths.

I had many companion mice. But miraculously, there were no ants and no bedbugs.

That July, Abraham Vital decided to begin bringing the house up to 20th-century, Western standards. Remodeling began with the cellar so that I wouldn't be too disturbed.

On July 18, workmen came across a secret lair, two-feet deep and four-feet square, which had been covered with wood planks and a cement casing. Inside this hiding place sat a *tik,* the small cylindrical chest used by Sephardic Jews to house the Torah, the first five books of the Old Testament. Decorated with elaborate silver filigree and enamel peacocks, it was found to contain not a Torah, but a leather-bound set of handwritten manuscripts, nine in all.

The manuscripts were in the square, Hebrew script typical of Iberia, the language largely Jewish-Portuguese—an old Portuguese written in Hebrew characters. Portions of the early works, however, were in medieval Hebrew itself. The writing was done with a calamus, the reed pen used in Iberia. The paper was in excellent condition.

All but three of the manuscripts bore polished vellum covers on which a title is illuminated with bird-headed letters. Hoopoes, owls, thrushes, European goldfinches and peacocks predominate. One species of hummingbird (remarkably, a New World family of birds) is also pictured. Lacy, intricate geometrical patterns and arabesques form the backgrounds to titles. Gold leaf is used liberally. A bright carmine and the blue of lapis lazuli are the dominant colors.

I found that all of the manuscripts were signed in a careful script in the form of an Egyptian ibis by a man named Berekiah Zarco. From the dates penned next to his signatures and references in the text, we know that they were written over the course of twenty-three years, from 5267 to 5290 in the Hebrew calendar—1507 to 1530 CE.

On the night of July 18, 1990, I began reading his work.

What I found were six treatises on various aspects of the kabbalah, the mystical philosophy which radiated out into the Jewish diaspora from Provence in the early Middle Ages and which has been passed down in subsequent centuries both orally and in texts. The most well known of these kabbalistic texts are the Bahir and the Zohar.

Three of Berekiah's manuscripts—those without title pages—were of a secular nature, however. Bound together by a leather strap, the first dated from 1507 and the last two from 1530. Right from my first inspection, it was evident that they concerned the Lisbon massacre of April 1506. Some two thousand New Christians—Jews forcibly converted to Christianity in 1497—lost their lives in that riot, many burned in the Rossio, the square that still centers the Portuguese capital.

Unfortunately, numerous sections and even single pages of Berekiah's manuscripts had been reassembled out of order by someone undoubtedly unable to read Jewish-Portuguese. It was maddening. Two months of rearranging were involved. Once back in order, however, Berekiah Zarco's work read smoothly.

The three historical manuscripts taken together form a single work telling the story of Berekiah's family during the tragic events of April 1506. In particular, they recount Berekiah's search for the killer of his beloved Uncle Abraham, a renowned kabbalist who is likely responsible for some of the hitherto unattributed works of the Lisbon School, including—for reasons that become clear in the story—*Knocking on Doors* and the *Book of Divine Fruit*.

Several other, more cursory accounts of the pogrom have reached us (including the one by Solomon Ibn Verga mentioned by Berekiah), and there can be no doubt about the historical veracity of Berekiah's story. All of the major events of his tale are confirmed by contemporaneous accounts. Many of the people mentioned, including Didi Molcho, Dom João Mascarenhas and Isaac Ibn Farraj are known to us through their writings as well as through documentation from the Church and the Portuguese Crown.

Some readers unfamiliar with Sephardic and New Christian literature of the 16th Century may have difficulty with my rendering of Berekiah's story in the form of a mystery and the use of colloquial language. Berekiah Zarco is, however, like many of his contemporaries, a modern author in outlook and style. The second manuscript in particular reveals a straightforward technique resembling that of the Spanish picaresque novel, the earliest of which were published a short time after Berekiah completed his work. Interestingly, many of the Spanish picaresque authors were converted Jews as well.

Unlike the picaresque novels, however, Berekiah's tone is hardly ever ironic and never slapstick. In addition, his central character—himself—is neither a rogue nor a hero. He is simply what Berekiah Zarco must have been: a intelligent and confused young manuscript illuminator, fruit seller and kabbalist; a young man devastated by the murder of his uncle.

Berekiah's frank language includes the use of swear words, openly blasphemous statements and even slang—all of which I have tried to retain.

Clearly, if Berekiah had intended to write yet another mystical tract or even staid historical text, he would have. He had the talent and the knowledge. The fact is, he didn't. He wrote a mystery in three parts, the last of which contemporary critics might call an afterword. For the modern reader, I have spaced these three parts over twenty chapters. Chapters I through VIII correspond to the first of Berekiah's manuscripts; IX through XX, the second; and XXI, the third.

Although *The Last Kabbalist of Lisbon* is more than a translation, I have stayed rigorously faithful to the content of Berekiah's writing except in two areas: where he includes extended prayer recitations and chants; and where he digresses to substantiate arcane spiritual points relating to kabbalah. Although of scholarly interest, these would probably prove troublesome and boring to the reader, and I have largely excluded them from my rendering. Also, several sections have been re-arranged into chronological order which originally were linked by the spiritual point Berekiah was trying to make. I believe that this, too, has not altered Berekiah's work in any fundamental way, and my revised structure will certainly make more sense to the modern reader.

In general, I have tried to strike a balance between contemporary language and the occasional use of an antiquated word or phrase. The entire work is, I hope, faithful to the spirit of the author.

Berekiah is not completely consistent in his Portuguese spelling, perhaps because of the trouble of transliterating the language of his homeland into Hebrew characters. When Portuguese is quoted, it is therefore done with modern spellings.

Where Hebrew words are retained, they are written using Latin characters so that they can be pronounced by American and European readers.

Berekiah's manuscripts do raise some interesting questions about the history of Hebrew books in Iberia. Is the illustrated Torah which he discovers in his Uncle's *genizah* the so-called Kennicott Bible now belonging to the Bodleian Library of Oxford University? His reference to letters forming beasts and to Isaac Bracarense (undoubtedly the Isaac de Braga for whom the manuscript was illustrated) would seem to point in that direction. Nothing is known of the Bible's history from its 1476 completion date until its acquisition in 1771 by Oxford at the suggestion of the librarian, Dr. Kennicott. Perhaps it was indeed saved by Abraham and Berekiah Zarco.

As to the Hebrew and Arabic version of the *Fountain of Life* kept by Father Carlos, was it truly smuggled to Salonika? What, then, happened to it?; no Arabic original has ever been found, only Latin translations.

*The Last Kabbalist of Lisbon* is itself something of a puzzle. Why was it hidden away in Ayaz Lugo's cellar? How come there is no mention of it in contemporaneous Jewish manuscripts? Was it never published? Surely, given his stated purpose of alerting New Christians and Jews to the continuing danger they faced in Europe, Berekiah would have tried to give his writings the widest possible dissemination.

Several theories were offered to me by Professor Ruth Pinhel of the University of Paris which were later echoed by most of the other experts in the field of medieval Sephardic literature with whom I consulted.

Firstly, Berekiah's disparaging characterizations of Old Christians and his open call for Jews and New Christians to abandon Europe would certainly have angered the European kings and religious authorities, particularly the Inquisitors of Portugal and Spain. Had he brought his work into Christian Europe, any copies discovered would have been suppressed and burned.

It is also probable that his passionate plea for Jewish emigration would have enraged the leaders of the region's fragile Jewish communities, whether secret Sephardic groupings in Portugal and Spain or more open communities in the Ashkenazic lands of northern Europe. Those Jews or New Christians who had a spiritual, emotional or monetary stake in remaining in Europe might have suppressed his writings as well.

In addition, Berekiah's treatment of such topics as sex and the schism between kabbalists and rabbinical authorities may simply have been too forthright to endear him to certain readers. His writings would certainly have been taboo to many conservative Jewish leaders trying to resist the coming age of the secular Jew.

Although I have my doubts, another theory should be mentioned: it is possible that Berekiah himself suppressed his writings; not only might he not have wanted to expose secret Jews mentioned in the text, but excommunication for so-called heresy was not unknown. Despite his passionate need to warn the Jews of Europe of the fate foreseen by his uncle, he may have feared being cut off from his community, as was another Jew of Portuguese extraction a century later, Baruch Spinoza. Perhaps he circulated copies of his book in secret, imploring his readers not to divulge its contents or even mention its existence. Maybe that is why it bears no title.

One other, more disheartening possibility: Berekiah might very well have been killed trying to re-enter Portugal and save his cousin Reza. Any copies of his writings which he scripted and transported to Iberia would have undoubtedly perished with him. Only the works hidden back home in Constantinople would have survived.

As to their hiding place, very possibly all the manuscripts were sealed up to protect them during the Nazi period; the cement casing dates from this era. It must be remembered that Portuguese New Christians did indeed emigrate in mass numbers during the 16th, 17th and 18th centuries, primarily to Turkey, Greece, North Africa, the Netherlands and Italy, areas later threatened or overrun by the German Reich. For instance, as a result of New Christian emigration, by the end of the 16th century, Constantinople alone boasted a Jewish community of 30,000 persons and 54 synagogues—the largest in Europe.

During World War II, most of the Iberian Jews living in Greece, Yugoslavia and the rest of southeastern Europe, 200,000 or more, were arrested and gassed. In view of Berekiah's plea for the Jews and New Christians to leave

Christian lands, it is interesting to note that the Jewish community in Moslem Turkey was protected by the government and wholly escaped destruction. Even so, the owner or owners of Berekiah's manuscripts, perhaps Lugo's parents, would have rightly feared the spread of killing to Turkey, just as Berekiah feared the spread of the Inquisition from Castile to Portugal four hundred years earlier (the Inquisition was definitively established in Portugal in 1536, some 50 years after it began in Spain and just six years after the last of Berekiah's manuscripts was completed).

Did Ayaz Lugo know of the existence of the manuscripts? He makes no reference to them in his will. Possibly, they were hidden by his parents without his knowing it.

Thanks must first go to Abraham Vital, who generously offered me his home and, subsequently, his permission to work on Berekiah Zarco's texts. I wish to express my appreciation, too, to his wife, Miriam Rosencrantz-Vital, who got me through many a late night with her Port wine and home-cooked couscous.

Thanks, too, to Isaac Silva Rosa, for encouraging me to take time off from my dissertation to work on this manuscript; Ruth Pinhel for her help with historical references; Ari Diaz-Lev and Carl Konstein for helping with Hebrew translations; and Joseph Amaro Marcus, an expert in Spanish and Portuguese kabbalah, for deciphering the undecipherable.

This book is published in the memory of Berekiah Zarco, his family and friends.

# Preface

Grief was pressing hard at the tip of my reed pen when I first began recording our story. It was the Hebrew year of fifty-two sixty-seven, the Christian year of fifteen and seven.

Selfishly, I abandoned my narrative when God would not grace my soul with relief.

Today, twenty-three years after this feeble attempt to record my search for vengeance, I have again caressed open the pages of my manuscript. Why have I broken the bonds of silence?

Yesterday, around midday, there was a knock at the front door to our home here in Constantinople. I was the lone member of my family in the house and went to see who it was. A short young man with long black hair and dark, tired eyes, swathed in a handsome Iberian cloak of scarlet and green stripes, stood on our stoop. In clipped, hesitant tones, he asked in Portuguese, "Do I have the honor of addressing Master Berekiah Zarco?"

"Yes, my boy," I answered. "Pray tell who you might be."

Bowing humbly, he replied, "Lourenço Paiva. I have just come from Lisbon and was hoping to find you."

As I whispered his name to myself, I remembered him as the youngest son of an old friend, the Christian laundress to whom we'd given our house in Lisbon just before our flight from that benighted city more than two decades before. I waved away his continuing introduction as unnecessary and shepherded him into our kitchen. We sat at benches by a window giving out on a circle of lavender and myrtle bushes in our garden. When I enquired about his mother, I was saddened to hear that she had recently been called to God. In somber but proud tones, he eulogized her for a time. Afterward, it was a delight to share a small carafe of Anatolian wine, to talk of his sea voyage from Portugal and his first, astonished impressions of the Turkish capital. My ease left me unprepared for what was to follow, however; when I asked him why I'd been granted the pleasure of his visit, he pulled from his cloak two iron keys dangling from a silver chain. Immediately, a shiver of dread snaked up my spine. Before I could speak, he showed me the eager smile of a youth presenting a gift to an elder and pressed the keys into my hand. He said, "Should you desire to return, Master Berekiah, your house in Lisbon awaits you."

I reached out to his arm to steady myself; my heart was drumming the single word *homeland.* As the teeth of the keys began biting into the fist I had formed around them, I caressed open my fingers and leaned down to sniff the old-coin scent of the metal. Memories of serpentine streets and olive trees swept me to my feet. The hairs of my arms and neck stood on end. A door opened inside me, and a vision entered: I was standing just outside the iron gate to the courtyard at the back of our old home in the Alfama district of Lisbon. Framed inside the gate's arch and standing at the center of the courtyard was Uncle Abraham, my spiritual master. Draped in his vermilion travel robe of English wool, he was picking lemons from our tree, humming contentedly to himself. His dark skin, the color of cinnamon, was lit gold, as if by the light which heralds sunset, and his wild crest of silver hair and tufted eyebrows shimmered with magical potential. Sensing my presence, he ceased his melody, turned with a smile of welcome and shuffled closer to me with the duck-like walk he normally only adopted in synagogues. His warm green eyes, opened wide, seemed to embrace me. With an amused twist to his lips, he began undoing the purple sash to his robe as he walked, let the garment slip away onto the slate paving stones of the courtyard. Underneath, he was naked except for a prayer shawl over his shoulders. As he continued to approach me, rays of light began issuing forth from his body. So bright became his form that my eyes began to tear. When a first drop slipped salty into the corner of my mouth, he stopped and called to me using my older brother's name: "Mordecai! So you have finally heeded my prayers!" His face was framed now by an aura of white flame. With a solemn nod, as if he were passing on a verse of ancient wisdom, he tossed me a lemon. I caught it. Yet when I looked down upon the fruit, I found instead tarnished Portuguese letters knotted into a chain. They read: *as nossas andorinhas ainda estão nas mãos do faraó*—our swallows are still abandoned to Pharaoh. As my gaze passed over these words of New Christian code a second time, they lifted into the air, then broke with a tinkling sound.

I found myself looking once again upon the keys. Warm tears were clouding my eyesight. The door upon my vision had closed.

Lourenço was gripping my shoulders, his face pale and panicked. Reassuring words somehow found their way to my lips.

To understand the revelation which then came to me, the Hebrew words *mesirat nefesh* must be explained. They mean, of course, the willingness to sacrifice oneself. And their occult power resides in the tradition among some kabbalists to risk even a journey to hell for a goal which will not only help to heal our ailing world but also effect reparations inside God's Upper Realms.

With the keys throbbing in my hand, I began to understand for the first time the sacrifice Uncle Abraham had made, how the concept of *mesirat nefesh* had given his heartbeat its passionate but fragile rhythm. And for reasons that will become clear in the telling of our tale, I saw, too, that my vision had been a summons from him to return to Portugal in order to fulfill the destiny he'd prepared for me long ago—a destiny I'd not followed, never before even understood.

I began to see, as well, that in returning to Lisbon I would have the chance to make up for my deviation from destiny, to live up to *my* pledge of *mesirat nefesh*. For the journey back will surely put my life at risk. With Spain in the grip of the Inquisition and Portugal drawing ever closer to its flames, my return may well mean that my time with my wife, Letiça, and children, Zuli and Ari, has come to an end.

So it is with them in mind that I have again picked up my pen. I would like for each member of my family to read of my reasons for leaving; and of the events of twenty-four years ago which forced these reasons into my heart. The story of the murder which darkened our lives forever and my hunt for the mysterious killer is too long and complex to be heard from my lips. And I would not wish to risk leaving anything unsaid.

I write, too, in order to clear the cold air of secrecy from our home, so that Zuli and Ari may finally understand my vague responses when, as children and adolescents, they asked of the events which preceded my escape from Lisbon. It has not been easy for them having a father with a past clothed in sordid speculation by many in our immigrant Jewish community. With tears in their eyes and their hands balled into white-knuckled fists, they have heard me called a murderer and heretic. How many times, too, has my wife suffered rumors that I was seduced in Lisbon by Lilith in the guise of a Castilian noblewoman, that even today this demoness owns my heart?

A murderer, yes. I admit to having slain one man and contracted to end the life of another. My children will read of the circumstances and form their own judgments. They are old enough now to know everything. A heretic, I think not. But if I am, then it was the events which I will shortly describe that forced the arrows of heresy into my flesh. As for my heart, I leave it for my loved ones to name its governess. May truth emerge from these pages without fear, like the trumpeting call of a shofar welcoming Rosh Hashanah. And may I, too, finally free myself of my last delusions and from the vestiges of the mask I donned to hide my Judaism as a boy. Yes, I expect to learn much about myself as my pen follows my remembrances; when memory is allowed free reign to probe the past, does it not always gift us with self-knowledge?

Of course, guilt for my ignorance and failings—and for my more terrible sins—has accompanied me into exile in Constantinople, clings to me even now. Some would say it is even the deepest of my motivations. Yet as I gift Hebrew letters onto this polished sheepskin, I realize that I am most inspired by the chance to speak across a span of decades to still others as yet unnamed—my unborn grandchildren and those of my sister, Cinfa. To all our descendents, I say: read this story and you will know why your ancestors left Portugal; the great sacrifice my master made for you; what happened to the Jews of Lisbon when this century possessed but six Christian years. To ensure your survival, these are events to which your memories should cling like orphaned children.

Most importantly, if you follow the melody and rhythm of these words toward their final cadence, you will learn why you should never set foot in Christian Europe.

So make no mistake, under the surface of this story lies the razor edges of a tale of warning. I am convinced that it is your safety which prompted Uncle Abraham to appear to me and summon me to Portugal. Were I not to write, were memory to end in tepid silence, I might have your deaths on my hands as well.

As for the weave of the mystery which I will unfurl for you, my enemies would say that it is sure to include intricate arabesques out of a desire to conceal the blood staining my own hands. The evidence will point in the other direction. Uncle Abraham has gifted me with this chance to live fully as myself, and I will not disappoint him again. So if you find complication—even contradiction—amongst the twill of my more modest phrases it is because I wish for you to see the events as they truly occurred, to see me as I am. For a Jew is never the simple creature the Christians have always wanted us to believe. And a Jewish heretic is never so single-minded as our rabbis would claim. We are all of us deep and wide enough to welcome a river of paradoxes and riddles into our souls.

There is a last confession which I must now make: I have no idea why Uncle Abraham called me by my elder brother Mordecai's name in my vision, and I find my ignorance disquieting. It is as if there is some deeper significance to my master's appearance, an inner layer of meaning to the deaths of twenty-four years ago, which I still cannot grasp. Why, for instance, has my uncle shown himself to me only now? Clearly, I need more time to consider this matter. And yet, perhaps he meant for the light of understanding to penetrate my darkness as I record our story. Will I come to comprehend the subtler connections between the past and present only when my manuscript nears its end? The possibility makes me smile, calms my doubts a little; it would be just like my uncle to demand a day and night of earthly work before presenting me with the last core of his heavenly meaning! And so, I continue forward...

When I first considered tracing our tribulations across a page of manuscript, my family and I were hiding in our cellar. The mystery had just opened before me in all its complexity. It is there where I began my story twenty-three years ago. And it is there where we will start again.

Of three events we shall speak before we come to the murder which changed our lives: the passing of the flagellants; an injury to a dear friend; and the arrest of a family member. Had I understood the meaning of these portents, had I read them as verses of a single poem scripted by the Angel of Death, I could have saved many lives. But ignorance betrayed me. Perhaps, as you follow my words across these pages, you will fare better. May you be blessed with clear vision.

So sit yourself in a quiet room graced with a circle of fragrant bushes or flowers. Face east, toward beloved Jerusalem. Untie your knots of mind with chant. And let a soft candlelight shadow these pages as you turn them.

*Bruheem kol demuyay eloha!* Blessed are all God's self-portraits.

Berekiah  Zarco, Constantinople
Sixth of Av, 5290 (1530 CE)

# BOOK ONE

## Chapter I

When I was eight, in the Christian year of fourteen ninety-four, I read about the sacred ibises who helped Moses cross an Ethiopian swamp riddled with snakes. I drew a scythe-beaked creature in scarlet and black with my Uncle Abraham's dyes and inks. He held it up for inspection. "Silver eyes?" he questioned.

"Reflecting Moses, how could they be any other color?"

Uncle kissed my brow. "From this day on, you will be my apprentice. I will help you change thorns to roses, and I swear to protect you from the dangers which dance along the way. The pages that are doors will open to our touch."

How could I have known that I would one day fail him so completely?

Imagine being outside time. That the past and future are revolving around you, and you cannot place yourself properly. That your body, your receptacle, has been numbed free of history. Because I feel this way, I can see clearly when and where the evil started: four days ago, on the twenty-second of Nisan; in our Judiaria Pequena, the Little Jewish Quarter of the Alfama district of Lisbon.

It was a jeweled morning much like any of the opal beads on the necklace of that spring month. The year was fifty-two sixty-six for the New Christians. April the sixteenth of fifteen and six for the accursed Christians of heart.

From the darkness of early Wednesday morning, hiding here in the cellar, I remember the dawn of Friday as if its sunlight heralded the first notes of an insane fugue.

*Concealed behind one of these notes of melody, camouflaged in memory, is the face I seek.*

The day of our first Passover seder began dim and dry, like all the dawns of late. We hadn't been blessed with rain in more than eleven weeks. And would have none today.

As for the plague, it had been sending shivers through our bodies and souls since the second week of Heshvan—more than seven months now.

King Manuel's half-made Christian doctors had resolved that cattle were perfect for soaking up the airborne essences which they blamed for the disease, and so two hundred dazed and overheated cows had been let loose to wander the streets.

Manuel himself had long fled our misery with most of the aristocracy. From Abrantes, three weeks earlier, he'd issued a decree establishing the construction of two new cemeteries outside the city walls for the scores who were taken to God each week.

The souls of the dead were beyond being encouraged by such a gesture, of course. And one could hardly blame the living for regarding the decree as simply one more indication of the King's ineffectual pragmatism and cowardice. Was it a turning point? Certainly, daily life began to take on an edge of cruel and despairing madness. In the last three days, I'd seen a collapsed donkey blinded with his master's dagger, his eyes spurting blood, and a girl of no more than five hurled shrieking from the rooftop of a four-story townhouse.

The poor, to dispel their hunger pangs, had taken to eating a mash of linen fibers and water.

I had just turned twenty years old. Proof that I was a little too devout for my own good was my belief that our city had been gifted generously with the stark significance of Torah. To me, there was a terrible, timeless beauty and horror to everything. Even the filthy feet of the recently deceased sticking out from the burlap of their sour-smelling plague carts possessed a sad and reverent grace. For they made our thoughts turn to Man's mortality and our covenant with God.

Only Uncle Abraham had the confidence to disregard completely the goat-ribbed preachers roaming the streets screeching that God had abandoned Portugal and that the end of the world was but five weeks away (though it could be postponed, they noted, if we were generous with our handouts of copper coinage). With an irritated frown, he had told me, "Don't you think that the Lord would show me a sign if He were about to close the last gate upon the Lower Realms?"

Father Carlos, a priest and family friend, could not yet be counted among those unfortunates who'd succumbed completely to the insanity gripping the city. But it seemed only a matter of days. "Drought and plague . . . they are the Devil's twin birth!" he told me in a conspirator's whisper as we stood in the archway of St. Peter's Church.

I had brought my little brother, Judah, to him that morning for religious instruction in the ways of Christianity. The three of us were watching a candlelight procession of flagellants whipping their backs with leather scourges whose ends trailed wax balls laced with filings of tin and splinters of colored glass. Behind them marched friars from Lisbon's monasteries unfurling blue and yellow pennons sewn with images of the Nazarene crucified. At the rear, proud-postured guildmen in flowing, silken fineries hoisted up litters bearing effigies of saints.

Crowds had gathered to watch, lined both sides of the street, formed two ragged ribbons against the dusty white façades of the townhouses as far as the cathedral. Shouts for water and mercy rang up like antiphonal choruses. All the variety of our town was there: horsemen and peasants, whores and nuns, beggars and black slaves—even blue-eyed sailors from the north.

Waifs and barking dogs suddenly began running past Father Carlos, Judah and me to the west to keep up with the moving spectacle. The priest closed his eyes, murmured nervous prayers. I inhaled deeply on the chilly perfume of danger in the air. *And tonight,* I thought, *into the unpredictable currents of this sea of madness, we will be launching the forbidden ship of Passover.* Yes, our celebrations should have started exactly one week earlier. But most of the secret Jews, including our family, had postponed Passover in the hopes of sailing safely through the tainted waters of Old Christian gossip around us.

A filthy, mop-haired woodcutter standing near us suddenly screamed at the top of his lungs, "For heavenly rain, we must have more blood! Lisbon must be the Venice of blood!

Judah pressed back against my legs, and I gripped his shoulder. Father Carlos rubbed his hands over his domed forehead, as if in defense. He was a corpulent man, squat, with soft, pale skin, a bulbous nose, webs of red veins on both his cheeks from too much drink. Few people took him seriously, but I found him a good friend. His droopy eyes settled on me. He said, "Men like nothing more than profaning the sacred, my boy."

I was suddenly laden with sadness for our fate. The scent of Indian pepper turned me around, and blood splattered across my pants and Judah's face. A shrieking initiate had pulled skin loose from his shoulder blade, was spraying spices over himself to capture the sting of God's love. In my brother's terrified eyes, I believed I recognized the look of a Hebrew child about to flee across the Red Sea. A fleeting premonition, unusual in its certainty, shook me: *We Jews of Lisbon have waited too long to re-enact the Exodus, and Pharaoh has learned of our escape plans.*

As I came to myself, Carlos hid his gaze in the wing of his cape, whisper-screamed, "That young initiate's moans...you can hear the wailing of the Devil's children in them!"

Judah was looking up at me with stunned, breathless curiosity. When tears caressed his eyes, I picked him up, wiped him, tousled the thick locks of his coal-black hair. He hugged his arms around my neck. "Thanks ever so much," I told Carlos. "Between you and these madmen, I think we've had all the religious instruction we need for today."

I lifted the woolen hood of Judah's mantle over his head and patted him as he sobbed and sniffled. After the last penitent had dragged himself past our former synagogue, Carlos led us across the square. At the corner was our house, a single story of whitewashed stucco whose rectangular perimeter was traced with a rim of deep blue. An affinity between colors lifted my gaze to the gauzy turquoise of the dawn sky, then down to the spine of the roof, a horizon of mottled fawn-colored tile pierced near its center by our chimney, a soot-blackened white cone notched with air-holes. From its point rose the tin silhouette of a troubadour pointing east, toward Jerusalem. Thin scarfs of smoke from our hearth were wafting around him and unraveling into the southerly breeze leading toward the river. "Just as well we cancel our lessons today," Carlos said as I pulled open the gate of iron tracery that served both our home and the house belonging to my beloved friend Farid and his father. "I've got some unhappy business I've been putting off with your uncle."

We stepped into the secret landscape of our courtyard. Enclosed by white façades and walls, paved with gray slate, it was centered by a venerable lemon tree circled by oleander bushes. Farid was standing on his stoop in his long underwear, barefoot, combing his hands back through the  black locks falling to his shoulders. To me, he had always seemed gifted with all the attributes of a warrior poet of the Arabian desert—a slim, muscular build, sharp green, hawklike eyes, soft olive skin and an agile, unpredictable intelligence. The stubble he always left on his cheeks made him look sleepy but seductive, and men and women alike were often captivated by his dark beauty. Now, he signalled good morning to me with a twist to the forceful hands he'd developed as a weaver of rugs. Though deaf and mute from birth, he'd never had the least difficulty making himself understood to me in this way; as toddlers, we'd developed a language of gestured signs, undoubtedly because we were born just two days apart and grew up holding hands.

Returning my friend's greeting, I led Father Carlos to the kitchen door, an ogival threshold exuberantly marked with a rim of green and rust mosaic stars. In a doubtful voice, he said, "Might as well get it over with."

Can a house possess a body, a soul?  Ours was bent and fatigued from centuries of rain and sun, but fiercely protective of its residents.

As manuscript illuminators, Uncle Abraham and I had often modeled biblical dwellings on our home. For its walls we applied a milky ceruse, and to approximate the low and sagging chestnut wood ceilings which creaked alarmingly during the rains of Av and Tishri, we applied the rich brown made from vinegar, silver filings, honey and alum. The sandy floor tiles which scratched one's feet were given a moderated vermillion obtained from a marriage of quicksilver and sulphur.

Cracked foundations sloped the floors toward Mother's tidy bedroom at the sunset side of the house, little more than a corridor but with the advantage of an entrance to Temple Street for her sewing clients. Facing sunrise was my aunt and uncle's cozy, light-filled chamber. Between the two were the kitchen, centered by the great oaken table around which our lives passed, and the bedroom I share with Judah and my little sister, Cinfa. Our fruit store, added on two centuries ago judging from the masonry, jutted out from this room toward Temple Street.

As Carlos and I stepped inside, he grimaced at the sour scent of fresh whitewash on the walls. While he and my little brother checked the cellar for Uncle, I went to my room to peer through its inner window into our store. Down the center aisle, beyond baskets of figs and dates, raisins and sultanas, bitter oranges, filberts and walnuts, all manner of fruit and nut then to be found in Portugal, were Cinfa and my mother, Mira, spooning olives from wooden barrels into ceramic bowls for display. I leaned in and called out, "Blessed be He who has illuminated our Lisbon morning!"

Cinfa showed me a quick smile. A gangly, wild sort of girl, with a voice forever seemingly squeaked between knuckles jammed into her mouth, she'd been gifted with grace of late. Almost twelve she was, and an adult beauty was awakening in the secretive fullness of her lips, her high cheekbones and postures of reserve. The girl who had spent hours chasing hares and capturing tadpoles was giving way to one more interested in puzzling over the modest, hazel-eyed twin in the looking glass.

As Cinfa and I kissed, my mother offered me a dull, antagonistic look. A small, puffy woman of lowered eye and bent shoulder, her contours were concealed as always inside a loose-fitting olive tunic and black apron. Her deep-brown hair, streaked a brittle gray at the front, was crowned by a toque of gray lace and clasped into a bun at the back of her head. The bun was tied with a black velveteen ribbon from Jerusalem given her years ago by her elder brother, my uncle Abraham. Its stringent hold seemed to draw the color from her face, which, over the last few years, had swollen into an expression of wan defiance against any possibility of happiness; she would forever be grieving her long-buried husband and first-born son, my elder brother Mordecai. To all who knew the playful young mother she'd been, her wasted state was a reminder that life saved its sharpest arrows for women, the bearers—and mourners—of departed children.

"Either of you seen Uncle?" I asked.

Cinfa shrugged. Mother licked her cracked lips as if displeased by my interruption, shook her head.

Father Carlos and Judah met me in the kitchen. "No sign of him," the priest said.

We sat together at the table to wait. Aunt Esther appeared suddenly at the courtyard door, dressed in a high-collared black jupe which seemed to light her tawny face. Her dramatic, darkly outlined almond eyes opened in horror. "What are those stains?!" she demanded, pointing to my pants. "Has Judah been crying?!" She clamped her jaw into an expression of judgment, glared at me while tucking wisps of henna-tinted hair under her crimson headscarf. Slender and tall, possessed of a deeply lined and shadowed beauty, she could dominate a room with a single glance down the length of her elegant nose.

"Just a little blood," I began to explain to her. "The flagellants were..."

She thrust out her hand and sucked in on her cheeks so that she looked like a Moorish dancer. "Don't tell me! I don't want to hear it! Dear God, can't you even clean yourselves? And whatever you do, don't let your mother see Judah like that. We'll never hear the end of it!"

"Yes, go wash," Father Carlos agreed with a dismissing twist to his hand. He turned to Aunt Esther and added, "I told him it's the first thing he should do when we got back."

I shot the priest a dirty look. He curled his lips into a wry smile and lifted his eyebrows as if we were rivals for my aunt's affection. To her, he said, "Now, about my little problem..."

I took Judah with me to our bedroom and slipped off his clothes, then my own. As I cleaned him with the vinegar and water solution which my mother always insisted upon, his body went limp in my hands. A compact five-year-old, already muscular and possessed of seductive gray-blue eyes, he seemed destined to grow into a milk-skinned Samson.

Never one for bathing, he dashed back to the kitchen the moment I'd finished dressing him. When I entered the room, he was clinging to the fringe of Aunt Esther's jupe while fingering his wooden top. She was preparing her beloved coffee with almond milk and honey the way she'd learned in her native Persia.

From outside, the sour rumbling and creaking of refuse carts was suddenly drowned out by a woman's shrieks. Opening the shutters to listen, I spotted a familiar vermilion carriage careening down the street. As always, the horses were caparisoned in blue-fringed silver cloth. The usual driver, an Old Christian with pockmarks cratering his cheeks, had been replaced, however, by a fair-haired Goliath in a wide-brimmed, amethyst-colored hat. "Guess who's coming," I said.

Aunt Esther nudged me partially aside and peered out. "Oh dear, Dona Meneses. More work for Mira," she grumbled. She squeezed my hand. "You shouldn't stand here staring out at her."

I rolled my eyes, turned away. The carriage pounded to a stop and the door squealed open. Dona Meneses' pattering footsteps trailed toward the Temple Street entrance to my mother's room. As she entered the house, she began to describe the qualities of the fabric she'd brought in false, lyric tones. Her voice trailed away to a soft murmur as my mother's door was closed.

Aunt Esther leaned toward us as if to disclose a secret and said, "It'll be a miracle if Mira can turn that hideous puce velvet she brought with her into anything presentable!" Marching to the hearth, she carried our matzah to the table with a linen mitten.

"It pays our debts," I said.

"True. And with the drought..."

"It's the Devil!" Father Carlos exclaimed suddenly in a voice of warning.

"I grant you that Dona Meneses isn't lovely, but she's hardly from the Other Side," I replied.

The priest squinted his eyes and glared at me. His tongue darted between his thick, soft lips. "Not her, you fool! It's the Devil who's behind the plague and drought!"

"You're an absolute lunatic," Aunt Esther told him in Hebrew with that frown of hers that could freeze bathwater. "And keep your voice down—we don't want to scare her away!"

The bells of St. Peter's began tolling tierce. Father Carlos mumbled to himself as if succumbing to the religious call, said a quick grace and picked on a piece of warm matzah with his chubby fingers. In a tone of disgust, he continued in the Holy language, so that Judah wouldn't understand, "You mean to say, Esther dear, that the Devil doesn't exist?"

"I mean to say that if you scare my little nephew one more time with your nonsense..." And here, Aunt Esther lifted her iron poker from the fire and aimed its red-glowing tip toward the priest's bulbous nose, "...I'll see to it that you meet your Christian savior sooner than you intended! Find someone else to scare!"

"Your aunt has always had a way with threats," Carlos whispered to me with a lecherous smile. "Remember her the day they dragged you out to be baptized in the cathedral? She cursed them in seven different languages...Hebrew, Persian, Arabic, Portuguese..."

"We remember," I interrupted, holding up my hand in a gesture of disapproval so that we could all avoid the memory. Too late; Esther's eyes, dimmed by isolation, were focused on an inner landscape. She had slipped her hand below her crimson scarf, was tracing the outline of the cruciform scar given her on the accursed morning of our forced baptism. Then, she had fought hardest of all against the bailiffs sent by the

King to drag the Jews to the cathedral. As an example, a guard had thrown her to the ground, pinned her legs and arms to the cobbles on the Rua de São Pedro. A Dominican friar had pressed a red-glowing iron cross vertically to her forehead. He'd shouted, so all could hear: "I hereby gift you with the sign of our Lord!"

As for me, I was covered with pig blood and sawdust by Christian children on my way home from the baptism ceremony. But they never learned of the gift they gave me; my burning humiliation summoned the grace of God to me, and I had the first ever of my visions.

This preternatural occurrence began when Farid saw me in the courtyard. Out of shame, I ran from him. As I reached the  kitchen door, however, a presentiment of eyes watching over me forced me to stop. When I turned, a white light appeared to me in the sky, far away, above the Moor's castle. As it drew closer, wings sprouted, and I saw that the luminescence had been but a supernal egg. A radiant heron of ruby red, black and white took form, and as it flew over the Little Jewish Quarter, wind from its flapping blew fiercely against me. When I looked down at myself, the blood and sawdust were gone.

Uncle told me that God had shown me my continued purity and had revealed the Christian stain to be simply an illusion. I answered, "It wasn't God; it was just a bird."

"But Berekiah," he said, "God comes to each of us in the form we can best perceive Him. To you, just now, He was a heron. To someone else, He might come as a flower or even a breeze."

Indeed he was right; at my darkest moments, the Lord has always appeared to me as a kind of bird, perhaps because I most easily see the beauty of creation in those creatures gifted with flight.

Recalling other words of Uncle's wisdom, I said now to Aunt Esther, "The Devil is just a metaphor. It's religious language. You can't expect all words to have everyday meanings."

"As God is my witness, it's too early for kabbalistic philosophy!" she answered.

Aunt Esther's harsh tone of voice moved Judah to climb up next to me on the bench. His lips were pressed together into that slit of forced silence which Mother's shrieks and slaps had taught him. Of late, he'd learned to do everything he could to avoid being her last, impossible burden—to tiptoe, not run, through childhood.

The trap door to our cellar, located at the southwest corner of the kitchen, suddenly opened. Uncle Abraham, my spiritual master, rose from the staircase, his forehead bathed in sweat and his hair waving off in a hundred different directions, as if he'd been caught in a spiritual storm. A small finchlike man of darting movements, his pointy face was centered by a long, angular nose that gave him an amusing look to strangers, but which connoted a probing intelligence to all those who knew him. His smooth dark skin, the color of cinnamon, seemed to highlight his wild crest of silver hair and tufted eyebrows. Graying stubble softened his cheeks, and where they looped inward, added a shadowing of sagely age to his face. Always, but particularly after prayers, his eyes burned with that secret green light, that piercing strangeness, that distinguished him at once as a powerful kabbalist. "Who's that?" he asked squinting. "Ah, it's our friendly priest!"

"Where'd you come from?" demanded Carlos, still unused to my uncle appearing out of nowhere. "We looked in the cellar not five minutes ago. Sometimes I think you're a *lez*."

"What's a *lez*?" Judah asked.

"A ghost that comes back to play tricks—a spirit jester," I answered.

Uncle grinned appreciatively and wiggled his right hand in the air to show his five fingers; in Jewish lore, *lezim* were reputed to only have four. "My movements parallel life's mysteries," he said with a dismissive wave. Raising his eyebrows, he nodded inquisitively toward the muffled voices coming from the back of the house.

"Dona Meneses," I explained. "She's brought fabric for another dress. Purple, this time."

He took coffee and, after a quick blessing, wolfed down a hard-boiled egg. We'd already finished *shaharit,* morning prayers, together, but he again wished me good morning with a kiss on the lips. Lifting Judah onto his lap, he assaulted him with little popping kisses and growling noises. Not usually demonstrative, the coming of the Passover made Uncle giddy with affection.

"I just came to tell you that I decided not to sell the sapphire," Carlos said with a sigh that seemed to request forgiveness.

My master's lips suddenly curled in that way that made him look menacing. He said, "I think you should reconsider."

"You're buying gemstones?!" I asked. I looked to my aunt for her protest. But she was busy tracing her glance over a Book of Psalms she'd recently copied for an Old Christian nobleman, proofreading carefully.

Turning back to Uncle, I added, "If we had that kind of money, we could close the store, leave this desert for a few weeks."

My master gave me a challenging look. "A sapphire cut during the time of Rabbi Solomon Ibn Gabirol," he said. He spoke in Hebrew except for the word *safira* in Portuguese.

Solomon Ibn Gabirol was a master Jewish poet of the eleventh century from Málaga. "I'm afraid I've lost the trail of your thoughts," I said.

*"Petah et atsmehah shetifateh delet.* Knock upon yourself as upon a door," Uncle replied.

That was his condescending way of saying I was to keep quiet and look inside myself for an answer. "Way too early for your mystical advice," I countered.

He answered by filling my cup with water. "Keep drinking and you won't get angry. The fluids will carry the white bile from your system."

"Any more liquid and I'll drown," I replied.

"You'll drown when you disappear in God's ocean." Lifting a finger to his lips, he requested silence. Turning back to Carlos, he said in a grave tone, "The *safira* could be lost, you know."

"My responsibility."

My master lifted Judah from his lap and sat him on one of our Persian pillows. "Off you go," he said. To Father Carlos, he added, "Lost forever, I mean. Your position puts you in danger."

As he spoke, I realized that we weren't talking about a gemstone at all. *Safira* was code for *Sefer,* Hebrew for book. He was undoubtedly negotiating to purchase a work of Rabbi Solomon Gabirol's and smuggle it out of Portugal. But why talk in code inside our house, where we were safe from the spying eyes and ears of the Old Christians?

Father Carlos nodded with a gesture of excuse and stood up to take his leave.

"One warning—I'm going to keep trying to convince you," my master said with fierce determination in his voice.

The priest crossed himself with a trembling hand. Trying to mollify Uncle Abraham, he offered a misguided effort at humor and replied, "Your kabbalistic sorcery doesn't scare..."

My master jumped up from the table, glaring at Carlos. Motion in the room seemed suspended by his rage. "I never practice magic!" he said, using the Hebrew term, *kabbalah ma'asit,* practical kabbalah, to designate this forbidden activity. "You should know that well, my friend."

He was referring to the time Father Carlos had requested an amulet to kill a slanderer spreading rumors about the priest's continued allegiance to the faith of Moses. Uncle had refused, of course, although he had personally appealed to Rabbi Abraham Zacuto, the King's astronomer, to see that the evildoer was silenced. Now, he walked to the hearth and stared at the backs of his fingernails in the light of the fire. His topaz signet ring etched with the form of an ibis, symbol of the divine scribe, glowed with an inner sunset. "When Adam and Eve were born in Eden, they were covered with nail from head to toe as armor," he said. Turning back to Carlos, he added, "And now, our fingernails are all that remain from this primal protection. A tiny border, don't you think? Not much against the weapons of the Church."

The priest shrugged off the implication and lowered his eyes.

"It won't be enough to save you if they find out about the sapphire."

"I need it," Father Carlos said, a note of sadness in his voice. "Surely *you* should understand. It's the last..." His words trailed away. He added dryly, "I should be going now. I've a Mass to prepare."

"You bastard!" Uncle shouted. "Holding back a *safira* our children will need, that God will need!" When he turned the wall of his back to Carlos, the priest bowed his head as if to request forgiveness from the rest of us and left.

"You could be more understanding," I said to my uncle. When he waved away my criticism, I added, "So why were you speaking in code with Carlos? There's no chance Dona Meneses can hear us way back there. Besides, she must know we still practice Judaism. If it bothered her, she'd have reported us to the authorities by now."

"The priest trusts no one. 'Even the dead wear masks,' he says. And the more I learn, the more I think he's right." He scratched his scalp and frowned. "I'm going to pay my respects to Dona Meneses." He shot me a commanding look and marched out.

"How quickly people forget," Aunt Esther sighed.

"What do you mean?"

She dabbed some rosewater on her neck, then tied a linen kerchief around it. "The plague. It disappears for a couple years and people think it's something new the Devil's conjured up." She brushed a trembling hand over her forehead, reconsidered her words. "Maybe it's a kind of grace that we can forget. Imagine if..."

"Not a word, not a gesture, not a single lesion do I forget!"

Aunt Esther grimaced; she knew I was referring to my father and elder brother, Mordecai. During the winter of fifty-two sixty-three, a little more than three years ago, the knife of plague had peeled them open to the moist northern winds of Kislev. My father, lost under running black sores and pustules, shivered to death on the sixth day of Hanukkah. A month later, the living skeleton that had been Mordecai was dead in my arms.

My aunt and I sat in silence. After a few minutes, Dona Meneses left our house with the large basket of fruit which she always took away from her visits. Esther said, "I'll go to see if Cinfa needs help in the store," then trudged out of the room with that stiff, forward-tilting walk of hers. I watched Judah playing in the doorway with his top until Uncle returned to me and said, "I need your help in the cellar."

Below the trap door, we descended five coarse granite steps, one for each book of the Torah, to a small landing centered by a menorah in green and yellow mosaic. Passing through the next entranceway, we started down another stairway of twelve thinner limestone steps—one for each of the books of the Prophets. Since the forced closure of our synagogue in the Old Christian year of fourteen ninety-seven, this had become our temple. As we descended, I picked a blue cylindrical skullcap from a shelf and placed it atop my head. Uncle reached back to his shoulders and lifted his prayer shawl over his head, giving it the form of a hood. Together, we chanted, "In the greatness of thy benevolence will I enter thy house."

The cellar was low-ceilinged, five paces wide, double that in length, floored with the same rough slate as the courtyard. It had witnessed at least a thousand years of chant, and its cool, musty air, guarded hermetically by walls shimmering with knotted patterns of blue and yellow tile, seemed scented with ancient memory. Window eyelets at the top of the northern wall—at the level of our courtyard paving stones—let in only a soft, dim light. From the bottom of the staircase, which flanked the eastern wall of the room, spread our circle of prayer mat. Around its circumference were seven verdant bushes in ceramic pots, one for each day of creation. Three were myrtle, three lavender and one, symbolizing the Sabbath, was an intermingling of both plants. The half of the room beyond the mat, facing sunset, was our realm of earthly work, where Aunt Esther scripted manuscripts and where Uncle and I illuminated them. Our three desks of the finest polished chestnut faced the north wall, were spaced only a foot apart so we could view one another's work. Each was gifted with its own high-backed chair. Opposite, against the south wall, were two granite bathtubs sunken into the floor. In between was our hulking storage cabinet of coarse-grained oak. It had lion's-paw feet and possessed eight rows of ten drawers, each of them thin and long, like the receptacles for type in a printer's studio. A last row, the lowest, had only two drawers. We kept our gold leaf and lapis lazuli in these.

The most unusual item in the room was undoubtedly the circular, platter-size mirror on the wall above the middle desk belonging to Uncle. Inside a chestnut-wood frame, the looking glass' silver surface was concave, and hence reflected squashed and distorted images. We stared into it oftentimes at the start of meditation as a way of loosening the mind from its accustomed landscape, particularly from its familiarity with the body. The mirror was somewhat famous locally because on the sixth of June of thirteen ninety-one of the Christian era, it was said to have seeped blood at the death of tens of thousands of Jews killed in the riots then raging across Iberia. In fact, great-grandfather Abraham held that it shed an infinitesimal amount of blood—invisible to the naked eye—whenever even a single Jew died. He believed that the blood had become visible at the time of the anti-Jewish riots only because so very many of us had been murdered. From his time forward, therefore, it had been known as *O Espelho a Sangrar,* the Bleeding Mirror.

We all hoped it would never reveal its talents to us again.

As Uncle motioned me toward the sunken bathtubs, he said, "I need you to pee."

"Now?" I asked.

From the rim of a tub, he picked up a jug. "In here. It's spring. I need a virgin's pee."

Each year, just prior to Passover, my master made new dyes and colors for our manuscript illuminations. The acid in the urine ate at certain elements to create varying colors, particularly a fine rose when mixed with Brazil wood, alum and ceruse, and a brilliant carmine when mixed with the ashes of vine branches and quicklime.

"I'm no longer a virgin," I said, picturing Helena as she had been in the hills overlooking the vast monastery being built just west of Lisbon. I'd waited so long for her decision. Until it seemed as if sex and life would not happen to me as they did to other people. And then, when all was lost, when the ship set to take her to Corfu was already anchored in Lisbon, her arms opened to me like the gates of God's grace.

"A whore at the Maidenhead Inn?" Uncle asked, awakening me from daydream. He had often recommended a certain house of ill repute outside the city walls.

When I answered, "Helena," he raised his eyebrows like a rogue and said, "In any event, you're the closest thing to a virgin I can get without revealing that we're still illuminating Hebrew books. Judah's too young and I'm too old, and women's pee is too strong—especially your aunt's. I tried it years ago when we were married. Turns everything black as Asmodeus' soul."

We shared a silly grin. "Now I know why you loaded me with fluids," I said.

As my water cascaded hot and musty into Uncle's jars, he shuffled to our desks with the modest, duck-like walk he adopted in synagogues and began to dust them.

After I'd peed in six different ceramic jugs and closed their lids securely, we placed them in the sunken bathtubs. Uncle washed his hands and brushed them through the Sabbath bush of myrtle and lavender. With a puzzled frown, he said, "Diego the printer is so late—I don't understand."

Diego was a family friend whom Uncle was initiating into his threshing circle, his group of mystics which met in secret to discuss kabbalah. Although a robust man with the graying beard and commanding brown eyes of a patriarch, he'd had his heart reduced to ash in the Inquisitional flames of Seville which had claimed his wife and daughter four years earlier and from which he'd barely managed to escape. Often, Uncle and I sought ways to renew his spirit, and we had convinced him to go for a walk today through Sintra forest so that we might sketch the great white cranes before their migration north.

"Perhaps Senhora Belmira's family has kept him behind," I said. A neighbor and friend of Diego's, she'd been beaten to death in Xabregas, one of the city's eastern districts, two months before. Diego had been spending a lot of time with her loved ones of late.

Uncle shrugged and cupped his hands around my nose. "Refresh yourself," he said, and as I sniffed at his myrtle-scented fingers, he added, "If he isn't here soon, we'll go to his place and check. Oh, and when we do go out, I'll need to pass by New Merchant's Street. I promised Esther I'd deliver the Book of Psalms she's just finished."

My master had a way of turning business transactions into disputations on the sex lives of angels and other esoteric matters. "You have precisely the time it takes Diego and me to down a cup of wine at the Attic Inn!" It was a tumbledown garret, but it served kosher wine on the sly.

His lips sculpted a dismayed but amused frown. "Look who's giving orders!" he observed.

I met his challenge with the bored expression I used to practice to irritate my father when he spoke of Talmud classes. He nodded his agreement. "All right, no more than a half hour." He motioned for me to bend so he could bless his hand over me. Then, as I picked dyes and colors from the storage cabinet, he unlocked the *genizah,* the traditional hiding place for old books in a synagogue. Ours was a pit—three feet wide by four feet long—sunken into the floor at the western perimeter of the prayer mat. Its contents were constantly changing; books smuggled out of Portugal were soon replaced with others my master discovered and either bought or begged.

Uncle stepped one foot down into the *genizah* to retrieve our work. By the time he'd climbed back out, I was at my desk, arranging my brushes and dyes. Placing my manuscript neatly on the slightly inclined surface of the desk in front of me, he circled his hand around the back of my neck and advised me with a parable on the coloration for my most recent illumination, one of the tales from the famous collection of "Fox Fables." As I began to offer an analysis of his words, his lips began to tremble and his hand grew cold against my skin. "What is it, Uncle?" I asked.

He rubbed his eyes with both his hands, like a child, took a long inhale of breath as if to ready himself for a challenge. "You're so grown up," he said gently. "Already my equal in so much. And yet in other matters..." He shook his head, smiled wistfully. "There is so much I'd like to tell you... Beri, God may soon demand that we take separate paths." He reached into his pouch and took out a scroll of vellum. Handing it to me, he said, "Be so kind as to accept this little gift."

The scroll unfolded into a vellum ribbon on which were scripted both our Hebrew names in elegant golden lettering. "Esther made it for me," he continued. He gripped the back of my neck and, in an urgent

voice, added, "If ever you should need me, wherever you are, no matter how far or how desperate the circumstances, send this ribbon to me
and I will come for you." He placed his other hand atop my head, stared
pressingly into my eyes. "And if, for any reason, you find me beyond
your earthly reach, pray over it and I will make every effort to appear
before you."

So touched was I by his grace, by my master's generosity, that my
throat parched with a kind of desperate yearning. Tears clouded the
room. I had to swallow several times just to whisper, "But we will never
be separated. I will always..."

Uncle told me, "Youth is meant to be separated from age for a time.
You will go your way as it should be, then return. But no demon, however powerful, shall stand in my way if you are in trouble!" He took his
hand from atop my head and caressed my cheek. "Now come, let's work
together."

"But is there nothing that I can...?"

He held up his hand and pointed to my manuscript. "Woe betide
the kabbalah master who answers every question posed by his apprentice! Now get to work!"

A few minutes later, as I was highlighting the powerful legs of a
young dog in my illumination with minute strokes of black, a shriek like
shattered glass cut the air. "Go!" my master yelled.

I bounded up the stairs. The kitchen was empty. Harsh voices
from outside pounded against the walls. I climbed through my bedroom
window into the store, dashed out onto Temple Street. As I removed
my skullcap, I spotted Aunt Esther kneeling over our friend, Diego
the printer. He was moaning. Blood was spilling from a gash on his
bearded chin into her hands.

# Chapter II

Diego the printer was the first to contribute to the river of blood which would, over the next few days, lead us into a desert landscape bordered everywhere by grief. But at the time, this geography of death was still a secret from us.

Streams of sweat stained his temples and cheeks with a residue of the city's endless dust. Blood sluiced over his neck from the gash at his chin. Coughing, he fought for breath. "I was walking here...just walking," he said in Portuguese. "By the river, I stopped by the King's Well to wash my hands." Aunt Esther unbuttoned the top of his crusted doublet, cleaned his chest with fabric rent from her blouse. I noticed the brown line of an old scar on his chest, just under his collar bone, almost as if a worm had burrowed there.

Around us, neighbors were beginning to gather now, to whisper together. "Two boys..." Diego continued, "...they yelled that I was poisoning the well with an essence of plague. They ran after me. I fell. They threw stones. 'Get the long-tailed rabbi! Get the long...' A swarthy man in a blue cape saved me. Tall, strong..."

In Diego's desperation, his last words sought the comfort of Hebrew. "Speak Portuguese," I whispered to him as we laid him back onto the cobbles.

Diego's turban slipped off, and I saw for the first time the wisps of thinning gray hair over his ears, the brown birthmarks dotting his scalp. A folded paper dropped free as well. Believing it might contain a personal message or a prayer formula which would incriminate him as a practicing Jew, I snatched it up, hid it in the large drawstring pouch I keep around my neck and which functions as a kind of knapsack. Judah brushed against me, icy with fear, and I had to shake him to get him to run to Dr. Montesinhos. Uncle had joined us, and, after a rushed prayer, said, "I'm going inside to see what medication I can find."

I tried to hold Diego's gash closed by pressing my finger into Esther's makeshift bandage, but soon the linen was soaked crimson. Esther ran off for clean water as I substituted cloth ripped from my shirt. Uncle arrived with Farid. They carried extracts of comfrey and bayberry and geranium, sizings and bole, gum arabic and sulfur water. But none of the styptics could effect a clotting. "It's his accursed beard!" Uncle grumbled. "I can't get to the wound." He told Diego, "Dr. Montesinhos is going to have to shave you."

Diego, who was from the Jewish priestly caste of Levi, pushed us away when he heard that. "I won't allow it!" he shouted in Hebrew. "I must have my beard. It is forbidden to…"

"There are Levites without beards," I pointed out, but Diego simply moaned. I turned to Uncle, whispered, "An attack in daylight. It's a bad sign. A few more weeks of drought and…"

"How can you be sure it wasn't planned?" Uncle demanded angrily.

I began to ask what he meant, but a shadow crossing over us halted my words. Two horsemen leading a white and gold carriage glared at us from above. Silver morions and greaves gleamed in the sunlight. Scarlet and green pennons decorated with the King's armored spheres flapped in the dry breeze. "What in God's name is the disturbance?!" one demanded gruffly.

It was then that I noticed that my master was still in his prayer garb, a white and blue shawl over his shoulders, his left arm circled by the straps of his phylacteries, a leather prayer box on his forehead above his spiritual eye. For such an infringement, he could have been exiled as a slave to Portuguese Africa. Behind my back, I signalled to Farid in our language of hands to spirit him away. "A man has been hurt," I said.

"Are you a New Christian?!" the horseman demanded.

My heart boomed as if to force a denial. Out of the corner of my eye, I saw Farid tugging Uncle back through the crowd.

"I've asked if you're a New Christian!" the horseman repeated menacingly.

The door to the carriage behind him swung open. Silence swept the crowd. Out stepped a thin, delicate man in a violet tunic and bi-colored leggings, black and white. A ruffled collar of gold silk seemed to offer his gaunt, evil face to me as if on a platter. His black eyes surveyed the crowd as if in search of an innocent to punish. While dangling a hand weighted with twin rings of emerald cabochons the size of almonds, he said in imperious Castilian, "We'll take him with us. There must be a hospital near the Estaus."

The Estaus Palace, a turreted edifice of shimmering stone, played home to noble guests on official visits to Lisbon. "My lord, the new All Saints Hospital is right on Rossio Square," I said. "Not a hundred yards from your destination."

Diego was a bear of a man, over six feet tall, and it took a guard and one of the nobleman's Moorish-looking drivers to help me lift him. Inside the carriage, a young woman with a peaked, violet tress and a rose-colored silk jupe sat opposite the Castilian nobleman. She was blond, fair-skinned, round-faced. She reached for Diego with stringent concern, looked at me with intelligent eyes burning for an explanation.

"Attacked by foreign seamen," I lied.

Her sudden look of surprise, the impossibility of her desperation, the kinship of her face to my own banished time. A piercing of meaning it was—a *shefa,* influx of God's grace. Akin to a verse of Torah suddenly shedding its clothing and revealing itself in a sparkling of naked understanding.

By the girl's side was a pug-nosed dog in a blue and yellow troubadour's suit. A coffer of silver rested on the crimson floor of the carriage. These last details I only noticed as the Castilian called to his driver to make ready. I surveyed the scene as I often do to imprint life in what Uncle calls my Torah memory, backed away. When the door closed, the nobleman leaned out the window to me and whispered with a wine-scented voice, "Have no fear. Your friend won't die on this holiday." To his two drivers, he called, "Make haste! We've a wounded man here!"

A curiosity akin to dread tugged at my heart as the drivers whipped the horses. Who were these Castilians? Did they know we were secret Jews?! Was the nobleman mocking me or acknowledging his kinship? For a moment, I saw fingers as tiny as a child's straining in the window of the carriage as it throttled down the street. A curtain lowered, silencing my questions.

I found Uncle in our courtyard, playing chess with Farid. His prayer shawl was neatly folded in his lap and topped with his phylacteries. After I explained what happened with Diego and the Castilian nobleman, he looked up at me and said, "Before my forces are decimated by this heathen's let us get to the hospital and make sure Diego is treated right."

Farid read his lips and grinned. Uncle and I wanted to change into street clothes, and as we entered the kitchen I enquired about what he meant about the attack on Diego being planned. By way of reply, he asked, "What lives for centuries but can still die before its own birth?"

I rolled my eyes and said, "No riddles, just an answer."

He frowned and marched to his room.

A week later, I came upon the answer to Uncle's paradox. Had I understood earlier, could I have changed our leaden destiny to gold?

My master and I chose a route along the river because the shifting wind was now punishing us with the odor of one of the municipal dungheaps beyond the city's crenelated walls. The public cemeteries were full, and as of late, dead African slaves had been tossed on top of the heaps. What the vultures and wolves couldn't pick quickly enough putrefied and mixed with excrement into a nightmare smell that burned into your skin and bones like an unseen acid.

As we passed through the Horse's Well Gate, I recalled the metallic shiver the gates to the Judiaria Pequena made when the Old Christian guards locked the Jews inside for the night. A shout from above turned us. Our former rabbi, Fernando Losa, was waving at us to wait from the top of the Synagogue Steps. He'd become a dealer in religious Christian garments since the conversion, outfitted even the Bishop of Lisbon, may his tongue turn to powder. "Oh no, not Rabbi Losa," I moaned. "For what terrible sin are we being made to atone?"

Uncle laughed. A woman suddenly shrieked, "Water!" and we pressed against the wall as a rain of waste cascaded from her third-story window.

Losa joined us puffing for breath, an exquisite scarlet cloak embroidered with a collar of pearls draped over his narrow shoulders. Thin and beak nosed, with deep-set treacherous eyes, a shiny bald head and a frowning slit for a mouth, he looked to me like a vulturine golem constructed for hunting down subterranean rodents. As a boy, I expected him to have talons rather than fingers, and in my dreams, he never spoke, always hissed. "Those wretched, filthy cows are everywhere!" he said now in a false, patrician voice.

"At least they're kosher," my master noted.

Rabbi Losa sneered and said, "This bad fortune of Diego the printer's is what comes from talking to you about the *fountain*, you know." He was referring in code to the kabbalah; it was no secret to him that Uncle wanted Diego to join his threshing circle.

My master made a deferential bow and whispered in Hebrew, *"Hakham mufla ve-rav rabanan*, you are a great scholar and a rabbi of rabbis." He glanced at me to be sure I'd catch his play on words; he was insulting Losa by accenting the letters h, a, m, and r. Together, they formed the Hebrew word for jackass.

Uncle turned to leave, but the rabbi said, "Wait one moment!" He licked his lips as if savoring a tasty sauce. "I've come to give you a warning. Eurico Damas says that should you ever so much as whisper his name in your sleep, he'll chop you up and serve you inside sausage casing. Best keep your beak out of private affairs, little man!"

My heart sank; Damas was a New Christian arms dealer who'd won contracts from the King for spying on his former brethren and who had recently taken a child bride. Two weeks ago, Uncle had barged in on a secret meeting of the Jewish court and demanded to have him judged for drowning the newborn infant of a flower seller he'd raped and refused to marry. The investigation ended a week ago, when the flower seller herself mysteriously disappeared. Uncle's name was to have been kept secret by the rabbinical court, but apparently someone—probably Losa himself—had given it to Damas.

"Is that all you came to tell me?" my master demanded.

"That should be quite enough. If it weren't for my intervention, he'd have come himself."

"Many thanks, oh great scholar and rabbi of rabbis," Uncle answered with an ironic bow.

Losa pulled in his chin like a hen, watched us leave with the bitter but patient air of a man who has lost the battle but will continue to wage the war.

As we rushed toward the city center and the hospital, I daydreamed about protecting my master from a succession of kabbalistic demons and Biblical giants. Perhaps I'd never outgrow such fantasies. And yet, passing the clamor of Lisbon's great fishmarket and port, they seemed suddenly fitting. After all, Uncle had sworn protection over me as a boy in order to take over my mystical guidance. Did it imply a reciprocal promise I'd never before realized?

When we explained our mission to a bailiff at the All Saints Hospital, he informed us proudly that the nobleman who had brought Diego in had been none other than the Count of Almira. The name meant nothing to me, but I wrote it in gold in my Torah memory because of my attraction for his traveling companion. A girlish nun escorted us to Diego's room. It was gloomy and low-ceilinged, stank of vinegar, amber and death. Over each of the twelve cots hung a bloody crucifix. Yellowing linen curtains opened to show men tied with leather belts to beds, peering white-eyed and hungry for life, encrusted in bandages, stinking like manure. Shutters were partially opened for a view of the Dominican Church across the square.

Diego was in the last bed. Recognizing his large sombre eyes and saffron-colored turban, I smiled with joy and nervousness. But he was wholly changed. His shaved cheeks were the white of marble, nicked here and there with blood. Jowls previously hidden gave his face a heavy, pendulous attitude. He looked suddenly like the kind of tender man who gave presents easily, who doted on children, but who paid a price for neglecting himself—the kind of man he may have been before exile and isolation.

The gash across his chin had been cauterized and stitched. When he spotted us, he gasped and sat up. Involuntarily, he turned his face to the wall as if preparing for death.

My uncle stopped, his penetrating emerald eyes seeking to exchange places with Diego's. When I prodded him forward, he walked to his friend and offered an encouraging smile. From here, we could see he was feverish with sweat. I prayed it wasn't plague. "You look well— the bleeding's stopped," my master said.

"You shouldn't have come, seen me like this." Diego faced the wall again and closed his eyes.

"You can start growing back your beard as soon as your chin has healed," I observed.

He whispered, "I thank you for coming, but I must ask you both to leave."

Uncle nodded at me to accede to his request. When I reached the hall, he was sitting at the foot of Diego's bed. Their whispered conversation was giving my master wild, whirling gestures. Diego hid his eyes behind his hands, bent his head sadly. I said prayers until my uncle came to me. He sighed his frustration. "A bad situation. Diego shall have to suffer for a while."

"I guess it's a good thing we're not all subject to a Levite's restrictions," I replied.

"We're each of us subject to outside influences. One must accommodate them or live in the wilderness as a hermit. And even there..." My master's voice trailed away as he scratched his scalp. "Let's get out of this dungeon," he said. "I'm beginning to itch all over."

"Maybe some manuscripts would cheer him up," I said. "We could ask to borrow those Latin treatises he wants so badly and..."

"No books!" Uncle said, holding up both his hands as if to stop an onrushing carriage.

Outside, a droning chant was shivering the warm air of the Rossio; the daily procession of flagellants was on its way to the Riverside Palace. The sun revealed in Uncle's drooping eyes that his soul had been brushed with Diego's despair. He said, "Truth did not come into the world naked, but came clothed in images and names. And lies? What clothes do lies wear?"

"The same ones as truth," I said. "It's up to us to distinguish."

"Yes," he agreed in a dry voice. "And are all crimes seen by God?"

"You mean, will those boys who attacked Diego be punished?" I asked.

"If you like."

I was considering my response when Uncle squeezed my hand. "Sorry. I can't bear to talk any more about this. Let's go for the walk we'd planned."

"But I haven't brought my sketchbook," I replied.

"Draw the birds in your Torah memory, my son."

Uncle and I spent a lovely afternoon together, watching our beloved cranes. To see creatures so large and gangly, so white, descending from out of the blue like feathers—it took our breath away. Breezes swept by us with the gentleness of flowers, and when my uncle told me it was time to get back home, I was surprised to find myself separate from the day itself.

When we reached our house, Cinfa and Aunt Esther were preparing our Passover seder in the kitchen, had spread a netting of rice kernels across our best white tablecloth to search for impurities. The house was heavy with humid, intoxicating scents; a magnificent lamb was roasting slowly on a spit in our hearth, its fragrant juices dripping and hissing against the braziers. From its heady scent, I knew it had been basted with the grease from those pouches of luxurious fat that are ewes' tails—a cooking secret brought by Esther from Persia. "Smells heavenly," I said.

"Prayer before food," Uncle scoffed. He slipped down into the cellar.

I took a mortar and pestle, apples, walnuts, dates and honey with me to the store; in between customers I'd prepare *haroset*.

Waiting on customers freed my mother to help Cinfa and Esther in the kitchen. The store was quiet until I was taken with the idea of displaying our recently arrived bananas from Portuguese Africa nearest the door. Perhaps it was a coincidence, but suddenly we were the place to be. Secret Jews kept me busy all afternoon with last minute orders for that evening's Passover seder. By the time pink and gold clouds began lighting the sky as heralds of sunset, I was exhausted. I bolted the doors, drew the curtains and sat alone in silent prayer until Uncle called me into the kitchen. He looked splendid under his white robes, had his hair combed forward into its Sabbath swirl. "By any chance, did Reza stop by the store?" he asked in a hopeful voice.

My cousin Reza, Esther and Uncle's only living child, had married recently and would be spending Passover with her husband's family. "No, was she supposed to?" I asked. "I thought that she said she wasn't sure she'd be able to come at all tonight."

"I just thought that maybe..." Uncle took my hand, and it was with sadness that he told me, "I found the face of Haman for my Haggadah. Perhaps all our work will proceed smoothly now."

My master was illuminating a Haggadah for a family of secret Jews in Barcelona, had had a difficult time finding a face amongst our acquaintances which could serve as a model for Haman. But why was he sad? Because of Reza's absence? Before I could ask, he began his blessing over me. I hugged him, and for the first time in memory, he let his body bend to my love. Had I won a greater trust from him in the last few days? Suddenly infused with that resolute force of his, as if he'd drunk in my energy and concern, he kissed my lips and gripped me. "Passover is here!" he whispered. We shared an exultant smile.

Cinfa and Judah set the table. The saffron-colored ceramic Passover plate which our neighbor Samir had made for us was set with the cilantro, lettuce, roasted egg and grilled lamb bone which were symbolic parts of the meal. With Esther's approval, I added a spoon of my *haroset*, representing the mortar with which the Israelites, as slaves, built the tombs, palaces and pyramids of Egypt. Our matzah was set under a linen napkin. The silver goblet traditionally set aside for Elijah crowned a corner by my uncle's place.

How to explain this first night of Passover? Words and faces of relief? Of giddy joy? Sadness for those now departed? We took our places linked by a shared aura of preparation. Uncle, as always, was our guide through the ritual. For although Passover is at its center a festival of remembrance, a re-telling of the story of how God brought the Jews out of bondage, it also has a hidden core. Inside the body of Torah, folded like a phoenix in its egg, is the story of the spiritual journey each of us can make, from slavery to sanctity. The Passover Haggadah is a golden bell whose singing tones tell us: always remember that the Holy Land is in you!

To begin, my mother lit a candle at the hearth, then set flames dancing up and down the tiny steps of candelabra at each end of our table. The present and past were linked. We were the Israelites awaiting Moses at Sinai, just as the table, draped in white, was rendered our altar and the kitchen our temple in the desert.

It was Uncle then, acting as our leader, who opened the initial, most-sacred gate of holiday by intoning a blessing over the first of four cups of wine we traditionally drink. "Blessed art Thou, O Lord our God, King of the Universe, creator of the fruit of the vine." Uncle sang in Hebrew, his gentle voice a tender echo of the trumpet call with which he used to begin our service in the days before Old Christian informants might eavesdrop. After repeating this and the following verses in Portuguese so that Judah—whose Hebrew lessons had fallen behind—would understand, the voices of all those assembled wove together into a single ply of promise and solidarity: *"Quem tem fome que venha e coma. Todo necessitado que venha e festeje Pessá. Este ano aqui, no próximo em Israel. Este ano escravos, no próximo homens livres.* Let all who are hungry come and eat. Let all who are needy come celebrate the

Passover with us. This year we are here; next year may we be in the land of Israel. This year we are in bondage; next year may we be free."

A bit later, as Uncle began to cut steaming pieces of lamb atop our matzahs, he commented that each letter of the Hebrew alphabet is ruled by an angel and that it is the angels, assembled in our written and spoken words, who work the wonders at which ordinary men are amazed.

Surely, our prayers and stories had a winged grace that night.

Yet how fragile angels are; their magic was dispelled in a single moment. Cinfa had gone to open the courtyard door for Elijah, the prophet, whose spirit is said to enter each home during Passover. Ragged shouts from far off came in with the rush of cool air. My master jumped up; the words were in Hebrew. Again, there was a long-journeying shriek. Then silence.

"What could it be?" my mother asked.

Uncle was pale. "Nothing," he said absently, as if he were entranced by a vision. And for the rest of the meal he wouldn't utter a sound except to conclude the ceremony. "Next year in Jerusalem," were the words of eternal homecoming with which we concluded, but they fell hollow between us.

The next day, at cockcrow, a scroll was left mysteriously at our courtyard door giving us the answer to my mother's question. In New Christian code, it read: *Sixteen swallows failed to mark their nests last night and were taken by Pharaoh. Your bird, Reza, was amongst them.*

As it turned out, my cousin Reza, along with all the other guests at her clandestine seder, had been arrested the evening before and carted off to the municipal prison. Someone must have informed on them. Had Uncle witnessed this through a mystical window or only guessed that something terrible was happening?

As I read the note that dawn, my mother said, "Esther and Uncle have gone to call on the New Christian aristocrats who serve at court. They're hoping that one of them will see fit to help."

It was the Sabbath, the day before the second holy night of Passover, and I was terribly pious in those days, so I resolved to do my part in hastening Reza's release by chanting all morning and afternoon. Yet it was to no effect; just before sunset, my aunt and uncle returned home dusty and disheartened. "One of the court Jews will try to inter-vene," my master said without conviction, scratching his scalp angrily.

"All the others...they drip tears and mouth false words."

The next evening, totally disheartened by Reza's continued imprisonment, Uncle came to me in our cellar and mentioned for the first time
the possibility of our leaving Portugal. "If I asked you to leave this country forever, would you go?" he asked.

"Yes, if I had to," I replied.

"Good. But your mother...could she leave?"

"She's frightened. An enemy one knows is often easier to bear than
one who is unknown."

"True. And if your mother doesn't leave, I doubt Esther would. Nor
Reza, now that she's married and trying to start a family. If we can just
get her home."

"Is that why you've been doubly upset? You want to leave? But if
you demanded that..."

Uncle waved away my questions, began to chant Queen Esther's
prayer, verses of special meaning to us because she, too, had been
forced to hide her Judaism: "Help me who has no helper except the
Lord. For I am taking my life in my hands..."

His own hands had formed white-knuckled fists and his lips were
trembling. Jumping up, I reached for his shoulders. His eyes gushed
with tears. Poor Uncle, I thought, Portugal is driving him to the limits
of his body's tolerance. "The Jewish courtiers will effect Reza's release,"
I said. "Then, if you want to, we will make plans to leave. Somehow,
we'll convince everyone. But now you must rest. Come, I'll take you
upstairs. You may lean on me until we are out of the wilderness."

"Let us stay here," he said. "Please." Nodding his acceptance of my
aid, he said, "Lead me to the mat. The atmosphere of prayer helps me."

We sat together in silence as he wiped his eyes with the sleeve of his
robe. When he laid his hand on my head, he said in a breaking voice,
"Where is the vellum ribbon with both our names on it which I gave
you?"

"I put it in my chest for safe keeping."

"Good." He smiled sweetly. "It is a great comfort to know that you
have it."

I gripped his arm. "Look, Uncle, whatever it is that's..."

He silenced me by pressing his hand to my forehead. "You are a
worthy heir," he said. "In spite of what I may shout at you in anger, I

have never regretted you being my apprentice. Never. Once you have lived more and put more of your prayer into deed, you will be a great illuminator. Your father once told me, 'There is a lion of kabbalah dwelling in my Beri's heart.' And he was right. Of course, it is a blessing to carry such a lion around with you. But a wild beast, even one born of kabbalah, may become inconvenient at times. Now listen closely. Up until now, it has been of little concern, because you have lived a life of study. But when you go out into the world, when action in the Lower Realms takes its rightful place beside prayer, you may have difficulties. Because you will never be able to wear masks like the rest of us. Every time you try to slip one on, you will hear the growling of the lion inside you. That was why you were in such deep despair at the time of the conversion—why, perhaps, God granted you a vision. You will not have it easy. You may have to live apart from people for a time. Or suffer their earthly judgments. But hold fast and embrace the lion inside you. Do you understand what I'm saying?"

When I nodded, he continued: "Then that is enough talk. Woe be the spiritual guide who fills his apprentice with pride. We are being threatened on all sides, and if we are to survive, we must work hard. That is more important than natural talent or inclination. Your lion needs to work!"

Uncle and I sat at our desks. As he painted his panel of Haman and Mordecai, he began to study me with tender eyes. I sensed that he was caressing my form with his gaze to remind himself that—despite Reza's imprisonment—the world was still good and beautiful.

The next day, Sunday, just after the cathedral clocktower had struck sext, there was a knock on the outside door to my mother's room. She shrieked for me. I ran up from the cellar armed absurdly with an ermine brush. In her room stood a black slave, as handsome as midnight. He wore a jacket of fine blue silk, yellow leggings. He was holding a note sealed with thick red wax. "From Dom João," he said in halting Portuguese, meaning one of the Court Jews we'd petitioned for help.

Esther came running in, understood immediately. She nodded for me to take the message, covered her mouth with clasped hands, began mumbling in Persian. I took the note and ripped it open. "We have seduced Pharaoh with gold," it read. "Swallows will be home before nightfall."

While I pushed raisins left over from my morning deliveries of fruit on the reticent slave, Esther left to tell Uncle. When I got to the kitchen, they were hugging. "I'd like to be there when she gets out of prison," my master was saying.

Esther caressed his cheek. "I'll heat some lamb for her." She glared at him suddenly and waved a judgmental finger. "But when you get home, you sleep!"

Uncle closed his eyes, nodded like a little boy. To me, he said, "Beri, there are two errands I need you to do." He took a manuscript from his pouch, handed it to me. "First, deliver this Book of Psalms. Do you know where the nobleman lives who ordered it?" When I nodded, he said, "There's a note inside." He fixed me with a grave look. "Give it only to the master of the house. Only him! And make sure he reads it in front of you." In a more casual tone, he added, "Then get some kosher wine from Samson Tijolo." He handed me a scroll tied with a red ribbon. "This letter is for him."

Uncle and I left the house together, but he turned north, toward the prison, while I headed west. We exchanged kisses. Nothing more. Had I understood that after the events of the next few hours I would never again feel myself moving through a world watched by a loving God, neither man nor demon could have kept me from clinging to my master and imploring him to use all his powers to change the future. Could he have mixed some powders and potions together to create another destiny for us? How afraid I am to knock upon myself and listen for the answer.

I first tried to deliver the Book of Psalms, but was unable to do so because the master of the house was not at home. Then, on my way out of Lisbon to buy wine, God granted me with the foresight to purchase *alheiras* for our celebration. *Alheiras* were sausages invented at the time of the conversion to save our necks and Jewish dietary laws. Although similar to pork concoctions in shape and taste, they contained smoked partridge, quail or chicken, breading and spices.

I left the city through the St. Anne's Gate, and some two hours later, to judge by the descent of the sun, I was knocking at the door to Samson Tijolo's farmhouse. No one answered, so I slipped around to the cellar door. It was open. I let myself in and took a small wine cask. Having neither ink nor pen to write with, I merely left payment on a table by the door. For a calling card, I left a matzah from my pouch. Samson would understand that it was I who had left my uncle's letter and taken the wine.

It was a good five miles back to Lisbon, and on the road back, my load had me drenched with sweat and dust in no time. I rested twice inside the long, late-afternoon shadows of wavering olive trees before entering the city. In a grove of pines about a half-mile from St. Anne's Gate, I took my shoes off to feel the needles, prickly and dry, beneath my feet. While reaching for a matzah to nibble, I re-discovered the paper that had fallen from Diego's turban. It unfolded into the talismanic form of a Magen David, and it read: "Isaac, Madre, the twenty-ninth of Nisan." Today was the twenty-fourth.

At the time, I thought nothing of the message.

By my reckoning, it was around four in the afternoon when I saw the walls of Lisbon again. Certainly, it was at least an hour after nones; I had heard church bells calling the faithful to prayers from neighboring villages as I walked. A pungent, smoky odor met me as I entered the city. A vague murmuring as if from a distant arena crowd. Odd it was; houses were shuttered tight, stores locked, as if for night. All around me were empty streets, highly shadowed by the afternoon sun. I crept forward, easing my feet into the cobbles. Beneath the granite walls of the Moorish Castle, two young laborers brandishing scythes ran to me. I tensed to run, realized it was useless. One curved his blade around my neck. He held up the severed head of a young woman by her hair. She dripped blood to the street. She was unknown to me. "Are you a *Marrano*,?" he demanded, meaning converted Jew. His right eye was a milky white, bulging, reflected my fear with a glint of evil. "Because we're going to get all the *Marranos* this time!"

My heart was pounding a prayer for life. I shook my head, handed my pack to him. "Look!"

He passed it to his bearded friend. Peering inside with a sniff, he growled, "Sausages." He handed it back.

As I offered thanks to God, the dead-eyed man lowered his scythe and asked, "Is that wine?" When I nodded, he took it from me.

My breaths came greedy and trembling. "The smoke . . . where's it . . .?"

"A holy pyre in the Rossio. The Dominicans want to send a signal to God with a flame created from Jewish flesh."

A dread for the fate of my people curling in my gut prevented me from asking more. Both men filled themselves with drink, then closed the spigot. I stared at the woman's head. Her eyes were not vacant. What then? Recoiling from this world? Taking back the cask now offered me, a shiver twisted through my chest as if made by a fleeing spirit. The bearded man held the dangling head up, licked her cheek twice as if savoring the sweat of a lover. Opening the draw string of his pants, he allowed the filth of his uncircumcised penis to unsheathe into the air. The woman's black mouth was pried open by fingers cracked with dirt. To his waist she was held. He began to do something unspeakable. The other watched while pressing against himself with the palm of his hand. I dared not close my eyes, but I turned away. When his grunting had finished, he laced his pants together and said, "Be careful where you go. People are being mistaken for Jews!"

I squatted under an awning when the laborers had gone. My dizziness slowly subsided. Wine took some of the furry, acid taste in my mouth away. Were all the former Jews being hunted?

Down across the staircases and alleyways of the Alfama I raced until I reached the Rua de São Pedro. The gate to our courtyard was lying on the street, bent and twisted. Our donkey was gone. The kitchen door was open. I burst inside as if across a threshold of departure. Silence swelled around my gaze. The hearth was dying away into embers, and the table was set with two cups. Beside one was a matzah, broken in half. Our tattered rug was drawn over the trap door to the cellar. "Uncle!" I yelled. "Mother!" Chilled, confused, I crept into my bedroom, found a landscape of smashed beds and pillaged chests. Peering into the store, I discovered overturned barrels. Spilled olives formed a black and green rug leading out the doorway onto Temple Street.

My mother's room was empty, undisturbed. As I touched the eagle-shaped vellum talisman she always kept on her pillow, I thought: *In the cellar. . . . They're all hiding together!*

I pulled the rug gently away from the trap door so that I would not break the cord which enabled it to be pulled into place from below. Then, peeling open the door itself, I slipped down the stairs onto the landing. The cellar door was locked. "It's me," I called in the dark line between the door and frame. "Uncle, open up." Silence. I rapped on the door. "It's me," I called. "Mother, whoever's there...it's just me." When I looked back up the stairs into the silent kitchen, a weighted anxiety trembled my legs. I banged against the door, called out again. No response.

I was sure that nothing could have happened to Uncle, our man of wonders, the kabbalah master who played fugues with Torah and Talmud and Zohar. You couldn't kill such a maestro of the mystical with man-made tools. But Judah or Cinfa... What if they were inside, afraid to call out? Or was the cellar empty? Had they all fled? Perhaps my master had a secret way of locking the door from the outside. To protect the books. Yes, that must be it.

Was it a premonition? Simple logic? A tremor linked to the possibility that something dreadful *had* happened to Uncle shook me. Standing atop the mosaic menorah, I was suddenly battering the door with all my strength. Till its iron bolt flew from the wood.

I was inside.

The hard, dry stink of lavender and excrement packed my nostrils. I was staring at two nude bodies cloaked by blood. Uncle and a girl. They were lying a few feet from each other, she on her side, he on his back. Their hands were almost touching. It looked as if their locked fingers had slipped apart after they'd drifted into sleep.

# Chapter III

When I saw them, the air was suddenly ripped from me, and my body receded. I was racing down the stairs into a warm cavern bordered by muffled noise and wavering light, breathing in rhythm to the swaying of the walls. Naked, Uncle was. A curtain of blood had closed over his chest. The girl beside him was also free of all covering, and also drenched with blood.

The rotten stench around me seemed to moisten my eyes. Moaning, kneeling over my master, I reached for his wrist, felt for a pulse; it returned a frigid silence.

Old Christian rioters had taken his life!

I looked frantically between the two bodies as if upon unknown scripts. Had they been making love? Who could she be?

Necks and torsos were contoured by liquid brown ribbons. I crouched by Uncle's head. On his neck, two lips of skin had peeled away from a deep slit still wet with blood.

Someone help me, I thought. Dearest God, please help me.

A cold dread curled up from my bowels and pressed out against my chest when I realized I was alone, that I'd be forever without my master. A wave of sickness rose inside me, and I vomited across the slate of the floor till a stinging liquid dripped from my nose.

For warmth, I wrapped my arms about my shoulders. Nothing must be changed, I thought. Not before I had imprinted the scene like a Biblical passage in my Torah memory. I must not faint!

The prayer mat was blotched red, had soaked up the syrup of life they'd spilled.

But the door had been firmly locked. How could the killer have gotten out?

Or was he here?!

I jumped to my feet, reached for my knife. Holding it in front of me like a flame in darkness, I turned back for the stairs, then swiveled around. The silence of expectation trembled my legs.

Yet the wall tiles and window eyelets, desks and chairs returned my gaze without the slightest quiver of motion. The room was empty, seemed hollow, like the rib cage of an animal whose heart had suddenly ceased beating.

The memory of Uncle handing me the vellum ribbon on which Aunt Esther had scripted both our names came to me framed by the silence which follows a wintertime chant. *Of course,* I thought, *he must have known that the Angel of Death was approaching. It was why he warned me of our coming separation.*

I stood with my back against the southern wall of the cellar, pressed hard to its granite by the immensity of my loss, and stared at them.

Now, twenty-four years later, every detail is as clear to me as the first lines of Genesis.

My master was lying flat on his back, his head tilted to the left in a solemn and restful pose. The girl was lying on her left side, her body the span of a man's arms from his.

Uncle's feet were at the center of the circular prayer mat, his head just short of its perimeter. His eyes were open, darker and glassier than in life, staring at nothing. Blood was smeared on both his cheeks and on the wild silver tufts of hair above his right ear. His left arm was by his side, his hand palm up, his fingers curled. His right arm, however, seemed to be straining toward the girl, and his fingertips were but two inches from her outstretched hand.

If, in the moment before death, he'd been hoping to comfort the girl with his touch, wouldn't his body and head have been turned to the right side to give him greater reach?

I reasoned that he'd already been dead before reaching this final position, and I imagined a hooded Dominican friar braced behind him, stripping him, slitting his throat, blood splashing down across his chest, cascading onto his feet. Then, for some reason, he'd been lowered gently, respectfully even, to the ground. His right arm had fallen toward the girl by accident. Or had been positioned there to make it look as if he'd been trying to soothe her agony. Why? Were the men who took his life artists of death?

Shit was smeared on Uncle Abraham's buttocks. More excrement, bloodstained but untrodden, was lying just inside the fringe of the prayer mat by the Sabbath bush of myrtle and lavender.

The stink in the room was an evil marriage of the floral and putrid.

The girl couldn't have been more than twenty. She was thin and pale, a slip of a girl. With long brown hair, now matted with crusted blood. Perhaps five feet tall, she possessed small, firm breasts, as white as marble, and they, too, were ribboned with blood.

I had so rarely seen a woman's form unencumbered by clothing that the effect of her graceful contours and deep shadows was to distance me even further from the present. Already numb and disbelieving, I stared at her for a time as if I'd forgotten everything from my past.

Shit soiled her thighs and ankles. Like Uncle, two lips of skin lifted away from a lengthy slit across her throat. She had been treated more cavalierly than he had, however, and after the edge of a blade had freed her soul from its confines, must have been discarded to the ground like *tref.* She fell heavy and hard, with her nose slamming into one of the lavender bushes; a flower pot was lying smashed by her head, and soil and ceramic pieces were scattered as far as the staircase. Her nose itself had broken, was twisted grotesquely to the right and crusted with blood. She was lying on her left side now, with her head tucked down into her armpit, as if she were seeking to hide her eyes. Her left arm was extended straight toward Uncle; her right was splayed awkwardly behind her back. Her legs were pulled in slightly toward her chest, as if she were seeking to retreat into the protected sleep of childhood.

I found myself staring at a ring of bruises around her neck some two inches higher than the crusted slit. These contusions looked like shadows made by a choker of beads, and at first, without logic, I thought that they were indeed marks made by a decorative necklace.

Then I looked to Uncle and saw that he, too, possessed such shadowing. Bruises circled his neck just above his Adam's apple.

Had they been strangled with a knotted cord?

I crouched by the girl, held her left hand. It was frigid, but not yet stiff. She wore a wedding band of braided golden filaments on her index finger. Slipping it off, I placed it in my pouch and whispered: *May her husband still be alive to cherish it.*

It was the sound of my own voice which suddenly pierced the darkness of my initial disbelief; with an audible gasp, I realized that their throats had been cut just below the large ring of the windpipe, as if by a *shohet* killing in the ritual manner of all Jewish butchers.

Had a traitorous New Christian led the followers of the Nazarene to my uncle, then slit his throat? I pictured a Dominican friar rousing the mob to break into our cellar, my master taken and handed over to this Jewish mercenary like a sacrificial lamb.

The name of the New Christian arms dealer Eurico Damas sounded inside me. His recent threat against Uncle's life had been relayed to us by Rabbi Losa: *Should you ever so much as whisper Damas' name in your sleep...*

Had Damas accepted a pouch of gold sovereigns from the Dominicans to reveal the hiding places of our most honored community members? Had he penned Abraham Zarco's name at the top of his list?

But could Damas have killed like a *shohet?*

My gaze was drawn to the staircase. Light from upstairs was glistening off the tiles decorating the cellar's eastern wall, was revealing to me a pattern of twelve-pointed stars seeming to possess a secret. Stars. Light. Patterns. Secrets. Years of training in Torah and Talmud had taught me to sense when my own reasoning had veered from the path of logic, whether Greek or Jewish, and my mind was searching out a fixed pattern in the tiles with which to cleanse itself. Staring at the whirl of blue, white and gold glazes, I permuted the word *azulejo,* tile, until the meaning of the word slipped away, until there were only eyes fixed on a glassy surface. Graced with the freedom that is emptiness, a realization tugged me breathless to my feet: Uncle's soul could not have been set loose by Christian rioters; I'd found the trap door closed, our tattered Persian rug in place. The rampaging mob would not have murdered two people, then closed the door neatly behind them and slid our rug into place. They'd have been emboldened by the Jewish blood warming their hands, stormed out of here overturning everything in sight. Our cellar would be a shambles!

I looked around to certify that the room had not been trampled by Christian feet. The desks and storage cabinet appeared to be untouched. Of the furniture, only the distorted looking glass on the wall above Uncle's desk bore an obvious bloodstain. A single rivulet of brown descended from its upper rim across the concave silver surface.

Had the murderer held a dripping hand to the mirror's frame as he peered at his distorted image? Or was the legend of the Bleeding Mirror true?

Whatever the case, no Christians had penetrated; their search had been confounded by the secret threshold of our trap door.

*And no Jewish butchers have been here either!* came another inner confirmation. For no butcher knew of the existence of our secret entrance. Nor would Eurico Damas have known of it. So the trap door must have been left open. Could Uncle have been so careless?

I placed the palm of my hand flat on my master's chest, as if seeking the answer from his presence. A faint residue of warmth stilled my breathing. Examining him for blemishes, I found only a dark bruise on his left shoulder, a slight swelling around it. His whitened skin felt thick to my fingertips, like leather, but still retained a terrible trace of the suppleness of life.

I would have guessed that he had been dead no more than half an hour, since just before four o'clock in the afternoon. And that there had been little struggle.

I gripped his right hand, his hand of blessing and illumination, began examining its pores and lines as if seeking to decipher the language scripted on an ancient parchment. Suddenly, for the first time in my life, I could actually feel God's presence leaving my body. I prayed that the curtain of blood on Uncle had been a dream, counted to five, the number of Books of the Torah, then swiveled my gaze back... The air squeezed in my throat as if a fist had closed. I could not look at him; my sobs, sharp and deep and endless, had begun.

How long did I cry? Time ceases under the pressure of such emotion.

When the blessing of silence descended to me again, I sat, began to rock back and forth. I remembered a deaf and blind little boy I'd once seen swaying like this in the street, and now I understood why; pervaded by an isolation and loneliness so wide that it has no borders, the body seeks to console itself with the grace of its own movement.

Awakening to my own presence, I found myself holding a jagged piece of flower pot. I sat by my master's chest. Ripped my shirt off and started cleaning the blood from the warped mask of his face. My lips sculpted his name as if in incantation.

I noticed his bloody shawl balled up by the base of one of the myrtle bushes and drew it over my shoulders. Like a reminder. Of what, I had no idea. I was sitting barechested. Shivering. Cleaning ink again from the fingers of his right hand with my shirt, slipping his topaz signet ring off; the crown of God had trapped the emerald glow of my master's eyes inside, and I needed that light with me always.

After I'd whispered a *kaddish* for him, then one for the girl, I took his left hand to begin cleaning it. A single thread was caught on the thumbnail. Lifting it to my eyes, I found it was black silk. A name hesitated at the edge of my hearing, was framed by my whispering lips: *Simon Eanes,* the fabric importer.

Simon was a family friend and member of my uncle's threshing group who had been ransomed years earlier from the Inquisitors of Seville with a fortune in lapis lazuli paid by my master. His hands appeared before me now, fisted inside the black silk gloves which my mother had sewn for him from remnants of Dona Meneses' fabric. These gloves were meant to protect his tender grip from calluses; he had only his left leg—the right one having been amputated in his youth—and he walked heavily upon wooden crutches.

Had the thread been pulled from one of these gloves?

As a member of the threshing group, he obviously knew of the existence of the cellar and the location of the trap door. But did a man with only one leg have have the strength and balance to kill like a *shohet?*

Placing the thread in my pouch, I examined my master's other nails for particles of skin or hair. Nothing. Then his face. Capillaries in his lips had broken, formed jagged webs. I brushed his eyelids closed. They were dark, seemingly bruised.

The feel of my master's bloody prayer shawl on my shoulders moved my eyes to our desks, our place of earthly work. Uncle's slippers and white robe were on the floor below. On walking there, I discovered that one slipper had tumbled over on its back. The other was a good four feet beyond. It seemed that they had been tossed carelessly from some distance away.

All his clothes were deeply stained with blood. Uncle had been killed while wearing them, then stripped.

As I turned in a circle, I surveyed the cellar for other garments, pausing only momentarily to see my dwarfish reflection in the Bleeding Mirror. How vile and ugly I appeared just then, a being of crumpled features and snakelike eyes, my hair knotted like a Gorgon's.

In the room, I could find nothing belonging to the girl. Not a blouse or scarf. Not a single ribbon.

A possibility harshly lit with shame closed my eyes. Uncle had been deeply troubled of late. For reasons which he'd never fully clarified. What if the girl had been the source of his worries, a lover who'd informed him that this would be the last of their secret liaisons? Or one who was pregnant, who'd given him an ultimatum: divorce your wife or I reveal who the baby's father is!

Did Uncle strip her upstairs, lead her down to the cellar, turn the bolt on the door, kill her, then take his own life? But the slit across his throat... Was it possible that such a wound was self-inflicted? Was Uncle capable of killing another being bearing a spark of God in her chest?

And where was the knife?! Had he made it disappear by whispering an incantation?

I held my breath as I pried my hands under the bodies to search. Nothing but the sickening feel of cold dead weight pressing toward burial.

I was unable to find the knife anywhere. Yet in the bottommost drawers of our storage cabinet, I discovered that the lids of our two blackwood boxes had been pulled off; our small fortune in gold leaf and lapis lazuli was gone; the killer—or another thief—had passed right over the lesser ingredients and headed for our most precious minerals.

The important thing, of course, was not *what* the killer had taken, but that he had known *exactly* where to find our treasures. The number of people so intimately familiar with our storage cabinet could be counted on the fingers of my hands: the family; Farid and his father Samir; and the threshing group members.

The killer had to be one of them.

The names of the four members of Uncle's group sounded as if read from a kingly decree:

Simon Eanes, the fabric importer and manuscript illuminator.

Father Carlos, the priest, the man to whom we'd entrusted Judah's education in Christianity. Had not he and my uncle argued about the manuscript of Solomon Ibn Gabirol's which Carlos had refused to give up?

Diego Gonçalves, the printer and devout Levite who'd been attacked by boys with stones two days earlier, on Friday morning.

Samson Tijolo, the powerfully built vintner to whom I'd gone this morning for kosher wine.

As Samson's name sounded inside me, I remembered bitterly the note Uncle had sent to him, cursed myself aloud for not having read it.

I faced the eastern wall and stared into the pattern of tiles; for the first time, I realized the powers of disguise gifted to the man I needed to bring to justice, understood that he had fooled us all with a mask of friendship. I sensed that if I were to catch him, I'd have to know everything that had occurred in this cellar.

Slowly, with the careful steps of a mantis, I began to creep across the room, to imprint the scene in my mind, inch by inch, as if moving my fingertips over an unscrolled portion of Torah.

A single bead with traces of blood was sitting behind the leg of one of our desks. It was dark, grained with thin, serpentine bands. When I picked it up, I imagined a rosary or chaplet tightened around Uncle's neck. Had it belonged to Father Carlos?

I slipped the bead in my pouch.

Two thick markings of blood stained the bottom fringe of one of the two leather wall hangings gracing the western wall of the cellar. In between these stains was a straight line where the hide had been slit. Undoubtedly, the killer's hand had folded this section of hanging around the blade, and pulled the knife sharply downwards to clean its edge.

Bloody sandal-prints led back and forth between the western wall, prayer mat and stairs, but did not continue up. The killer had been trapped, was looking for a way out, then simply disappeared.

How many different people had left footprints? Uncle's and the girl's were easily visible on the mat. As best I could tell, the killer had worn sandals, and his feet were an inch longer and much wider than Uncle's.

Might these tracks not have belonged to Diego or Samson?; both of them possessed feet like Goliaths.

Or had there been more than one killer? The rough surface of the mat picked up imprints but imperfectly, and against the dark slate it would have been impossible for me to separate the footprints of two or even three killers if their size and shape were similar.

Simon the fabric importer... I considered him again. Even a man with one leg could kill like a *shohet* if he'd used surprise as a weapon against a chanting kabbalist. But he would only have created a left footprint. At least two *right* sandal-prints not made by Uncle were clearly visible.

So if Simon were involved, he had had a partner.

But I was getting ahead of myself; the thread could have been planted to point blame toward Simon, and the bead might easily have been dropped by a cunning hand wishing to focus the hollow light of doubt upon Father Carlos. Even the footprints could have been faked.

I crouched again over Uncle's chest and lifted his left hand to examine the thumbnail. As is decreed proper, it was neatly filed, except where a tiny slit encrusted with blood had caught the thread. Wasn't it likely then that the thread had been placed there by a thresher desiring to implicate Simon?

Without considering the consequences, I lifted the hand I'd been holding to my lips, to receive Uncle's touch and blessing one last time. When I pulled him to me, I began kissing his cheeks and lips.

I was covered with blood. Dyed with it. Like an illumination come to life.

When I closed my eyes, a cold wind of presentiment swept me to my feet. Sweat beaded on my forehead. The hairs over all my body seemed to stand on end. A scream building in my chest pushed open an inner door, and a vision entered:

Around me was a scorched landscape of stoney hills. It was hot, dry. Sunset was casting jagged shadows across canyons and slopes, giving the scene the stark clarity of Torah. In the distance, from the eastern horizon, a white light was rising and approaching. It twinkled as it continued to ascend in the sky, as if expressing code, and it seemed to me that it was surely journeying to deliver a message. As I stood in a position of prayer, there now rose around me a great swooshing sound. It was as if an invisible creature—or the air itself—were breathing. The white light suddenly showed wings and took on the form of a great, luminescent ibis. It was as if the pigment of its white plumage had been distilled from the moon itself. With its black feet braced in front of its body, this bird swooped down and landed just in front of me, ran for several feet to get its balance, drew its wings closed, then poked its scythe-like beak in its chest to ruffle its feathers. It was the size of a man. Standing regally before me, its great silver eyes seemed to contain liquid mercury, to possess the spiritual allure of Moses. With its beak opening and closing, it spoke in my Uncle's voice. "Turn around!" As I obeyed, I found that I was at the edge of a body of water, perhaps a mile across, and that the curious breathing sound which had risen up around me was simply the noise of waves crashing and falling away. On the far shore, tens of thousands of men had formed columns like ants, were running up the slopes of faraway hills. "Turn back for me," the ibis said. I obeyed again. "As you suspected, you have come late for the Exodus this year, and you have been left behind. If you are to get across now, you will have to fly; you have no time to wait for Moses to return." When I replied, "But I have no wings," the ibis said, "A kabbalist does not need wings to fly, only the will to do so." His pronunciation of the word "will"—*vontade*— was purposely ambiguous and was also intended to imply *bondade,* "goodness." The ibis then said, "Now face south." As I did, the landscape froze in time. The scent of vellum was all around me, and I saw that the sea and hills and even the ibis itself had been but figures painted on a page of an illuminated Haggadah. I was standing on a panel depicting the Exodus, on the Egyptian shore. I had been left behind with Pharaoh.

Shouts from the street woke me into the present. *Of course,* I thought, *the premonition I'd had while watching the flagellants two days earlier had been a precursor to this vision. God had been trying to gain entrance to me and show me this since Friday. How poorly I listened when it was truly necessary!*

The question now was: had I the *will* and *goodness* to shepherd my family safely across to the Holy Land?

Suddenly, under an instinct of bodily fear, my hand craved the concise certainty of my knife, grabbed it from my pouch. Judah and Cinfa... Mother, Esther... My hands formed fists about their names. The need to find them swelled me with a clenched force so strong each breath seemed to jump within my lungs.

As I raced up the stairs, I lifted from my pouch the Book of Psalms which Uncle had asked me to deliver; the excess weight was suddenly irritating me out of all proportion to its significance. A thought pressed me back against the wall, however: *The note inside for the nobleman which Uncle had written! Might it not end some of my confusion?*

This letter was slipped in between the cover and the first page of manuscript. Standing on the cellar stairs, pervaded by a feeling of dread, I ripped the wax seal:

*Dear and honored Dom Miguel:*

*Before you, you see your Book of Psalms and my nephew Berekiah. I ask you now: are they so very different? Both beautiful. Both containing worlds worthy of being remembered.*

*If you have any doubts, look into my nephew's eyes. Would you condemn such a good and intelligent gaze to death?*

*I told you that there are some creatures created in God's image who have no feet, only pages. Then, I stopped short of asking these following questions so as not to scare you. But desperation is propelling my pen across this page and I cannot hold them back.*

*Can you be sure that a book does not breathe? Can you be sure that it does not reproduce? If not here in our lowly world of veils, then perhaps in the Upper Realms.*

*Can you be certain, even, that angels are not books gifted with form by God?*

*Is not the Torah itself God's body?*

*I say one name to you: Metatron.*

*Repeat this name to yourself. Say it one-hundred and sixty-nine times if you dare.*

*Will the angel Metatron yet record your good deeds or pass his gaze over your name?*

*You are a shipwrecked man trapped on an island. I am on a boat throwing a rope to you. It is not the rope you wanted and I am not the savior you had hoped for. Will you lament your fate and moan your disappointment until I pull up anchor and leave you behind? Or will you realize that none of us gets exactly what we want in this life? Will you not make do with what God has given you? After all, a rope from a Jew on a boat crossing the Red Sea at Passover is not something to spit at!*

*You may even find that you like traveling.*

*Look at the covenant which has always been with you if you have any doubts. May God bless you whatever your decision.*

*Abraham Zarco*


*P.S. I was waiting for you next to tell me that Christian doctors could give my wife, dearest Esther, her virginity back!*

A door seemed to open inside me as I finished the letter; Miguel Ribeiro, the renowned Christian nobleman, must have been a secret Jew as well! What else could Uncle have meant by *the covenant which has always been with you* except the circumcised crown of his sex? Clearly, I thought, Uncle had made a difficult request of Dom Miguel, one that he must have refused. Otherwise, my master would not have made reference to Metatron, the Talmudic angel who records the good deeds of Israel.

As for the request to repeat Metatron's name one-hundred and sixty-nine times, that was typical of my uncle; it was the number of times the verb *zakhar*, to remember, appeared in the Old Testament in its various forms. Whenever my master wanted someone of little experience in philosophy to understand a difficult reading of Torah, he gave them a holy phrase related to the verse in question to repeat this many times. Slowly, through kabbalistic channels, comprehension would take shape in the subject's mind.

That Uncle's request of Dom Miguel had something to do with books was obvious. Was he soliciting more funds in order to purchase some recently uncovered manuscripts? Had he found a book so special, something so valuable that it provoked greed within the threshing group? Was that the connection between this note and the kabbalah masters?

As I continued up the stairs, I felt for the first time that I was stepping along a path toward the truth. A thresher *was* involved. Perhaps with someone outside the group. They had murdered Uncle because of a priceless manuscript he had found, something so valuable, so magically empowered that it could turn the golden heart of one of my uncle's friends to tin.

At the top of the stairs, I gazed down on my master and the girl. Both lying on the mat. Reaching toward each other like... The thought that they really could have been lovers twisted away from me, and doubt added a terrible depth to the gulf of death separating me from Uncle. Had I truly known him or only glimpsed him through his mask?

A woman's scream suddenly came from down Temple Street. I whispered goodbye to the bodies below as one would to sleeping children.

In the kitchen, I could hear the ragged voices of a crowd just outside the door to my mother's room. Creeping footsteps coming from our courtyard. Peering outside, I discovered a weedy boy without shoes, his hair a mop of brown. He was picking lemons from our tree. I stepped forward and whispered in a voice of warning, "Leave this place now!"

He gasped, whipped around and tore off through the gate.

I started to peer over the wall after him, but ducked down immediately; to my right, descending Temple Street toward the river, were a hundred or more peasants in rough linen, carrying scythes and hoes, picks and swords. My heartbeat was swaying me from side to side. I sat for a minute or so to end my dizziness, then dashed to the shed for nails and a hammer.

Working with the speed of desperation, I joined the trap door to its wooden frame with the nails and drew the tattered rug into place, all the while thinking: *No one must be allowed to defile the bodies.* In my room, I slipped on new clothes; although my chest had been ransacked, there was still a ragged old linen shirt and pants lying discarded at the bottom. My previous clothing, heavy with Uncle's spilled life, met the lime stench of the outhouse pit.

Before leaving home, I slipped into Farid's house. Since he was deaf, I could not shout to him to draw him out of hiding. I called in whispers for Samir, his father. The silence of tile and stone met me. I checked the kitchen and bedrooms. The house had been pillaged, their loom hacked to pieces. But there was no sign of either of them. They must have fled. To make sure, I stamped on the ground thrice, then once, then four more times. I was forming the magic Egyptian number *pi,* the signal Farid and I used in emergencies. If he were here, he'd feel the number in the soles of his feet.

There came no reply.

Back in the courtyard, Roseta, our cat, trotted to me, the two sour cherries my mother hung from her neck as identification swinging wildly. Lifting her back into a luxurious curl, she purred as she brushed her gray fur against my leg. I shooed her away with a gentle kick and walked to our gate. Stepping into the Rua de São Pedro, I saw the sky to the west, over central Lisbon, clouded with smoke. I clutched my knife as I thought of my family. And yet, I did not move forward, looked instead back across the empty square to the two-story townhouse just beyond St. Peter's granite archway. Father Carlos' apartment was on the top floor. The shutters were closed tight. As a member of the threshing group, was he involved in Uncle's murder? Or was it even possible that my family was in hiding with him?

I took the steps of his stairwell three at a time, found his door locked. I called out for him. "Open up!" I said. "You'll be safer with me. Just tell me if you have Judah with you. Damn you, answer me!" Nothing. The sin of wanting someone to be have been killed so that they could not possibly be responsible for murder entered my heart.

Outside again, in the eerily empty square, listening to shouts from down by the river, my feet began to move me closer to the cloud of smoke rising from central Lisbon. Like a shell of being, I trudged on, my lengthy shadow retreating behind me as if my footsteps were tainted.

As I passed the south wall of the cathedral, a group of women ran by as if fleeing an invasion, but none of them tried to stop me or warn me. Were they swallows fleeing Pharaoh? I did not look at faces, and despite what bishops may say, the sound of a Jew fleeing death is no different from that of a Christian.

A group of youths with hoes and picks was standing outside the Magdalena Church, so I cut quickly left and headed to the river. I found myself on the Rua Nova d'El Rei by the Misericordia Church. Simon the fabric importer's store was only fifty paces west. As I rushed there, four men in merchants' dress, conversing in a doorway across the street, gazed in my direction but made no move toward me. Further away, a group of waifs was kicking a wicker basket back and forth as if it were a leather ball.

How to explain the effect of seeing every shutter on the street locked tight, balconies empty, not a carriage in sight? *Such is the look of a city under invasion from within,* I thought. *Of a city without a future.* I imagined myself a phantom, wondered if my fist would make a sound when it knocked at the door to Simon's store. Of course, it did. Shutters opened above. A bearded man in a wide-brimmed blue hat peered out. It was Master João, Simon's landlord and an Old Christian. "Stop that banging!" he shouted.

"I don't know if you remember me...Master Abraham Zarco's nephew. I've come for Simon Eanes. I need to find him. Is he in?"

"You're two hours late. The Dominicans came for him. Slit open his belly, then dragged him away toward..." He flipped his hand in the direction of the smoke ribboning above the Rossio. "Now go away. You'd be in hiding if you had any sense!"

"He's dead then?"

"Do you have eyes, you idiot! You see the smoke. That's him. Now get away from me, you *Marrano* dog, before the Dominicans come for me as well!" The shutters slammed closed.

On walking away, the names of the three remaining threshers were whispered inside me as if summoning me into a biblical wilderness: Samson the vintner, Diego the printer and Father Carlos.

I would have to find Samson next; his wife Rana, an old friend from the neighborhood, would not be able to hide the truth from me. If he'd come home soaked in Uncle's blood, her eyes would give the truth away.

Rossio Square opened like an infected wound maggoted with swarms of shouting people. They crowded around trapped carriages, traced their way through the great arcades of the All Saint's Hospital, leaned laughing across balconies and window sills. Gulls circled overhead, calling in shrieks. A man in rags was dancing with crusted sores oozing yellow on his feet. "Bit by a tarantula!" a leather-skinned old woman shouted at me. "Can't stop, even for this!" She laughed, then gagged with a hag's cough.

Above the heads of the crowd, columns of dark smoke were rising in front of the Dominican Church.

It was the heat of emotion that drew me forward. To have turned then would have been like walking away from God himself. Or the Devil at his moment of attack. Only saints have that kind of power.

Suddenly, I saw Master Solomon the goldsmith at the edge of the chaotic crowd. His hands pinned behind his back by a burly giant with a blacksmith's muscular sheen. Shit smeared in his hair, across his neck. A grimace of recognition for me trembling his legs. His darting eyes begged for me to run. I imagined his voice: "Now, Berekiah, before it's too late!"

Pushed forward, he was suddenly swallowed by the swarm.

I dove in after him, was carried by a sudden surge toward the center. A terror that I would find my family captured at the core of this mob pervaded me. And yet, a heat akin to sexual desire took my strength. Passed ahead, endlessly, like falling through the arms of a dream, there was suddenly space. A pyre. Crackling with flame. Orange and green tendrils unfurling toward the roof of the church. In the bell tower, a Dominican friar with a bloated goiter holding a severed head out to the crowd on the tip of a sword, exhorting the rabble in a raging voice: "Kill the heretics! Kill the devilish Jews! Bring the Lord's justice upon them! Make them pay for their crimes against the Christian children! Make them . . ."

The fire was giving off a terrible heat as it fed on the mass of Jewish bodies with which it had been gifted. Numb, far beyond thought, I stared until I recognized Necim Farol the interpreter and money-lender seeming to peer out at me through a window of flame. His head was charred black, he had white fish-eyes. To spare myself, I lowered my gaze, but there by my feet was the head of Moses Almal the ropemaker resting like a bust of John the Baptist atop a liquid crimson platter. All around the perimeter of the pyre were pools of blood from which bodies were growing.

Seconds or maybe minutes later, for such a scene defies sequential memory, Almal's head was swooped up and carried off by a bearded, racing figure.

As I followed his mad dash through the crowd, a shirtless man sweating like a miner began hacking with an axe at the body of an old woman splayed on the ground. First the left hand, then the right were severed. This last one bore a ring: the aquamarine of Senhora Rosa-monte, an elderly neighbor who always gave me lemons as presents. The axman was so lost in the joy of killing that he didn't notice the gemstone. He laughed and shouted, "The ash of the Jews will make good fertilizer for our fields!" He tossed the Senhora's hands into the crowd. A cheer rose up, and I pushed after them. A pale and pimpled sailor from the north was now wearing the hand with the ring on his head, dancing, singing a drunken song in a language spurting up from his gut. When I faced him, he ceased his jig. I poured all my coins at his feet, pointed to his find. He nodded, spit out guttural words, tossed the hand high in the air, straight up toward the gulls. It fell, splattering blood. I snatched it up, sealed it in my pouch. From the granite steps of the Dominican Church, shouts in a voice of doom turned me: "Kill the heretics! Kill them now!" It was a squat, owl-eyed friar swathed in his robes of evil. Like a heraldic shield, he held a bloody Nazarene stick out to the crowd. Solomon the goldsmith was there, lying on the cobbles at the foot of the church steps. Belly up, bleeding like a wounded dog. As I stepped forward, he shouted my name, once clearly. Crimson ribbons streaked his white robe. Two grunting men soaked in sweat and blood were hitting him with planks of wood formed into Nazarene crosses and driven through with nails. Solomon, who caressed gold leaf into whispers from God. Solomon, who kissed me full on the lips and sobbed when he saw the illuminated Book of Esther I'd made for him. Solomon, who...

It was hard work this killing. At each whack, spurts of life emerged from the goldsmith as if from fountains viewed from heaven. The ripped meat of his punctured hands was outstretched to make it stop. Screams. Hebrew screams for King Manuel. Now to Abraham, Moses. To God. "Make it stop! O God! Make it stop!" A gurgling blood from his mouth choked him.

"Let's shave the Jew before he dies!" one of the men shouted. Lifting a blazing branch from the pyre, he held it to Solomon's gray beard, set it afire. The tortured goldsmith's eyes were wide with pain, looking ferociously into the world for help.

As if an arrow of heresy had split my mind, I was thinking: *It is a failing of God that we cannot draw such physical pain away from another human being and make it our own.*

A hulking giant with a red cross painted on his forehead, carrying a rusty ax, suddenly came forward shouting for mercy and rain. With a great swing over his head, he sent the jagged blade crashing for Solomon's neck. Life splattered as far as my feet and his ragged body collapsed like a doll's, his neck spurting blood like new wine from a cask.

When I awoke to my own presence, Christian men were staring at me; it was idiocy, but in my horror, I had involuntarily begun to whisper prayers to myself in Hebrew!

A hand caught me suddenly, tugged me back. Jerked me hard. A face I knew. David Moses? We ran through walls of reaching arms with the weightless speed of nightmare. Raced through a forest of movement. Around corners. Up stone staircases. Down shadowed alleys. Into a house. Through a closing door into welcoming darkness.

A hand fell over my mouth. Breathing came hard against my cheek. A voice I knew was whispering my name. "Quiet, Beri," he said.

It was David Moses, our former chazan.

"Master David, did you see Solomon, the goldsmith?" I asked.

"I saw many of us," he replied.

"But Solomon. Did you see..."

Shouts from just outside the door: "Down by the river! Let's get going! Bring the cart!"

Master David covered my mouth with his hand. We crouched down. Our breathing ebbed together, then separated.

"Have you seen my family? My mother, Judah..."

"No. But they could be anywhere."

"I must go back...maybe they've made it home. I must find them and..."

He gripped my collar. "Listen, the only way to find them is to stay alive. You must get away."

"How did it start?! Who's responsible for this..."

"In the Dominican Church. A crucifix with a hole covered by mirror. A lit candle slipped in from the back by the friars. They tell everyone that the light is a sign from the Nazarene, a miracle. About an hour ago, a New Christian, Jacob Chaveirol, the tailor, he was..."

"I went to school with his son, Menni. He's brilliant in Torah. A man of wonders. He has a shop up..."

"He's an idiot! He said how much better it would be if Christ gave us rain instead of fire!"

"And...?"

"Beaten to death. They slit his abdomen and pulled out his... Two priests called on the congregation to kill the Jews. His brother, Isaac, killed as well, ripped to pieces. The head in the bell tower, it's his. Northern sailors contributed money for the wood of the pyre. And soon...and soon..." David's words faltered.

"And the King, why doesn't he come to our defense? Twenty years we were given to..."

"King Manuel?!" Master David sighed. "He a coward, but he's not stupid. He knows that if he sends troops to our aid, the mob will call for his head. The people hate him almost as much as they hate the Jews. He'll give the riot time to burn itself out, then take control of the city again."

He and I clung together in silence. I could not speak of Uncle; my revelations would have confirmed that he would never return to me. And I could trust no New Christian until I learned more about the murder. I asked, "Have you heard anything of the fate of Father Carlos or Diego the printer?" When David shook his head, I added, "And Samson the vintner?"

"Not a word," he replied.

My eyes were adjusting to the gloom; we were in a spiral stairwell. Above us, dim light filtered through a thin portal covered by a grill. Suddenly, I could distinguish a face above us peering around the central axis of the stairs. I lunged. Caught a leg. Stifled a scream with my hand. It was a girl. She struggled, but I held her with the force of my stored fear. "Stop! I won't hurt you!" I said.

She fought me for a moment more, then shook free of her terror. Her breathing came warm against my hand.

"Damn her!" the chazan whisper-screamed.

"We can't stay here anyway," I said. "We're too close to the Rossio. You go now and I'll meet you outside the *Porta de Santa Ana,* St. Anne's Gate. Past the monastery, on the crest of the next hill, is a single large oak. Meet me there. I'll stop her from shouting till you have had time to get away." I could see my friend clearly now. His prayer shawl had been tugged through his ripped mantle. "And for God's sake, toss away your *tallis.*"

"But what about you?" he asked.

"You've saved me once. I'll do the rest. Now that I've awakened to what is happening, I'll get away. Just get rid of your shawl."

"I can't," he said. He hid it back inside his mantle.

"And you think that Jacob the tailor was crazy? Look, I'll meet you beyond St. Anne's. Go!"

Master David paused as if to speak, then squeezed my arm and dashed out the door.

Power and fear produce a color of emotion unlike any other, and with the girl in my grasp, I felt my body to be silver, reflective, beyond confinement. "I'm going to let you go in a minute," I said.

She breathed hot against me. As I unfurled my hand, she straightened up and tugged my fingers back to her mouth. Her tongue flicked like sexual prayer against my palm, traced edges of desire along my thumb and forefinger. She reached fingertips to my sex. Squeezed once with the pressure of curiosity. The in and out of our intertwining breathing gave rhythm to our tongues dancing together. Two sinful lunatics we were, swelling together in a stairwell with a riot just outside. She took my hand. "Upstairs," she whispered.

Does the body have its own life separate from the mind? How could I have let her lead me on after having seen my uncle? Or does sex serve a healing function which we refuse to admit?

I followed her into a room grayed by a drawn curtain. The lock of the door clicked like a bolt in a dream. Lines of light at the window drew me from her. From here, I could see we were on a side street about fifty paces from Rossio Square, just inside the Moorish Quarter. Shouts filtered up as if through layered fabric. My heart suddenly skipped a beat; Master Solomon's face was burning before me. Except that he had Uncle Abraham's emerald eyes. They were vacant, cold, staring beyond me. So much death, so much blood. The girl's hand was stroking my behind. I turned for her mouth, but she ducked below, began caressing my desire with a liquid warmth, swirling with a wild craving, hiding me inside a gulping shadow with no form and all need, moaning desperately as I held her to me and swirled her hair over my quivering chest and licked the petals of her ears. As if mounting the contours of darkness itself, I gripped her shoulders and fondled the tickling desire of her breasts, thrust harder and deeper into the warm wet darkness until she was gasping as if crying and I was exploding as if free-falling into a bottomless cavern.

When she had taken everything from me with the maddening tip of a flicking tongue, she caressed my face. "To wash," came a breeze of whisper. The door clicked open as I lay in bed. Racing footsteps down the stairs. "*Marrano!*" came her shout. "A Jew in my room!"

I tied the string of my pants together and opened the curtain. She was on the street by a carriage, surrounded by men in cloaks, pointing up toward me. I grabbed my pouch and jumped onto the landing, crossed to the roof, slid down to a verandah opposite. Screams propelled me forward. I ran across rooftiles, dashed down gutters. Voices from the apartment below brushed like gusts of wind at my hearing. The last ledge came up as sudden as the closing of a book. A blank drop of forty feet led to the cobbles below. The height of two men separated me from the next rooftop. "Stop, Jew!" I turned as if to confront all of Christianity. A young, long-haired nobleman was navigating awkwardly down the roof. He was tall, thin, possessed a gaunt face which jutted forward at the chin with the arrogance of the high-born. His yellow leggings were wiped with blood, like the markings of a demonic script. He carried a horsewhip in his long, elegant hands.

*A young hunter out to prove his prowess to his friends and family,* I thought. *And I am to be sacrificed for the good of his arrogance.* As I waited for him, my feet sought sure footing. He stopped twenty feet away and faced me with a bemused look. I felt strangely at an advantage.

"This is going to be a pleasure," he observed in a voice of false ease. He braced his feet and arched his whip back, then swung it forward with a shout. Its tip slapped by my feet. Two rooftiles exploded. Moments later, the bitter clacking of their shards below spread a look of satisfaction across his smug face.

A rush like a ghost passed from my toes into my chest and up through my head: the grace of God was ascending. I clung tight to its hold.

"They say if you hit a Jew hard enough you can hear the gold rattling in his rib cage," he said with a smirk. "I aim to find out!"

It was a legend based on a horrible truth; Jews expelled from Spain in the Christian year of fourteen ninety-two were forbidden from taking valuables. Some of the tens of thousands crossing the border into Portugal dared to eat coinage.

As I spired up to the pinnacle of the roof, a tile came free. I picked it up, held it as a shield in front of my chest. An image of Moses and his tablets entered my mind. The burning sun of the age of Torah seemed to be pulling me toward the sky. My nemesis laughed. He took awkward giant steps, joined me on the apex. We faced each other across a silence of ten feet. His face was twisted with scorn. I began chanting the names of the Unnameable.

"A magical *Marrano* incantation?" he questioned.

To defend myself, I was tempted to invoke a kabbalistic prayer for his death. Forcing my words silent, I withdrew from thought until there was only a light presence weighing my soul.

"Crazy Jew," he said. "We'll kill all of you. Peel open your skin and take out your gold!"

A sudden visceral force pushed me. I charged. He lifted his whip slowly, as if mired in a liquid time. Was he surprised that a Jew would attack without warning? He never tried to dodge me. With my tile as a shield, I plowed up into him like a bull, took the very air from him. He flew to the end of the roof, slid past the ledge and screamed all the way down. A sound like a gloved fist knocking once at a door rose up toward me when he hit the ground.

When I peered below, I saw him lying at a crazy angle on the cobbles, twisted like a discarded marionette.

There was still the roof to cross if I was to get away. Space seemed to recede from me as I jumped, however. Crashing against the wall, I began a free fall, landed hard on a slatted verandah below. My arm was scraped badly and my face stung with blood. The apartment must have belonged to former orthodox Moslems; I was atop the gallery from which their women had surveyed the world below without being seen in the days before their forms of worship were outlawed as well.

I kicked against the blue slats till they gave, then dropped below.

Out of the light, I felt strangely distant from myself. I was in a bedroom of pallets and leather mats. As I trudged breathless into a whitewashed hall, voices came through walls. A family was gathered in front of a smoldering hearth. A tall, cinnamon-complexioned man in green robes and a white skullcap faced me. He had broad, powerful shoulders. His light brown eyes were close together and menacing, like an eagle's. A tuft of dark hair sprouted between his eyebrows, gave him the look of a man of mystery. The thought came: *I am too tired to fight. If this man chooses to take my life, I will offer it to him like a prayer.*

"You seek sanctuary?" he asked in hesitant Portuguese.

I answered in my Hebrew-accented Arabic: "They're after me." We watched blood dripping from my arm onto a leather mat. I cupped it with my hand. "I'm sorry for staining your..."

He called his wife. She rushed to me with a young girl clinging to her robes. Her hair and fingernails were dyed red with henna. After smearing an olive-green ointment on the cut, she bandaged my arm with a linen remnant. Her black, thickly outlined eyes regarded me fearfully till I complimented the grace of her daughter with an Arabic couplet which Farid had written.

My right shoulder had dislocated when I crashed, however, and now, calmer, I realized I could barely move it. It ebbed with pain, then grew numb.

"My name is Attar," the man said. "I am a potter. I come from Tavira."

"Berekiah Zarco. I am a fruitseller, and I have always lived in Lisbon."

He sat me down on a pillow and gave me water. When I mentioned Samir, Farid's father, a welcoming smile lit his face; they knew each other and had even studied Koran together in Granada when it was still the capital of an Islamic kingdom. "I'll get you some more water," he said when I'd finished my cup. He stepped behind me, grabbed me suddenly. Pushed hard. My shoulder popped. Pain broke over me like a tide, then receded. "You'll feel better now," he said. "But no more jumping across rooftops for a little while."

His wife cleaned my face with warm water as I tested my arm. Attar said, "You're welcome to stay till the trouble passes."

"I must try to meet a friend, then get back to my family."

My pants were badly ripped at the inseam. He made me change

into a tawny aba fringed at the collar with delicate arabesques in chartreuse thread.

"How will I ever repay you?" I asked.

He waved away my concern. "The possessions of nomads are meant to leave their hands," he observed. "It is better. What is without wings has a way of dictating our thoughts." He placed a knitted skullcap on my head.

"Allah be with you," he said at the door.

I echoed his closing and bowed my thanks. "I'll return your clothes as soon as I can."

He lifted the hood of my robe over my head and bowed back.

The street was empty when I slipped outside. Rushing along the cobbles, I tried in vain to fade my footsteps to silence. The acid smell of burning Jewish flesh was everywhere now. I was sure that a plume of smoke was rising just above me, but would not look. I breathed through my mouth, crossed the Moorish Gate under the scornful eyes of two sentinels on horseback. Dressed as I was, however, these representatives of the crown would not dare to touch me; if there was official violence against former Moslems, there might be reciprocal bloodletting against Christians in Turkish lands and North Africa.

As for the mob, all I had was my knife. I prayed I would not have to use it.

Once outside the city walls, I lowered my hood and ran across the fields fronting St. Anne's convent, then crawled through thickets of broom and tall, scorched grasses as I approached the great oak crowning the coming hillock. Master David was not there, however. A small crowd of worried Old Christians had assembled just beyond the Roman bridge below; they told frenzied stories of how the mob had turned on anyone even remotely connected to Jews. Some cowards, they said, were even using the riot as an excuse for personal vengeance, or a way of freeing themselves from debt.

"It's the New Christians' fault—they caused the drought!" a crone in black kept shouting to anyone who would listen.

A group of peasants armed with the hammers and iron rods of a looted blacksmith's shop suddenly marched out St. Anne's Gate in search of *Marranos,* primping themselves with the good humor of hunters scenting blood. I pressed my chest to the ground and waited. The sun had already set, and the sky was pearly with dusk. Crows flapped in the branches of the lone oak above me. I imagined death as an inky pool spreading from my stomach into my hands and feet. For what sin, I began to wonder, was God taking from us the best of Israel? Why was he using these Christians of Lisbon to punish us?

Soon, the voices of the Nazarenes were gone. Fear gripped me again only when I remembered Senhora Rosamonte's hand in my pouch. Beside her fingers was the note that had slipped out of Diego the printer's turban, stained now with blood. Reading its words again—*Isaac, Madre, the twenty-ninth of Nisan*—I wondered if it didn't have something to do with Uncle's murder. Had his death, in fact, been originally planned by Diego for five days hence, on Friday the twenty-ninth? Could Isaac have been the name of a killer hired with a handful of coins taken from an ecclesiastical coffer, from the Mother Church, from the *Madre?*

I realized, of course, that I was weaving a complex story from mere threads of evidence, that such a scenario was but a remote possibility. I felt so alone, however, so free of my family and Lisbon and the love of God that I needed to believe in a tale—however unlikely—which placed the events of this most terrible day in a sensible order.

Such is the power of isolation. And I understood then that freedom, of the kind bequeathed to abandoned orphans and apprentices without masters, could be the most dreadful state of all.

# Chapter IV

It was late Sunday, the third holy evening of Passover. Long after midnight. Master David had not met me, was either dead or in hiding. St. Anne's Gate had become ever more clogged with Christian rabble. Not so the Monks' Gate to the east. Past a few sleepy peasants slurping soup from wooden bowls, I strode across the fortified Visigothic bridge there back into Lisbon, my hand gripping my knife inside my pouch. A crescent moon was skimming over the stream below like a heavenly boat. Pricks of sound prompted me on like ivory needles. I realized with a bitter dread that I was fighting a fever. Yet had I ever been more alive? Every nerve in my body was craning into the present for the touch of sensation.

Was the city safe yet? The answer didn't seem to matter; a dreadful longing in my chest as powerful as Uncle's chanting of Torah was pushing me home.

Beyond the gate, a dim music of contrapuntal horns seemed to dance like shadows along the high Moorish walls surrounding the oldest part of the city. As I climbed, the Alcáçova Palace rose above me, its garlic-bulb towers beaming with an orange light that slid into the darkness as a mist. Hundreds of feet below me, seeming to protest against my movement, slept central Lisbon and our largest Jewish quarter, Little Jerusalem—twenty thousand moonlit homes reclining across the hillsides and valleys and nestling into a bend of the Tagus. As I prayed for my family, the downy gray moonlight behind my eyelids separated and coalesced as angels.

I descended through the steeply falling labyrinth of ancient stairs and alleys. By the Church of São Martinho, the smell of smoke chilled me. I slowed, crept along whitewashed walls. Loios Square opened to me. In front of the brittle arcades of the convent, a raging bonfire was sending jagged butterflies of light and darkness across a crowd. At the center, a group of New Christians from our Little Jewish Quarter had their arms and legs bound with nautical rope. They stood in a ragged line, their clothing tattered, their heads hanging from exhaustion. No one spoke. Wan, hopeless expressions showed they'd been paraded around the city like this for hours.

Rugged men with swords and halberds fixed them in place. I crept back and hid around the flaking wall of the corner tavern.

"I beg you not to do this!"

"Kill me if you want, but save my children!"

A hundred supplications pounded me as I searched the caustic orange torchlight for the faces of my family. Blessed be His name, none of them was there. I recognized all of the linked prisoners, however, including Solomon Eli the surgeon, and I imprinted their faces in my Torah memory.

A monk with a beaked nose was swinging a smoking silver censer and cursing the Jews in Latin.

How many had already been dragged from our neighborhood and rendered ash? Little Didi Molcho, whom we all believed would grow up to be a great poet? Had his future been pried from his mother's hands and...? Or Murça Benjamin, who gave me my first look at a girl's dark place out behind St. Vincent's? Was it her glorious body, within the crown of flames, that was beginning to...? *Please,* I chanted, *let no one be burned tonight.* Yet into the breathing spaces of my prayer burst the question: why has He allowed any of His self-portraits to be so desecrated?

Samuel Bispo the blacksmith was tied to the monumental stone cross that centers the square and was about to be whipped. I drew away into the darkness without looking back. Empty streets returned my hollow heartbeats. What a coward of Biblical proportions I was to have abandoned him and the rest of our prisoners!

My chest and injured shoulder were aching with a revolving, knotted pain, and I was shamed by my terror. I squatted to catch my breath, prayed for deliverance. A sweet scent stung my nostrils. Reaching my hand up, I discovered my nose was bleeding. Men following? Jumping to my feet and pressing into a slatted doorway, I listened. The plunk of dripping water reached me. When a bat sliced through the air and dove

into an open window across the street, fear like violent Moorish drumming struck at me. I set off again. Paupers in rags were sleeping
amongst sheep in *Praça do Limoeiro*, Lemon Tree Square. One was
awake, watched me with idiot-curious eyes.

Cutting in front of our old neighborhood inn and hostelry, I
descended the steps past the accursed house where Isaac Ibn Zachin
murdered himself and his children after the conversion. I cut into the
alley behind the Church of São Miguel. As if landing from a tumbling
fall, I found myself trudging along the Rua de São Pedro. A thousand
onions and garlic heads were scattered by my feet; a cart had been overturned. A tumbling island of black rats was forming over the opened
gut of a headless man without clothes. I rushed toward home. Since I had
last been here, half a day earlier, our neighborhood had been defiled. Shit
had been smeared against all the walls, stores looted, doors and shutters
smashed. At the entrance to our former schoolhouse hung a body: Dr.
Montesinhos. A cross of blood was finger-painted on his chest. A gold
sovereign peeked from his mouth; a daring Jew must have put it there to
pay for his ferry ride across the River Jordan. One of his sandals had
come free. A sprig of oleander peered over the lip of its heel. I took it.

I crept toward home, slipped through our gate. Two hens loosed
from neighbors' coops scuttled and cackled around the courtyard. Our
lemon tree had been felled by an ax. In my mind, I chanted our religious injunction from Deuteronomy against the felling of a fruit tree
even during a siege: *You may eat of them, but you must not cut them
down.* Out loud, I whispered: "Cinfa, Judah, Esther..."

I almost called Uncle's name, but an image of him lying stiff and
white pressed my lips toward silence. As I gripped the handle of our
door, Roseta hopped gray and ghostly onto the low wall next to me. The
cherries were gone from around her neck. "Wait," I whispered to her.
But she leapt inside as the door opened.

"Mother...Esther..." I called in a low voice.

The darkness of night held its breath.

The hearth in our kitchen was cold. I felt along the tile floor. It was
wet. Blood? I lifted my fingertips to my mouth. Only water. I cut my
hand on the tip of a fallen knife, cursed, then blessed He who gives
power to iron. I held it in front of me as I groped my way to the bedroom which I shared with Judah and Cinfa. Caressing the cold, barren
mattress where they slept, I whispered a prayer for their safety. I bal-

anced on tottering feet to my mother's room, whispered for her, felt the taut emptiness of her bed in my fingertips. I swirled her blanket over my shoulders to end my shivers.

Where could they all have gone?

Robbers had rifled through my chest again, but had still left behind most of the frayed hand-me-downs I'd inherited. Discarding the blanket from my shoulders and slipping out of Attar's cumbersome aba, I put on a pair of my father's linen pants and one of my elder brother's shirts. In Uncle's chest, I found his ancient woolen cape. Was I alone now, the inheritor of all his clothing, the narrator of his story?

Crossing the courtyard to Farid's house, I whispered for his father, Samir. Heavy footfalls from outside made me duck. I peered out the window. Two men carried swords. They were swiveling their heads to survey the courtyard.

The soles of my feet suddenly recorded three taps on the tile floor. One more. Then four. It was Farid, signalling *pi* from back in his house. I crept through his front room to the kitchen. A sweaty hand reached out for my arm. We kissed, and I held Farid until his silent sobs seemed to leach across my skin into my heart. I couldn't allow him to peel me open to emotion and pulled away. "I can't find anyone," I indicated against the palm of his hand in our language of signs. I considered telling him about Uncle, but guarded the knowledge of his death as if it might not be true. Was my master a powerful enough kabbalist to cast such an illusion?

Farid started to signal in wild, frenzied movements. I was unused to reading his words inside my hands. "Slowly," I begged.

"When the Christians came, I tried to escape the Little Jewish Quarter," he indicated. "But there were too many. It was like a cloud of locusts. I came back and hid. I saw Judah for a moment. Only him. Father Carlos was running with him down the Rua de São Pedro. They disappeared into his church. I tried to call, but my voice..."

So Carlos was alive! Perhaps he was indeed in hiding when I knocked at his door! But what then of Judah?

Farid's palm flattened and pressed against mine. His pulse raced. Space and time dropped away until there were only two presences meeting at a warm border.

I signalled, "I tapped *pi* for you once, this afternoon, an hour or two after nones, but there was no reply."

"I was looking for Samir."

"Any luck?"

He shook his head. "He was at one of the secret mosques in the Moorish Quarter when they came. I couldn't make it there. I don't know."

"Two peasants with swords have breached the sanctity of our courtyard," I indicated. "Let's sneak out and get to St. Peter's, look for Judah and Carlos."

Farid stood, guided me through squares of light and darkness toward their back door. As we stepped outside, a long-haired man with a lance surprised us. His blade swept at me. I dove to the cobbles. My right forearm burned. A gash near my elbow dripped blood.

Farid tugged me up, and we ran like madmen toward the river. At the Jews' Steps, I realized our nemesis was running after us, shouting for help, and would attract a mob if we didn't silence him. I stopped, caught Farid, signalled to him my plan. He nodded, ran down the steps and cut into the alley past Senhor Benadife's apothecary.

Dripping blood onto my left hand, I waited on the top step for my assailant. I kicked off my sandals so my footing would be better on the cobbles. He came to me panting. I could see now that he was younger than I, with a round, farmboy's face, a mop of wild black hair. Yet for all his ferocity, he had frightened eyes. Dangling from his belt were human ears, and a filigree earring twinkled from a lobe by his hip. In another time and place, I would have depicted him as one of Saul's terrified sons. So what sense did any of this make? It was as if Lisbon had thrown open its gates to a disease of ever-increasing lunacy. Yet my breathing came easy, from an eerie landscape beyond fear. "Go back to your millet and rye," I told him.

"You stole my father's best acres!" he answered. He crouched as if preparing to spring. "Don't you move!" he warned. His lance blade bobbed awkwardly; he was unused to carrying such a weapon.

"I'm a manuscript illuminator and fruitseller. I've never stolen anything."

Strange how humor can come to you at the worst moments; I thought, *Hmmmn, that's not quite true…a sponge cake once with a friend…*

"*Marranos*—over here!" he shouted at the top of his lungs. In a voice of bound rage, he added: "Land that was ours for centuries!

Your people... You live off of us, bring us plague, drink the blood of our children!"

"Your grievance is with whoever stole your land!" I told him.

"You do their bidding. You manage their estates, collect their taxes!"

Behind him, Farid dropped down from a rooftop like a cat and crept forward on cottony feet. I said to the boy, "Drop your lance and go. You won't be injured."

He lunged suddenly. I ducked away, but a wound burned open on my good shoulder as it was grazed. Watching my blood sluice, I thought: *I will never again let an Old Christian hurt me.*

Farid took him from behind. His powerful forearm locked around the boy's neck, the arching blade of his Moorish dagger cut into his cheek. I grabbed the lance and said, "If you threatened the nobles as you threatened us, then all would be well!"

Bellowing cries from down the street turned us: "Hold 'em son! We're coming!"

I signalled for Farid to let him go; we had to trade him for our lives. As he was released, the boy spat into my face. "When we catch you, I'm going to slice off your 'chestnuts' and hang them on my belt!" he announced.

I slashed the lance across his thigh. He fell. Blood curtained his leg as if seeking to cover his agonized screams. Farid grabbed me and turned me. We raced down the Jews' Steps to the river. I tossed the accursed weapon on which my blood had mixed with an Old Christian's into the silver waters.

As we ran, I wondered about the violence which seemed to rise up in me so easily. Had I, too, not simply been wearing a mask of piety and gentility all these years? Was there a true Berekiah whom I'd only glimpsed during moments of rage and desperation?

Dawn rose in tones of pink and rusty gold. We were hidden on a sand bar inside a lagoon of rushes between Lisbon and Santa Iria. I slept without dreams, awoke into Farid's arms startled, surprised by the return of the sun. As he wiped my brow and sat me up, I was struck by his unadorned beauty, in particular by the dark, youthful stubble bristling on his cheeks and standing out like ornamentation against his olive complexion. Thick ringlets of wild, coal-black hair framed his face like a mane, ribboned over his forehead, cascaded onto his broad shoul-

ders. The look of a schemer, people used to say who feared his silence
and the assessments of his light green eyes, who believed in their ignorance that the deaf were evil. But the only schemes Farid ever dreamed
up applied to rhymes. A born poet, he was, and more often than not, his
eyes were simply focused inward, judging only the curve of a phrase or
contour of a rhythm. Now, his lips thinned to a thoughtful slit. He fingered
the long lobe of his right ear as he always did when upset. He looked as if
he were yearning to speak. But that, of course, was impossible.

For a time, prompted by Farid's beauty, I stared at my own image
in the gentle waters around us. In comparison, my form was graceless,
and it seemed as if I couldn't possibly know this reflective twin looking
back at me with the hunted look in his eyes, the dirty stubble on his
chin, the mean, knotted hair falling to his shoulders. The young scholar
who shared his uncle's probing profile seemed to have been swallowed
by a gaunt, wild-faced youth of the forest, a Pan of vengeance. Had I
become the half-human creature the Dominicans believed us all to be?

Farid tapped my shoulder, offered me bread from his pouch. I
refused; it was only the third day of Passover and we were still cele-
brating the Exodus.

"Your fever broke in the night," he signalled. "You feel better?"

My separated shoulder was stiff with that dull, knotted pain which
I would forever associate with that Passover of death. The wound on my
forearm was tender with crusted blood. My right foot stung; gashes
scarred my toes. I gestured to Farid, "We've been abandoned by Moses
and will have to get to the other shore of the Red Sea by ourselves.
We're all alone."

As Farid ate, the reeds around us swayed in unison with the gentle
tide. The waters made the lapping sound of fawns drinking. All was
calm, as it should be. I began crying as if at the gates of God's compassion, gestured to my friend, "Which is the real world? This or...?"

He signalled back, "Heaven and hell are the sea and sky. And you
are the horizon."

His words meant nothing then. It was the elegant dance of his powerful hands which was too lovely to bear. And when he caressed my
face, the sobs knotted in my throat broke. Memories of the pyre cascaded, molten and furious, onto us both. Even so, I was still unable to
talk of Uncle. Farid took Senhora Rosamonte's hand from me. So frightened he was. Trembling. And yet, he touched its fingertips of blood-

stained marble to his closed eyelids as he prayed. I noticed then the bruises and welts on his neck. "We will bury her in a lemon grove," he signalled. "She will always be able to gift us with her fruit."

"What happened?" I gestured, pointing to his tender wounds.

"Nothing," he replied.

"Tell me."

"In the alley last night—a man tried to stop me. I killed him."

It was the first time either of us had signalled the verb "to kill" in the first person. We both realized our language of gestures had to change to keep up with this new, Old Christian century. As if unequal to the task, we walked along the Tagus back to Lisbon without conversing. Distanced from my own emotions, I remembered the young noble I'd pushed from the roof. Where would I find forgiveness for removing from the Lower Realms a being imbued with a spark of God's love?

Just outside the Santa Cruz Gate, we came upon docked salt boats. Women with knobby, blistered feet balancing ceramic jugs of the white crystals on their heads smiled at us. Children played, dogs wagged their tails. A merchant in scarlet and green robes tipped his cap to us for no reason I could fathom. Farid purchased sweet rice and grilled sardines from one of the women who sold food down by the river. He gorged himself, but I, of course, could not.

Coming into the Little Jewish Quarter was like leaving a theater. Suddenly, the image was not born of denial or separation, but as it was, bordered with shit and stinking of violence; etched with the barking of saliva-dripping dogs, centered by folding islands of rats and mice.

Vacant-eyed survivors swept blood from their doorways, wore tear-less masks, shuffled on bare, dispirited feet. Bodies waited for our notice: Saul Ha-Kohen folded over the slats of his bedroom window, an arm, stiff as salted meat, moving back and forth in the wind, tapping an unknown code against a shutter. Raziela Mor gutted, an onion in her mouth being pried out by her daughter, Nafa, clouds of flies seeking to lay eggs in her womb. Dr. Montesinhos hanging rigid and bloated from the coiled tracery above our schoolhouse door. A nameless baby without a head sitting in a shovel.

Faced with the unthinkable given physical form, no one dared speak.

Do you know what it means to look at a headless baby sitting in a shovel? It is as if all the languages in the world have been forgotten, as if all the books ever written have been given up to dust. And that you are glad of it. Because such people as we have no right to speak or write or leave any trace for history.

The doors to our store were now lying at oblique angles to each other on the cobbles, like entrances to a cockeyed underworld. Muffled moans in Hebrew were coming from across the way in Senhora Faiam's house. Her dog Belo's beseeching blue eyes stared out at me over the wall. In his mouth he now carried a gnarled and splintered bone, yellow with age; it appeared that he had once again found something resembling the remains of his recently amputated left front leg, buried this time by Senhora Faiam in the yard behind St. Peter's Church. His nose was twitching as if he were on the trail of someone to show it to.

My mother and Cinfa met me in the courtyard. They had been picking up broken pieces of slate. Cinfa ran shouting my name and clawed at me as if afraid to fall. Mother dropped to her knees and wailed. Two vellum talismans dangled from her neck. When I lifted her up, she gripped me with white-knuckled desperation. She sobbed as if she were vomiting. When she had her breath, she said, "Judah's missing. I don't know what..."

Mother gripped me so tight that her heartbeat seemed to pound from inside my chest. Dizzy with her presence, I said, "I'll find him."

She dragged her disbelieving hand through my hair, over my chest. Cinfa hugged herself into Farid.

"You're unhurt?" my mother asked. "Nothing happened that you won't..."

"Yes, I'm fine. What about Esther and Reza?"

"Esther's bruised but alive. Reza, we don't know." Mother turned toward Farid. Although she'd never fully approved of my friendship with him and was terrified of his silence, she looked at him now with anxious concern, raised her hand and approximated our gesture for greeting. "*O Farid está bem,* are you all right?" she mouthed.

He smiled gently and bowed his head in thanks.

"He's fine, too," I said. "Where were you all last night? I came back but the house was empty."

"We were here! I was hiding in the store with Cinfa. It was siesta when the Christians first came. We were spending it with Didi and his mother. Rushed back home only to find that..."

"Didn't you hear me?" I interrupted.

Mother held up hands blotched purple. "I surrounded Cinfa and myself with barrels of beans, then covered us with basketfuls of over-ripe figs. We stayed that way for as long as we could stand it, couldn't hear much."

Stained with violet skin and smelling of fermented sugar, she and Cinfa suddenly seemed possessed of a holy beauty; they glistened with survival. I was laughing with an absurd relief. I kissed her forehead. "Clever girl!" I said, as if I were my father.

"Old Christian men pinned Esther's arms to the cobbles in front of St. Steven's Church," she whispered conspiratorially. "And then..."

As I nodded my understanding, she lowered her eyes.

"Mother, have you seen any of the threshers? Father Carlos, Diego, Samson..."

"No one."

After searching his rooms, Farid signalled that Samir had not returned. We entered my house. Esther was seated in the kitchen with her hand wedged between her legs, her bare feet in a puddle of water. I kissed her forehead. She was cold. She would not talk. I covered her with a blanket from Cinfa and Judah's bed.

I whispered fearfully to Mother, "Then...then you have not seen Uncle?"

"No. I thought he might be in the cellar. But the trap door, it's nailed shut. He must have sealed it. And the curtains on the window eyelets are drawn. We can't look in. We've knocked and screamed for him a dozen times. No answer. I'm afraid to break through. He may have had a reason why he wanted it shut, to protect the books, or something more...more occult. I hope he's all right. He probably went out looking for us, then couldn't make it back home."

"When was the last time you saw him?" I asked.

"After lunch on Sunday. Not long before...before they came. He went to the cellar to chant. And Cinfa and I went out to..."

"Mother, I nailed it shut," I said dryly.

"You? Why?"

"When I came back, I went downstairs and... Wait." I went to the court-yard, took the hammer from our shed, smashed at the trap door. The last slat of wood dropped free with a cracking sound which seemed to imply a terrible finality, as if we would never again find safety in our house.

"Don't come down yet," I said to my mother as I stepped onto the stairs. "Let me take a look."

It was insane, but I wanted to see Uncle first because in those days I put very little beyond the range of a kabbalah master's powers. Might he not have swallowed a piece of paper bearing a special prayer formula before his throat was slit, a secret name of God which would effect his revival?

"Why...what is...?" Mother grabbed my arm. "What do you know? Is he down there?!"

"All right, come," I said, and in the quivering of my own voice, I heard the simple truth of his disappearance forever from the Lower Realms. "But I must warn you, Uncle is with us no longer."

Mother reached for her mouth to stifle a scream. I reached for her hands but she drew them away as if I were tainted.

She crept downstairs with one hand forming an awning over her eyes, the other gripping the talismans dangling from her neck. But she did not cry. A moan when she saw him. A rasping inhale. As if she were choking for breath. That was all.

As she knelt to put Uncle's fingertips to her cheek, she began to pull her hair. Her face peeled open to sobs. I turned away; it was a moment which could bear no witness.

# Chapter V

Time is like a seal certifying existence. And like a seal, it is artificial. As Uncle used to say, past, present and future are really just verses of the same poem. Our goal is to trace its rhyme scheme back to God.

And yet it was already Monday afternoon, a day since Uncle's death. The fourth evening of Passover would be descending soon.

My mother had just left the cellar, had told me that she'd never seen the girl before. "You're sure?" I'd asked her.

"Never," she'd whispered shamefully, and I could see her thinking: *It was carnal sin which drew death to him.*

I was now standing above the bodies, my aunt by my side. She wasn't howling or crying, had simply picked up a shard of pottery and was scarring her fingers with its razor edge.

"Esther, stop that!" I said. "Esther..."

Her transfixed stare, remote and childlike, showed she had severed herself from the finality of Uncle's death seeking to penetrate our hearts. A groan rising from her belly splintered suddenly into gagging. She looked between him and the girl, leaned forward as if tugged downward by his grip, began slashing at her index finger—the finger graced with her wedding band. I ran to her, ripped the ceramic piece away. Blood sluiced burning over my hands.

Farid rushed from the stairs and folded his arm protectively around Esther's waist. As he steered her away, she turned, stared at me over her shoulder as if to say goodbye before a long voyage. With Farid following closely behind her, she carried herself up the stairs with a ghostly grace.

Although its exact route is hidden to us, the pathway between sadness and insight must be paved carefully by God; I suddenly realized that the killer, who had been intimately familiar with the contents of our storage cabinet, would also probably have known of our *genizah!*

Taking a key from inside the eel bladder hanging behind the Bleeding Mirror, I lifted the rim of our prayer mat skirting the north wall and peeled away a piece of slate to reveal a lock. Half a circle to the right I turned. At the sound of a click, I lifted a wooden lid flanking the wall, three feet by four, camouflaged with slate. Our *genizah* opened with a groan of protest.

I'd been right; smudges of blood stained the top two manuscripts: the "Fox Fables" which I was illustrating and the Book of Esther which my aunt was lettering. Below, for the most part clean, but still tainted here and there with the red finger-shadows of the killer, were family Torahs, Haggadahs and prayer books; a map of the Mediterranean by Judah Abenzara; religious commentaries by Uncle's friend Abraham Sabah; poetic works by Farid ud-din Attar; and two mystical guidebooks by Abraham Abulafia—our spiritual father—which my master had not yet summoned the courage to entrust to his secret smugglers. Below these, seemingly untouched, there rested a Torah illuminated with magical beasts bequeathed to my master by his late friend, Isaac Bracarense; a Koran from Persia; three piles of my master's personal correspondence; our woolen sack of coinage, still heavy with copper and silver; and finally, the marriage contract between my aunt and uncle, scripted by one and illustrated by the other.

I locked everything below the *genizah* door.

It seemed clear to me that the killer had stopped his search before reaching the lower manuscripts; they were unstained. And if he *had* continued that far, surely he would have taken our money.

The only work missing opened the petals of a new mystery: it was the Haggadah Uncle had been completing just before his death. For all the daring of its knotted patterns and bird-headed letters, it was worth nothing in comparison to the Abulafia manuscripts, portions of which were centuries old and in the master's own hand.

So my uncle's Haggadah must have possessed a hidden value to the killer.

That certainty gifted me with another, and I turned around so that I could face our desks: the killer had found the key to the *genizah* in the eel bladder hidden behind the Bleeding Mirror. This was confirmation that a member of the threshing group was involved. But why had the *genizah* been re-locked? Out of a simple desire for order?

Seeking a power to enhance my own, I took out Uncle's ibis ring from my pouch and slipped it on my right index finger.

Farid had returned to the cellar now, was standing between the bodies, staring at the lips of crusted blood peeling away from my uncle's neck. He began wavering as if foundationless. When he looked at me, something he saw... His eyes rolled back in his head to show a sickly white. His body melted. I jumped up and reached out to break his fall. I held him till he awoke.

Cinfa stood on the landing now. The girl's eyes, like Torah pointers, were fixed on Uncle. Her hands gripped the hair at the back of her neck. Liquid was dripping down the legs of her pants.

Afraid that she wouldn't be able to cope with death viewed from any closer, I shouted, "Go up the stairs and guard the door! Let no one down!"

She did as I said. Farid was waking now, and I began to blot his brow with my sleeve. He sat up. "I'm okay," he signalled. "It was suddenly too much to bear. And something I saw..."

"What?"

"On your uncle's right thigh..." Farid clasped his hands together and took a deep breath.

"What?!" I demanded.

"*Semente branca.*" Farid used the kabbalist's term, white seed, for semen.

"What are you talking about?"

"Come," he signalled. We crouched together. There, on Uncle's inner thigh, in between smearings of blood, were patches of crust, like bits of mica.

"That could be anything!" I gestured wildly. "Spilled honey, almond milk. Uncle didn't pay attention to..."

"It's *semente branca,*" Farid repeated with an impatient, downward thrust to his gestures. "I sniffed it and..." Before I could stop him, he peeled a tiny piece free and placed it on his tongue. He tasted it as one might sample a new spice. Gagging suddenly, he spit it back into his hand, wiped it on his pants. "They had just made love," he signalled with definitive gestures.

It wasn't shock that Uncle could couple with someone other than Aunt Esther that made me gasp. But that he had brought a lover to his prayer cellar, our synagogue... It was impossible. It changed everything. And yet...

"Listen, I need your help," I gestured to Farid, realizing that we had reached the appointed time when I needed to count on his singular talents. I pulled the prayer rug off the girl and told him what I already knew and suspected, showed him the note Uncle had written to Dom Miguel Ribeiro, the nobleman for whom Aunt Esther had scripted a Book of Psalms. When he finished reading, I grasped his powerful hands and placed them flat against my chest so he could feel my heartbeat. I signalled, "Farid, I've been thinking that God may have brought us together for just this Passover. Perhaps he needs us to find Uncle's killer together. I must go look for Judah soon. But for now, I want you to walk around this room, gift your gaze to every form and shadow and tell me if you spot anything I haven't. Anything! You must give me your interpretation of what happened."

Farid did as I said. And when he was ready to tell me what he'd found, he motioned me to follow him to Uncle. We crouched by his head. *When will we be able to bury him?* I suddenly wondered, recalling with a jolt that we had to see him safely into sanctified ground as soon as possible.

"There is a slight slope to the slit across his throat," Farid signalled. "I'd say that the killer twisted your uncle's head to the left from behind, and with a razor-sharp knife in his right hand..." Farid tugged his arm across his chest to indicate the motion that must have ended my master's life.

He stood up, walked over to the girl, crouched by her hands, leaned over and sniffed at them eagerly, puffing like a dog. Looking up at me, he signalled, "She worked with olive oil and rosemary. Something else that's almost disappeared, possibly lemon oil." He touched her thumb with the tip of his index finger. "There's some ash there. I'd guess she was a baker. The ash may come from the ovens."

I nodded my agreement; I would be a greater fool than I am to discount Farid's nose or eyes.

"And look at her right temple," he gestured. "There's a small circular indentation there. One on the left as well."

"What do you think they are?"

"I've no idea. But the symmetry is most unusual. Now follow me." He led me to the leather hanging on the western wall where the knife had been cleaned. Lifting its fringe over his head, he showed me five slashing strokes of blood coming to a sudden end at a clean edge of tile. It was as if a hand with fingertips but no palm had been wiped there.

Was the killer a being able to disappear by fingerpainting arcane symbols in blood? Had one of the threshers summoned a demon or ghost to slay my master? Could such a creature from the Other Side have gotten past the mezuzah on our doorframe?

"What do you make of it?" Farid asked with anxious gestures. When I shook my head, he dropped the hanging back into place and signalled, "Now give me the rosary bead and the thread."

I took them from my pouch and handed them over.

He sniffed and licked at them. "The bead is carob wood, well polished. Expensive. Made locally, I'd say. But it does not belong to Father Carlos. At least, it's not from the rosary of his with which I'm familiar. The thread, as you know, is silk. Very fine quality. I would have to see Simon's gloves to know if it's a match. And even then... There must be more miles of black silk in Lisbon than paved streets." He let his hands fall to his sides.

"Nothing more?" I asked.

"Just that you were right about your uncle being murdered while still wearing his clothes. Inside his robe, there are stains from excrement and from *semente branca.*"

It was as if my master's body had released all its fluids. Perhaps, at the moment of a violent death, the body seeks to cleanse itself so the soul can depart quickly to God.

"Is that it?" I asked. When he nodded, I signalled, "Then how do you think he escaped? I know for certain the door was bolted firmly from the inside. He'd have had to pass through the cellar walls. There was no way..."

"Only one very poor thought has sought to dispel my ignorance," he gestured.

"Which is?"

Farid pointed up to the window eyelets. There were three, oval in shape, and each no longer than ten inches and no wider than a man's hand. They were covered by tiny shutters which could be locked and highly polished hide flaps which allowed only a dim light to enter the room.

I signalled, "Not even a child or dwarf could slip through one of those. Unless the killer was a mink or viper..."

"I told you it was a pauper of an idea." Farid shrugged, held his thumb and forefinger to his lips, then swirled them upward in a graceful arc. He meant that we had to wait for Allah to give us an answer.

"Can't wait for Him," I replied. Walking to the stairs, I sat to consider the mystery. I thought: *How strange that I feel nothing but a vague emptiness and weakness of body.* It was as if my love had died with Uncle. As if—cut loose from my past and present—I were floating free of everything but an unstoppable need to find the killer.

Suddenly, my heart seemed to leap against my chest; someone was scratching at one of the shutters over the eyelets we were just discussing. I ran up the cellar stairs, dashed through the kitchen to the courtyard. And found Roseta smacking her paw against a ball of vermilion wool which Uncle had recently made for her. She was all wet, looked like she'd been tossed in a well.

"You soulless idiot!" I hissed at her.

I took a long deep breath, apologized to her and walked out our gate to the street. To the east, about a hundred paces down the Rua de São Pedro, Dr. Montesinhos' body was still hanging in the doorway to our old schoolhouse. A small man in a long violet cape stood before him, was raising his right hand to offer a blessing. I could see him only in profile, but he had my master's wild gray hair and cinnamon complexion.

*It's Uncle!* I suddenly thought, as if all my previous conclusions about his death had been sheer idiocy. *Of course, he's used magic to fool us all!*

It was insanity, I know, but relief swept through me, and I started to advance toward him. I may even have begun laughing. On hearing my approaching footsteps, however, the small dark man turned toward me, froze, then bolted around the corner toward the back of the Church of São Miguel. By the time I reached there, he was gone from sight.

Desperately confused, I trudged back to Dr. Montesinhos' body. The gold sovereign which had been placed in his mouth to pay for his heavenly ferry across the Jordan River was missing. With a jolt like that which comes after jumping from a high wall, I thought: *The man in the violet cape was not my uncle, had reached up not to bless the body but to steal the coin. He had been just a common thief.*

On walking back home, I was pervaded by the sensation that history had taken off on an errant path unforeseen by God Himself. All of us in Lisbon—Jew and Christian alike—were now dependent only on ourselves for survival. It was then that a chilling thought came to me which I never imagined would ever penetrate my mind: *There never was any God watching over us! Even at its kabbalistic core, the Torah is simply fiction. There is no covenant. I have dedicated my whole life to a lie.*

On descending into the cellar, I sat again on the bottom step of the stairs and hid my head in my hands. Farid came to my side, rested his hand atop my head. "We're all doubting God right now," he signalled. "Do not think about the greater troubles which we all have. We have a murder before us. Let us return to that. Now, what special value might your uncle's missing Haggadah have had to the killer?"

I reminded Farid that my master had always modeled the faces of his Biblical characters on famous Lisboners, neighbors and friends—including his beloved colleagues in the threshing group. Always, he attempted to match them to characters possessing their own predilections and interests, of course.

"Had any of the threshers just been illuminated as an evil man?" Farid gestured.

"No," I signalled back. "I don't think he suspected any of them. Or had only learned very recently of the treachery against him. Probably, he wouldn't have gone back and re-illuminated their panels. It would have been simply too much labor for results..." I stopped in midsentence; everything was falling into place. Last Friday, just before our Passover seder, Uncle had told me that he'd found the face of Haman for his latest manuscript. In his voice, sadness and relief had woven together. Now, to Farid, I gestured that he must have discovered the perpetrators of some sort of plot against him that very day. I signalled, "And I think that he used the face of his principal enemy for the villain Haman...the face of the man who would kill him. It's the only possibility. And that's why his last Haggadah was stolen. The murderer knew of his characterization. Or suspected it. Or even accidentally came across it as he paged greedily through the manuscripts in the *genizah*. He panicked, took it with him. That's why he didn't leave blood stains on the bottom manuscripts or take our coins."

Farid tugged on his ear lobe, looked down at me gravely over his broad nose. "We must consider each of the threshers in turn," he signalled. "Father Carlos, what could have been his motivation? Could he have been Haman?"

"Uncle and he had argued about a *safira* of Solomon Ibn Gabirol's which Carlos had refused to give up."

"And Samson Tijolo? Had Uncle spoken of him lately?"

"Just before I went to his house to buy wine, Uncle told me that he wished to talk to him, gave me a note for him."

"What was the subject he wanted to discuss?"

"Don't know," I gestured. "But there's another thing. They only ever saw each other for threshing meetings. Was it simply the distance between our houses? I wondered about that sometimes."

"A spark of dislike?"

"More like rivalry. Two intelligent, powerful kabbalists. Competition may exist even amongst the angels."

"And then there's Diego," Farid gestured.

Diego had not yet completed his initiation into the threshing group. I replied, "I don't know if he'd been informed yet of the secret *genizah*."

"You could find that out from one of the other threshers."

I took out the note fallen from Diego's turban, showed it to Farid and explained how it had come into my possession. "What do you make of it?" I asked.

"*Madre* is mother, of course, particularly when used to discuss Our Lady. So I would say that it seems to be a half-Jewish, half-Christian talisman—a prayer to the Virgin for something good to happen to an Isaac on the twenty-ninth." He handed it back. "Very strange things you Anusim are making of late. You're like sphinxes with Jewish hearts and Christian heads."

"There's another thing, Farid. Diego was injured at the time. After being stoned and chased, could he have mustered the strength to slit two throats?"

"If he felt he'd had to; Diego is a survivor, fled Castile with the Inquisitors salivating over his imminent capture. His injury would be the best of excuses should anyone begin to suspect him."

"But he lives blocks away. Would he have risked setting sail through a sea of Old Christians to reach us? Unlikely."

"If, however, he had combined skills with Eurico Damas..."

"Or with Rabbi Losa," I noted. "He always hated Uncle. And he deals in religious garments, undoubtedly rosaries as well."

Farid breathed deeply. "And lastly, there's Dom Miguel Ribeiro," he gestured.

"I think he'd gone to Dom Miguel for funds to purchase a very valuable manuscript. A book that may have provoked an argument in the threshing group. This time, Uncle's need to save every last page of Hebrew from destruction may have gotten him killed."

"The girl's husband," Farid signalled. "What about him?" He caught my hands to stifle my protest. "I realize that it's almost impossible that she and Uncle had been lovers," he gestured. "But not everyone is blessed with your faith. Perhaps her husband had been convinced she was giving him the sharp horns of a cuckold. She might have come to Uncle for help of some sort, to ask a religious question. The husband could have tracked her under the mistaken assumption that whomever she was meeting was a secret lover. After watching her disappear through the trap door, he burst in and leapt upon Uncle. He took his own wife's clothing so she couldn't be traced to him."

"An obsessively jealous husband, mistrustful, faithless, prone to rage."

"Lisbon is up to its towers in such vermin. How many men do we both know who do not understand the way of love?"

"But he would have had to realize that his wife's very face would give him away. Taking the clothes would be an absurd gesture."

"Unless they possessed a hidden value," Farid signalled. "A jewel or a letter of credit. Beri, there's one more possibility." Farid licked his lips nervously.

"Who?"

"Like amateur beekeepers around an angry hive, we are avoiding the topic of Esther." He waved away my protests. "No one we know is more prone to rage than her, right or wrong?" he demanded.

I nodded.

"Her silence is most strange. Perhaps upon discovering the girl with your uncle in the cellar..."

"It's ludicrous!" I interrupted. "Do you think she could have strangled them in a jealous rage with some rosary she just happened to find lying about the courtyard?! Then slit their throats, stolen our lapis lazuli and gold and raced out of here so she could get raped on the street?

Farid, it's a house of cards built on a slanted table! No, her silence is not strange. I understand it perfectly. It has been born of forever disbelief, not of guilt."

"A house of cards on a slanted table *during a sandstorm*," Farid replied with an apologetic grace to his hand movements. "But I had to let the thought into the air, so it could fly freely from us. Now tell me this, Beri... Why would a thresher collaborate with Eurico Damas or anyone else outside the group?"

Blackmail? The word swept into my mind so violently that I jumped to my feet.

"What is it?" Farid gestured. "What have you heard? Who's coming?!"

"It's not what I've heard." I signalled for him to wait a moment so I could think. Could Eurico Damas have blackmailed one of the threshing members to help him slay Uncle and rob our storage cabinet and *genizah?* Perhaps he imagined that we kept barrels of gold, coffers filled with rubies. Could he have even brought the girl to the house, killed her there to make us think that she and Uncle had been lovers— to convince us that her husband had done the evil deed?

Another terrible thought occurred to me: perhaps the killer had spilled his own seed on Uncle! It was unspeakably dreadful. But even if we had been gifted with no other knowledge these past two days, we had learned that such evil was always only a single spark away from the present tense.

"Blackmail," I told Farid. "During our accursed reign of masks, everyone has a secret or two for which he can be made to pay!"

He stood and took my shoulder. "But that, too, presents us with a quandary. For if all of us have secrets to hide, could not anyone have been coerced? How do we proceed if we see everyone wearing the veil of suspicion?"

It was then that the most unimaginable terror spilled into my gut. Sweat beaded on my forehead. I felt sick, moaned aloud. So disturbed I was that I spoke to Farid rather than use our signs. "Father Carlos was with Judah! Might not the boy have witnessed the murders? Carlos couldn't bring himself to end his life. He took him away!"

Farid read my lips, closed his eyes as if to shut out the possibility. "I hadn't thought of that," he signalled weakly. His hands twirled together in a dance of prayer.

I took his shoulder, signalled, "Did you see if Carlos was covered with blood?!"

"They were far away. I don't think so, but I can't be sure."

A grave silence held its fingers to our lips. We were left with Eurico Damas, Rabbi Losa and Dom Miguel Ribeiro. One or more of them had joined forces with a threshing group member.

"We will need to speak to all of them," Farid said.

As I nodded, my mind began to construct an explanation for the clues we'd found:

Uncle had been in the house all alone, was visited by a girl whom he had known years ago, a baker's assistant, the daughter of an old friend perhaps. She was greatly troubled. Her husband had beaten her recently. What should she do? My master sat her at the kitchen table and poured her a cup of wine moderated with water, offered her a matzah. They talked of her desperation until shouts from the street drew their attention. Understanding immediately what was happening, Uncle told her to remain quiet, crept cat-like to the courtyard and then the store to look for our family members. But I was on the way back from my journey to buy kosher wine and Esther was at the market in front of St. Steven's. Judah was with Father Carlos. Mother and Cinfa were taking siesta with a neighbor. As Old Christians battered at the doors to the store, he took the girl into the cellar, slipped the tattered Persian rug in place over the trap door from below. Curtains were drawn over the window eyelets at the top of the northern wall so no one could see in. The tiny shutters were locked.

Sometime later, during a brief quiet spell in the riot, there was a knock on the cellar door. A familiar voice calling for help. Rushing up the stairs, Uncle opened the threshold to our synagogue to a brother from the threshing group. This man had argued with Uncle about a valuable manuscript, may even have plotted to purchase it behind my master's back. Whatever the particular nature of his sin, he had earned the face of Haman. And yet, with a riot raging outside, all bitterness would have been forgotten for the moment.

Eurico Damas suddenly strode in behind the thresher. He lunged without warning, pushed Uncle down the stairs. Hence the deep bruise on his shoulder. As my master rose to one knee, he was grabbed from behind. A rosary was wrapped around his neck. "Give up easily, and I swear on the Torah that I'll spare the girl!" Damas shouted.

Uncle acceded, understanding in that moment the nature of the sacrifice he had been called upon to make. Life was squeezed from him. The thresher, a former shohet, took my master's body, slit his throat to make sure he would not revive. He was laid gently to the ground. Blood sluiced freely across the prayer mat.

A black thread was placed around his thumbnail to implicate Simon.

By now, the girl had backed to the eastern wall of the cellar, was crouching in fear, begging for her life. Damas broke his promise to Uncle, grabbed her, but as he was strangling her, the rosary broke. He slit her throat, then threw her down. Her head smashed against a flower pot. Her nose broke, was twisted grotesquely out of shape. Within seconds, she had bled to death.

The rosary beads were scattered across the slate floor of the cellar. Damas ordered the thresher to pick them up. One was left behind, lost under our desks.

The thresher then took the key to the genizah from our eel bladder, opened the camouflaged lid. Uncle's last Haggadah was discovered on top, paged through greedily until the killer came upon his own face as Haman. Terrified, he concealed the manuscript beneath his cape, informed Damas that they had to make an early departure.

Damas had been told where to find our gold leaf and lapis lazuli, had just lifted them from their blackwood boxes.

Together, they stripped the bodies so it would look as if Uncle and the girl had been making love. It was intended to be a last cruel joke to play on our family. And, of course, to point blame toward the girl's husband. The thresher may have protested. But he was reminded of the seemingly terrible secret for which he was being blackmailed.

All this killing provoked excitement in Damas, for there are men in whom sex is intimately woven with violence. Or perhaps he believed the scene was missing one last, perversely poetic touch. He wished to defile Uncle's body even more foully.

He unsheathed his sex, spilled his own seed onto Uncle.

As for the girl, she was also known vaguely by the thresher.

Her father was not just a good friend of Uncle's, but one of his as well. And there was something in her clothing which would give this connection away. So he snatched up her dress and blouse, her undergarments even.

Had Judah stood at the top of the stairs witnessing all this? Was he encircled by the killer's arms and carried away?

A secret name of God was then drawn by the thresher on his own forehead and that of Eurico Damas. On Judah's as well, perhaps. A powerful name which had been lifted from a manual of practical kabbalah and which would enable them to pass through walls.

And then they were gone.

# Chapter VI

As I repeated my scenario to Farid, I heard a man's voice coming from the courtyard. I ran up. It was a neighbor, Rabbi Solomon Ibn Verga. His bearded face was framed in the kitchen doorway, and he was talking to Cinfa of God's mercy in comforting tones. He carried three slate tiles in one arm, a basket of onions in the other. "You made it, my boy!" he told me with a smile. As if afraid to cross the threshold into our home, he did not come toward me.

"But most of us haven't. Judah's missing. And Uncle..."

"Yes, Cinfa was telling me." He put his basket down, motioned me over. Taking my shoulder like an elder, he said, "Never forget that your life has been preserved so you can remember. As for me, I shall make this perfidious riot the culmination of the book I'm writing on the history of the Jews."

"A history book?" I questioned, never having heard of such a work written by a Jew since the days of Josephus.

"Exactly," the Rabbi replied. "An account of all the gates of nettles we have passed through on our way to the Mount of Olives."

*We are truly emerging into a new era,* I thought. *It will be a world defined by history texts, not the works of God. The rabbis and kabbalists shall become obsolete.*

"I suggest that you make use of what you've experienced during the past two days in your illuminations," the Rabbi added. "Translate what you've lived through into images. As Jews, that is our process of artistry." He handed over the slate. "From your courtyard, I believe. It was on the street."

After I'd thanked him, he wished me peace and started to turn away. "Oh, and if you need any onions..." He held up his basket.

"Someone overturned a cart. They're not much, but they've come to us at bargain prices."

Again, one would not think humor is possible at such moments. And yet we shared a smile.

Does insanity, like insight, comes in flashes?

Then I heard them. The first of the screaming waves of Old Christians approaching. I pushed past our guest and ran to the gate. From the swelling murmurs and shouts, I reasoned that they were approaching from the west, from the cathedral. And rapidly.

"What is it, my boy?" Rabbi Solomon asked.

I turned for him. "You better get home, Rabbi. I don't think it's over."

He flipped the hood of his cloak over his head. As he passed me, he paraphrased a verse from Proverbs: "'God punishes the one whom He loves, like the father the son he delights in.' We are his chosen people. We shall yet see the Temple rebuilt."

I gathered the family together and told them they had exactly one minute to collect belongings. Rushing to the outhouse, I scooped up a clump of filth with a wooden bowl, then smeared it into the fibers of the tattered rug which covered our trap door; in this way, I hoped to deter robbers or intruders. From my room, I took with me a candlestick and a flint, several blankets and a jar of water. In a secret panel at the bottom of my chest was the vellum ribbon on which was written my name and Uncle's. I grabbed it and tied it around my wrist, turned the golden writing flat against my skin so that it could not be read. Then, I led us down into the cellar, cursing myself all the while; the minutes I'd used talking with Farid could have been spent searching for Judah. And now...

Atop a weak voice, I lifted a prayer begging forgiveness toward God when I realized that we would not be able to bury Uncle that day. Eyes closed, my body swaying with my heartbeat, I asked that this breach of duty in no way impede his soul's journey.

For the rest of Monday, we waited—Mother, Esther, Farid, Cinfa and I. We sat in our own separate worlds, no one talking.

The royal blue of the prayer mat which covered the dead girl; the warm thick scent of Cinfa's hair as she tucked her head below my shirt and breathed hot against me; the nervous buzzing of the cicadas in the courtyard. Every traitorous sensation underlined the same question: why was I here to see, to listen, to smell, when so many had died?

"I almost wish I had died with them," I whispered to my mother.

"Guilt clings to us like God," she answered. "How could it be otherwise?"

Every time that I believed my mother wasn't worth fighting for, she surprised me with such a verse.

"We live to remember," Cinfa said, repeating Rabbi Solomon's words.

Is it through mimicry of adults that children are able to cling to hope?

Suddenly, there were shouts coming from the street, accusing the *Marranos* of having summoned the drought with witchcraft.

It was the first of three separate occasions that day when we heard the followers of the Nazarene. Hundreds of them descended upon us in waves, led by Dominican friars shouting with the strident, high-pitched voices of eunuches for us to come out and be cleansed through flame, shrieking epithets against the devilish Jews. *"Bichos meio-humanos,* half-human creatures," they called us. Once, in the late afternoon, the music of bagpipes vibrated the chestnut beams of our cellar ceiling as if to summon us to a fair. The last time, by my reckoning about three hours after the fourth evening of our Passover had descended, sharp squeals reached us in our darkness—as if a pig were being whipped through the streets. I prayed that that was all it was.

Twice, they trampled through our house, shattering what was left of our furniture.

Cinfa huddled between Farid and I. Esther sat stoically. Her eyes no longer had any of their dark make-up, and her graying hair fell carelessly onto her shoulders. *An actress whose fellow actors have all died, whose theater has been burnt to the ground,* I thought.

Mother gripped her talismans and prayed silently. Whenever she looked at me, I could see her studying my resemblances to Judah.

If the Christians had discovered the trap door, all would have been lost; the planks were hastily nailed back into place and the bolt on the true cellar door was broken when I burst inside to find Uncle. One false step onto the center of the rug above and they'd have literally fallen upon us.

After darkness descended, I painted Uncle and the girl with myrrh to subdue the rising odors that signify the soul's departure. Covered them again with prayer rugs.

The gash in my arm from the boy's lance finally closed with the aid of extract of comfrey. I painted it with a thin layer of marigold juice to ensure healing, wrapped it with a linen handkerchief.

I gathered my courage once and whispered to Aunt Esther, "Had you ever seen the dead girl before?" She was seated on a bench we'd brought down from the kitchen, my mother's thick mantilla of brown Flemish wool blanketing her shoulders. Her right hand, wrapped in a bloody linen towel was wedged between her legs in protection of what had been defiled.

She would not utter a sound, and I knew that her soul had fled deep inside her body.

Was it a cruel question to ask Esther? I didn't care; I had to know if she knew. Not for the prurient reasons she probably thought.

I kept the girl's golden wedding band in my pouch to give to her husband, prayed that he was still alive to cherish it.

Uncle's signet ring I kissed and placed in the blackwood box which had held our gold leaf; I felt it might have pained Esther to see me wearing it.

When mother asked me about the whereabouts of this keepsake, I thought it might be a propitious time to talk with her. "Who knew of the *genizah?*" I asked her.

She pulled her head in like a hen, stared at me as if I were insane and told me to ask no more questions.

After the cathedral had tolled midnight, we heard Brites, our Old Christian laundress, calling desperately for us from the courtyard with the shrill voice of a lost gull. I was about to shout up to her when my mother thrust her hands at me and formed a cross.

I realized then that hell was being unsure if a little brother was in the clutches of torturers with respect for neither the beauty of the human body nor the sanctity of the soul.

And I wondered who it was who was etched as Uncle's murderer on the Enduring Tablet of Moslem tradition. I vowed to discover the girl's identity. More than ever, I believed that she was the key.

Early Tuesday morning, I found I had had enough of darkness and hesitancy. My legs and arms were clenched with the need for air and movement. In the purplish haze before dawn, I resolved to start looking for Judah, Reza and the members of the threshing group. I reasoned that there would be few Christians about at that hour of the morning.

"You mustn't go!" my mother whispered to me. Her nails dug in to the pulp of my flesh. "No! It's not safe. And you have to recite morning prayers. Uncle will be angry if you haven't done your work for the Lord."

"Morning prayers will have to wait!" I told her. I broke free, entrusted everything in my pouch save my knife to Farid.

He accepted my offerings without gesture. His eyes were blood-shot, and lines of sweat were sliding across his cheeks. When I kissed his forehead, it burned, tasted of foul disease. He turned away from my probing stare, and I saw that the bruises on his neck had soured to black and yellow.

"What is it that you feel?" I asked with my hands.

"A spiny animal is scraping my gut, trying to get out," he signalled weakly.

Was it plague? If he were to depart, who would speak my inner language, help me to find Uncle's killer?

Fixed by hopelessness, I continued to watch him, remembering that it was our old friend Murça Benjamin who first said that he and I were twins gifted to different parents. Dearest Murça was to be re-married soon, after the illness and death of her first husband. Had she even survived?

As I started my search, I grabbed the hammer from our shed and whispered to God, "Return Judah to us and take me in his stead."

For a shield against Christians, I inner-chanted verses from the Zohar.

Nearest me, the Rua de São Pedro was empty. A dark, cottony haze blanketed the city. Those shutters which had resisted the onslaught of rioters were locked as if never to be opened. Gulls flew overhead, lumi-nescent, as if about to burst into flame. Down by St. Peter's Gate, a stout woman carrying a wicker basket atop her head began running with a painful, bobbing gait. High above her, beyond the twin towers of the cathedral, ribbons of smoke were unraveling into the air; the pyre in the Rossio must have still been raging.

The door to Father Carlos' apartment was still locked. Inside St. Peter's, hanging oil lamps sputtered with flame. In the the nave lay corpses splayed like drowned fishermen washed to shore.

Senhora Telo the seamstress was on her back under the fresco of the Annunciation which decorates the transept. Her face was white and waxen, her eyes closed. No blood. None at all. Her tin whistle, meant for calling her children, dangled over her shoulder.

A growl turned me. A pink-nosed, tawny mongrel had its front paws across the stomach of a man whose chest was soaked black. Ears pricked, he raised a crusted, throbbing lip to show fangs, growled from his gut as if I might challenge him for the body.

I headed to St. Michael's Church. Many lay stiff and silent before the altar of the Nazarene. I took a candle from a side chapel and searched. Judah was not among them.

At St. Steven's, I found a body of an adolescent girl in the courtyard garden, inside a circular bed of the most perfect marigolds. She was being picked by a hunched, methodical vulture with an indifferent gaze. Watching him, I learned that these birds rip first at the soft tissue—the lips and tongue, the eyes. The girl was beyond recognition.

The caretaker of the church, an Old Christian, came out from his hiding place in a side chapel before I left. To my question, he shook his head and said, "No, not Father Carlos. Others. Most were heading for the river. There was talk of boats carrying Jews to the other side."

I found that the only thing which could now upset me was kindness. When he hugged me, my foundations slid away. I pushed him away and reached out for a wall. Then I ran.

Dawn was spreading a gauzy light over the horizon. Swallows were scooping great arcs of air all around me, twittering as if in hurried speech. Cutting down to the Tagus, I described Judah to the fish-mongers setting up their stalls to sell last night's catch. They'd seen nothing. "Were Jews killed?" one asked me. As if bored with the very idea, she yawned.

When I overturned her table, she shrieked like a parrot. But no one dared confront me; people recognize madness and draw away.

Then I walked toward the city center as far as the inner rim of the Terreiro do Trigo, Wheat Square. I dared not go any further; at the quay-side, two Portuguese longshoremen and a group of blond northern sailors were exchanging shouted curses. Four men were sprawled dead between them. A pack of murdered dogs lay scattered around the orna-mental cross at the center of the square, their blood soaking into hay strewn from recently unloaded bales. Further away, on one of the piers used for repairing vessels, a cheering crowd had gathered to watch the violation of an African slave girl. Pressed face-down to the slimy wood planks, she grunted at the crude madness of the little man thrusting against her back. Inside the floating city of ships, sailors and merchants watched and laughed. I turned back for the relative safety of the Little Jewish Quarter. My first steps seemed to pose the question: *Do the Old Christians hate us so violently because we gave them Jesus, the savior they never really wanted?*

The single-story house Reza shared with her in-laws centered the northern perimeter of Lemon Tree Square. The sun had just poked its eye over the eastern horizon when I reached there. Her door was closed but unlocked. The great chestnut wood table in the kitchen was kneeling; it had lost two of its legs.

A neighbor heard me searching and peered at me from the front doorway. He was a tiny man with razor-reddened cheeks and sleepy eyes. He spat up at me when I asked if he'd seen her.

Did these Christians always expect us to wipe their scorn away with a meek hand and continue shuffling into an uncertain future?

I shoved him so hard he crashed into the street and fell with a shriek.

A girl, perhaps four years old, was sitting stoically on a pillow in Reza's vegetable garden, naked. A square cross had been finger-painted with charcoal on her forehead. She was nibbling raisins, had dark hair cut straight at her shoulders, secretive brown eyes framed by long and elegant lashes. She had no nail on her right thumb. "I run away," she said.

"What's your name?" I asked.

She looked up at me with distant eyes and shook her head.

"And where are your parents?"

She pushed raisins into her mouth. I ripped a sheet in two and covered her. "I'll bring you to my house," I told her. "You'll be safe." She wanted to be carried on my shoulders. So strange it was to hear a child's laughter. I lowered her to the cobbles and made her walk.

At home, I realized for the first time that the kitchen was a shambles. A few precious drops of vinegar were left at the bottom of a cracked pitcher by the cold hearth. I dripped them over my hands and the girl's forehead. Rubbed off her cross completely. We descended to the cellar.

"Who's that?" my mother demanded, staring at the girl as if she were an affront to her grief.

"I found her at Reza's house. But Reza wasn't there. Just her."

Mother cursed under her breath, then took the girl from me and held her fast. "And Judah?" she demanded.

I shook my head. "I lost his trail."

She turned her gaze toward the wall. It was the same agonized movement my elder brother Mordecai made just before death. When he finally stopped breathing, I drew his last tear to my fingertip and traced it across my lips. An aching relief swept through me like a desert wind as I tasted his salt.

It was then that I had the second of my visions, the first since our forced conversion. It burst up from my feet to my head and pushed through my mouth as a scream. In it, I was standing in our courtyard. Mordecai was sitting on our roof, next to the tin weather vane of a troubadour. I wanted to join him, was pervaded with longing. My gaze was drawn by the same faraway light I've always seen in my visions. As it approached, it transformed itself into a great, fan-tailed eagle of glowing colors. Its head was a ghost-like white, and its eyes shimmered from violet to red, like prismatic crystals. Its gorget was yellow-green; right wing silver, left gold. Its chest was the purple of murex. Swooping down to our rooftop, this great bird extended its talons and snatched up Mordecai effortlessly. I called to him, "What about me?" Mordecai answered, "Years from now, we will need your help. You still have work to do for God." Safe inside the eagle's powerful grip, he continued east, toward Jerusalem and the Mount of Olives.

So had my true work always been to free my family from Pharaoh, to see them safely out of Portugal? Is a man born to accomplish one great goal in his lifetime?

To Mother, now, I asked, "Did you hear anything curious from Uncle about his threshing colleagues in the last few weeks? Any doubts...anger?"

She would not answer, began twirling the hair by her temples and pulling it out.

The girl I'd found in Reza's garden had plopped down to the slate and was looking up at me blankly. Cinfa stood facing her, staring and squinting, gathering the hair at the nape of her neck. Before the mood of despair could claim me, I ran out to search for the threshers.

Diego lived alone in an apartment adjacent to the St. Thomas Church, less than a hundred paces from the city's eastern walls, in a predominantly Christian section of the Alfama. As I climbed through the streets toward it, house shutters began clanging open. Townsfolk in stocking caps pulled low over their foreheads peered out at me, yawning and blinking. Gloomy laborers began trudging off for work. My stomach started growling for a braid of cheese or bit of matzah. But I had forgotten money. Perhaps I could have begged a crust of leavened bread, but it was the day preceding the fifth night of Passover. *Chametz*, of course, was still forbidden to me.

A pretty girl with bits of hay in her sleep-mussed hair was standing in a closed doorway. She had swathed herself in a blanket, couldn't have been more than Cinfa's age. Hailing me with a whisper, she opened her covering for a moment. She was naked, had tiny breasts and slim, boyish hips. "For two eggs, I'll carry you into my solitude," she whispered. "Why not just..."

Such is what happens when children are abandoned to the god of Lovelessness in our most noble and loyal city.

Just ahead, at the steep lip of hillside which fronts the tiny square by the Church of São Bartholomeu, I planned to look out across central Lisbon to see if the Christian storm had ended. Naïve I was even to have entertained this notion; centering the valley below was the Rossio, a mile or so distant. At least a thousand Old Christians were already assembled there. Two great conflagrations were blazing into the sky.

From my vantage point on the crest of hillside, the Old Christians shed their human disguises for a moment and looked like ants feeding in a ragged cluster.

Suspecting that small groups of marauders would soon begin to spread through the city, I rushed off to Diego's apartment. The door to his townhouse was locked. He lived on the second floor, so I called up to him. Across the street, a skeletal old cobbler holding two mallets in a claw-like hand began to watch me with suspicious eyes. He looked away abruptly when I returned his gaze.

Picking up pebbles from the street, I began tossing them at Diego's shutters. A wan old woman with bloodshot eyes and a pointy chin bristling with gray hairs poked her head out of the third-floor window just above. She clutched a black shawl about her head, had a blunted red nose eaten to nearly nothing by some disease. "Who ya want?!" she snapped with a Navarese accent.

"Diego Gonçalves. Have you seen him?"

She shook her head with exaggerated motions and smacked her lips. In a voice which seemed to glue all her words together, she said, "Ain't my place to interfere in other folks' business, ya understand. Lord knows, just takin' care of my husband's a day's work. But sometimes, the Lord brings someone with a question and we gotta answer. Because the Lord is watchin' and if we don't, we..."

I guessed she was drunk or insane. "So is he here?" I interrupted.

"*Ojos*," she said gravely and slowly, as if years of experience were behind that one word.

"What?

"Eyes! These Portuguese people got eyes the size a walnuts. And they stare like they want to see what color yer soul is. Ever wonder if that ain't the problem?"

"Look, do you know if Diego has been here today?" I asked.

"God's always watchin'. The Devil's always watchin'. And with these walnut-eyed Portuguese everywhere, ya can't escape. When I was..."

Under my breath, I whispered, "Go sing it to the goats, you witch!" Picking up some more pebbles, I began pitching them harder at Diego's shutters.

"He ain't here!" she shouted defiantly.

"Where is he then? I don't have much time!"

She looked up skyward and crossed herself. "The people on his floor were taken away yesterday," she cackled. "By men with Portuguese eyes."

"May I take a look inside?" I requested.

"Who are ya?"

"His nephew," I lied.

She leaned out and surveyed the street with her top lip lifted up like an irritated donkey. The cobbler must have been staring at her because she raised a fist toward him and shouted, "Get back to work ya lazy old turnip!"

He flapped a hand at her like she was crazy, squinted and gave her the sign of the evil eye with an extended pinky and index finger.

She blocked his malediction by crossing herself, then shouted at him again. Lifting a key from inside her blouse, she dropped it into my cupped hands. "Don't eat it, now," she warned me, "it's my only one."

I expected her to cackle, but she was deadly serious. "You have my word," I assured her.

When I reached the second floor, I tried the handle to Diego's door and found it locked. The door to the apartment belonging to his neighbor, however, had been torn away. A strange smell, like brackish water, was wafting out. Before investigating, I returned the key to the upstairs neighbor. "You a Jew?" she asked. "'Cause they was Jewish ya understand."

"I'm a Jew," I admitted dryly.

She gripped my arm. "Now ask me if I'm one too!"

"I've got to go," I said.

Her nails bit into my flesh. "Ask me!" she demanded, the spray of her sudden rage hitting me in the face.

"Are you a Jew?" I repeated matter-of-factly.

Before I could duck away, she slapped my face with her callused old hand. "You Portuguese bastards never hesitate to insult a Navarrian lady!" she shouted. "But I'm not about to..."

She was still yelling when I reached Diego's apartment again. I knocked and called for him, but received only silence. Growing fearful for his safety all of a sudden, I began shouting, "Diego! Diego! It's just Berekiah!"

Not a sound was returned to me.

I entered the apartment next door. Old Levi Califa, the retired pharmacist and Talmud scholar, lived there with his widowered son-in-law and his two grandchildren. The state of his quarters did not bode well for Diego's safety; the canopied bed in the front room had been stripped. A cross had been finger-painted in blood on the eastern wall, and below it, in foot-high letters, were the words: *Vincado Pelo Cristo!* Avenged for Christ.

With contempt for the legions of Old Christian illiterates staining the landscape of Portugal, I noted that the word *vingado* had been spelled incorrectly. How could they expect to even catch a glimpse of God when they could neither write correctly nor read with any perception?

"Master Levi?" I called out warily.

Silence.

At the far wall, the door to the rest of the apartment was splayed on the ground. Stepping over it and creeping through the open entrance, I entered a tiny room, square, no wider or longer than three paces, with a parquet of the coarsest oak and a single wooden stool as the only furniture. Yet had I ever entered a room more filled?

Immediately, I knew I'd walked across a holy threshold.

On the whitewashed walls, written in black, in tiny Hebrew letters, was Exodus. All of it. From the names of the Israelites who entered Egypt with Jacob to the flight of Hebrew slaves across the Red Sea to the raising of the Tabernacle by Moses. The verses began at the top of the eastern wall, continued south in a straight horizontal line, then west and north to form a ring. I guessed that more than two hundred such rings had been written. Lettering covered the entire top half of the room like a holy arbor.

Leviticus, too, had been started, but had ended abruptly with the commandment not to burn honey to the Lord. That's when the Christians must have forced their way into the room and taken the scribe.

There was no need to puzzle over his identity. I knew with certainty it was old Levi Califa. Who else would have been so devout as to spend his time in hiding by recounting the central story of Passover?

I was so awed that I simply turned and read, my eyes quickening their pace like a dervish finding the rhythm of his dance.

I didn't expect to encounter Califa himself. But on the kitchen floor, on a piece of broken plate, was a right hand. I knew it belonged to him because the index finger on which he'd always kept his carnelian signet ring had been sliced away. Close by was the last piece of charcoal with which he'd been writing and which must have fallen from his clutches.

A severed hand does not look real. But why? Is it because our minds refuse to believe such cruelty possible?

And why is it that the Christians do not merely kill us, but cut away our body parts? Is it an effort to render us inhuman, to force us to better correspond to their image of us as devils?

Not far from his fingertips were the hyssop-blue heads of Califa's beloved Brazilian parrots, whom he'd named *Ternura*, Tenderness, and *Empatia*, Empathy, the Talmud scholar's two-word motto.

The bodies of Tenderness and Empathy must have been stolen for their precious feathers. Already, perhaps, they were decorating the hat of a Christian nobleman.

As I leaned over to retrieve the hand for burial, a footfall across a snapping piece of wood turned me. In the front room stood the old cobbler from across the street, patient gray eyes fixed on me. He was thin, tan, wore only a sweat-stained undershirt and the crudest of linen pants. He had to be at least fifty, had thin wrists, narrow and bent shoulders. Wisps of tangled gray hair tufted up from behind his ears.

In one hand he held a gouging tool, in the other, a mallet.

I reached for my knife and held it in front of me. *They will force me to fight again*, I thought. Unwilling to engage him amidst the sanctity of written Torah, I stepped to the front room. As I did so, he said in a hoarse voice, "You haven't much time."

I didn't respond, thought: *Why do Christians always expect Jews to speak before they fight?*

Anger rose in me, and I felt as if hot mercury were running through my veins. Stepping to within three paces of him, I awaited his first lunge, imagining that he would crumple under my knife.

Even so, I did not desire to hurt him; it is said that the distance between the righteous taking of a life and a cold-hearted murder is but a hair's-breadth, and I did not presume to have the eyesight necessary to always know the difference.

He scratched the bald vale centering his head with the end of his mallet. "You don't understand my meaning, I'm a friend," he said.

"Then drop your arms."

To my utter amazement, he laid them neatly at his feet. With lines of worry ribbing his forehead, he said, "You haven't much time. They're coming up from the river. You've got to get home. I came to warn you."

"Why?" I demanded.

"Let's just say that Master Levi was a good friend."

"When did you last see him?"

"Come on, son," he said, holding out a hand to me.

"Tell me when you last saw him, please. I need to know."

"Yesterday," the cobbler replied. "The Dominicans came for him and his family." He reached his hand out again and brushed my arm.

Involuntarily, I backed away. "And Diego Gonçalves? Was he with Master Levi?"

He turned nervously for the door. "Look, you've got to go! Can't you understand?"

"Have you seen Diego Gonçalves?"

"No. He hasn't been here that I've seen. Maybe he was captured." He shrugged, then continued angrily, "Look, I'm going. You can leave with me or wait for them to come and get you. And don't worry, the Navarrian hag will make sure they find you quickly. She's the one who opened the door so they could get Master Levi without working up a sweat." He leaned forward to pick up his mallet and gouging tool. A sudden urge to stab him in the back of his neck swept through me. What purpose would it have served to hurt this righteous Christian?

Did the mercury flowing through my veins possess its own desires?

"Come," he said, straightening up. His voice possessed the supplicating tone of my father calling me to study. A shout suddenly reached us from behind the house. The cobbler lifted a crooked finger to his lips to suggest silence.

Together, we crept into the stairwell like children off to a dangerous escapade. The Navarrian hag, as he called her, was standing above us on the staircase, an expression of contempt twisting her wrinkled face. The old man raised his mallet and hit it once lightly against his own head to indicate what he'd do to her should she give our positions away. We made our way down the stairs like cats stalking their prey. I wanted now to find Samson, to read the letter which my uncle had sent him. My plan was to get to the *Porta de São Vicente,* St. Vincent's Gate, exit the city and head northwest to his house.

In the street, swallows were still swooping madly through the morning chill. A murmur coming from the west was pierced with the caustic laughter of young men hugging danger to their hearts.

The cobbler pointed down the street to the east, to the wavering eye of sun. "Go with God," he said, gripping my shoulder.

I mouthed my thanks. Then I ran.

I cannot emphasize enough how deeply clouded my judgment must have been by Uncle's death; any Jew in my position should have realized that the Dominicans would close off all the exits to the city as their first religious calling of the morning.

It was also a mistake to run. The claps of my footfalls drowned out the sounds of the Old Christians and gave my position away.

A mob of one hundred or more was fronting St. Vincent's Gate. When they spotted me, arms pointed toward me like arrows.

I had stopped, my gut clenched with fear. Even so, a sense of sliding toward doom made me extend a hand as if to seek the assurance of a railing or wall. I grabbed only air, of course, then instinctively sought the protection of my knife. For a breathless moment, I even wavered at the edge of taking my own life. It would have been easy; in those days, I still believed in a personal God and did not fear death. Dying, yes. But not the glorious journey back to the Upper Realms. A last prayer, a single thrust, and then I would have been released. The thought was: *better my own hands setting my soul free, than those of men who've held a cross.*

Of course, they couldn't have known for certain by my outward appearance that I was a New Christian. But if they'd stripped me, my covenant with the Lord would have made my allegiance obvious.

The urge for life is more powerful than thought. Or perhaps my need to find Judah was too strong.

I turned and ran as if there'd been no other choice. Were my enemies after me? I couldn't tell; my senses had been dispelled by my quickened pulse. Imagine standing beside a leaden bell tolling madly during a howling windstorm. That was my heartbeat and that was my breath.

All that comes to me now is a general sense of descending outdoor staircases, the odor of my own terror. The next image that penetrates my Torah memory is of a bell tower. I was in front of the façade of the Church of São Miguel, not two hundred paces from home.

Without warning, the tower seemed to crash to its side. I had been shifted in space, was on my back against the cobbles.

Although I was fighting for breath, there was no sense of pain, only silent confusion. My head seemed imprisoned inside an amphora of glass. It was as if the hand of God, without warning, had simply moved me through space.

A fleeting image of a water lily surrounded by sand, bursting suddenly into flame, seared my gaze. Later, I understood that I had been unconscious for an instant, and upon waking, had caught a glimpse of the dream world flowing beneath the current of my usual thoughts. Even then, however, that image—of a lily in flames—seemed vital to me, a gift from God to which I needed to cling. (The clue to its significance came while illuminating a Book of Esther one day in Constantinople, when I realized that the Lord must have seen Lisbon as a burning flower that fateful Passover.)

To my left, six or seven feet away, I now noticed a man in a cape of polished hide kneeling, holding his shoulder as if he were wounded. I realized he must have lunged for me from a hidden doorway and knocked me flying, hurt himself in the process.

Two lanky men in ragged clothing were running toward me from down the sloped street. They appeared to be identical twins. Closely cropped black hair crowned their heads. They both held axes, and I sensed that they wanted to split me like a block of wood.

Behind them, a rampaging group of men and women was rushing toward me. Everything seemed a whirl of noise and wind, shadow and contour.

When the two axmen suddenly merged together, I simply could not understand. Then I realized the obvious: my vision had been distorted by my fall.

Cold iron glinting in the sun has a way of summoning one's body to arms. I was up in an instant, gripping my knife.

The serpentine alleys and pathways of the lower Alfama had long ago been incorporated into my interior map, and I cut away to the west just as my wounded assailant struggled to his feet. I reached the steep staircase leading down to Cantina Square in seconds. From the highest step, one can jump easily onto the neighboring rooftops. I took the leap correctly, then spired up and down four rooftops to the next alleyway. Three men were following me. The two closest, perhaps twenty feet away, held swords. The third was a friar using his crosier as a staff. "Get the *Marrano!*" he was shouting in a hoarse voice. "Bring me his covenant with the Devil!"

By that, I assumed he wanted my sex for a personal trophy. Having been educated to view the world symbolically, I wondered, of course, if the Dominicans wanted to end our possibilities for reproduction once and for all.

The alleyway was empty. Dropping down, I scaled a low wall into Senhor Pinto's courtyard. As I suspected, his kitchen door had been smashed in. The house was a shambles. I cut through his kitchen to the corner of the Rua de São Pedro and the Rua da Adiça. Farid's house was just across the street. I took his wall with a single leap to the top, then jumped to the courtyard and ran for our kitchen.

I did not descend to the cellar, however. After verifying that I hadn't been followed, I lifted away the false frontpiece to the chest in Uncle Abraham and Aunt Esther's room, took out a dried eel bladder containing a few coins to be used in an emergency. I waited a few minutes for shouts to disappear from Temple Street. Then, when all I could hear was my own heartbeat, I headed to the river. Near to shore, a fisherman whom I have seen since childhood but never spoken to was seated in his blue rowboat, cutting a braid of cheese with a rusty knife. He was old, perhaps fifty, squat, had a suntanned, leathery face and the gray eyes of illiteracy. When he met my gaze, I held up a coin and looked west, down river; once there, beyond the city gates, I planned to walk the five miles to Samson Tijolo's vineyard.

The fisherman nodded, rowed toward me and maneuvered his boat alongside the riverbank.

"I need to get out of the city," I told him.

With two of my copper coins sitting in his crawling bait, the fisherman rowed us out a hundred feet or so into the river, puffing and tossing away curses. Above the big toe on his right foot, an angry red sore had eaten into his grayish waterlogged skin.

"Bit by a crab," he grumbled. "Never healed properly."

Weaving through two large fishing boats and cutting around a galley flying the red Portuguese cross, he turned the boat until we caught the current. As his rowing gained rhythm, Lisbon's defensive walls trailed behind and became but a ribbon threading through church towers and the tangle of the city's outer districts. He dropped anchor beyond a rocky outcropping of beach and lifted his hand to bid me good luck.

I nodded my thanks, rolled up the legs of my pants and waded into the cold water.

On the beach, two Andalusian pilgrims to Santiago de Compostela wearing scallop-shaped hats approached me and asked me where a tavern might be. I made believe I couldn't speak their language and walked away.

# Chapter VII

Two hours later, Rana, Samson's wife and an old friend from the neighborhood, answered my knock on her door with her newborn baby, Miguel, suckling at her breast. "Beri...oh my goodness, you're alive! Come in!" She grabbed me and pulled me into the house, closed the door behind me and locked the dead-bolt. "I can't believe it!" she smiled.

We kissed, and I reached out to rub the baby's downy hair. So young he was that his eyes were shut tight as if never to be opened. "Handsome little thing," I said, for who could tell a first-time mother that her baby would look like a squirrel until it was at least a month old?

Rana replied, "Handsome? Have you been meditating too much again?" She tried to smile, but tears trapped in her lashes. Her lowered glance showed a desperate isolation, and I understood that Samson, too, had been lost in the Christian storm.

We sat by her hearth. "How did you find out about the riot?" I asked.

"Some neighbors came to warn me."

"Maybe we should leave here together. Go back to..."

"You know I can't," she interrupted.

For protection against dangers from the Other Side, Rana would not leave her house for the first forty days after Miguel's birth—the number of years Jews wandered in the wilderness and days of the Biblical flood. I replied, "When did you last hear from Samson?"

"I've had no word since Sunday. He was going to Little Jerusalem to buy fabric we needed for..." She nodded toward Miguel. "He was going to Simon Eanes' store. You haven't seen him or heard anything? Or spoken to Simon?"

"No, nothing. But I don't think Simon made it."

She turned to face the wall, and her lips mouthed prayers. I said, "There's still a chance that he's found safe haven. Samson was clever. And imposing. He'd frighten away many a Christian. Sure used to scare me when I was a kid. He may yet come back." I gripped her arm to impart strength, realized I was really trying to convince myself that Judah could be safe.

"No," she said. "If he were alive, he'd be back by now."

"He could be in hiding."

"Samson, in hiding? Beri, a father for the first time after fifty-seven years is not going to go into hiding when his child's life may be in danger."

Rana was one of those rare people who refused to lie to herself. It was why most people found her aggressive, even heartless. She nodded her resignation, rubbed her free hand through her curly brown hair. "If I must go it alone then..." Her words faded and she bit her lip to keep from crying. "All hunger and sleep," she said of Miguel, trying to smile. Her nipple had slipped free of his mouth, and she pushed it back into place as he fidgeted with his arms. He made a warm, satisfied noise as he suckled. Rana looked up at me with hopeful eyes. "Beri, have you heard anything about my parents?"

"Nothing. I'm sorry. I should have checked before coming. I didn't think."

"It's okay. I suspect they'll come when they can...if they can."

"Rana, I dropped by last Friday to get some wine. I took a cask and left a note."

"Yes, we knew it was you because of the matzah." She patted my arm. "How reassuring it is that some things never change. I must have been asleep. I don't sleep much. But when it comes, I'm lost to the world. Except when Miguel cries. Then, it's like a hunter has shot an arrow into my heart."

"Listen, do you still have the letter I left that day?"

"Of course I do," she answered. "Is it important?"

"I have to read it. Something Uncle may have told Samson... Where is it?"

"Taking care of Miguel has made me a bit absent-minded. But I'm sure it's somewhere in the bedroom."

"Can we take a look?"

"Hold him," she said, lifting Miguel and handing him to me. As Rana looked through their chests and desks, I held the little boy in the cradle of my arms and remembered the tender feel of Judah. So many late nights Mordecai and I had spent walking with him to keep his tears away; he had not been an easy baby, had been burdened with fluid in his lungs that gave him a harsh cough. I closed my eyes and the feel of the baby's soft skin tingled my fingertips. *Judah, my Judah,* I whispered to myself. *Please, dear God, let him still be alive.*

To banish the dread descending over me, I engaged Rana in conversation as she searched. We talked of Miguel's stomach problems. "His turds look like magpie droppings," she said in a worried tone. "Dr. Montesinhos says it's nothing to carry on about, so I suppose..."

"Forget it," I said with a wave. "Judah's did, too. I think all babies are part bird."

She laughed, but the ensuing silence showed all the more clearly the sullen mood that weighted the air inside the house. We shared a look in which we acknowledged that Samson might never return, and she reached up to caress my face. "Dear Beri," she said. "I miss the neighborhood." Our gaze was linked by memories of demons banished together by our children's army.

She went back to her hunt, headed to a chest of drawers by the bed. From a small wooden box with a metal lock, she lifted away a scroll. "Got it!" she said in triumph. She handed it to me. "That's it, isn't it?"

"I think so." I placed Miguel into her arms. The scroll curled open into five sheets of paper.

As if inviting me to share an adventure, Rana said, "Listen, Beri, take a look at the note and I'll get some challah bread and wine...no, of course, you must be reliving the Exodus. Just some wine, then? You can stay, can't you? Till you finish the note, at least? You must stay."

"I'll stay till I finish it. Then I must go back to my family. But Rana, if you have *chametz* in the house...then you haven't celebrated Passover yet?"

"No. We were waiting a little while longer to be safe."

She led me back to her kitchen table, brought me a cup of wine, then took my free hand. Uncle's note read:

*Dearest Samson,*

*Miguel Ribeiro has refused. So I shall tell you a story. In it, you will find my hopes that you discover the need for all of us to make a sacrifice at this decisive moment. If we do not perform as Rabbi Graviel did during this present fulcrum in time, then all may be lost.*

*No matter that your belief is crumbling, it is your acts which count.*

*Shall Samael win the day?*

At the top of the next page was written: *A História da Crestadura do Sol do Rabbim Graviel*—The Tale of Rabbi Graviel's Sunburn. It was the same story my master had told me on his last Sabbath, and as I mouthed the title, his hand seemed to reach for the reins at the back of my neck. His voice whispered: "Yes, read it again, Berekiah, so you, too, may see its significance. It is no accident that I offered this story to both you and Samson."

"What is it?" Rana asked, sensing my sudden agitation.

"A tale. Of Rabbi Graviel, one of my ancestors. Of how he had to suffer imprisonment in Spain in order for his daughter to survive. I think that my uncle saw in a vision that he'd have to make a great sacrifice as well. Yes... In order for the girl in the cellar to survive, he had to give up his life. He made a deal. But the murderer did not keep his word."

"Beri, you mean your uncle... Oh dear, Oh my God." Realizing for the first time that my master was dead, Rana's shoulders jerked backward. She placed Miguel on the table, then stood up and covered her ears with her hands. She stared at me in horror.

When she began to shake, I went to her, peeled her hands down. "Rana! Rana!"

She looked at me as if trying to decipher my face, to learn my identity. In a monotone leached of apparent emotion, she said, "Samson.... And now Master Abraham... Esther, is she...?"

"No, she's safe. With Mother and Cinfa. But Judah's missing."

I sat Rana at the table and fed her wine. She held both her hands around the cup like a child, gulped at the liquid, began rambling about the vineyard's wells. When silence came to us again, I asked, "Did Samson mention any trouble in the threshing group?"

She shook her head.

"An argument with my uncle, perhaps?"

"Nothing," she replied.

"But then why did Uncle mention Samson's loss of faith? Was he in some sort of trouble?"

Rana gripped my arm and whispered, "Samson says the baby should be raised Christian, that it's no good to be a Jew anymore. We won't have Passover this year. Even if..." She opened the fold in Miguel's swaddling clothes to show me the foreskin of his penis; he should have been circumcised on his eighth day. She closed her eyes to despair. Tears bathed her eyelashes. As if in solidarity with his mother, Miguel, too, began crying. I took him and rocked him gently to little avail. Rana's words flew out suddenly as if tossed in different directions: "If I'd known... how could he change so? When we were married...and then the baby coming along. We were so...so good. Remember Passover as it was? Remember, Beri?! Before the...wait, let me show you something."

From the alcove above her hearth, she grabbed a thick book. The intricate, lacy border on the cover identified it as a printed edition of the Old Testament produced when I was a boy by Eliezer Toledano. She held it out to me. "Look!" she ordered.

Taking it from her, I asked, "What do you mean—what do I look for?"

"Anywhere! Open it anywhere!"

I handed Miguel back to her, let the manuscript fall open naturally. The Book of Ezra faced me, verses about the rebuilding of the Temple. Each and every name of God had been crossed out with brown ink. It was chilling, as if a talisman of evil.

Rana spoke in a hurried voice, as if stalked. "Samson told me, 'We must bury the Jewish god. After Passover, we'll say prayers for the Lord and then we must bury Him and then we must forget Him.' Samson crossed out all His names!"

I stared at the defilement, then caressed the pages closed, vowing never to look again. I put the book on her table.

"I can't live as a Christian!" Rana suddenly yelled. "I'd sooner kill myself!"

Her shout seemed to split the air between us. "But your son?" I asked. "Who would care for him?! Now that..."

"I'd rather he were dead!"

Some Jewish parents had murdered their children, then committed suicide to avoid the forced conversion nine years earlier, acts which were written in a script I'd never comprehend. "You can't mean that," I told Rana.

She leaned forward, placed Miguel in my arms. Her eyes glowed with frightening resolve. She grabbed a thick bread knife from the table, jumped up, pointed it toward me, her body clenched with rage. "I would do it now if you told me that I must sew a shroud for my God!"

"You would be sinning gravely if you were to ever harm this baby. He is God's ambassador to us. Would you kill Abraham, Isaac, Moses if they stood here before you?"

She held her knife in place.

"This child is Abraham, Isaac, Moses. He is the Lord our God!" I exclaimed.

Rana dropped her weapon and began to sob. I sat her down and caressed her hair. The baby seemed entranced by her wails. Yet when she calmed, he began to kick and fuss. I gave up on trying to soothe his discomfort and handed him back to her.

Without giving myself time to consider, I took the defiled Old Testament from the table, held my breath and threw it into the hearth.

Rana gasped. "Berekiah! No! What you've done..."

As smoke and flame crackled from the curling, yellowing pages, I spoke in a voice that seemed to come from Uncle: "I don't need words written for me. Not even the Torah. And you don't either. Keep an internal Judaism. God will meet you inside, just beyond where you speak to yourself. If Samson returns...and we will all pray for his safety, then let him talk of Christianity while you breathe Judaism. Your son will know the difference. And when he is old enough to keep secrets, you shall tell him of the bride that is the Sabbath who has been waiting inside him patiently all through his childhood. And you shall celebrate their wedding together."

The baby sought her breast again. Rana fed him, stared at his face as if seeking a glance of that future ceremony beyond his eyes.

*How wonderful,* I thought with burning jealousy, *to be able to offer your own nourishment to another being.*

Does one's life goal always appear without warning, in the space of a single instant? For I knew then that I sought to offer myself as fully as Rana to someone before I died.

She shrugged as if unconvinced. "We'll see," she said.

At the door, we kissed. "Rana, was Samson angry with Uncle or any of the other threshers? Did that have anything to do with his loss of faith."

"No. It was the baby. It's one thing to live in terror yourself, quite another to condemn one you love to a similar fate. He took a long look at the baby's future as a Jew, and he didn't like what he saw."

"Do you want to come with me?" I asked. "You know you're welcome to stay with us for as long as you need to. And you mustn't be afraid of the Other Side. It's superstition. You've no need to fear leaving the house."

"No. Thank you." She caressed my arm. "My parents will try to come to me. If they can..."

"I understand. Remember, build an inner garden where you can hide, where you can invite Miguel when he's old enough." I brushed the baby's wisps of hair again. "And if Samson returns, send him to me. We can all still use the future tense when speaking of Jews in Portugal. Perhaps he will regain his faith."

We kissed. Yet she called me back as I set out. Her hand was trembling by her lips. "Do you think that the Lord has taken Samson in revenge...for what he did to the Old Testament?"

I closed my eyes to search for an answer, and with a chill, realized I no longer trusted God. I inscribed the sweeping gesture Farid and I make to express the unknowable.

# Chapter VIII

As I walked away from Rana's home, my descent into a hollow world unwatched by God made me cling tightly to Uncle's story of Rabbi Graviel. On reading his words again, I recalled the last lesson he had given Judah and me; in it, my master had spoken of the need for making a sacrifice, as well. This lesson was spoken during our Passover seder, last Friday. As turnip and saffron soup was being ladled by Esther into our wooden bowls, he had nodded to me and said, "The Lord showed favor upon Sarah..."

His words had been a cue for me to chant Torah from memory beginning with that verse in Genesis. In Portuguese, so Judah would understand, I began: "The Lord showed favor upon Sarah as He had promised, and made good what he had said about her. She conceived and bore a son to Abraham for his old age, at a time..."

My uncle had me continue through the following fifty-two verses. Pausing only to wet my lips with wine, I recounted the story of Isaac, son of Abraham and Sarah, whose name means "he laughed" in Hebrew—a reference to Abraham's great pleasure at having been able to sire a son despite his one hundred years of age.

When I recited the verse, "The time came when God put Abraham to the test," Uncle nodded with lifted eyebrows for me to talk directly to Judah. Cupping the boy's chin, I received the gift of his gaze. In my best theatrical voice, I continued the story:

"'Abraham!' the Lord called, and Abraham replied, 'Here I am!'

"God said, 'Take your beloved only son Isaac and go to the land of Moriah. There you shall offer him as a sacrifice on one of the hills which I will show you.'"

Judah wriggled in his seat and bit his lip, disturbed by the prospect of Isaac's death. I could sense him recoiling from the memory of our mother's cursing, wounded in his soul by the way she denied him a place in her life. I took his hands in mine and told him how Abraham had bound Isaac and laid him atop an altar he'd built of wood, and how just as he raised his knife to cut life from his son, the Lord in the person of an angel intervened: "'Do not raise your hand against that boy; do not touch him! Now I know that you are a God-fearing man. You have not withheld from me your son, your only son. I shall bless you abundantly and give you descendants until they are numerous as the stars in the sky and the grains of sand on the seashore.'"

Judah was hardly put at ease by this peaceful ending; his face swelled with yearning for reassurance. My stomach sank as I realized it was cruel of Uncle and me to have thrust a sword of Torah through his fragile defenses. I fixed my hand at the back of his neck as he looked down and away from the eyes of the family, trying to caress encouragement into him. "Eat some more soup," I said. "It's getting cold."

Uncle frowned, waved my advice away and said, "Now Judah dear, I had Beri tell you this story for a reason. Tell me what you think of it."

Eyes focused on the little boy. But his lips were sealed tight. My hand began to pat encouragement at his back; he was near crying. I stared at Uncle with bound anger, wanting to shout, "Hasn't he been through enough in five short years! Leave Judah be or so help me...!"

"I want to know what you think," Uncle prompted. "I will never judge you badly for telling me the truth. Never! On that you have my word."

"Tell us, Judah," Esther said. She smiled maternally.

Mother was looking at him with a stoney face, had begun picking nervously at the wisps of hair by her temples. When I pinched his neck for him to get it over with, Judah whimpered, "I didn't like it."

"Me neither," I interjected.

"Why didn't you like it?" Uncle asked, shooing away my help with a flapping wrist.

Judah balled up his fists and rubbed his eyes. "Because...because I don't know. Because I didn't."

"Tell me why?" Uncle said softly.

"Because Isaac didn't do anything wrong!" Judah blurted out.

"Exactly," Uncle said. He stood up and leaned toward the boy, his hands braced on the table. "Now I'm going to tell you a secret, Judah.

And secrets are very powerful things. So you must not tell it to anyone. It is only for us. Okay?"

Judah nodded, and his mouth fell open as if he were suddenly entranced; he loved Uncle's secrets.

"Many people say that this story means that sometimes it is necessary to make a sacrifice for God," my master began. "A terrible sacrifice, if need be. And on one level they are right. Abraham was willing to kill his son. Then there are some people who say that it was wrong of God to have asked this of a man. And wrong of the man to have agreed. Maybe they are right. I sometimes believe so myself. But here is the secret..." Uncle lowered himself across the table so that his face was but a foot from Judah's. His eyes were flashing. Lifting a finger to his lips, he whispered, "Do not forget that Isaac means, 'he laughed.' That is the proof we need to be sure that the Torah is speaking metaphorically, in riddles of a very particular sort. Isaac is not Abraham's son in this world. He is a kind of son inside Abraham himself. He is a child made up of Abraham's laughter and sorrow, anger and tenderness, fears and dreams. And what was God asking from Abraham? That he be willing to give these up. That he be willing to give up his innermost emotions and thoughts, his dearest possessions. That he untie the knots of his mind. That he extinguish part of himself. And why? So that a door might open inside him through which God could enter. Dearest Judah, this story is asking you to open yourself to God and nothing more." Uncle reached out to tousle his nephew's hair, then twist his nose. "God loves you so much that he is willing to tell a terrible story and have you think bad of Him. All this so that you may one day meet Him inside yourself. He wants to be able to hug you, nothing more. Okay?"

Judah, still entranced, gave a great big nod. With gratitude, I noted how children's moods could be altered so easily.

The lesson for me in all this—at the time—had been to think twice before doubting Uncle. But now, as I walked toward home, I thought of what he had been telling us all about sacrifice. God had asked the Biblical Abraham to give up his most cherished possession. Had He asked Uncle to give up his own life? Why? Was it so that more books could be saved from Christian flames?

Such speculations were interrupted a few minutes later by a man shouting my name. Rana must have had intuition concerning her parents; her father, Benjamin, and mother, Rachel, were rushing toward me from the top of a coming ridge. "Beri," Benjamin shouted, running to me, his dark eyes wild with fear. "Rana, is she...?"

"She's fine. And Miguel is fine, too. They're safe for now."

"Thank God." He placed his hands against my chest. "Listen, we cannot talk, we must get to her. Give our blessings to your entire family."

"I will." I held his arm. "Just one thing. Have you seen Samson? He was supposed to be in Lisbon buying..."

Benjamin raised his fingertips to my lips. "As of Sunday, my daughter is a widow," he whispered. "Samson was captured when the riot broke. He was unprepared."

Rachel twirled her hand in the air. "Smoke. Samson is nothing more than smoke."

"And are the pyres still burning in the Rossio?" I enquired.

Benjamin nodded. "The fires will never go out as long as we remain ourselves."

His words seared through the numbness which seemed to advance and recede inside me at its own pace, and I realized that I had been too long away from my family. Rushing back to the city, I found the eastern and northern gates clogged with crowds of Christians and Dominican friars. The young men among them were hitting one another, cursing, preparing like bear cubs for a chance to test their prowess. To the west, however, at the St. Catherine's Gate, I found only a small crowd of drunken old men. Later, I discovered that word had spread through the city that the King would be sending troops from the east to re-establish order in his capital; hence, this negligence of the western gates.

Apparently, I looked less like a *Marrano* than even my mother imagined; the Old Christians whom I passed raised not a single sword, instead entreated me to share their crude jokes about women and Jews. For the sake of my life, may God forgive me, I acceded to their wishes. "How is a Jew like a praying mantis?" asked a man with a thin and empty face. When I shook my head, he said, "Spit at it, it continues praying. Lock it away, it still continues praying. Only solution is to take out your sword and cut off its head!"

Amazing that anyone could find that sort of thing amusing. But the Christians stained the air with their toothless howls, and I joined them as best I could.

As I strode away from them, I began to suspect that God had

allowed me to enter Lisbon at this gate so that I might visit the New Christian arms dealer Eurico Damas on my way back to the Alfama; his home was in the wealthy Bairro Alto neighborhood crowning the slope above the great shantytown just ahead. As to this enviable location, Damas told my uncle shortly after his own voluntary conversion, when the two men were still on speaking terms, "I never want to forget where I came from. No faithful New Christian would."

Honorable sentiments. But when he was out of sight, Uncle plucked a hair from the middle of my head. Shushing my yelp, he said, "Berekiah, that man's noble words are as anchored in his soul as this filament was in your scalp. One little tug and it's..." He swirled his hands in the air and feigned amazement at the disappearance of the hair. "Never trust anyone who gains by the death of another. Especially such a man who later shows off his prayer shawl in public."

With the sun low in the sky, I climbed up the tangle of unpaved streets that switchback across the western hillsides toward the Bairro Alto. Passing the jumble of wooden barracks where the poorer classes spent lives of dreamless servitude, dirty faces regarded me over shoulders as if I were an unusual sight. Children scattered dust as they chased chickens and cats. Flies fed at the corners of their eyes. A tall African slave chained at his ankle to a rusted anchor, stared at me with the intense eyes of a storyteller recording the passing of a character. I recognized a kinship in him and nodded, but he turned from me as if he'd been suspected of a crime. The air was modulated with the scents of shame and anger. Yet here and there, a few homes sprouted gardens planted with marigolds and lavenders, cabbage, turnip and fava beans.

A cobblestone plaza umbrellaed with powerful chestnut trees marked the end of the King's tolerance; beyond this point, the pinewood planks and cloth patches of these wretched squatters ended and the polished stone of Lisbon's aristocracy began.

I recognized Damas' house immediately; sprouting from the limestone cornice were horned, cavern-mouthed gargoyles which had petrified me as a child. From beyond the roof, where the courtyard undoubtedly was, smoke was rising in tufts. I slipped my hand in my pouch and took out my knife, concealed it in the waistband of my pants.

To my banging on the iron grating that fronted the door, a delicate boy with a sweet round face answered. He stood on his stoop, hands on his hips. A green silk shirt and scarlet vest billowed from his chest—

presumably, hand-me-downs prematurely given. With an irritated gesture, he swept a long lock of amber hair away from his cheek and tucked it under the rim of his blue beret. His hands were ash-stained. He seemed to think I was a foreign peddler; in his lilting voice, he said slowly and definitively, "We don't have any need of whatever you're selling." Rubbing his chin, he left a sweaty black streak behind.

"I'm not selling anything. I'm looking for Eurico Damas."

He looked up skeptically into the sky, then down to the ground and shrugged. "I'd start digging if I were you." He twisted his lips into a sneer and jerked his thumb upward. "He ain't gonna make it up there if I got any say in it."

"Dead?" I asked.

The boy knocked against the stone doorframe. "Couldn't be no deader."

"You're sure?"

"Saw his body myself. Opened his mouth and spat in it to make sure."

"Was he killed during the riot against the New Christians?"

He shrugged. "Look, Master Eurico had lots of enemies. Did you really expect him to survive? He should've hidden himself like a bedbug in a mattress seam." He nodded up at me. "Who are ya, anyway?"

"Pedro Zarco," I replied, using the Christian first name I'd accepted under the sword of conversion. "I live in..."

"Ah, Master Abraham's nephew!"

"How do you know who I am?!"

The boy approached me, slipped his fingers around the grating of the gate as if planning to scamper up. From here, I saw that bruises and scrapes were what reddened his cheeks. "Master Eurico hated your uncle," he said. "Talked all the time about capturing him and giving him the *pinga* just to see what curses and drivel would come out. Strange, but in a way, I think he kinda liked him, too. In the way that he liked anyone. But he thought your uncle was a little crazy...and dangerous."

*Pinga,* meaning "drop," was a torture in which droplets of boiling oil were dripped one by one across your body. Sometimes they spelled the victim's name with the burns; Portuguese appellations can be very long and most people will confess to just about anything before a boiling drop even touches their family name.

"Are you a servant?" I asked.

"I've sent them away." He peeled off his beret with the grin of someone revealing treasure. A cascade of silken amber hair dropped across his shoulders. *He* was most definitely a *she*. "I'm his widow," she said with a great nod. She shrugged as if to excuse her previous disguise and unlocked the gate. She took my arm as if inviting me to dance. "Come!" she said.

So this boy was Damas' child bride! She ran me into a bloodstained kitchen and tugged me through the larder into a courtyard shaded with orange trees thick with fruit. On the brick terrace by the back of the house, a raging pyre of clothing and wood was crackling. A colorful pile of shirts, coats and trousers was heaped nearby. Flakes from the flames were drifting up into the sky and falling back to earth like feathers. "I've been burning his things all night," she said with an exhale of triumph. "The boots were the first to go. Eight pairs he had. One for each day of the week. And an extra one of sharkskin for Mass on Sunday. If he didn't like my polishing, he'd change his water on them and make me start over. And let me tell you, that man's pee smelled like a cat's! Only problem now is that they stink when they burn! Just like he did!"

Tendrils of flame were jumping like tugged marionettes. "You threw Eurico Damas into the fire?!" I demanded.

"I think you'll find his teeth if ya look hard!" she grinned. She licked her lips as if tasting a treat. "He had more than his share so I'm sure they're there somewhere." She fixed my stare with a bemused look, burst into laughter. "He went to kidnap your uncle, you know."

"Did he find him?! What did he..."

"No, he came back all snarly. Couldn't locate where Master Abraham was hiding. I heard him say so."

So my intuition was wrong; Eurico Damas had not been involved. And Samson was dead. That left Father Carlos and Diego as the only threshers who could have betrayed Uncle; Miguel Ribeiro and Rabbi Losa as those who might have stooped to blackmail.

"He wanted to *pinga* your entire group of kabbalists," the girl continued. "Force 'em to admit it was all a lie. Lately, he was kind of obsessed with it. Getting old, I guess. He didn't believe in that sort of thing, ya see."

"What sort of thing? I don't understand."

She laughed as if to ridicule me, tugged with showy pride on the ends of her silken vest. "An ever present God, stupid!" As she spoke, a black-haired, weedy teenager with wisps of mustache on his upper lip ran out of the house trailing a bloody sword. His eyes were targeted upon me.

"It's all right, José," she said. "He's Master Abraham's nephew." To me, she whispered. "It was José who killed him. He's not much good with a sword. But when a man's as drunk as a pig in a trough of grapes, it don't take more than one little skewer and..." She thrust her hands down in imitation of a swordsman delivering a deathblow, grinned, then left me to toss a cloak onto the fire. José acknowledged me with the serious nod of an adolescent who has assumed the role of a protector, and in an eerie, reverent silence, we three watched the garments smoke and twist and blacken. The girl's expression hardened. She touched her cheeks as if blotting stains. She turned to me. "I've other marks on my back, you know. For a year, I was his whipping post. Used to flap his 'bird' himself while hitting me if ya know what I mean." She grinned, "I want to erase the very memory of him." She took my hand. "You can understand, can't ya?" When I nodded, she looked at me gravely, pointed to her chest. "Do kabbalists really believe God resides in here?"

"There and everywhere else. And nowhere. God will come to you in a form which you can perceive—clothed as you can see Him. It depends on His grace...and your vision."

"Then He won't come to me as a man—I've no need for a male God. I've already had one, and I hated him! I'll kill the next male god that shows his 'purple head' to me!"

"A female emanation then. Or neither sex. Or both more likely."

"A woman. Yeah, I'd prefer a woman." She made a fist, and with gritted teeth, shouted, "I'll never have another man thrust inside me!" Her look became haughty as she twisted her beret back on. Tucking in her hair, she said, "Grab any of his clothes you want, then go!"

We stared at each other as if to take in the world's cruelty. In a trembling voice, she said, "Once upon a time there was a happy girl who swam in the Tagus and who was spied from afar and sold by her parents into slavery." She closed her eyes and folded her arms about her chest, as if comforting her own despair.

I replied, "And a young man who lost his uncle and little brother."

Her eyes opened in understanding, and we nodded at each other like siblings who must part. The weight of our solidarity held me in place another moment, then I turned and strode away.

Sunset had washed the sky with rosewater and copper. As I surveyed the massive crowd still assembled in the Rossio from afar, Uncle's hand held the back of my neck. "If you dye your hands red, no one will bother you," he whispered. I knew what he meant and pulled off the scab which had formed on my shoulder where the boy's lance had caught me. The blood sluicing out came warm against my fingertips. I coated my hands and arms with it. "Now descend to the river," Uncle whispered. "Walk along the bank, and to any one who hails you, tell them you are hunting *Marranos!*"

As I knew I would, I made it home without incident. The shit-stained rug over our trap door was still in place. Yet I descended into the cellar as if into imprisonment. I was young and proud, and such a hideaway only provoked shame.

Cinfa ran to me as I reached the bottom of the stairs and said that only a half-hour before men had stood in the kitchen above them, offering clemency for any *Marrano* who showed himself. "Don't go out again!" she begged.

"Judah?" my mother asked breathlessly.

"Nothing," I replied.

Farid and the little girl with no thumbnail were sleeping under blankets by our desks. Esther was sitting in silence, her profile that of a limestone sculpture.

After I'd comforted Cinfa, I lifted up the prayer rug over Uncle, and as I did, his putrid odor stung my nostrils. *Dear God, how long until we can get him into the earth?* I thought. I painted him again with myrrh, told myself with each brush stroke: *Keep looking at his face; you must remember everything in order to take revenge.*

As I chanted to myself, my body, miraculously, began to shed its accumulated frustration, to vibrate and flex with a holy force. Such is the power of Torah—or so advanced were my powers of self-deception, perhaps—that I was growing convinced that it was I who had been chosen to save Israel from Lisbon's Philistines and that by solving the mystery of Uncle's murder, I would somehow be turning the key in the door of our salvation. What exactly the connection was between my master's death and the survival of the Portuguese Jews, I hadn't a clue at the time.

As I looked up at the leather blinds drawn down over the window eyelets at the top of the northern wall, I wondered again about the killer's escape. *There must be a hidden exit,* I thought, *a tunnel—some way out that was known only to the threshers. That was why Uncle never wished me to enter the cellar without his permission. I hadn't yet been initiated into the secrets of our temple.*

"Did you bring any food?" Cinfa asked me suddenly. "She's hungry."

The little girl with no thumbnail stood by Cinfa, was staring up at me with yearning silence. "I'm sorry, I forgot," I answered. "I'll go up now and see what I can find in the store. There must be..."

"No. You sit!" my mother ordered. Her hands were balled into fists and her eyes were flashing. "We wait now until it's over for good!"

Cinfa and the little girl nibbled on the one matzah I had left. It was blood-stained, but it disappeared all-too-quickly. So hunger accompanied us as well.

Needing something with which to busy my nervous hands, craving to learn the identity of the girl, I took a sheet of paper from our storage cabinet and began to draw her.

Farid awoke maybe an hour later, after I'd finished her face and was beginning the first lines of her hands. Cinfa tapped me on the shoulder and said he was asking for me.

I brought him a cup of water and held it to his lips. He gulped greedily. He was sweating profusely, and his fever had gone up. His pants were stained with flecks of blood and shit. "How are you feeling?" I asked.

"Something is peeling me open from the inside out. And I'm afraid I couldn't hold back. My pants... I must stink so bad that even Allah is holding his nose."

Despite his protests, I cleaned Farid's behind and thighs, then covered him with his blanket again. We hadn't any extra pillows, so I buttressed his head with several manuscripts from the *genizah*. What better purpose for Hebrew writing at this point could there have been?

As he descended into sleep, I sat by myself against the eastern wall, in the spot where I imagined that the girl had begged for her life. I brought my knees up by my chest into a position of self-sufficiency and solitude; something cold and calculating was drawing me away from my family. Was it my longing for vengeance? They talked in whispers now, but I could not. I needed to run, to shout for all to hear that I would avenge my uncle. I could live no more enclosed in murmurs, enchained by coded conversations. My master had been right; the lion of kabbalah inside me would not let me live as a secret Jew any longer.

And so I learned that the spiritual journey for me that Passover would be an unveiling of my own true face.

I returned to my sketch, and for the rest of the hours of light, disappeared into the contours of first the girl, then Uncle. When darkness came, I found I was unable to say evening prayers. The little girl slept between my legs, using my thigh as a pillow. Cinfa huddled with us under a blanket.

In my sleep that night, it was my own screams which came to me; I was tied to the fountain in Rossio Square and baptized with a burning palm branch.

I awoke into darkness with the smell of smoke, thick with memory, permeating my clothes—an impossibility, I know, for the pants and shirt I was wearing had not borne witness to the pyre in the Rossio. From the viewpoint of kabbalah, however, illusions like this are not so easily dismissed, and later I understood the odor as an indication that some part of me had not advanced past Sunday. Now, however, I simply undressed and doused my clothes with fennel water from our storage cabinet. But the odor, stubborn as an engorged tick, clung tight.

I couldn't get back to sleep. In the darkness, moonglow shapes of yellow and violet started folding around my family and me in icy sheets. Yet their touch was comforting. It was as if we were enveloped in a blanket that sealed our fates together. (How dearly I would have liked to have said, *a blanket bequeathed by God,* but such poetry was lost to me by then.)

And so, the world reached the early hours of Wednesday morning, the morning before the sixth evening of Passover.

Worry brought me back to Farid. His breathing rose against my fingertips, regular but shallow. I recalled how when we were children, he would cry at the scent of spring rain against the oleander bushes in the courtyard; the sweet smell, to him, was overwhelming.

Yes, he has always been more sensitive than me.

And I remembered then how when Judah was born, he and I had danced our prayers by the river.

Judah... Farid... Uncle Abraham...

Names... Are they arbitrary signs or something more meaningful?

When I was despondent over my forced name change from Berekiah to Pedro, Uncle covered my head with his prayer shawl. "God has many names," he whispered. "So we who are made in His image should have many as well. And what is beyond your name will always be the same."

My master told me many times that we were all God's self-portraits. Would that even include his killer?

Now that I'd seen a pyre of Jewish flame curling high above the steps of the Dominican Church, you'd think that one life—Uncle's life—wouldn't matter so much. Perhaps horror must be localized in a single soul, a diamond of pain.

As my thoughts reached a sudden impasse, I looked up to see dawn light beginning to filter through the window eyelets at the top of the northern wall. I took a sip of water from the jug on the storage cabinet, nodded good morning toward my mother who had just woken. Cinfa was lying asleep against her thigh. My mother's hands were caressing her hair absently. Esther was sleeping on her chair, her head fallen to her right shoulder, her arms hanging limply. Farid, too, was still asleep. His forehead was burning. I wiped it with water, but he did not wake.

Lifting the prayer rug from the girl, I kneeled by her face and made some final adjustments to my drawing of her; the mouth which I had given her was too wide, too melodramatic.

A sketch of a person is a powerful thing; as I stared at it, her image took on the contours of a talisman bearing her unfulfilled hopes.

A few minutes later, while still engaged in correcting her lips, I heard Reza and her husband, José, calling to us from the courtyard. Mother sat up, and her mouth dropped open. Yet she did not get to her feet. It was as if she could not trust her ears. I ran to them. Cinfa followed.

Reza was opening the trap door when I reached the top of the stairs. I motioned for her to let me climb out. "I looked all over for you!" I said, hugging her. It was good to feel her compact, feminine solidity. And I needed the light and air.

Even so, Reza looked as if she'd been hunted. Her great gray eyes, normally so aristocratic—even distant, some said—were lit with burning anxiety. José hadn't been to a barber in several days, looked ill, bloated with a kind of restrained terror. His eyes were rimmed by deep, dark circles and his thick red lips were badly chapped.

"You're okay, Beri?" Reza asked hesitantly.

"Fine, fine. But where have you two been? I went to your house, but there was..."

"We tried to get here, but the way was blocked," José said, taking my shoulders. "So we left the city for Sobral. Stayed there. Each time we tried to get back till now, the gates..." He shook his head. "We couldn't risk it."

Reza removed the toque from her head, asked in an urgent voice, "Is...is everyone here safe?"

"I can't find Judah," I replied. My heart throbbed against my chest as if to seek an escape as I added, "And your father, Reza...he's left his body and returned to God."

The toque dropped from her fingers. Her eyes opened wide to seek understanding. I moved to take her hands, but she pulled away. I whispered, "What once gave home to your father is lying in the cellar."

Her face was suddenly white, her eyes glassy. She descended to him as if straining at a yoke.

Downstairs, my mother, Cinfa, José and I stood back as she kneeled to touch hesitant fingers over his form; if death is to be accepted, then it must be met alone for a time.

When she sagged like a child to the floor, I rested my hand atop her hair. I felt her silent tears enter me as if through a whisper. She turned for Esther. "How did it happen, Mother?"

My aunt wouldn't respond, was still in hiding within herself.

"Do you know if King Manuel has retaken the city?" I asked José.

"Not yet. They say that he is afraid to return. The people are now clamoring for his death."

Reza prayed over Uncle. When she turned away, Esther rose like a ghost, glided to his body and covered his face again with the prayer rug. She sat back down and returned to stone.

A wall crumbled inside the little girl with no thumbnail when Reza picked her up. She wailed as if her insides were being torn.

"You know her?" I questioned.

"Aviboa. The daughter of my neighbor, Graça. Is she...?"

I shrugged. "The girl was the only one there."

It was a sin, I know, but as I replied I was thinking: *Why could I not have found Judah instead?*

# BOOK TWO

# Chapter IX

It is near noon on Wednesday—seven hours from the sacred descent of the sixth evening of Passover—and I have done all the drawings I will need.

Reza has assured us that the city has quieted, and so she, José, Cinfa, Aviboa, Mother and I creep upstairs in a line, unsure of our footing, as if returning from a long sojourn abroad. To cool Farid, I walk him to my mother's room and wash his face with brandy. I hold a compress to his forehead. His eyes cannot resist closing, but he remains awake; fingertips cross my arm over and over again asking for Samir.

Esther has remained below to commune alone with the gloom of the cellar.

We are preparing my master and the girl for burial. We chant our prayers as we wash. Seven times I clean Uncle's face with cold water, three with warm. And as it is written, we cleanse first his stomach, then his shoulders, arms, neck, genitals, toes, fingers, eyes and nostrils.

A warm tide of sadness and joy sweeps over me as I hold the marble hands of Uncle's old armor; he has escaped to God. Then I am alone again with a murdered man. Insight comes in flashes, says the Zohar. And so it is.

The slit which splits his neck has turned black. The blood has clotted to a ceramic crust.

Four times I wash his fingers, and yet they are still dyed with ink. Just as it should be for an artist meeting God.

Aunt Esther takes a scissors to her hair and places her hennaed locks upon his chest.

Which Hebrew poet was it who said that a widow's clipped hair consists of tears of blood drawn into filaments?

When my master is dressed in his white robes, Mother sprinkles the symbolic dust of Jerusalem over his eyes and private parts.

I hold Cinfa's hand as she says goodbye. "We'll never see him again," she nods to me. Her weary, bloodshot eyes are wide open and curious, not sad or frightened.

"Not like this," I agree. "When you next see Uncle, it will be when he holds out his hands to you and welcomes you to God."

My confident words belie a stiff terror which forces my eyelids closed; I have forgotten the feel of my master's embrace.

We lay him upon his prayer shawl, then cover him with the linen shroud Reza and Mother have sewn.

When his face disappears from me for the last time, my eyes close to capture him in their darkness. He is only a violet shadow now; I cannot summon his glow. Will he fade until I can no longer even summon his voice?

We wash the girl with no less care. Reza helps now; she has sent Aviboa to play with Roseta in the courtyard.

Brites, our laundress, appears suddenly at the kitchen door. Gifted with an optimistic nature, she generally has a bright sweet face. Today, however, she is glum and hoarse-voiced. In her cart is our last load of laundry, cleaned and pressed. She has brought us a salted hide of codfish the length of a man's arm.

We kiss, and there is no need to talk. The silence of our solidarity sits in my chest like a heavy stone. "I called for you in the night," she finally whispers.

"We couldn't answer. But thank you." My lips press to her cheek again, then I leave her and mother to mingle their tears together.

There are no coffins to be bought in our neighborhood, no New Christian carpenters left alive to work. And I refuse to pay an Old Christian for this. So we carry Uncle and the girl in their shrouds into the cart I've borrowed from Dr. Montesinhos' widow. The donkey belongs to Brites; she insisted on the loan. When I protested, she whispered, "Please, Beri, you could be my child."

The urge to draw away from the present tense into a happier past tugs hard at me. I must fight it to perform my religious duties. And more importantly, to find Uncle's killer.

Esther sits in the cart atop a wooden stool, her lands folded in her lap, her hair chopped at hopeless angles. Mother, Reza and I walk beside the donkey. We leave Lisbon to the east. Christian eyes without questions watch us as we depart; everyone knows our mission. Cinfa remains at home with José, Reza's husband.

Many Jews have made their way to the *Quinta das Amendoas*—the Almond Farm, as we call the  large property centered by a haunting tower of weathered limestone about two miles east of the city. Aaron Poejo, the owner, was a mountain Jew from Bragança who moved here because his Algarvian bride was shivering to death in that frigid north-eastern climate. To remind him of home, they brought along almond and chestnut saplings and rooted them here. The original cottage, now no more than waist-high rows of cragged stone, was abandoned in favor of an octagonal storage tower following one of Poejo's visions. Apparently, he saw long-haired blond seafarers in iron masks sacking Lisbon and setting fire to all of its Jewish quarters. The crude structure was redesigned with a third floor belfry to be used as a lookout sight; from there, as Farid and I discovered one day on a mission of childhood espionage, one can see the Tagus and its own granite lookout towers, get an advance warning of attack. The irony, of course, is that years later, during the conversion, Poejo's wife was stoned to death by dark and squat neighbors whom they'd known for years. In any case, as the story goes, Poejo and his two daughters tried in vain to knock down their tower-home the night his wife was killed. In the morning, exhausted, desperate, they hollowed a great chestnut trunk, hauled the woman up and buried her inside. Although the trunk has filled in over the years, that tree, directly south of the tower, grows with mottled and denuded branches even today, as if poisoned by remorse. It is said, too, to give off a rotten stench on *Yom Kippur.* Hence the farm's local notoriety as a place of arcane power fitting for those martyred for Judaism.

As for Poejo, after his wife's burial, he and his daughters collected cuttings once again, continued south right across the Algarve, survived the sea crossing and settled in Morocco near Tetuán. In consequence, the almond trees of the Quinta das Amendoas, like so many in Portugal, have long gone untended. Yet today, as we pass, we can see that their green fruit have defied neglect, have sprouted like musical notes in the scruffy, overgrown branches.

From Little Jerusalem and the Judiaria Pequena, even the small Jewish street on the other side of town near the Carmelite Church, we drag our dead. A few have donkey carts like us. Most have folded their loved ones into wooden wheelbarrows.

Our elders direct us to the fields that have not been used in the past for graves. I nod my solidarity to all who pass but do not talk except to ask after Judah and the two living threshers—Father Carlos and Diego Gonçalves. No one has seen them.

I dig two pits with the help of three Moorish laborers who've come to earn extra money. They have silent black eyes and ask no questions.

Reza insists on helping. "Beri, I need to *do* something," she says. "The world starts caving in every time I sit still." She stares up at me with lost eyes and chews nervously on the ends of her hair, a habit from childhood she has regained.

For Uncle, Mother chooses a spot by a young almond tree whose candelabrum arms are upraised in prayer toward the turquoise sky. The girl has found rest by a broad cork tree whose branches unfurl like the arms of a welcoming grandfather.

The scribe Isaac Ibn Farraj chants with us. He is here burying Moses Almal's head; it seems that Isaac was the lunatic who had raced in front of the pyre in the Rossio to steal his friend's last vestige from the flames and spare his ghost from a wandering afterlife in the Lower Realms. "I've seen enough Christians for one lifetime," he confides to me. "I'm learning Turkish. It's easy, written with Arabic characters. I'm going to get on the first boat to Salonika I can find. They say it's becoming a Jewish city. Anyway, I suggest you do the same."

"And what of your home here?"

"Pretty soon all our friends will be gone from Portugal anyway. And believe me, I won't make the same mistake Lot's wife made!"

Thinking of the note which slipped from Diego's turban, which mentioned the name "Isaac," I ask, "Before the riot, did you set up any special meeting with Diego Gonçalves the printer?"

"Not that I recall."

"And the twenty-ninth of this month, this coming Friday—does it mean anything special to you?"

Isaac scratches the white, fungus-like hairs on his chin and folds out his lower lip. "Beri," he says, "I can see you're in trouble and need help. But you'll have to talk plainer if you want me to understand." He takes my hand, and his eyes focus upon me with tenderness.

It suddenly seems ridiculous to have suspected him of being the

Isaac mentioned in the note; he has never had any connections to the threshing group, nor any reason for antagonism toward Uncle. I realize that I'm beginning to mistrust everyone. "Never mind," I say. At my request, he then tries to revive Esther by beseeching her in Persian. She replies with eyes of glass.

Seven times I circle Uncle's grave praying. As it should be for a *Ba'al Shem,* Master of the Divine Name. My Hebrew prayer voice, rising and falling like water across walls of weathered sandstone, seems to originate in an ancient past. Forced to walk, I leave my family to bury Senhora Rosamonte's hand below a lemon tree. With my thanks, I take her aquamarine ring as her last gift and place it in my pouch with Diego's message and the girl's wedding band; it may one day redeem the life of another swallow taken by Pharaoh.

On my way back to my family, I pause for a moment to place the palm of my hand flat against the trunk of a massive cork tree whose valuable bark has recently been peeled away. For some reason, perhaps to better feel the power of the verdant giant, I close my eyes. Immediately, a great light sets the darkness ablaze with an orange-black fire and a humid warmth seems to pass right through me. A great rustling of leaves comes to me from high above, as if an eagle or heron has alighted on a topmost branch. "Yes, we are here," comes Uncle's voice. "But do not open your eyes. Our radiance would overwhelm you."

As I squeeze my eyelids closed in protection, he says, "Berekiah, the bark of a tree is not merely a symbol to be used in poetry. It is a real presence which shares the Lower Realms with you. It grows, it dies, and it can be removed by a woodsman. Feel your hand meeting the solidity which lies beneath such bark."

I squeeze the trunk between my hands, sense a fluid power rising from the earth up through my legs and into my head.

"You have been drawn to this tree because it has reminded you that a mask can be something other than a metaphor," he says. "It can be a real adornment, as well."

As I think, *Please, Uncle, address me as simply as you can,* he replies in a tone of anger: "We speak in the language of the Upper Realms and know of no other way to converse!" Regaining a tone of compassion, he continues: "Remember, our shadow is your light. Our simplest clarity is your greatest paradox. Berekiah, listen. You must never send your illuminations with a courier who doesn't recognize himself in his mirror from one day to the next. And remember the eyesight of he who speaks with ten tongues."

At that, there is a quivering in my hands and a flapping sound from above. The blazing darkness behind my eyelids fades to gray; the bird—Uncle—has flown away. Opening my eyes, I stare through the empty canopy of branches above into the great blue sky.

His words repeat inside me: *Never send your illuminations with a courier who doesn't recognize himself in his mirror from one day to the next.* Was he referring to a man with no self-knowledge? Or someone without memory, perhaps, who has sought to leave behind his past, to deny its existence. A man who cannot recognize himself because he does not wish to recall the personal history which helped to make him who he is today.

*And remember the eyesight of he who speaks with ten tongues.* Farid. Uncle could only have been referring to his fingers—his ten tongues. My master meant for me to count on his discernment in learning the identity of this man who could not even recognize himself.

For a moment, I am tempted to pray over the vellum ribbon on my wrist for my master to visit me again, to give me a clearer answer in the language of the Lower Realms. Deep in my gut, however, I fear entering the realm of practical kabbalah; Uncle must have had his reasons for speaking to me in riddles.

"Beri!" It is Mother, calling to me from across the field.

As I start toward her, I think: *More and more, the world is intruding on my inner life of contemplation. Just as Uncle knew it would.*

After Reza and I wash our hands in a nearby creek, we leave the Almond Farm right away; I am afraid for Farid's life. And the Old Christians could descend like locusts at any time.

Just before reaching home, I jump down from the cart to enquire about Father Carlos at St. Peter's Church. There is still no sign of him, and his apartment remains locked. So I climb the streets and outdoor stairways of the Alfama to Diego's townhouse. The cobbler who helped me avoid capture the day before hails me from his doorway, nods for me to come to him. "Don't go in," he whispers.

"Why?"

"A man came looking for your friend Diego. He left a little while ago. But he's been here before, watching. He may be here even now. Hiding, waiting. Just smile and nod at me, then go away."

I do him one better and feign a laugh, then ask, "Who is this man?"

"I don't know. A Northerner. Blond, strong."

I bow my thanks and leave, my steps repeating the question: *Could the same man who killed Uncle now be hunting Diego?*

At home, hard-boiled eggs are being prepared for lunch by Reza. Of course, cooking should be a neighbor's duty during our initial mourning period of seven days, but there is no one left who isn't grieving. All the ceramic debris has been swept from the kitchen into the courtyard, the floor mopped. Even the leg of our table which had been knocked off has been nailed in place.

"Brites did it while we were gone," Reza explains. "She's cleaning the store now with the others."

"Esther's with her, too?" I ask.

"No, she's sitting vigil over Farid in your mother's room."

"And Aviboa?"

"Yes, she's helping clean up, is sticking close to Cinfa." Reza chews on the ends of her hair and sighs. "I'm going to have to adopt her, you know. I can't leave her to fend for herself. Graça, her mother, was a widow and an only child."

"Is she Jewish?"

Reza's eyes flash. "A four-year-old girl? Who are you, Berekiah Zarco, to ask such a question about an orphan? You think kids are born knowing Hebrew or something? What difference could it possibly..."

"Reza, you misunderstand me. I don't care. It's just that it could create complications."

"I live with nothing but complications." She sighs again, brushes her hand against my arm as an apology. "Her father was a New Christian, Graça was Old."

"It's safer not to tell my mother that...for now, at least."

As Reza nods, I kiss her cheek. Caressing open the door to my mother's room, I find Farid lying on his side under two heavy blankets, shivering. Aunt Esther sits on her stool by the foot of the bed, still staring at nothing, her hands folded in her lap. I kiss her cool forehead.

A rumpled and bloodstained sheet has been pulled from the bed, is tucked against the wall.

Farid's eyes open, but he does not smile or acknowledge me in any way. I take a woolen blanket from my bed and cover him with yet another layer, kneel beside him, move to take his hand. He waves me away. "It could be plague," he signals.

"Your gestures are stronger," I lie. We lock fingers, and his eyes close again. I sit picturing map-contours of Portugal, Greece and Turkey as if shapes on a chessboard where my family and I serve as pawns.

When Farid's shivering subsides and he falls asleep, I caress his hair for a time. Grabbing the stained sheet and balling it up beneath my arm, I tiptoe out and across my bedroom to hide his incontinence from my mother, fearing that she may demand that the family abandon him because of his worsening illness. Reza starts when she sees me, but her subsequent stare denotes solidarity. Behind an oleander bush to the side of our outhouse, I hide the sheet. Later, I will tell Brites that it is there and to be careful of the evil essences it has absorbed when washing it.

Lacking vinegar, I clean my hands with black soap and water, go to the cellar and write my list of suspects—beginning with the two remaining threshers—on a piece of vellum in micrographic letters forming Uncle's name:

Father Carlos.

Diego Gonçalves.

Rabbi Losa.

Miguel Ribeiro.

With my last stroke, I think: *the girl we have buried will point like a vane toward the correct name.*

I take my drawing of her, slip my hammer inside my pouch and walk to all the bakeries in the Alfama and Graça neighborhoods, sensing that she is the key, that if I can find her identity, I will also learn who it was who destroyed my future.

Now that calm has returned, my eyes see that Lisbon has become a city of staring Christian eyes, of garbage and dung, of splintered wood and bloody stone. None of a half-dozen bakers or their assistants whom I question knows the girl. I cut down past the cathedral and head into Little Jerusalem. Stores are closed, streets littered with refuse. Women sweep blood from their stoops. A burnt bed sits smoldering right in the middle of the Synagogue Square as if waiting for its owner. Simon Kol's bakery behind the Riverside Palace is boarded up. I slip around the side, past a pile of rotten cabbages and onions being picked through by feral cats, one of whom has furry testicles swollen to the size of lemons. When I pound on Master Kol's personal entrance, he peers down from a window. His unshaven cheeks and bewildered eyes are the symptoms of the illness we all share. "Pedro Zarco?" he asks. When I nod, he points to his courtyard. I wait at the gate. As he lets me in, he hugs and kisses me. His chest heaves like a bellows as he sobs.

He is dressed in the coarse linen of mourning. "Kiri?" I whisper, naming his only living child with the same, trespassing fear as I would a secret name of God.

"Yes," he answers. We hold hands. "How's your family?" he asks.

"Uncle Abraham is dead."

Simon gasps. "How could he have..."

His words trail off because we both know that in this world even a *gaon,* a genius, a man of wonders can be killed by a simple blade.

To my question about Judah, he shakes his head. "Many are missing," he says. "And they will never be found. Swallowed by Leviathan. And mark my words," he says in a prophetic voice, "the monster will only be sated when it has taken all of us. Wait and see!"

I hand him my drawing. "This girl...ever see her? I think she may work in a bakery."

He squints. "Looks a little like Meda Forjaj when she was young," he says. "Same sloping eyebrows that come together over the bridge of her nose. Like butterfly wings. But I don't know her."

"Who's Meda Forjaj?"

"Fled Little Jerusalem about the time of the conversion. But she'd be about fifty by now. A widow. Couldn't be her."

"Where'd she move?"

"Out near Belem, I think." Belem was the nearby town from which the Portuguese caravels left for Africa, India and the New World. "I think she was hoping to meet a rich explorer if you know what I mean," Simon adds. He shrugs, gestures that he makes no judgment. "We do what we need to in order to survive."

"A woman her age—she can't earn a living just from that," I say.

"Her husband imported woolens from Flanders. She helped out, kept the books. Maybe she takes in sewing like your mother."

"Thanks." We hug lightly, as if afraid to admit we may be parting forever. "You won't open your bakery again, will you," I observe.

Simon shakes his head. "I no longer want to feed this country," he says. "A bleeder," he whispers. "It's a much better profession for Portugal."

The collective gaze of the Old Christians massed at St. Catherine's Gate chills the hairs at the back of my neck, but this readiness of my body to break into flight is unnecessary; their eyes are calm, their breathing easy. Their fear of plague and drought and all the myriad demons who rule their knotted thoughts has been purged, at least for the moment.

I reach the outskirts of Belem in less than an hour. Here, hundreds of Africans and day laborers ruled by the whip are hard at work building a monumental new monastery for King Manuel that should take well into the next century to complete.

A ragpicker in soiled pants points me to a local bakery. A lean woman with an accusing, bitter face meets me at the door. "Can I help you, Senhor?" she asks in harsh, Castilian-edged Portuguese.

From her accent, I know that she is a Castilian New Christian, one of the thousands who fled here after King Ferdinand and Queen Isabella expelled the Jews in fourteen ninety-two. In her fierce eyes, I see that she loathes being seen with a compatriot. I show her my drawing. "I'm looking for this girl."

She turns her back to me and begins transferring buns from wooden pallets into sacks.

"It's important," I add.

"If you've nothing to order, then leave."

"She's dead," I say. "I'd like to tell her parents."

She turns, and mistrust gives her a squint. "She's Senhora Monteiro's girl. Why do..."

"And Senhora Monteiro lives...?" I interrupt; I've no more patience for fear, even that which belongs to a Jew.

"Down the street, on the right. A house with yellow trim. But it might be better..."

"Tell me, does Senhora Monteiro have any relation to Meda Forjaj?"

"Her sister-in-law," she replies. "How did you...?"

"Eyebrows like spreading butterfly wings. And the memory of an old Jew."

Down the street, a dwarfish, fish-eyed woman with a scaly, leathery face glares up at me from her door as if I've interrupted a card game. She wears a ragged wig made from waxed, black-linen thread.

"Are you Senhora Monteiro?" I ask.

"Who wants to know?"

"My name would mean nothing to you." I hand her my sketch. "Do you recognize this girl?"

"It's Teresa. What are you doing with this?"

Her husband, a squat, rabbit-like man, appears at the back of the house. He is soiled with white powder, perhaps quicklime, and puffs rise from his bare fat feet as he strides toward us. Above his sleepy dark eyes sprout winged brows.

The woman says, "This man's got a drawing of Teresa. Look."

His jaw drops as if he's never seen artwork—or as if he understands. When I force out clinging words about her death, fists raise to his cheeks. Tears gush in his eyes. When I reach for him, Senhora Monteiro intercepts my wrist. "What are you saying?!" she demands.

"She was killed in the riot in Lisbon. On Sunday."

The Senhora's hand muffles her gasp. Terrified eyes focus inside. Silence seals the three of us together till she screams, "I knew it would come to this! Killed with those Jews, wasn't she?!"

Her husband shoves her, runs back into the house before I can answer. She crashes up against the wall and crumples to the ground. "You bastard!" she shrieks. She cackles, spits after him.

I help the Senhora to her feet, retrieve my drawing from the ground. She has no tears to give, so I say, "She was killed in the Judiaria Pequena. Do you know what she was doing there?"

She snatches my drawing from me and surveys it as if forming a criticism. "That's her all right. You make this?"

"Yes," I reply.

"Artist, huh? Filthy goat should never have run off. But girls from mixed marriages...cause that's what she was, you know...I'm not Jewish. Thank God." She waves toward the back of the house as if shooing away a fly. "He's a Jew...was, I mean. It's the mixed blood. Makes girls want a man as soon as they start to bleed. The moon, it causes friction, they say, in the children of mixed marriages." She rubs her filthy, callused hands together. "All that swirling of blood, the pure with the tainted." She shakes her head. "You got talent, you know. You're not Jewish, are you?"

"I was. Now I'm just trying to survive. Like pretty much everyone else in this dungheap."

Her stare is fixed by inflamed contempt. I try to remember that she, too, is an emanation of God, a ripple from the sapphire of love he cast eons ago into our world. I see only the spittle on her lips and her raven-black wig. "Do you mind telling me what Teresa was doing in the Little Jewish Quarter?" I ask.

"Aren't you listening? She was getting it between her legs! Wanted a bird that was circumcised!" She sees her tone bothers me, laughs, makes her hand flap. "Liked the way it felt when a big fat Jew-quail hopped all the way up her and began spreading its..."

"Who's her husband?" I interrupt.

"An importer with lots of brains, big balls, too, they say. Furry...like wool. Only tasting like Moroccan dates." She licks her lips greedily. "But no money. You don't all have a talent for making money. Hah! I found that out twice in my life! That husband of mine... And now Teresa's." She shakes her head and frowns. "Name's Manuel Monchique. You'd think she could at least have found one who..."

My heart seems to pound through my chest. *Of course,* I think, *Uncle's former student—Teresa was his Old Christian bride!*

We'd learned only a month before that Manuel had obtained a card of pure blood from the King, effectively erasing the "stain" of his Jewish past. Uncle had recently insulted him on Temple Street because of this seeming betrayal. Now, framed inside Senhora Monteiro's revelation, this confrontation appears dyed with sinister colors.

Cold fingertips brush against my arm. I focus again into the present tense, see that Senhora Monteiro is grinning up at me, has lifted up her skirt and is pounding her hand between her legs. I tug off her wig, toss it to the floor behind her. Underneath, sickly tufts of gray hair sprout from a louse-infested scalp.

Her clucking laugh accompanies my escape. The streets of Belem, then outer Lisbon open to me, yet I seem to race only into the mystery of my master's murder. Maybe Manuel had found Teresa with Uncle, taken his knife and...

And yet, a high barrier blocks my way toward an answer; how would Manuel have learned of the location of our trap door and *genizah?*

Blessed be He who opens the arms of grace; I discover the São Lourenço Gate to the north of the city guarded only by a lazy rabble.

Marching through, I skirt the scruffy hillside that holds aloft the battlements of the Moorish Castle and descend quickly to the Alfama; I must check on Farid again before confronting Manuel Monchique. My mother meets me in the kitchen. Diego stands behind her. The gash across his chin is now obscured by several days' growth of beard, the stitches barely visible. His saffron-colored turban crowns his head. He stares at me over his broad nose as if hoping to glean my thoughts, limps to me like a wounded dog. We hug. But the knowledge that he could have conspired against my master gives me the careful, self-conscious movements of a bad actor.

"I'm so sorry about your uncle," he says. "And to have been killed by the Christian rabble, it's almost too much to believe possible."

Diego's words are unable to penetrate the rigid gates I erect around myself; not only do I not trust him, but I now see that a stranger stands at the corner of the room by the hearth, and I cannot allow my ripped soul to be seen. A barrel-chested, stone-faced man in the coarse livery of a mercenary, he holds the handle of his sheathed sword with both hands and is fixed at attention. I nod questioningly in his direction.

"My bodyguard," Diego answers.

"New Christian?"

"Yes. With a card of pardon. I figured that was safer. And now that the mob has killed your uncle and so many others, I think..."

"My master was murdered by a Jew!" I declare.

"What?"

"Uncle's throat was slit as if by a *shohet*."

It is the first time my mother has heard my reasoning. She reaches out for the table as if the world is receding from her.

Diego gasps for breath. He covers his mouth with his hands as if seeking to prevent the possibility of such treason from entering him.

Does he manifest the shock of an innocent philosopher or the dramatic flare of a murderer?

"But why would a Jew take your uncle's life?!" he demands.

"Maybe jealousy, maybe robbery," I lie, wishing to test his reaction.

My mother suddenly shouts, "What in God's name are you talking about, Berekiah?! How could you believe that one of our own people would take my brother's life?!" Her voice possesses that hysterical tone which indicates that she is but one step away from accusing me of being a bad Jew.

I gulp water from a jug on the mantle, stare into her eyes and say, "A manuscript was stolen. No Old Christian even knew that we had any in the house."

My mother begins pulling at her hair.

"Are you sure?" Diego asks.

When I nod, he takes my arm. "From where was the manuscript taken?"

"From the cellar."

"He had books in the cellar! What are you..."

"His last Haggadah," I explain.

"He was keeping Hebrew books?"

"Yes."

"Had he lost his mind?!"

Either Diego is skilled at feigning ignorance or he really hadn't yet been fully initiated into the threshing group, hadn't yet learned of the *genizah*. I will have to check with Father Carlos, if he is still alive. And yet, what if he lies in order to implicate his brother philosopher?

"He was smuggling the books out of Portugal," I tell Diego. "Saving them from flames."

"Dear God. With whom?!" he demands.

"Don't know. Listen, when did you last see Uncle?"

"Last Friday. At the hospital. You were there. Why are you..."

"And Sunday?" I ask. "Did you see him then?"

"No. What are all these questions about?"

"I'm trying to trace his movements," I lie. "Where were you from Sunday until now?"

"Hiding. With a friend." Diego's expression hardens into the look he gets before delivering a stern lecture. "Berekiah, I think you need to explain yourself. What makes you think that..."

"I don't have to explain myself to anyone!" I answer rudely. "Uncle's death gives me new rights, and one of them is to be able to disregard that surly face you're now hoping to subdue me with. Judge me if you want. Frown, pray, invoke Torah against me. I don't care."

"You should care. What if..."

"Be quiet, Diego! Just tell me if you know who the man is who has been making enquiries about you at your apartment?"

"What man?! What are you talking..."

"When I went to look for you this morning, your neighbor across the street, the cobbler, he told me that a man had been enquiring after you...blond, strong...a Northerner, perhaps."

Diego's eyes betray terror.

I ask, "Do you know why someone would be following you?"

"No," he whispers. He takes my shoulders, grips them hard. "Unless...unless the same man is after me who killed your uncle!"

"Yes, I thought of that. But why would anyone want both of you dead?"

He shakes his head.

"Think!"

"There's nothing!" he moans. "What could we know that..."

"Had Uncle mentioned any special book he'd discovered? Anything at all?"

He shakes his head. I take out my drawing of the girl murdered with Uncle. "And her?" I ask, unscrolling the sketch for him. "Do you recognize her?"

"Never. Who is she?"

"It doesn't matter." I put the drawing back in my pouch. "How about Dom Miguel Ribeiro? What do you know of him?"

"He's a nobleman, isn't he? The son of old Rodrigo Ribeiro, if I recall correctly."

"Yes. Did Uncle mention him?" I ask.

"Not to me. But Beri, you must have other clues to the killer's identity. What did you find in the cellar? Anything that would indicate this Northerner who's been looking for me? I must know. If he's after me, then I will have to..."

"Nothing," I lie, unwilling to trust him just yet with the knowledge of what I'd discovered. I turn away from his skeptical eyes toward my mother. She stares into the fire dancing in the hearth. I pat her arm. "How's Farid?" I ask gently.

She turns to me with startled eyes and says, "Berekiah, I need to know more. Was the Haggadah the only book stolen?"

"Yes, I think so. Now how's Farid been doing?"

"Don't you think we should..."

"Mother, just tell me how Farid..."

She pulls in her chin and turns away in defiance.

"You're insane!" I shout. "All your 'shoulds' and proper ways of being. What good has it done you?!"

Tears well in her eyes and she says with desperate force, "How could you treat me like this when Judah...?"

"Go sing it to the goats!" I yell. I march away from her and Diego, realize with a mixture of aching regret and pleasure that it is I who have started this argument. Uncle's death has released me from my past personality and my future, and it seems that rage and frustration are all that I have left of my inheritance.

I peer in on Farid in my mother's room. He sleeps, breathes in jerks and starts as if possessed by nightmare. I rub his neck and arms with a wet towel till his inner-struggle calms. Hollowed by fear for his safety, I march out of the house.

"Where are you going?!" my mother calls after me.

"Out!"

Diego exhorts me to stop, limps to me by the courtyard gate, rubs the stubble on his cheeks thoughtfully. He says, "If you're right about your uncle, then perhaps you're in danger, too."

"It's of no importance. No Old Christian will ever hurt me again." Staring into his eyes, I add, "Or Jew, for that matter!"

He reaches tenderly for my arm. "So innocent you are, my son. You don't know what they can do. Berekiah, I think you and your family should just pack up and leave. That's what I'm doing. I'm settling business matters, selling what I can and then getting away any way I can. The King won't dare to stop us now that..."

"Peace be with you," I interrupt, then remember the note that belongs to him. I lift it from my pouch, press it into his hand. "This fell from your turban when you were lying on the cobbles. I'm afraid it got a little stained with blood from Senhora Rosamonte. I'm sorry."

Diego reads it, nods his understanding. "Yes, Isaac. An acquaintance from Andalusia. From Ronda. Reminding myself to meet him on that date. My memory is not what it once was. Your uncle knew him."

"And *Madre?*"

"The Fountain of the Mother of God. It was to be our meeting place. We were..." His words trail off and he grabs my arm as if clenched by fear. "But now maybe I understand! Isaac talked about selling your uncle a book! I assumed it was in Castilian, but now that you say he was keeping Hebrew books..."

"When?"

"A few days before his...before Sunday. We met here. You were in the store, I guess. Isaac said he owned a copy of Judah Ha-Levi's 'Book of the Khazars' and your uncle inhaled as if scenting myrtle."

"I'd very much like to meet him," I say.

"I'll try to locate him and bring him by tonight after dinner."

When I thank him, Diego adds, "Maybe it doesn't pay to go around Lisbon right now. You should..."

I wave him away, exit through the courtyard gate and start down the Rua de São Pedro. When I take a last look back, I see Diego's head bobbing above the courtyard wall as he limps back to the kitchen. What if the boys who'd stoned him had been in the pay of someone, another thresher perhaps?

*There are no accidents and no coincidences,* I hear my uncle say. *Everything possesses significance.*

A man in white hops out suddenly from a doorway and thrusts a leather book in front of my face. My knife is already at his throat as he begins to scream my name. "Beri! What are you doing?!"

I lower my blade; it is only António Escaravelho and his worm-eaten New Testament. A former Jewish councilman and silversmith of astounding dexterity, he became a fervent Christian after the forced conversion and an even more fervent lunatic a short time later.

António reeks like old garbage. His gray beard is crusted with dirt, and his tan, leathery skin is riddled with red blisters. His gospels exude the smell of cardamon and dung, an unsympathetic combination. I hold my nose.

"God be with you," he crows, as I put my dagger away. He winks his mad, darting eyes, presses his book up to my chin as if correcting my posture.

"I wish you wouldn't keep accosting me like this," I answer. I push the gospels down to his side and sigh at the sight of lice eggs dotting his frayed ropes of hair. Hoping that he can point me further along the trail to my uncle's murderer, I ask, "Were you in your usual spot near my house when the riot began?"

He disregards my question, replies with a toothless grin, "I've petitioned again to go to Rome and see the Pope. It seems that this time I may get my exit card."

"You're not still at it!" I shout, for he'd been asking to leave Portugal for years. The King's decree of the twentieth of April, fourteen ninety-nine, had closed all borders to New Christians.

"Indeed I am!" he exclaims as if hurt by my implication of hope-lessness. "And you must join me, my boy. You and Master Abraham!"

"No more journeys for my master," I whisper to myself, unwilling to risk António's reaction to his death. With a smile of wistful sadness, I remember that my uncle always used to tell him, "Why make such a long journey to a man so short on holiness?!" To my surprise, I repeat to the beggar another phrase of Uncle's, "The very thought of seeing the Pope makes my scalp itch."

So will I now begin to imitate my master's words? Is that how I will keep him with me?

António observes, "I think you would find a trip to Pope Julius II most liberating. The Moslems throughout the Italian peninsula are friendly, they say."

Moslems in Italy? I figure the drought has parched his sense of geography. "Listen closely, my friend, were you here Sunday, the first day of the riot?" I question again.

"Nearby...hidden," he replies. He raises a finger to his lips. "With a four-legged friend."

"Could you see the gate to our courtyard?"

"Yes," he replies. "From the cobbles to the sky, it's all part of the..."

"And did you see anyone enter? Maybe with a knife...or a rosary. Manuel Monchique perhaps? You remember him, one of my uncle's old students."

"There may have been a dragon-fly or two," he says. "And some toads. It's not always easy to spot them when they hop inside the..."

"But a man?" When he shakes his head, I say, "You're sure? How about Diego Gonçalves? You know him, he's a printer...a friend of my uncle's."

"No."

"What about Father Carlos? Or Rabbi Losa?"

He shakes his head after I pronounce each name. It seems that the killer must have entered and exited through our fruit store—or through my mother's separate entrance to Temple Street. "Then peace be with you," I tell him, and bow my departure.

As I start away, he screeches, "Have you no lamb from Passover? There's a hole in my stomach bigger than the one in my soul!"

"Go to see Cinfa," I call back. "She'll give you all the fruit you want."

"Bless you, my boy."

Ahead, mendicants are clamoring by the cathedral wall; despite threats of death made by the Crown, one of the cows let loose by the King has been slaughtered. A wiry man is slicing its skin away with a rusty sword while a juggler drenched in sweat entrances a group of waifs and dogs by whirling three of its bloody hooves in the air.

Around the corner, Manuel Monchique's house remains silent to my knocks. The shutter of a window suddenly opens just a whisper. "It's Pedro Zarco," I call, using my Christian first name for safety. When no one answers, I slip around the side. Tossing my hammer over the wall to their courtyard, I pry my body up and over. Manuel's elfin mother stands at the back doorway, robed in black, gripping a blue ceramic pitcher in gnarled hands. She has the expectant look of a frightened animal, a tanned face puckered by age. "It's me, Pedro," I say. "I went to school with Manuel for a time. My uncle is Master Abraham." When I pick up my hammer, she tosses her pitcher at me. It breaks into in two perfect pieces by my feet. She rushes inside.

Manuel comes to the doorway draped in a black-fringed scarlet cloak. The blade of a sword held straight up in both his hands splits my vision of his ruddy, youthful face. He seems just another of the great wonders of this era of falsehood with which we've been burdened; one would never guess that he'd been the kind of oversensitive boy whose eyes watered at the slightest trace of wind, forever doubled over from the meagerest chase through the woods after his beloved butterflies. Now, he puffs up his chest like a pheasant, designs a letter *yod* in the air with the tip of his sword and says in a false voice of command, "I don't know what debt you think you've come to collect, but you won't get anything from me or my family!"

"You can go sing it to the goats, too," I say. "Save all your Christian bravado for the virgins you seduce on Yom Kippur. I come only with this." Lifting the scrolled drawing from my pouch, I toss it to him. "Take a look, my brave and handsome crusader for Christ."

Manuel kneels, picks up my sketch with a wary hand. Immediately, his eyes light with surprise. As if I've handed him stolen property, he asks, "Where'd you get this?!"

"I drew it."

"You've seen her?" He sheaths his sword, rushes to me. Reaching for my hands as a friend again, he asks, "Where? When? Is she all right?"

"Manuel, I'm sorry...she's dead. Murdered at our house."

When I explain, his touch grows cold. Disbelief echoes inside his quivering breathing. Either he has a talent for lying or this is the first he has heard of her death. "It couldn't have been her," he says. "Even your hand might confuse an eye, the curve of a chin, a..."

"Is she a laundress or a baker?" I question.

"Neither," he smiles. "It's the wrong..."

When I take her ring of braided gold filaments from my pouch, he grabs it from me. The certainty in his voice falters. "It's the right kind. But really, it doesn't prove anything. I know other women who have rings just like it."

"Her hands smelled of olive oil, rosemary and lemon oil. She had ash stains. And two indentations on her temples. Like the marks made..."

The blood descends from Manuel's face. He kneels to keep from fainting. As if giving way to sleep, he closes his eyes and begins to weep. When he has his breath, he says, "Candles... She works with Master Bento. They make scented candles together. With floral essences. When the wax has cooled, they're coated with olive oil to keep them fresh."

"And the indentations?"

Manuel nods. "At birth. The midwife had to pry her out. With a forceps. She wouldn't come. Afraid to take first steps, she was. So very timid, as if the world were a steep, descending staircase into a dungeon. I was helping her see that there was a garden below. I was helping her walk to it. We were...we..."

As I wait for his tears to end, I consider the impossibility of a shy girl found naked with my uncle after making love.

Manuel suddenly says in a limp voice, "How was she killed? Was she violated by the Christians?"

"I don't know if she was raped. I don't think so. But, Manuel, her throat was cut."

"Dear God..." His buries his head in his hands for a time. When he looks up, he says, "I...I suppose you've already buried her."

"We couldn't wait any longer. I'm sorry. At the Almond Farm. I will show you the exact spot when I can. And we will say a *kaddish* together for her. But do you have any idea what was she doing in my neighborhood?"

"She left the house on Sunday to visit Tomás, her brother. He lives near you. She must have run from the mob and found her way to your place by accident."

"Did she know my uncle?" I ask.

"She knew of him, of course. But they never met that I know of."

"How about any of the members of Uncle's threshing group . . . Diego, Father Carlos?"

"I don't think she'd even heard of them."

"And did she consider herself a Jew?"

He shakes his head. "Not really. Mosaic law about the mother having to be Jewish and all that. Her mother's Old Christian, was born in Segovia, but has lived in Lisbon since she was little. A peasant really. But don't try to tell her that. Teresa's father is a Portuguese New Christian from Chaves. When she decided to marry me, they refused to have anything to do with her. So what do I do? I get a card of pure blood. Logical, no? Does the old whore care? She tells me that a Jew is like a pomegranate because the blood inside always stains what it touches. She has an answer for everything. Like the Devil." Manuel stands, twists his face away in anguish. "And your uncle, he never understood the pressure I was under."

"Manuel, Master Abraham is dead, too."

He starts, leans toward me. His eyes show panic.

I nod to assure him it's the truth. "Aunt Esther was violated and will not speak. Judah is still missing. And Uncle is with us no longer. Mother, Cinfa and Reza are safe."

Manuel turns around to hide his tears. Or is it his prior knowledge?

"Master Abraham never did forgive me then," comes his whisper.

I ask, "Was his forgiveness that important?"

Manuel whips around and glares at me as if it is criminal to pose such a question. "Berekiah, a card from the King doesn't remove your heart!"

"I did speak to him about you. After we were so rude on the street. He said he would honor you the next time you met. Hate for the concept of pure blood carried him away. He knew that he had acted wrongly. You had his full blessings."

Manuel's eyes drip silent tears. He picks up the halves of his mother's jug. "How did the Christians find him? Didn't he get out with you?"

I consider trying to trick him, but decide that the truth is riddle enough. As I describe the bodies, he hides his face in his hands again. "It's *impossible!*" he says. He moans the word over and over until his voice becomes a whisper disappearing into an ocean of silence.

I come to him and say, "We must find out exactly how she got to our cellar. Perhaps her brother can tell us."

"If he's still alive."

As we walk toward Tomás' apartment, Manuel whispers his wife's name as if in incantation. He hides behind an expression of rigid control, grips his sword handle. It is all wrong for him. Instead of polished iron, Manuel should have gone out into the world brandishing a butterfly net and notebook.

Our destination is the third floor of a squalid townhouse in the poor neighborhood below the hillock crowned by St. Steven's Church. Brittle bells are tolling vespers when we arrive, and Old Christians are shuffling inside. A caretaker is shooing away a pack of prancing dogs who want to join in services. Sunset has lit the horizon. The dark of the sixth evening of Passover is almost within reach.

Manuel's brother-in-law, a pillow-maker's assistant, is stuffing feathers into netting when we arrive. His garret smells like a chicken coop. He has no neck, red-veined cheeks like Father Carlos, a receding fringe of dirty brown hair. He wears a bull's expression of unknowing, obsessive rage, takes the news without looking up. A brief pause in his hand motion is all.

"She said she was going out," he says. "She was complaining of uncleanliness, the time of women's pain."

I motion Manuel outside; we have learned all we need to know.

"What do you know of that man?" I question.

"You need to ask? The half that is Christian has the manners and intelligence of a swine. You can imagine how crazy that makes the half that is Jewish. Teresa must have been adopted. It's the only explanation."

When I look up, Tomás is moving back from his window. Could he have followed his sister and killed them both out of some half-formed sense of religious righteousness bequeathed by his mother? Could he and a thresher entrusted with the secret of our *genizah* have come to kill my uncle at exactly the same moment? Was such a coincidence possible?

Two feathers float down toward us. I reach out for one. "I think Teresa considered herself more Jewish than you think," I say, gripping it tightly. To Manuel's puzzled look, I ask, "Where does a Jewish woman go who has just finished her rhythm with the moon?"

"To a bathhouse," he replies.

"And where's the nearest bathhouse?"

"On the Rua de São Pedro. Just down the street from your..."

"Exactly."

# Chapter X

Our synagogue in the Judiaria Pequena was built in the Christian year of thirteen seventy-four on a tiny hillock flanking the southern rim of Lisbon's ancient defensive walls. At the bottom of this slope is a tiny square centered by a great pear tree, a brother to the towering giant which used to shade the yard of our central temple in Little Jerusalem. A staircase of polished limestone rises twenty feet from the tree's octopus-tangle of roots to Samuel Aurico's tannery on the first floor and another fifteen to the synagogue on the second.

On the other side of the synagogue runs the Rua de São Pedro. It was here that our ancestors put the entrance to our *micvah*, a series of cascading pools—two for ritual bathing—carved out of the rock below and gifted with an underground stream as a source. Some nimble negotiation by Rabbi Zacuto and other Court Jews spared it from the mass confiscations of fourteen ninety-seven and enabled our chazan, David Moses, to remain as manager. Of course, our men and boys were no longer expected to immerse themselves in its waters before the Sabbath. But I've persisted. After all, a bath is pretty much a bath, and presumably even the Pope cannot prove what's in one's head. Now, of course, all that has changed; Portuguese curses have been strung into rope around our wrists, and proof no longer counts for anything. Throughout Spain, bathing on Friday has been declared enough evidence to turn a man to smoke. That Lisbon has begun to welcome the heat of this Inquisitional fire has become only too clear over the last week.

Naturally, our women have been similarly proscribed since the time of the conversion from purifying themselves after the moon has summoned the red of their tides. But Teresa, Manuel's wife, was apparently more faithful and courageous than he ever imagined. Was she surprised by Old Christians as she bathed? Possibly, she slipped away without time to dress and raced down the street to find safety in our house; it is only four doors east of the *micvah,* at the triangular corner the Rua de São Pedro makes with Temple Street, the Rua da Sinagoga.

The bathhouse door is locked, and no one answers our knocks. "I don't think Master David survived Sunday," I tell Manuel, and I explain to him how the chazan failed to meet me that afternoon at St. Anne's Gate.

Despite my words, Manuel calls to him in the crack of the doorway. The sixth evening of Passover has already descended gray and wind-blown over the city, and dust is kicking up from the cobbles in swirling sheets. Manuel covers his nose with his hand and kicks at the door with his foot. There comes no response. He asks, "Where to, now?"

"His apartment," I answer. "I know where he keeps his keys."

As we head off, he says, "I never understood why Master Abraham always treasured living so close to the bathhouse and synagogue. The way he and Rabbi Losa always fought, I mean. It seemed only to make things worse."

"Uncle always said that our location was prime for disappearing into God. The Rua de São Pedro and Rua da Sinagoga come together at our house. He maintained that a kabbalist should try to live at an intersection of lines—'where two become one.'"

"I suppose it's a blessing to be sure that life's made up of definite and discernable patterns," Manuel notes with a wistful smile, and in his tone I can tell that he, too, is questioning God.

We climb up a side street to the chazan's apartment and knock on his door. Perched on the eaves of his townhouse roof is an escaped hunting falcon, wary and fitful, a leather strap dangling from its right talon. When a gangly woman with a pointed chin hails us from upstairs, the bird takes wing. "We are all God-fearing Christians here," the woman says in a trembling voice. "*Old* Christians, every one of us, with the Lord Jesus risen in our hearts." She brings her hands together in front of her chest in a position of prayer.

Even from here, I can see that she has bitten her nails bloody. She must think that we, too, are on the hunt for *Marranos.* "We're simply looking for Master David," I say in a reassuring voice. "Nothing is wrong. We just want to know if you've seen him."

"Oh dear, I knew it. But you won't find him here. I haven't seen him since Sunday. I believe that he was scheduled that day to warm the heart of God himself from the pyre in the Rossio."

*Scheduled that day to warm the heart of God?* Often, in their effort to speak euphemistically, Lisboners gave voice to the most absurd and monstrous expressions. Was there any people on earth more capable of turning a scorpion into a rose with their tongues?

I ask, "Do you have the key to his apartment, by any chance?"

"Yes, yes, I do," she replies.

"Can we take a look?"

"Give me a minute and I'll help you."

She comes downstairs smoothing the front of her black smock with nervous hands. Her gaze will not rise to meet my own. She says in a hesitant voice, "When we first met Senhor David, we thought he was so gentlemanly. That's why we kept him as a tenant. Later, of course, we found out that he was just a *Marrano.* He assured us that he would be moving out by the end of this very month."

In her pathetic way, she is trying to distance herself from her tenant. In a reassuring voice, Manuel says, "He was the local chazan, you know." He utters these specific words because he suspects—as I do—that she is terrified because she has a Jewish background as well. His use of the Hebrew word "chazan" is his way of letting her know that we, too, know Hebrew—that we are New Christians who mean her no harm.

Due to a similarity of sound, however, the woman confuses "chazan" with the Portuguese word for a bad omen or instance of ill luck, *azango.* With a great nod, she replies in an excited voice, "Yes, yes, your excellency is right—all the Jews are *azango!*"

A week earlier and we'd have laughed at her ignorance. As it is, we both inhale deeply as if bracing ourselves for a fight that may last our lifetimes. Emboldened by the solidarity which she believes that she has elicited from us, she rushes to open the door. "Got it!" she says as the lock clicks. When the door squeals open, a foul smell wafts out. She says in a humble voice, "If you would only stay a few minutes, I would be most appreciative." She meets my gaze for but a moment. "I don't mean to be rude, dear sirs, but the stars and planets say that we're not to have strangers in our townhouse today. I'm sure you understand."

A worn leather runner leads from Master David's entrance to his cold hearth, five paces of a man distant. But we daren't move; all along its length, the precious ouds and lutes of David's collection lie gutted and shredded. A cittern banded with the most beautiful rose and cherrywood, like an agate carved for music, has been broken in half and dangles from a hook on the mantle like a dead crab. Below it sits a small mound of broken glass and ceramic potsherds topped by a tangle of phylacteries which will never again feel the pulse of any arm. The landlady points a stern finger toward us. "You should have seen it before I cleaned up. His fava beans were growing gray beards. Like their rabbis! And the stink... Lord, his people smell, don't they?"

"Just tell me if you've seen his clogs," I say.

She smooths the front of her smock again. "I'm afraid I don't keep track of his things. We were not friendly. In fact, we never even..."

I head to his clothes chest as she babbles on about the cold distance she insisted on maintaining from the "musical little Jew," as she now refers to David. His clogs are huddling together below a jumble of dated velvet caps from the time of King João. With a little prompting and silent cursing in Hebrew, the heel swivels open and three keys fall out. The landlady gapes. I say, "For four years, long before you moved here, I studied the Greek and Arabic modes with David right in this room. Couldn't you tell by my odor?"

"Ah, I understand," she whispers with an urgent inhale of breath. A grudging admiration deepens her voice as she says, "You people disguise yourselves well."

"It's no disguise," I say, "it's magic!" Remembering an old trick taught to me by Uncle, I show her an empty hand, then pull David's keys from out of her nostrils.

She gasps and crosses herself, falls to the ground in a position of prayer. "I beg you do me no harm," she moans, tears gushing in her eyes.

I say, "If the 'musical little Jew' should return, just tell him that Pedro Zarco has visited."

"Yes, senhor," she says, making a little bow with her head. "But I'm afraid that it would be better to tell him in your dreams tonight. That's the only way your excellency is likely to get a message through at this point."

The micvah is damp and slimy, and its windows have been nailed shut by some thoughtful Jew. As we descend, I lose my footing in the pure darkness. My behind is rudely introduced to the granite edge of a stair, and a raw pain stabs my shoulder. I cry out.

"I better get an oil lamp before you do yourself some serious damage," Manuel says. He climbs back up and out into evening, eases the door closed behind him.

As I sit inside the comfort of the black solitude, violet shapes condense, only to then shrink away into spotted shadows. "The lathe of darkness gives form to our wishes and fears," I hear my uncle say. So I wait. Framed by my soft breathing, Mordecai appears in his youth, then dances away on fawn's feet. A creak tugs me back from daydream. I jump up. A footstep? My heart pounds a code of warning. My uncle suddenly rises, blue with flecks of gold, an illumination painted by my memory. His expression is hesitant, pensive, as if he is considering the meanings of a difficult verse. Instead of stopping to greet me, he continues floating up and out into the false night of ceiling until he is gone.

*Pay it no mind,* I think. *It is not a vision, but only an illusion.*

Faint breathing from below prompts me forward. Or is it only the wind threading through an unseen shaft of cave? It is said there are a dozen different tunnels and borings that meet and surface here, the remnants of a subterranean network created by our ancestors in preparation for the Messiah. I call in Portuguese, *"Judeu ou Cristão?"* It seems to be the only question that matters anymore.

The breathing is gone. "I come in peace," I say.

Expectant silence returns my fear. I decide to ask the darkness a riddle; a Jew will know my meaning. "Who is the angel that offers his hands to Abraham?" The answer is "Raziel"; both his name and that of Abraham add up to two hundred and forty-eight in Hebrew, a language in which letters are also numbers. Raziel's hands are the equal sign that links them.

I ease two steps up the stairs in case a shadow should lunge for the source of my voice. But no movement pierces the darkness. I ask my riddle again, climb still higher. A door creaks open, a flame from above lights Manuel's face. The staircase below opens gray before me.

"Sorry I took so long," he says. "No one..."

"Sshhh...I think someone's here. I've heard breathing, a step I think."

He tiptoes down to me. "Jew or Christian?" he whispers.

"A footstep has no faith."

"So what is..."

"Raziel," comes a hoarse whisper. "...Raziel."

"What's he saying?" Manuel asks.

I put my finger to my lips to request silence. "Show yourself," I call below in Hebrew.

A tiny man with blinking eyes and tufts of thinning hair above his ears steps bare feet to the base of the stairs. A thick towel at his waist makes his chest appear shrunken. It is the surgeon, Solomon Eli. Before I realize it, I have bounded down the stairs. "It's impossible!" I say. "I saw you in Loios Square, roped together with your wife and..."

He pats my shoulders in exultation. *"Shalaat Chalom!"* he cries. "One of my little boys has escaped with his life!"

Solomon gives pet names to all the babies he circumcises. Mine has always been *Shalaat Chalom,* meaning "dream request"—a reference to my father's supplications for another son.

"But I saw you with...."

Solomon blocks my words with a finger to his lips. "My dearest wife, Reina, is dead," he whispers. He ribbons his hand upward in imitation of smoke. "All but me."

"But how?"

"How, you ask? A cyst, my dear *Shalaat.* I cut a painful cyst from one of the thugs who took us. A mason. About a year ago now. He recognized me after Reina had already... They made me watch. I told him I wanted to follow her across the Jordan River. He smiled furtively, hit me. When I awoke, I was lying on the roof of a house above the Church of São Miguel. Yellow wildflowers were growing from the tiles between my legs. Very strange. I thought I was dead. It was night. But when I saw the moon... I mean, I never read that heaven was circled by celestial bodies. Or is the *sahar só uma outra sohar,* the moon just another prison?" Solomon shrugs, forces a sour smile. "Maybe my mason thought it would be greater punishment to leave me alive. I had no clothes when I awoke. So where should I go? Not home. No one there anymore. I stumbled here. The door was open. Later, someone came and locked it."

"Has anyone else been here?" Manuel asks. "A girl?"

"No one," the surgeon replies.

I tell Manuel, "She would have died before Solomon arrived—back on Sunday. And somehow, she must have gotten from here to my..."

"What girl?!" the *mohel* demands. "Is it Cinfa? Is she...?"

"No, she's fine." I take Solomon's hands, explain about Uncle and the purpose of our search. "So have you seen anything, anything at all—jewelry, clothing, food...?" I ask.

"Come with me," he says in a grave voice.

The surgeon leads us past the men's ritual pool to the dressing alcoves for women that are tiled with six-pointed shields of King David. He walks with the careful, childlike movements of a man who has been fasting for days. Even so, the echo of his footsteps in these caverns pounds like drumming. He takes us to the small dressing room in which he's been sleeping. Manuel discards a towel that has served as Solomon's blanket. He lifts up a linen tunic that has been scrunched into a pillow and lets it dangle freely.

"Teresa's?" I ask.

A veil of shadow closes over Manuel's face as he lowers his lamp. He kneels. Dark sobbing quivers across the icy sheets of tile.

"She was nude when we found her," I whisper to Solomon. "I don't think she would run out on the street that way if she could have helped it. So how do you..."

Manuel suddenly marches out the door and down the hallway toward the central court. I call his name in vain and follow. My echo vibrates around us like a voice disclosing secrets.

Heading east, he races down a ramp into a meditation room, then descends past long-abandoned baths and dank-smelling grottoes. Finally, we reach the room which serves as Master David's office. Inside, we find his two turreted bookcases overturned, the bathhouse records scattered across the floor. At the far corner of the room, an oil lamp sits on its side. While Manuel inspects it, Solomon slumps to the stone floor. His chest heaves in the damp and heavy air. "My legs are tired," he shrugs.

"We'll get you food as soon as we leave," I assure him.

He holds up his hand to indicate that there is no rush.

"What was this all about?" I ask Manuel.

"Trying to see which way my wife would descend when the Christians came."

Solomon gazes around, sniffs at the air like a rabbit, leans toward the ground, then stands and raises himself up on his tiptoes like a deer straining to feed from a topmost branch. "Something foul in the air," he grumbles. He sticks out his tongue. "Like manure."

He's right; there is a fiber of evil trailing through the air.

"A dead squirrel or rat," Manuel says. "Drowned probably."

A key of understanding turns inside me and I reply, "No, it's no dead animal. I understand now. I'll show you what it is back in our cellar."

Manuel, Solomon and I descend the stairs underneath our secret trap door. The mohel huddles under the blanket I've given him, reaches his hand along the wall to keep from stumbling. He's never been in our cellar before, and he asks in a curious voice, "So how long has all this been here, my boy?"

"For as long as anyone remembers," I answer.

The prayer mat and myrtle bushes gift Solomon with the knowledge that the room has become our clandestine synagogue, and he chants, "Blessed be He who saves His temple from idolaters."

Aunt Esther is seated at Uncle's desk at the far end of the room, staring straight ahead into the Bleeding Mirror. She wears no headscarf, and her raggedly cut hennaed hair gives her a frightening appearance.

"Etti," Solomon calls to her, since he loves to call everyone by their pet name.

She neither replies nor stirs. Solomon puffs out his lips, looks at me questioningly. I say, "She will not reply for now. We must give her time."

The *mohel* nods, then sniffs at the air. "It's this cellar that's causing the smell," he says. "This place stinks as if..." His words end with a gasp when he thinks of the shell of putrefying body left behind by Uncle.

I step straight to the leather tapestries from Córdoba hanging on the western wall of the cellar, just behind Esther. Scrolling one up, I lift it off its hooks and lay it on the slate floor, then do the same with the other. Manuel lights our two silver candelabrums from his oil lamp. Pressing my fingertips against the wall just under the strange bloodstains which end abruptly at a line of tile, I say, "If Samir or Uncle were here, we could save some time. Even one of the threshers."

"What are you looking for?" Manuel asks.

"You'll see," I say. "I've just found out how a man—or even several men—can disappear from this room. And how a smell can be carried across space."

I begin tapping my fist against each tile in a horizontal row just at the height of my head, from the south end of the room by our sunken bathtubs to the north, by Esther.

Solomon whispers to Manuel, "Poor boy, Master Abraham's death has him thinking from left to right." It's local Jewish slang for the notion that I've lost all sense.

"I assure you that no gnat has flown in my ear," I reply, making reference to how King Nimrod lost his mind. "I used to wonder about my uncle appearing out of nowhere all the time. Father Carlos even suggested at times that he was a spirit jester. But now I know how he did it. And why I was never allowed to enter the cellar without his permission." I continue tapping, and when I don't find the sound I want, move to the row below. At the fourth row down, one which crosses the wall at the height of my neck, I find what I want—the hollow reply of a tile with only a thin backing of wall.

Cinfa bounds downstairs suddenly, halts on the bottom step, watches me with wary eyes.

Twenty or so more taps, and I have found the outline of tiles which have a meager backing. If I am right, there should be one tile near the right or left border which jiggles when pressed. A few moments later, I have found it. Prying it free, breaking a thumbnail in the process, I toss the tile to Cinfa. Below, there is a circular iron handle on which is crudely etched the Hebrew word, *rechizah*, bathe. After a deep breath and a prayer for success, I grab it and give it a yank.

When I pull, a break in the wall becomes the edge of a door revolving around a central fulcrum. A room of purest darkness confronts us. Solomon joins me, squats down on his haunches like a Moslem holy man and peers inside with a curious expression. I turn to Manuel. "Give me the oil lamp—I'm going inside."

"Where's it lead?" he asks.

"We shall see. But for now, just give me the lamp."

He hands it to me. We can see ahead into a stone corridor. "I'll follow you," he says.

Solomon pats me on the shoulder. "I'll stay here. And you, Cinfa," he nods up at my sister, "why don't you fetch me some matzah and water? A glass of kosher wine, too! And the softest, sweetest pillow you can find!"

We slip behind Manuel's lamp into the darkness as Cinfa dashes upstairs. The dank hallway ahead smells of cold stone and solitude. It narrows as the ceiling lowers until we are tucked into a crawlspace. We make our way like moles. After about twenty feet, when our limits flow outward and upward, we stand. A limestone door sprouts a rusted iron handle, also circular and also etched with the word, *rechizah*. Manuel tugs it open around its fulcrum. A humid wind rises against us. I lift our lamp. Blue and green tiles shimmer back at us. Countless papers are scattered across the floor. We are in the chazan's office in the bathhouse.

After Manuel and Solomon have headed for their respective homes, I go to my mother, armed now with the assurance that the killer was no sorcerer but simply a clever thresher. She is in our store, scrubbing the floor on her hands and knees by the light of a slender candle. I tell her what we've found. "Did you know about the secret exit?" I ask.

She puts down her brush and kneels. "Before you were born," she begins, "when the New Christians of this city were Jews, and your father was trying to establish..."

I close my eyes because it seems she is opening the title page to another endless story about my father and his struggles to develop a profitable business. She senses my irritation, snaps, "Our cellar was part of the *micvah!* It's where our granite tubs came from."

"How come you never told me?"

She turns away as if burdened with my presence. Her jaw muscles throb in anger. "You think that you have a right to know everything? Life doesn't work like that, no matter what my brother may have told you."

I stare at her with contempt even as I know she's right.

"Maybe he thought you knew and that he didn't have to discuss it," she adds in a conciliatory tone, picking up her brush. "Anyway, it wasn't important." The little wave of dismissal she gives me connotes exhaustion. She looks down suddenly, frowns; a pimply brown toad has hopped out from a hiding place. "What do you suppose he wants?" she asks.

"Food...a fly. To survive. Just leave him be."

"Leave him be? An unclean thing like this? One of the ten plagues of Passover?! Sent by God to punish the Egyptians who held us as slaves. In my house?!"

Mother seems to be ricocheting between somnambulism and a kind of vibrant lunacy. As she grabs her broom, I try to bring her back to more important matters and say, "I always thought he must have hid in the *genizah* with the books. How he loved their touch and smell!"

"Who?" she asks, and she furrows her eyebrows like I'm crazy.

I suddenly feel as if I could slap her. She lifts aside one of the unhinged doors to the store and sweeps the poor toad flying onto Temple Street.

"Can't you please..." I begin. But there is no point. Her very presence seems to sap my energy. She stares dreamily into the sky. The dazed toad wobbles upright. Roseta drops from out of nowhere, creeps stealthily forward, claws poised. "No you don't!" I say. I jump outside and sweep the toad into my hand, drop it into my pouch. I await Mother's protests against filth. But silver clouds rolling in from the west have transfixed her; night, like everything else, has reminded her of Judah.

I drop the toad in the fields upriver, wash my hands, nibble a matzah, then head back to our house to check on Farid. A sliver of crescent moon has risen over the horizon, and a story forms as I watch its halo: Manuel's wife is bathing in the *micvah*, hears the shrieks of New Christians being butchered on the street above. Racing through the maze of pools and alcoves, she reaches a cold wall of stars inside the chazan's office. Are the connecting doors open? Is my uncle, too, in the bathhouse, cleansing for prayer? Or does she scream as the torchlit Christians descend? Perhaps Uncle hears her, opens the secret door, crawls into the bathhouse and pulls her to safety.

Together, my master and the girl wait in our cellar for an end to Lisbon's madness. But the killers—a thresher and a blackmailer—come first. After they summon death to our home, they slip through the secret entrance to the bathhouse. One of them caresses the door closed, leaves the streak of blood from his fingertips behind, creeps through the tunnel to safety.

Farid is seated in the kitchen when I come inside. His face is etched with pale struggle. I know I should rush to him, but my own strength is eclipsed by despair. "Should you be up?" I signal from the doorway.

My friend nods, indicates with heavy gestures, "I found my house empty. You have not heard from my father, have you?" His arms dangle white, as if angels are already dressing him for...

"No. I've asked around. No one's seen him. In the early morning I'll go looking for him. Things have quieted enough so that..."

"A note came for you," he signals, holding up a scroll. "Actually, for your uncle."

I rip open the seal. It's from Senhora Tamara, a used book seller in Little Jerusalem with whom we had frequent dealings. It reads:

> "Master Abraham, a young boy tried to sell me what appears to have been a storybook from Egypt recently uncovered by you. Was it stolen in the riot? I'm sorry. Perhaps I should have bought it, but I wasn't thinking straight and chased him out of my store with some hysterical screaming. But I believe I can describe him—the boy who came. Perhaps someone will know him and we can get it back."

I feel as if I have hooked a great fish for Sabbath: the *storybook from Egypt* is code for Uncle's missing Haggadah! I have been informed that the killer has made a careless move. And now that I know how he escaped... It seems that a balance in the Upper Realms is now being weighted in my favor.

And yet, even before my discoveries have had their chance to fill my lungs with the fresh air of hope, Farid enchains me once again to despair; after I read him Senhora Tamara's note with my hands, he signals, "Another obstacle presents itself before us. I crept down to the cellar to try to find you when the note came and saw the secret door in the wall. I know what you think. But the killer didn't leave that way."

"What?!"

"Go there. Look for blood. You will see that there are stains before the passageway narrows. As if the killer were feeling his way along the walls. But all such marks end before one is forced to crawl. The killer did not pass through. He turned back for the cellar."

I take a deep breath. "Are you sure?"

"At sunrise, you can better verify what I say. Now, by the light of a lamp, your eyes may not be able to tell you what I have seen. But it is the truth. There is no mistake."

It occurs to me again that it is no accident that God has given me Farid; He knows that I will need the help of so talented a self-portrait of God. I signal, "But knowing that he could escape through the door, why would the killer turn back for the cellar?"

"Maybe he heard someone in the bathhouse...more Christians. Or perhaps, yes... perhaps he was too large or awkward to fit through the passageway. In all probability, he had never been that way before. He may have assumed he could fit. But then he discovered..."

Farid's hands fall to his sides. He signals weakly that his diarrhea is worsening. Ashamed of my own good health, I lead him to the out-house. The night air hits us, dry and chill. His face contorts in pain as I wash his raw behind. Fighting dread, I think: *not only do I not know how the killer escaped, but now I must battle once again for the life of another.* Looking inside myself into Farid's future, I see the Angel of Death, a shadow of a thousand gaping eyes, standing at my friend's deathbed. Skeletal hands clutch a sword with a bitter drop suspended at the pointed tip. As Farid sees this hideous being before him, he opens his mouth in terror, sculpts a deaf man's clucking scream. Quickly, the Angel of Death flings his foul-tasting offering inside.

And from this drop, Farid dies and discolors and putrefies.

There will be no escape.

My friend's rag-doll body leans on me as we shuffle back inside. "Farid, then where in God's name did the killer hide when I burst in? The door was locked. There was no one in the cellar. I swear, no one!"

As he gestures a poetic phrase about the will of Allah, I grab an oil lamp hanging from the central beam and head downstairs. Just as he said, drippings of blood and footprints stain the floor and walls of the tunnel, and there are finger-shadows in groups of five where the killer has felt his way forward. As it becomes necessary to crawl, matted bloodstains revealing a woven imprint of fabric are reflected back to me, must have been made by knees pressed to stonework. At the tightest spot, a slashing stain seems to indicate that a hand had reached desperately ahead. When the tunnel begins to open outward, when I can stand again, there is nothing. No bloody footsteps or finger-shadows.

The killer turned back. Or disappeared.

# Chapter XI

Farid places his hand against the wall to secure his fragile steps down the cellar stairs. He comes to me, squats down on his haunches to fight the pain carving through his gut, signals, "Now that you know the killer didn't leave through the secret door, tell me the sequence of your movements after you discovered Uncle...everything."

It is the magic of words gestured to a friend which gifts me with insight; after I've recounted all, the solution comes to me freely. It seems as if it were in me all along, hiding, curled like a sleeping cat in an unseen corner: "The *genizah*!"

Farid nods as if reading a verse of wisdom. With his hands, he says, "The killer must have hid there as you called through the door for your family. When you burst in, he was lying with the books, hugging the darkness. Later, when you went upstairs to get nails and a hammer, you paused to scare away a robber, to gaze down the street at the mob. You were dizzy and sat for a time. He must have used those moments to escape through your mother's door to Temple Street."

"Oh God...I didn't look...I mean, it didn't occur to me to look because I thought at first Old Christians had killed him. They would not have known of the *genizah*."

"We must check," Farid signals. "We can afford no mistakes."

Opening the lid of this hiding place with the key taken from behind the Bleeding Mirror, I lift out our manuscripts and letters—our sack of coins, as well. Inside the now denuded pit, it is then easy to spot the blood stains. They cover the floor like brown shadows of scattered leaves, bear the woven imprint of pressed fabric.

When I turn to Farid, I signal my interpretation of the stains: "The killer was lying on his right side, with his body folded around the pile of manuscripts. Hence all the stains on the floor from the bloody clothing. His legs were tucked up toward his chest, and the tips of his sandals made the smudges on the eastern base. His left elbow was held back against the northern side and left the petal-sized fabric imprint near the top rim. His right arm, held out, was holding his *shohet's* knife. As he was lying here, waiting for me to leave, he sliced the blade against the southern side a few times, gifting the plaster with the faint lines of blood."

Farid nods his approval.

To myself, I whisper, "Diego."

My friend reads my lips, signals, "What about him?"

"With his size, he might not fit in the crawlspace leading from the cellar to the bathhouse."

"True. But even Father Carlos might have trouble."

"Maybe. But look, Diego said he'd be back tonight with a man who wanted to sell Uncle a Hebrew manuscript. What if he told me that only to buy himself some time? I have to find him. Maybe he's trying to escape even now. And I promise to look for your father. I'll go to his secret mosque after Diego's apartment."

As I lift the books and letters back into the *genizah*, Farid shuffles to me, takes my arm. "You shouldn't go near the Rossio."

"I'll descend to the Moorish Quarter from the Graça neighborhood. It'll be fine."

"Speak only Portuguese." When I nod, his fingers say, "And take my best dagger. The one from Baghdad which can split even a Sufi's thinnest thought in two. Get it from my bedroom."

"What will you use?" I gesture.

"One of my father's. The long one from Safed. He would want..."

I nod as Farid's gestures tumble toward grief-stricken silence. We face each other across the distance of the dying. We both know that after a time, my hands will not be able to reach him. He will free-fall just like Mordecai and my father into the black-flame hands of Dumah, the soul-keeper of the world beyond. Farid quivers his hand by his gut, our signal for terror, then punches a weak fist against his chest; he is saying that his spiritual dikes are failing and he cannot continue alone.

When we hug, he has the sick-soft petal feel of Mordecai. His ribs, hard and cold, ripple outward as if seeking to emerge. I hear my uncle warn me: *Berekiah, do not abandon the living for the dead!* I signal, "I'm going to go for a doctor. The hunt for Diego will have to wait. If you should..."

"No doctors!" Farid interrupts. "All the Christians know is blood-letting."

"I'll find an Islamic one."

"Where?" he gestures skeptically.

"Somewhere...I'll go wherever I have to."

We argue for a time. But it is only a show; we both know that Dr. Montesinhos was one of the last who faithfully practiced the wisdom of Avicenna and Galen. Who could I find now who would risk illness to visit a poor and deaf weaver of rugs? He waves away my words with flapping motions. He moans as I wash his arms and legs with water. His skin is free of sores. It is not plague, not the sweating sickness. He is being sucked dry of life. Suddenly, he pushes me away. "Go find Diego!" he gestures angrily. "You're only wasting time with me."

"Farid, will you do what I say?" I ask with my hands.

He stills my request with a descending wave of gestures: "You have no oil of life that can be poured into my lamps."

"Your poetry is of no interest right now," I signal back. When he continues to protest, I raise my hand to feign a threat of violence. He smiles at the absurdity.

With a descent linked to the inevitable, I think: *This is the last time I will see him happy.*

I lock the *genizah* and place its key back in the eel bladder. "Upstairs," I tell Farid.

"What do you have in mind?" he signals.

"Patience."

In the kitchen, I boil an egg, pour salt on it and force him to down it with boxwood and verbena tea. Together, we suffer an hour of automatic chewing and agonized heaving. I feed him charcoal ash, more liquid till his belly is distended. On my instructions, he hugs his legs to his chest, and I give him a strong enema of linseed decocted in barley water, another of barley water and a single drop of arsenic. Once he's clean, Cinfa brings us from the cellar a special incense of poppy and camphor intended to induce drowsiness. Farid wheezes as he inhales. I talk him to sleep with the fables of Kalila and Dimna told me by Esther in my childhood.

After I grab the dagger from Baghdad from under his mattress, I climb through the cool air of the sixth night of Passover into the upper streets of the Alfama to find Diego. Just before I reach his townhouse, however, I spot a man of towering stature looming in the darkness across the street. He is leaning back against the flaking wall of the cobbler's workshop, wears a wide-brimmed hat and a dark cloak which curtains his body down to his booted feet. He is at least a hand's length taller than I am, well over six feet, a height almost never seen amongst the Portuguese. Straight hair falls to his shoulders. His right hand grips a rawhide riding whip.

He can only be the Northerner about whom I was warned.

His head raises up suddenly, and he stands upright; he has spotted me. We share a look in which I sense that he knows who I am. Neither of us make a move, however. Questions seem to root my feet to the cobbles: is he here to kill Diego or merely waiting to collect the payment he was promised by this thresher for the murder of Uncle?

What must he be wondering about me?

I don't stay to learn the answers; they must come from Diego himself, and clearly, he is not in his apartment or this Northerner would not be waiting so diligently outside. I back away and rush toward the Moorish Quarter, checking over my shoulder now and again to make sure I'm not being followed.

In the nighttime streets of Lisbon, harsh orange lights spray from the windows of taverns and brothels. Every time I hear a sound, my heartbeat leaps as if toward a secret refuge; it is that time of night when all noises and objects seem to have turned into oracles foreseeing death.

The secret mosque which Samir frequents is in the second floor of a blacksmith's workshop near the old Moorish bazaar. The great wooden door, carved with knotted patterns and centered by a horseshoe knocker, is locked. A dead goldfinch, of all things, lies on the cobbles below, a tear of blood near its beak. After a second tap with the knocker, a candlelight blossoms in the window above. "Who is it?" comes a woman's hissing whisper.

"Pedro Zarco. I'm looking for Master Samir."

The shutters bang closed. After a few seconds, a man in long underwear, with the wiry frame and squinting eyes of a Sufi ascetic, appears in a doubtful crack of doorway. Lit by a fluttering candle flame, his cheeks show hollow under the crescent moons of his cheekbones.

"I'm looking for Master Samir," I begin. "He comes here..."

"Who are you?" he asks in Portuguese. His voice is deep, sonorous, as if cut from granite.

"A friend. Pedro Zarco. We live on opposite ends of the same courtyard. If he's with you, tell him I'm..."

"He's not here." He speaks gruffly, as if being seen with me is a risk.

"Do you know where he's gone?"

"When the pyre started, we scattered. He ran home for Farid. Wait." He closes the door and bolts it. Footsteps trail off, then return in a rush. When the doorway squeals open, dangling sandals are offered to me. "Samir ran off so fast that he left these," he explains.

The knowledge that Farid's father, too, must be dead, prompts me to run to Senhora Tamara's bookstore and home in Little Jerusalem—to find out about the 'storybook from Egypt' which was offered to her.

There comes no answer to my knocks at her door, however. My feet turn me toward home. My body has the emptiness of a cavern, and the night air resonates inside my chest as if inside a leaden bell. I must eat something and pray for *nezah,* the lasting endurance which emanates at every moment from God into the Lower Realms.

At home, I wash my face, eat some stale matzah and two apples, then sit in front of the hearth and chant.

Beyond my prayers, solitude and slumber descend, catch me in their net.

Suddenly before me are Uncle's hands, gesturing wildly at the back of the hearth in a language I cannot fathom. Sweat beads on my forehead. A face suddenly leans toward me. Distended with dancing shadows, it burns with an orange light. My heartbeat leaps. I rear back, jump to my feet.

"Berekiah, I've brought the man I told you about." It is Diego, lit by the hearth. He unfurls his hand. "This is Isaac of Ronda."

I take deep breaths to calm myself, see that Diego's bodyguard stands with his back to us at the kitchen door. Isaac himself has the gaunt, dim face shared by so many of the New Christian merchants. Draped in scarlet robes, his shoulder-length straight hair is topped by a crested purple cap from which a long dark plume is arching back. When we shake hands, he stares boldly into my eyes as if trying to convince me of his strength or beckon me to share his bed. Peasants sometimes behave in such a way, and I realize that he may have only recently come into money.

My sudden descent from the dreams of half-sleep has left me heavy in body. I light two more oil lamps above our table to give me time to recover my strength. "Have you seen my mother or Esther?" I ask Diego, confused about the time and place into which I have awoken.

"Undoubtedly, they are asleep," he says. "Dawn will be with us in a few hours. I thought it was safer to come now, however. I suspected you'd still be up."

The illumination from the lamps has given our shadows more restful, human proportions. I beckon my guests to sit. "Some brandy, perhaps?"

My offer is accepted. Isaac clamps his lips onto his cup, jerks his head back and downs his drink as if it were water. "Toothache," he says. "Dulls the pain."

"We have some oil of cloves if you'd prefer," I say.

"Thank you. But I've got some myself." He reaches in his pouch, takes out a vial and rubs the liquid across his gums. His hands are thin, elegant, his nails immaculately pared. As of yet, it seems, only his hands have had time to adapt to riches. Soon, his lips will learn to caress the wine from his cup, and when he shakes hands, his will descend like a peacock feather in a soft breeze.

"Diego, where have you been?" I ask. "I went looking for you."

"With a friend. I thought it was safer than going home."

"It was. That Northerner...I saw him outside your townhouse."

"A Northerner?" Isaac asks in a voice of surprise.

"Blond, tall, with a rawhide riding whip of the kind made in Castile," I reply.

Diego shrugs. "I shall not go home. Perhaps he will grow weary of waiting for me and simply leave."

"What do you suppose he wants?" Isaac asks.

Diego brings his hands up over his face and shudders, stares me straight in the eyes with a look of dread. "We suspect that he wants to kill me. Some enemy whom we, the friends of Master Abraham, have made without being aware of it."

Isaac fiddles nervously with the hair falling over his ears. "I was sorry to hear of your Uncle Abraham's death," he says. His Andalusian accent is thick, his voice deep, slow and graveled like many of his kinsmen.

I say, "I have heard that you have a *safira* to sell that was cut by Judah Ha-Levi."

He paraphrases one of the poet's most famous verses: "'I shall not rest until the blood of the prophet Zechariah finds peace.'" He gives me a probing look which seems to seek understanding of my own motives.

"My uncle was interested?" I question, wondering how to categorize this Isaac of Ronda.

"Very," Diego says.

Isaac adds, "He said he would raise enough money to pay me for it over the next few days. But now I..."

"How did you get the *safira* into Portugal?" I question.

"It was always here. I bought it from a friend in Porto. He was about to burn it. I couldn't let that happen. I'm sure you understand."

"If you don't buy it, Berekiah, I'm afraid another person may get it who doesn't have your understanding of its importance," Diego observes.

"So you're no longer considering it at all?" Isaac asks Diego.

"I was really only interested in order to help Master Abraham until he raised enough money. I prefer Latin manuscripts, myself. Far safer. So I must defer to Berekiah."

"Was anyone else interested in the book?" I ask.

"I have made several contacts," Isaac replies. "But no one seems ready to make an offer."

"Not even Senhora Tamara, the bookseller in Little Jerusalem?" I enquire.

"She wanted nothing to do with it. Isn't buying anything in Hebrew at present—not even translations from Hebrew. After what happened, you understand."

Diego says, "Simon, among others, seemed to believe it could fetch a large price elsewhere. In Genoa or Constantinople or Ragusa. Even in Morocco."

"Simon Eanes, the fabric importer?" I ask.

"Yes," Diego replies.

My heartbeat sways me from side to side. Were they in competition over books? Was that it?

A perverse desire twists in my gut and rises through my mouth as a devilish prayer that the murderer not be Simon—that I may be granted the privilege of revenge.

Diego pats my shoulder and continues in a wistful tone, "Hard to believe so much effort for manuscripts that we once could take out from our libraries. Our heritage seems to be falling into private hands. One day, all our writings will belong to Christian nobles and be locked away in golden chests and glass display cases."

"I'm willing to sell it cheap," Isaac says. The pitch of his voice jumps in order to tempt me. "Or to make a trade even. A silver candelabrum at this point would be enough. I want no more delay in getting back to Ronda."

"You understand that I can't fulfill any verbal agreement my uncle may have made," I explain. "We'll need all our savings just to eat. But tell me this—did he say who was helping him buy his manuscripts and smuggle them from Portugal?"

"Don't you know?!" Isaac asks.

"No. My uncle wouldn't say in case he was ever exposed. The less we knew the better, as far as he was concerned."

Farid suddenly shuffles into the room. With his hands, he says, "I didn't realize..."

"Doesn't matter," I signal back. "Sit with us if you have the strength."

Diego and Isaac stand, bow in Farid's direction. He nods his head, drops next to me and rests a heavy hand on my arm. "My friend is deaf," I say. "He will read our lips. There is nothing you could say to me that couldn't be said to him."

"I'm afraid we didn't speak of your uncle's methods," Isaac continues. He rises to his feet. His smile seems practiced. "And if you're not interested in purchasing the book...?"

"No."

"Then I'm afraid our meeting is at an end. Thank you for the brandy."

At the door, he hooks his arm in mine. In a delicate whisper, as if trying to enchant a child toward sleep, he recites verses of a poem by Moses Ibn Ezra: "'My night is plunged into a silent, waveless sea of darkness, a sea that has no coast, no shore for those who voyage. I do not know if this night is long or short. How can a man oppressed with grief know such a thing?'" To my ear alone, he whispers, "Have courage!"

The peculiar gentleness of this stranger whom I doubted leaves me hugging my sorrow like a lonely widower. When Isaac and Diego are gone, I put Farid to bed. My mother is asleep in Esther and Uncle's bed, curled into a ball, breathing fitfully. From her hand has fallen a stoppered vial. I snatch it up from the curls of the blanket, caress a viscous drop onto my finger. Bitter comes the taste of extract of henbane and mandrake. To escape both herself and Lisbon's gates for a time, mother has summoned a twilight sleep akin to trance. Maybe it is for the best.

In the cellar, I find Aunt Esther still sitting at Uncle's desk like a statue, Cinfa shivering at her feet. I bring down a blanket from upstairs, cover the girl. Her eyes connote separation, fear. Yet she bends away irritably from my touch. In my room, sitting on my bed, I pray for Judah's safe return before daring to head again into Little Jerusalem to try to wake Senhora Tamara. But before I can summon my legs to help me, chant entwines with sleep and drops like a woolen quilt across me.

I awake in bed. Blind to my borders. The blackness all around seems a hiding place for evil. A hard warmth pushes against my ribs. I jump up. It is Cinfa, her face veiled by hair.

As I regain my composure, she wakes. "Where are you going?" she moans.

"To call on Senhora Tamara."

"You mustn't go!"

I caress her cheek. "Nothing will happen. Don't worry."

She sits up, ducks her head under my shirt and breathes hot against me. It is a refuge she sought as a child. "I'll be back sometime after dawn," I say. "You remember when I used to take you to Senhora Tamara's bookstore to read 'The Fox Fables' while I made my dawn deliveries?"

She nods against my chest.

"We shall do that again soon. Now while I'm gone, will you look in on Farid for me?"

She squirms her head into the air, alert to the task, just as I'd hoped. "And do what?" she questions.

"Feed him more boxwood tea when he wakes. It's in mother's blue pitcher. And an egg if he can eat. Wash your hands afterwards with soap."

She nods thoughtfully, stands up atop the mattress. Towering over me, she shows me the knowing eyes of an adult, the weighted stance of our mother. Does the girl secretly hate me for helping to take away her childhood?

Outside, the dawn of Thursday is upon us. The sun's chariot has already begun to lift into the sky. When it reaches the western horizon, it will beseech the seventh evening of Passover to gift mankind with its holy descent.

On my way to visit Senhora Tamara, I stop by the New Christian workshops on Goldsmiths' Street to see if anyone has tried to sell our gold leaf or lapis lazuli. My knocks are answered by the newly widowed and childless who kiss me and press their hands into mine as if I may be able to entreat God to bring back their loved ones. But no one has been offered any lapis or gold of late. They gift me with promises of help when I slip from their arms back outside. Numb, wary lest I be tempted to feel too much, I shuffle into sunrise.

When I ring Senhora Tamara's bell, she shouts,"A *tinta está quase seca,* the ink's almost dry!" It's her antiquated way of saying that she's on her way. Half a dozen locks clang open. A pale eye sitting above a deep pouch of skin peers through a crack of doorway. "Berekiah!"

Senhora Tamara shows her toothless smile, unhinges the last chain and pulls me inside as if a kid dragging a parent toward treasure. Silver hair frames her wizened face. "Let me look at you!" she exclaims. She takes mouse steps backwards, squints up at me, her heavy eyelids wrinkling. The wisps of dark hair on her upper lip bristle as she makes a puffing noise and says, "You need to go to a barber and get some sleep!" Her turned cheek invites me to proffer a kiss.

"Did I wake you?" I ask.

"Me? You kidding?! An old lady never sleeps soundly." She flaps her hand bitterly. "The curse of old age—all those memories clattering keep you distanced from sleep!"

"Where were you then? I came in the middle of the night. There was no answer."

"Next door," she replies. "Sleeping with a neighbor. These days, a Jew who still dares sleep alone is putting one foot in the grave!"

We talk of my family. She gasps at Uncle's death. "Come," she says, beckoning me to the desk by her hearth. "Sit on the stool." She shows me a stern but faraway look, as if she is wondering how to reconcile his murder with God's presence.

With quivering hands, she lifts away a Latin treatise on flowers which she must have been reading. She motions me to my seat, lights two candles sprouting from the cups of a seven-armed silver menorah. Manuscripts in varying states of decay line shelves up to the ceiling, form rickety towers on the floor. She pulls a chair next to mine, sits with her hands on her lap as if squeezing into herself the strength needed to fend off tears. She and the room both reek of vellum and the special dust which rare books dispel; the Senhora keeps her windows closed to forestall the decay of her Greek, Roman, Byzantine, Persian and European volumes. How I used to love the hermetic otherness of this store as a child, as if it housed my inheritance.

"He was just a child," she says with a pressing force.

"Who?" I ask.

"The boy who came to sell your uncle's Haggadah."

"Did he speak with any accent?"

"No, he's from Lisbon."

"Dark skinned?"

She leans into me, her jaws grinding. The bright scent of cardamon alights around her; she is chewing seeds. "Fair skinned," she says. "Tiny, thin. With wild hair. Like a thistle. Wait." She darts about the room like a hen, picks out paper, a reed pen and an ink well. She puts them down in front of me. "Start drawing, Beri," she says, and she stands like a Torah teacher over my shoulder as she commands my sketch: "...No, no, his nose was thinner, with nostrils like the sound slits in a cittern, very elegant you understand. And the lips were fuller, as if he were pouting. More curve...more shape..." She presses into the taut muscle between my neck and shoulder when I've captured a feature correctly and whispers, *perfeito* as if drawing the word into a silken thread. After an hour, she has lifted her hand away in satisfaction.

"And his clothes?" I ask.

"Poor. A ragged little nincompoop. The kind of kid who hawks esparto grass by the quays. He said he was selling the Haggadah for his master. I handed him a fable to look at while I examined it. But the little beggar couldn't even read." She frowns as if illiteracy were a Christian sin too beastly to tolerate. She walks me to the door with her hand in mine, says, "I'm sorry. I should have bought it. But all of a sudden I was screaming like a parrot. You know how I get." She motions for me to bend so that my face is at her level, speaks in a conspiratorial voice. "Berekiah, after all this... When do you think King Manuel will come to his senses and allow us Hebrew books again?"

"Never," I say.

"Then I must start smuggling, too," she concludes in a hushed voice.

"When I find out how my uncle did it, I'll tell you."

I scroll up my drawing and slip it into my pouch. We kiss goodbye. On the street, gazing over tawny rooftops into the distance, I wonder who would be bold or foolish enough to send an illiterate boy to sell a stolen Haggadah to Little Jerusalem's most experienced bookseller. The whisper of my uncle's voice rises with a swirl of dust from the cobbles, bearing the name Miguel Ribeiro, the aristocrat for whom Esther recently scripted a Book of Psalms.

When I ask, "Why him?," there comes the reply: "Precisely because the acts of a Portuguese nobleman cannot be questioned by a Jew."

# Chapter XII

The Rua Nova d'El Rei is a hell to cross, already a sweating stink of peddlers and animals and spices. I thread my way through the rabble to Goldsmith's Street and turn up toward Miguel Ribeiro's mansion. Two armored guards stand outside, halberds poised in gloved hands. The shorter of the two, a sickly looking man with a harelip, follows me with suspicious eyes. I plant myself in front of him and say, "Tell your master that Pedro Zarco wishes to speak with him."

A black footman with a shaved head is called to carry my message inside. He returns at a trot. The guard opens the gate. On the front steps, a squat servant with oily, copper-colored hair and a sweaty, pimpled forehead rushes to me. He wears blue leggings too tight for his fleshy buttocks, and his green brocade doublet is ripped at the collar. He takes my arm as if escorting me from danger. Up close, I see that his fat neck is scratched raw and red. Is he riddled with mange? He stinks of metal, like an old coin. Perhaps he has been eating antimony pills— a cure-all freely recommended by half-made Christian doctors.

"Inside...inside!" he whispers, his hands waving wildly.

He ushers me into a vaulted waiting room painted with frescoes of roseate gods and goddesses in the Florentine style, then looks me up and down with rapt, jaundiced eyes. In a conspiratorial whisper, he asks, "Is your God really a bull?"

"What?"

"Is the Jewish God a bull?" Forming horns atop his head with his hands, he speaks as if I might not understand Portuguese. "You know, a male cow...a cow's husband...bull..."

Of course, I'd heard of scholars at the University of Coimbra who believed we had prehensile tails; bishops in Braga who claimed we needed the warm blood of Christian children for Passover rituals; doctors in Porto who said that we possessed an odor similar to that of rotting whale meat—the *foetor Judaicus*. But this belief that we prayed to a bull was a new slander. An understanding of the misconception involved only came to me weeks later, when I realized that the servant had confused the Portuguese word *touro*, bull, with *Torah*. So in reply, I simply sigh and say, "Just let me speak with your master. He knows who I am."

He wipes his forehead with his sleeve and says in an urgent voice, "Don't you know where he is? He spoke of needing to find Master Abraham Zarco. He's you're uncle, isn't he?"

"Yes."

"Then you must know!"

"I assure you I don't," I say. "And my uncle can't possibly be with him—he's dead."

"Oh dear." He holds his head in his hands.

"What is it?" I ask.

He looks up imploringly, whispers, "Dom Miguel has been missing since Sunday. He had mentioned your uncle's name. I thought..."

"Have you searched for him?"

"Leave?! Leave this house?!" The servant paces the room, curls his hands together, braids and unbraids his arms.

I ask, "When was the last time you saw him?"

"Oh dear...Sunday afternoon. The riot was starting. Some men came looking for *Marranos*. He spoke with them, then rode out toward Benfica. He has a stables there. But we've had no word. I don't think he made it."

"Who was with him?"

"No one. I've sent messages there. No one's seen him." He begins clawing at his neck, then swipes at a chaffed scar below his ear with catlike ferocity. He squats on the ground as if about to relieve his bowels right into the seat of his leggings, continues scratching. "If he were a Jew, I'd understand," he groans. "But he's innocent! Completely innocent!"

I remember Uncle's comment about Dom Miguel's covenant with the Lord. Apparently, not even his household staff knows that he's a secret Jew. "Go sing it to the goats, you ignorant peasant!" I say, turning to leave.

The servant jumps up and grabs my arm. I rip it away. His eyes bulge fish-like in anger, and he hisses, "Yes, you're one of them! Right to the tip of your horns!"

Grinning cruelly, I say, "Have no fear. I won't curse you to our *touro* god."

He arches his back into a posture of command, peers up at me over his pug nose. "Begone, *Marrano!*" he shouts in an arrogant voice.

But I am beyond the contempt of mortal men. As I turn away, he calls after me in a terrified voice, "You're not going, are you?!"

I look back for his beseeching eyes. He is squatting again, swiping at his neck, drawing blood now. I watch him from across a distance which, to my surprise, will admit no sympathy for Christian anguish.

The road to Benfica skirts the quarry pits at Campolide where hundreds of yellow-eyed Africans mine limestone from gouged hillocks. Two breeds of slaves they've become: the *portadores* or carriers, backs braced with baskets woven from vine, who grunt and trudge under their burden of stone; and the *picadores* or hackers, wide-shouldered and lean-muscled, whose rose-pink hands grip the wooden handles of the iron picks which remove the hills a little at a time.

A third breed lives on a lower level: small, darting Portuguese slave boys known as *lebres,* hares, who scavenge scree and carry it from the worksite in reed baskets.

In Benfica's main square, a droopy-eyed grandmother wrapped in a black mantilla is hawking quince marmalade from the steps of the São Domingos Church.

"Do you know where Miguel Ribeiro has his stables?" I ask her.

"Never heard of him," she replies.

"The local blacksmith will know," I say. "Be so kind as to tell me where he works."

She points down the street to a dusty wooden shack and cackles, "So it's the Basque you're after, is it!" Her shoulders hunch and she giggles to herself as if a secret has been exposed.

A sorry-looking donkey is hitched to the shack's door handle. Flies have formed a buzzing nimbus around an enraged wound on the poor creature's snout. Inside, a pale-skinned giant with thick black hair and oak-branch arms is pumping a bellows the size of a carriage. He wears only sandals and a long, leather apron, and from the side his thick, muscular legs and even buttocks are visible. The bellows' cylindrical mouth glows red where it enters the forge. The air smells of smoke and metal and heavy toil. I cough to get his attention, excuse myself and ask, "Dom Miguel Ribeiro—do you know him? He's said to have a stables very near here."

He turns to me, and with a clipped Basque accent questions, "Who's asking?" A thick cord of scar tissue runs from his left ear lobe across his cheek. Droplets of sweat cling to his chin, fall patiently, one by one, to the floor.

"My name is Pedro Zarco," I say. "I've word from Lisbon for him. From his sister."

He turns away from me and returns to his pumping. In an irritated voice, he says, "If you work for his sister then you should know where he lives."

"She's had thick cataracts since childhood and couldn't describe the way."

My failure to lie convincingly is implicit in the patient, resigned way he lowers his arms and wipes the sweat from his fingers on his apron. "She doesn't need to see in order to describe the way to her brother's stables," he says.

"Look, she came down from Coimbra after the riot. She's worried. All she knows is that he's here somewhere in Benfica. Do you need to see my written pedigree to give me an answer? Or will checking my teeth be enough?"

He laughs from his gut, eyes me up and down. "You're really quite a nice looking young man." He thrusts out his legs, leans back and reaches his massive hand below his apron to his sex. As he fondles himself, his leering stare makes it obvious what he wants. "For a little price, I might tell you."

"For a little price, I could buy the information from someone else."

"My 'bird' is mighty nice," he grins, showing the remnants of a few brown teeth. "Big as a raven. And the way it can kiss your ass cheeks! Young man, I think you'd like it."

"I've a friend who'd love it. But I'm not interested."

He unstraps his apron and tosses it aside. He's completely naked underneath, all dripping, matted hair and muscle. His member sticks straight out from his abdomen, big and round as a rolling pin. "I could take you without your permission," he says, as if favoring me with a forewarning. His eyes are bright with seductive anticipation.

I show Farid's dagger. "And I could cut it off."

He laughs, steals forward like a stalking animal, runs his thumb enticingly across the length of his facial scar. "How do you know you won't like it if you've never tried?" he asks.

My heart pounds a code of dread as I back up. "I have tried. Once, with that friend I mentioned. But I prefer other unions. And I've grown exceptionally fond of my ass in just one piece if you don't mind."

He doesn't smile, but moves his hand to his lips for saliva. I back to the open doorway. Trying to seduce me with his lust, he begins pumping on his sex.

I chant, "Blessed be He who has given me an escape from satyrs," and race into the street. Looking over my shoulder, I see him by his donkey, showing the poor animal and a good deal of Benfica his private manhood.

Back in the central square, neither a soap seller nor a basketmaker knows where Miguel Ribeiro keeps his horses. "Don't you mind that your blacksmith shows himself?" I ask, pointing down the dusty street.

"It's good for business," the soapseller observes. "People come from all around to see it. 'The Basque blacksmith who's larger than his horses!'"

A gorse peddler joins our conversation and informs me that there are several stables along the road to Sintra, so I head through the town's western gate. After a long row of sumac bushes, a dirt road opens to the north fronted by a chapel to the Virgin Mary. A mouse of a woman enfolded in black prays on her knees to the benevolent effigy. The Nazarene child, in Mary's hands, looks fragile and solitary. The supplicant turns to me with a delicate face betokening warmth. "Saint Anthony once prayed here," she says.

If you added up all the Old Christian claims for their Saint Anthony, you quickly came to the conclusion that he covered more territory on his knees than Dias, da Gama and Columbus in all their ships combined. "Then it is a very holy shrine," I reply in a gentle voice, crossing myself. "Tell me, senhora, do you know where Dom Miguel Ribeiro might have his stables?"

"I believe it's just down this road," she answers, pointing to the north. "On the left after another two hundred yards. First you'll pass the stream where the Melo boy drowned in the flood a few years back, then that series of granite boulders which Father Vasco says was a temple to witches in the time before He was born. A little ways after that."

I cross myself again and thank her. The landmarks appear just as she said. A humid, putrid scent begins to waft toward me, however. It grows sickening just as I cross the gnarled shadow of a giant oak on which is carved the hollow-eyed skull usually painted above the doors of leper houses. A hare, quick as fear, suddenly darts across my feet. All my senses attuned to the present, I step over a cartwheel abandoned in the middle of the road. On the west side of the road, a grove of orange trees gives way to grasses, and I spot the stables—six arcades flanking a white and blue farmhouse. A low stone wall borders the property. The wooden gate which gives entry is unlocked, squeals open to my touch. Halfway up the dirt path, I call, "Dom Miguel! I am Master Abraham's nephew. I mean no harm!"

My voice seems to cut dangerously at the rotting air. Only the dull, staccato rapping of a woodpecker from a long ways off dares enter the ensuing silence. I cross the dry field fronting the stables fighting the urge to retch, breathe as lightly as I can. All but one of the sheds is empty. In it is the source of the maleficent odor; an eyeless horse being eaten away by waves of squirming maggots.

The front door of the house is locked. A muffled voice comes to me just as I touch the knocker. My hand peels open my pouch, creeps around the base of Farid's dagger. The door opens, and a gaunt, beak-nosed man in a rough linen cloak steps out. He points a crossbow at my heart. "Old or New Christian?!" he demands.

"Old," I answer.

Two more men emerge from the house. Arms grip me from behind, tear open the ache in my shoulder. *"Filho da puta!* Son of a whore!" a voice spits in my ear.

Using the Hebrew for whore, I say, "If my mother were a *zonà*, I'd be dressed a lot better than I am!"

"What was that?" The gaunt figure lowers his crossbow, steps to me.

The blue and white fringes of his prayer shawl dangle below his cloak. "Your *tzitzit* are showing," I say. "You're not going to fool many people that way."

"I'm not aiming to fool anyone," he says. "Jacob, let him go."

Set free, we bless each other and exchange names. "I'm looking for Dom Miguel Ribeiro," I explain. "Is this his stables?"

"Yes," he answers, unfurling his arm toward the door.

Inside, a man only slightly older than me, with spiky black hair and several days' growth of beard shadowing his cheeks, sits on the floor at the back of the foyer. He wears a blue brocade doublet that is open at the collar, leather riding pants torn at his thigh, the coarsest of Alentejo boots. The heel of one is missing. Offering me a nod of acknowledgment, he stands and walks toward me, limping a bit because of the missing heel.

"Dom Miguel Ribeiro?" I ask.

He nods. I begin to introduce myself, but the beak-nosed guard with the crossbow now standing at my side exclaims, "He's Abraham Zarco's nephew!"

Dom Miguel's eyes open wide and he takes my hands. His touch is frigid. "Come!" he says, his voice quivering with eagerness. He leads me to a warm kitchen smelling of grilled meat, and we sit alone at a granite table by a hearth of snapping embers. "Where's your uncle?" he questions.

When I tell him, he turns toward the wall and crosses himself.

"Why did he visit you recently?" I ask.

Dom Miguel continues to face away, however. So I say, "Maybe it's my lack of sleep, but I'm confused. Do you know that you're Jewish? Or, at least, that my uncle considered you so. Did that have something to do with his recent visit?"

The nobleman jumps up suddenly and takes down a wine skin from a shelf above the mantle. He pours the burgundy liquid into two ceramic cups and dilutes them both with water. He hands me mine and says, "To your health," then downs most of his in a single gulp. He drops heavily to his chair. "Drink!" he prompts with a twist to his hand, then quoting a famous Hebrew poem, adds, "'Drink all day long, until the day wanes and the sun coats its silver with gold.'" As I take a sip, he observes, "Wine is the only thing keeping me going. By now, it's replaced all my blood." To my questioning eyes, he adds, "No, I don't think I'm Jewish...not yet, but I'm learning. And that was indeed part of the reason for your uncle's visit."

"I don't understand."

"Me neither," he laughs in a single, ironic exhale. "We'd have to ask your uncle again to be sure. And now, that's impossible. But according to what he told me, I was born in Ciudad Real to Jewish parents. In the year fourteen eighty-two." He snaps his fingers, "Gained two years just like that. A miracle of sorts. Your uncle said that in fourteen eighty-four my parents were burnt at the second auto-da-fe ever held in Ciudad Real." He downs the last drops of his wine, scratches the whiskers on his chin. "Considered *negativos*, they were, since they refused to con-fess the names of other secret Jews. Your uncle, he said that he handled all the arrangements to have me smuggled into Portugal. He studied for a time with my father apparently, knew my parents well. He said that my mother forced him to pledge that I be raised a true Christian, that I not be told of my origins unless at some future date it were to become absolutely essential. Your uncle said that his attitude toward me at the time was, 'As long as you're going to be one of them, you might as well get the most out of it.' So he waited until he found childless aristocrats who wanted a little boy to inherit their holdings and who wouldn't ask too many questions about the baby's circumcised sex. I only found this all out a week ago when your uncle came to my house to inform me that the Book of Psalms your aunt was scripting for me was almost finished." Miguel pours us both more wine. "He gave me a letter signed by my adoptive father as proof."

"Why do you think my uncle told you now, after so many years?" I ask.

"Don't know." He leans toward me and stares into my eyes as if try-ing to elicit a reassuring response. I shrug my inability to provide it. He belches loudly, looks away. "Berekiah, I've thought about this a lot," he says without turning back. "Do you suppose that he knew the Old Christians would begin to kill the Jews of Lisbon...that he was worried for my safety?"

"He had powers, but I...." A shiver snaking its way up my spine binds my words to silence.

Miguel holds up his hands as if also unwilling to enter the danger-ous territory of prophecy. "Anyway, I lost my temper. After so long, finding out... Now I wish I'd had the chance to ask him more. You see, when it comes down to it, I don't doubt his word. I suppose that now I'll never know more about my real parents. Funny sometimes how understanding always arrives a little bit too late." Two gulps and his new cup of wine is emptied. "Come," he says, standing up. "I've some people I want you to meet."

As I stare into his drunken eyes, I realize that my master had presented this young nobleman with a dreaded truth. Was death his punishment for destroying an illusion?

"First, some questions," I say.

"As you wish." He bows forward, as if he's my servant.

"You say you were angry when he told you," I begin.

"Yes, wouldn't you have been?" he replies.

"For now, Dom Miguel, my hypothetical responses are irrelevant. Where were you Sunday when the riot began?"

"Ah, I understand the direction of your questions." He feigns pulling an arrow from his chest, laughs too deeply. "Very well. I was at home. Then, when the Dominicans started burning in the Rossio, I set out for here. Berekiah, I'd just been told I was a Jew. Wouldn't you have..."

"Who came with you?" I demand.

"No one."

"Then you've no witness who can confirm your story."

Dom Miguel grins, straightens up and unfastens the thick laces of his leather codpiece with the heavy clumsiness given to him by a stomach sloshing with wine. He reveals his sex, lifts up the circumcised tip as if offering me a rose and says, *"He'll* confirm my story!"

"Not good enough. *He* can't speak."

Dom Miguel laughs from his gut.

I roll my eyes at the man's drunken idiocy. Unconcerned, he begins to lace up his codpiece, his eyes squinting at his fingers as they stumble over their work. Finished, he drops to his chair with a great sigh, stares at me with a yearning expression for far too long, as if he's trying to invade my thoughts. Everything about this debauched aristocrat irritates me. What I dislike most is that he hasn't a clue as to who he really is.

As if shot from an arrow, the thought comes to me: *This is the man Uncle was referring to when he told me to beware of a courier who can't recognize himself from one day to the next.* Jumping up, I shout, "What would prevent you from killing my uncle with impunity?! You, a nobleman!"

"Look, my friend," he begins. "Would I kill the only man who could tell me the truth about my parents? If you believe that, you're a fool!"

"My uncle was the only one who knew you were a Jew...who could prove it! Kill him, and your secret is safe!"

"Berekiah, do I need to show you my covenant with the Lord again? And others knew about it. A boy growing up with servants...people see. They don't speak about it, but they see. In fact, my covenant is greater proof than all the documents in the King's archives." He stands, pounds his fist on the table. "I didn't kill your uncle! If I did, then why don't I kill you now?

To this, I can come up with no reply worthy of speech.

"Come with me!" he says. "I must show you something."

Dom Miguel leads me into a crowded sitting room. Tired-eyed men, women and children offer me solemn, acknowledging nods. Smiles blossom fleetingly, then dry and fade. My host whispers to me, "No need for fear, we are all New Christians here." To them, he announces, "This is Berekiah, a friend from the Judiaria Pequena."

A dark, almond-eyed man with a scruffy beard dotted with oat flakes stands and asks, "Do you know Mira and Luna Alvalade? They must live near you."

"Yes, but I haven't seen them lately," I reply.

"They're my cousins. They...I...." His words trail off.

"When I get back to Lisbon, I'll try to find out how they are and get word to Dom Miguel."

"What about Dr. Montesinhos?" asks a handsome woman with a shawl of russet-colored lace wrapped protectively around her head.

"I'm afraid he's dead. I'm sorry."

In quivering voices, most of the others gather the courage to ask about friends and relatives. I dispense the news that I can, record the names in my Torah memory so that I can find out about them after I have disembarked fully on the shores of vengeance.

Miguel takes my shoulder, whispers to me, "They're all from Carnide and Pontinha and other nearby villages. When riots broke out, they came here for shelter. I spread the word that no one would be turned away, armed some of the men as soon as they got here."

"The horse in the stables?" I enquire.

He grins. "Discourages both the curious and the enraged. Same with the skull carved on the tree." Miguel belches again, hits himself in the chest. He unfurls his hand to indicate his guests and shakes his head. He whispers into my ear, "They don't want to leave. One of these days, I suppose I'll have to kick them out."

"And is there no more killing in Lisbon?" an intelligent-looking teenage girl suddenly asks me. For a moment, it seems as if God has chosen her to ask this question of me; the room becomes eerily silent. It's as if we've become a congregation assembled to await an answer from the Lord himself. "It's reasonably safe," I say. I know that this isn't the answer they want, but it is all I have.

"What does 'reasonably' mean anymore?!" the man with the scruffy beard demands angrily.

"As safe as it's going to be for a while," I reply. "As safe as the world can be for Jews until the Messiah comes."

A murmur passes through the room as if I've now given the correct response. And yet, what if our faith in His coming is nothing but the hope of the forever shipwrecked?

Miguel and I settle onto a rug by the hearth as the guests talk amongst themselves again. He whispers to me, "If I had killed your uncle, do you think I would have saved all these people?"

"To atone for the sin of murder, you might save all Israel," I reply.

He closes his eyes tight, as if to shut out the world.

I can see I've wounded him. But in my state, the anguish of strangers means little to me, and whatever sympathy beats in my heart doesn't reach as far as my voice. "My uncle wrote you a letter," I say dryly. "I brought it to your mansion last Sunday, but your servants said you were out. Uncle Abraham said for me to show it only to you."

My host opens his eyes. They are red and weary. "Did he tell you what it said?" he asks in a hopeless monotone.

"The letter is guarded inside my memory," I reply, and I repeat it to him, word for word.

Inexplicably, he laughs from his gut when I've finished. "Your uncle asked whether I'd be interested in going into business with him," he says. He stares at me as if surprised suddenly by my presence. "Yes, you are handsome. It would have been hard to have refused you. He was clever. What he asked had something to do with parcels. And the angel named Metatron mentioned in the letter. And trips to Genoa, I believe. Somewhere on the Italian peninsula. I'm sure I said 'no,' but I don't really recall what exactly it was he was proposing. My mind was racing between the past and present. So many things began to make sense."

He grips my shoulder. "Berekiah, you know that moment when you stop translating a foreign language in your head and you understand the words without thinking? It was just like that. I suddenly understood the cool distance of my adoptive parents, their reticence to travel with me, the shadowed whispers behind closed doors as they put me to bed."

"So when the riot broke out, you...?"

"I panicked. I mean, I had just found out that I was Jewish and then there's this pyre in the Rossio rising toward the rooftops of Lisbon. It seemed like it was lit just for me. Strange the sensations you have when the past no longer is yours...when it's been changed and your own history has been rewritten. So I rode out here."

"Did my uncle mention anyone else when he spoke with you... other names?"

Dom Miguel shakes his head with exaggerated force.

"No one else? A priest...other Jews? Think hard."

"I wasn't paying much attention. He wanted me to travel for him. Because of my connections, it's easy for me to get overseas. To carry parcels for him. Yes, that was it! A *correio*, courier...that's what he wanted me to be."

"He used that exact word, *correio*?" I ask.

"Yes."

"And what were you to carry?"

"Angels," he said. Dom Miguel smiles. "Your uncle said, I remember now, that I would be carrying angels to safety. I had no idea what he meant."

"Hebrew manuscripts," I say. "He probably didn't want to tell you the whole truth until he discovered how you felt about being a Jew...where your allegiances would lie."

"I don't understand...angels...books?"

"Books are created from holy letters. Just as angels are, according to some. Viewed from this perspective—through a window of kabbalah, if you like—an angel is nothing but a book given heavenly form...given wings, to use a common metaphor. Apparently, you were to to be given the task of saving these winged manuscripts from flames. He didn't want to call you a smuggler, used a more pleasant word—courier. Which I suppose must mean..." Speech gives way to greater understanding about the betrayal which led to Uncle's death.

"What?!" Dom Miguel demands.

"Which means that someone who had been smuggling books with him was betraying him. The present *correio*. So my uncle needed to find a replacement. And he must have been desperate. That's why he decided to risk revealing your Judaism to you. Perhaps the courier even knew of the location of our cellar and the *genizah*. Or maybe he worked with a thresher. Perhaps they hired the Northerner who has been watching for Diego Gonçalves at his townhouse." Dom Miguel's puzzled expression shows me that I've confused him with my references. "It's simple," I say. "My uncle needed you precisely because his previously trusted courier had begun to betray him. How, I don't know. Nor for what reason. But this courier, this smuggler, may be the key."

"And who has he been until now?" he asks.

"I don't know. But I'm going to find out!" I get to my feet. "I've got to get back to Lisbon now. Will you be here if I want to talk with you, or back at your palace?"

"Here, it's where I'm needed." He laughs in a single exhale. "And where there's wine. It's not kosher, but it works just the same."

In the foyer, a last question which I hesitate to ask makes me pause before the door.

Dom Miguel says, "Would I have saved all these Jews had I not known about my true past? That's what you want to know, isn't it?"

"It's an unfair question. You've acted honorably, more than..."

"No, I wouldn't. Not that I would have applauded the killing, mind you. I'm not a cruel person, and I've never believed the Jews very different from... I was about to say 'us.' A case of understanding arriving a little late again, no? But I'd have sat in my palace in Lisbon reading by silver candlelight. And when the screams pierced my window frames, I'd simply have had the shutters closed."

Back in Alfama, irritated with my sweaty exhaustion and the passionate afternoon sun of Lisbon, I knock on Father Carlos' door to no avail, then enquire after him inside St. Peter's Church. According to the caretaker, there is still no word of him.

As for Diego, I wouldn't know where to begin looking for him; with the burly Northerner probably waiting outside his apartment, he is surely not at home. And his only friends that I knew for certain were the members of the threshing group.

Prodded by the hope of finding the names of Uncle's smugglers or even a suspicious reference to an acquaintance, I decide to check the correspondence belonging to my master which I earlier discovered at the bottom of our *genizah.* Before going home, however, questions about Rabbi Losa's whereabouts on Sunday tug me toward his door. In response to my sharp knocks, his gaunt face juts like a gargoyle out the window on the second floor. "What do you want?" he questions unpleasantly.

Strange, but I'm relieved to see his face and hear his crusty voice. I reply, "Just to talk to you, dearest rabbi."

Perhaps he thinks I'm being sarcastic. "Go back to your accursed kabbalah!" he snaps.

His shutters bang closed. I knock at the door, and sensing my good feelings for him betrayed, shout, "I'm not going away till we've talked!" As I wait, an irrational rage seethes in my gut. I begin kicking at the door. "I'm going to break it down! I swear, I'm going break your damn door down!" Fury rises into my head, burns my cheeks and temples. It is as if boiling alcohol has risen into the top chamber of an alchemist's alembic, and I cannot stop myself from kicking. Obviously, whatever makeshift masonry was giving me firm foundation has suddenly crumbled. Ragged children gather to watch. A scruffy wood carrier shoots me a look of contempt. He dares to say, "You, *Marrano,* what are you doing there?!" Squatting, he lowers his baskets to the street. His eyes, seemingly unrimmed by lashes, are dim, imply only the vaguest approximation of human intelligence. When he stands, he folds his spindly arms over his chest and leans back into a posture of disdain.

I must be crazed, because I march right up to him behind the silver of my dagger. "I'm about to hack your ears off!" I say, venom spraying from each word. "That's what I'm doing here!"

In an instant of clarity, I realize that I'm mimicking Farid's presence in my thoughts. Is that how one gains earthly bravery—by embracing an image of courage and making it one's own?

Do we learn by carrying into our interior what was once exterior?

The wood carrier continues to eye me defiantly but doesn't speak. Fear and hate give him a foul odor, redden his cheeks. I turn back for Rabbi Losa's house. An olive-skinned child with bangs of black hair curtaining his forehead watches me, waves. Suddenly, I realize it's one of our neighborhood kids, Didi Molcho. Blessed be He who saves the little children. I wave back. He gasps suddenly, points behind me. I turn, jump away from a flying log. Too soon, another one is racing toward my eyes. It catches my ear with a glancing blow. I'm on the ground. Blood stains my fingertips as I explore the wound. My nemesis leans back and grins with sated content. His mouth is a mossy brown ruins. He spits and coughs. I stand, feign wooziness. As he laughs, I run forward, barrel up into him. He is frailer than I expect, all bones and whiskers and yellow skin. Knocked onto his behind, he gasps for breath, then shouts, "*Marrano* dog!"

I stand over him menacingly and put a finger to my lips. "You've still got your ears. If you want to keep them then you'll keep God's silence."

He stands, brushes off his pants, looks away into the crowd. "He's just a Jew," he says to save face. "Not worth my trouble."

As I turn around to walk away, I catch Didi's eyes. He knows to signal to me should the wood seller approach. He nods that all is well as we come together. "He's gone?" I ask.

"Already down the street. But listen, Beri, while you were fighting, Rabbi Losa got away. He ran from the house."

My mother is sweeping the courtyard slate when I arrive at home. She doesn't ask where I've been. "Dirt everywhere!" she says to my questioning eyes.

Reza is preparing codfish and eggs at the hearth.

"Have you checked on Farid by any chance?" I ask.

"He's still in your mother's bed. Oh, and look on the table," she adds. "Something for you from Master Solomon."

Solomon, the *mohel* whom I found hiding in the *micvah*, has dropped off a hulking Latin translation of Averrões commentary on Aristotle's "*De Anima*"—perhaps in thanks for liberating him from the bathhouse. "When did he stop by?" I question.

"About an hour ago."

"Did he mention why he left it?"

Reza shows a fleeting smile. "'A present for my little *Shalaat Chalom*,' he said."

I lug the book to my room and drop it to my bed. Through the inner window, I see Cinfa scrubbing the floor of the store. She looks up with faded eyes as I climb inside. "In the night, I gave water to Farid like you told me," she says in a dry voice. "And he ate two eggs I made."

"Thank you. That was sweet. Are you okay?"

"Fine. Why don't you stay home for a while? Eat something."

"Listen, I'm going to go down to the cellar. You can come with me if you like. But then I've got to go out again."

"To find who killed Uncle?" she enquires.

"Who told you that?"

"Beri, I'm not stupid. I hear conversations, know what..."

A single knock on the door halts her explanation. Without waiting for our reply, Senhora Faiam, our neighbor from across Temple Street, rushes in. Her black dress is torn at the collar, red scratches arc across her cheek toward her lips.

"The Old Christians?!" I shout, rushing to her, thinking she's been assaulted.

"No, no," she says. "Nothing like that." She grips my hand. Her pale eyes are rimmed red with sleeplessness. Her jowls sag. "I saw you from my house," she continues. "I'm sorry about Master Abraham." When she lifts my hand to her lips and gives it a gentle kiss, I sniff at her odor of distress. "Beri, we need you," she says. "Can you come to my house?" So Cinfa won't hear, she tugs me down to her level, whispers into my ear, "Bring talismans. An *ibbur* has possessed Gemila and is clinging as tight as can be." She grips my hand hard. "And Beri, the *ibbur* says he knows who killed your uncle!"

# Chapter XIII

From our storage cabinet in the cellar, I gather what I need to exorcise an *ibbur* and head to Senhora Faiam's house. Gemila, her daughter-in-law, sits bound with rope to a wooden bench in the kitchen, her hands tied together, breathing in gulps, famished for air. How to describe the victim of a possession? Twice before I have seen the symptoms: the white skin like waterlogged parchment; the tormented eyes; the rims of crusted blood inside the lips and nostrils. Gemila is no different, perhaps even worse; she has already ceded a good portion of her human shell, begun to take on the demon's form. Her chestnut locks are matted with shit, stuck in clumps to her cheeks and neck. The pinky of her left hand has clearly been broken, sticks out to the side at an impossible angle. Her loose-fitting white frock is stained everywhere, looks as if she has been swimming in mud and blood. *A being from the Other Side has slithered around her soul,* I think, and my first urge is to run. But Uncle has taught me that *ibburs* are only metaphors—very powerful ones, it is true, but no match for even an incipient kabbalist. And if this demon truly knows who killed my master...

Gemila suddenly tilts her head back as if it is too heavy to control. When she gazes at me, her eyes lose their terror and connote only a contemplative depth of vision. They fix upon the wisps of incense smoke now rising from my censer.

Bento, Gemila's husband, touches my shoulder and shows me a lost smile meant to ask for help. His black hair is tied back tightly with a blue ribbon, and a week's growth of beard sprouts thickly on his cheeks. His forehead and hands, pants and shirt, are all streaked black with sweat and the grease of fleece. He earns a living as a traveling shearer and must have made it safely back into Lisbon only to find his wife like this.

Belo, their three-legged dog, normally tethered to Gemila by a fierce fidelity, has backed up against the door to the bedrooms and is staring at her with frightened eyes.

"*Sente-se bem?*, do you feel all right?" I ask Gemila in Portuguese.

It is a stupid question, I admit. She offers me only silence. Eyes as cold as obsidian resist my penetration. I lift her roped hands. Her pulse races unevenly, as if her essences are scurrying in all directions. She frowns and stares contemptuously at my touch. She gulps again for air. Cringing, she screams in Hebrew, "A bell is falling through my chest!" Her eyes roll white, then fix me with a frigid stare.

Senhora Faiam whispers, "She is ricocheting between our world and the demonic sphere. When I nod, she adds, "We have found that the *ibbur* speaks no Portuguese, only Hebrew."

"When did this pain begin?" I ask Gemila in the holy language.

Her chest heaves, then stills. "There is no pain—this vessel is frail but adequate," comes a voice. It is not Gemila's. It is monotone, leached of warmth. The Hebrew is Castilian accented.

"Who are you?" I ask.

"White Maimon of the two mouths."

I look away for a moment to gather my resolve; this is no ordinary *ibbur,* but a demon. "Why do you say, 'two mouths?'" I ask.

"One to devour the children of *Anusim,* the forced converts. Made of blood. With needles for teeth."

Biting at the air for breath, she suddenly spits red at me. Senhora Faiam gasps. As I wipe my neck, Gemila opens her mouth. Ruined teeth are coated with fresh blood. She laughs.

"God forgive her," Senhora Faiam moans. "She ate glass just before I ran to you. I tried to stop her but the *ibbur* can only live on minerals. He's..."

I wave away the Senhora's cascade of words, face Gemila. "Why have you come?" I ask.

"*Zedek* is divorced from *Rahamim.*"

This demon knows kabbalah! He refers to the break between female justice and male compassion that has given rise to a reign of evil in our era.

"I come with *Rahamim*," I say. "Together, *Rahamim* and I will marry this woman."

"You may enter and ride me, but you will not emerge!" the demon warns.

It is a double entendre on Gemila's sex and the chariot of mystical vision; few who ride it can return unscathed. Referencing a second-century Jewish sage who emerged safely back into our world after a journey in the chariot, I say, "I come in peace, like Rabbi Akiva." Raising my middle finger over the girl, I invoke the power of Moses.

She rears back. With challenge grounding his voice, the demon spits out, "I am neither Amalekite nor asp! And Moses is dead!"

"It is always Passover," I reply. "Moses parts the Red Sea even as we speak."

"Then soon he, too, will be on the other side unable to help you."

"So you refuse to let the woman guide her own vessel?" I ask.

"She has let me inside, and I will stay with her and give her the solace which your God has refused. Otherwise, I would be an ungrateful guest. Don't you agree?"

"As you wish." I turn to Bento. "Three things I will need. Cold water from the Tagus. Fill the largest tub or cauldron you can find with it. It must fit Gemila. We have one if you can't..."

"We have one! What else?!"

"A sole. Bring me the smallest one you can find. And for God's sake, keep it alive. And lastly, get Cinfa to show you where our magic dye is. Bring it to me and spill some into a plate."

"What will we do?" Senhora Faiam asks.

"All filth and dirt heighten the Other Side. So the Zohar says. And so this demon knows. Gemila must be cleaned."

"You may even pare my fingernails, it will do no good!" the *ibbur* hisses. "The Sabbath is just another sunset to me, and you are a shadow trying to hold a fire."

"And the sole?" Senhora Faiam whispers, so the demon won't hear.

"Fish are immune to the likes of Maimon," I answer. "It will help us in the struggle."

While Bento is out, I instruct Senhora Faiam on how we will chant Psalm Ninety-One to prepare Gemila. The Senhora grips the censer chain with both hands as she listens.

"Take that foul odor from me, you shit-filled goat!" the demon suddenly shouts. "And know this, Berekiah Zarco—if you attempt to remove me from my home you will never find your uncle's murderer!"

The evil being's words rip speech from me. I stare into Gemila's dark eyes to make contact with him. Her head swirls in a lazy circle as if plagued by irresistible sleep. When she straightens up, she laughs from her gut.

"So you've seen the murderer?!" I demand.

"I have! But if you raise Moses' finger against me again, I will cling as tight to the secret as I do to this woman."

"And you will tell me the identity of the murderer if I leave you be?" I ask.

"Yes."

"Why should I trust you?"

"Maimon does not lie," he says. "I have even dared to tell your Lord the truth. I do not fear him. I have nothing to lose. Only Jews like this sinning whore have a need to lie before their Lord!"

Senhora Faiam takes my arm, "Would you listen to an *ibbur,* Berekiah?"

"But he knows!" I shout. "He knows who did it!"

"Untie me!" the demon demands.

I pry myself from Senhora Faiam's fevered grasp. With fists raised to her cheeks, she shouts, "Would you serve Samael, the Devil, to avenge your uncle?!"

My confession clutches my throat: Yes! I would do anything to find him! Anything!

So what is holding me back? Gemila herself? She jerks upright with a grunt, her neck craning as she lifts up the bench to which she is tied. When she lets it drop with a crash, she writhes within her bindings as if impaled by a burning sword. She bites at the air for breath. When the tide inside her ebbs, she stares at me with her impenetrable eyes. "Untie me!" she demands.

Yelping turns me. Belo is scratching furiously at the door to the courtyard with his single front paw.

My uncle's voice sounds inside me: "Do not abandon the living for the dead!" His hands grip my shoulders as I turn back to the demon. I begin to chant Psalm Ninety-One: "You shall find safety beneath his wings, shall not fear the hunters' trap by night or the arrow that flies by day, the pestilence that stalks in darkness or the plague raging at noonday..."

"You will never find the murderer!" Maimon shouts. "Never!"

Senhora Faiam follows my lead, and the plies of our separate voices are united by the spinning wheel of psalm. We chant together: "You shall watch the punishment of the wicked. For you, the Lord is a safe retreat. You have made Him your refuge. No disaster shall befall you, no calamity shall come upon your home. For he has charged his angels to guard you wherever you go..."

Beyond my words, I turn inwardly from the demon, ascend the steps of silent prayer. Once atop a glowing parapet of inner vibration, supported by the bellows of my chest, I raise again my middle finger over Gemila. She looks around with darting eyes, strains against her ropes, mumbles obscenities in Hebrew, shrieks. Laughs squirt from her. She offers me a grin of beguiling enchantment pierced by a flicking tongue. But she is far below, entwined inside the psalm melody I now entrust to Senhora Faiam. God's secret names are rising from my throat, flowing in and out of my nostrils as I match my breathing to the rhythm of the words. Light and dark entangle, then separate into stark relief. The world is lit as if by black flame. Time recedes into the distance, and in my heightened state, I see that it is the terror of abandonment that gives rise to Gemila's laughter. Ascending still higher on the winged melody of psalm, I reach down to caress her cheek. Pain. A grip of evil. Cold wind. Blood sluicing across my hand. Shrieks. Senhora Faiam washing me.

"The demon has bitten you!" she shouts.

I wave her away, take up the chant again till the room grays and Maimon and I are staring at each other across a charged space which breathes slowly in and out. Bento approaches my body, touches its shoulder. "The bath is ready," he says.

Gemila struggles like an animal as we strip her. I turn toward the bedroom; Gemila's little boy, Menachim, is sitting inside, hugging Belo, crying. "You must leave us!" I say.

He jumps up, runs past us with the dog at his heels. Together, they dart out of the house.

The river water is pure and frigid. Gemila's shrieks cut the air. Fists form, tendons strain on her neck. Her arms flail free of the ropes. A blow catches Senhora Faiam and sends her crashing. Gemila's face contorts in banshee joy. Blood drips from her mouth, sends pink clouds through the churning water. She writhes as we hold her, every muscle slithering toward escape.

Soaked cold but heated by inner prayer, I chant as Bento holds his wife under. Until the airless cold numbs the fight out of her. Her teeth chatter. I hold the smoking incense under her face. Her lips go gray and her eyes glaze.

We lift her out. As Senhora Faiam dries her hair with a towel, she whispers soothing words. Bento kisses her hands.

"Please get back," I say.

With a prayer from the Bahir, I pick the fish from his jar. I dip it flailing in the magic dye. Gemila sits shivering in her chair. I press the vermilion-dyed wriggling sole to the lifeline on her forehead. She starts as if burned. Quickly, I brush it down across her shoulders and breasts, abdomen, sex and feet, till I have covered each of the ten *sefirot*— primal points—with dye. When the fish has soaked up her symbolic essences, I drop it to the floor. As it flips across the tile, I close my eyes and intone magic words from Joshua: "Stand still, O Sun, in Bebeon, stand, Moon, in the Vale of Aijalon."

With my eyes closed I roll my eyeballs until I can see the inner colors, jiggle my breath in and out until the wind of Metatron's wings spins me. When I open my eyes, the sole is flexing its gills like a bellows. I slip it back in Bento's water jar; the fish has written a message across the tile floor in exchange for its life.

I read as quick as I can. In a flashing spectrum of Arabic script, I discover the word: *tair*, bird. In this case, it is a veiled reference to the aperture through which the demon can be extracted.

Footsteps come from behind. Father Carlos faces me. From the mountaintop I have ascended on the inner wind of prayer and chant, it seems natural that he is here. I hold my finger to my lips. His eyes request judgment. I nod my ascent. He turns to Gemila, raises his middle finger over her and begins to chant our psalm in his commanding voice.

With blood from my fingertip, I etch *Elohim* along the fate-line in the young woman's forehead in *ketav einayim*, angelic writing, a version of which I learned from Uncle. Her head tilts back as if her neck has wilted. Her eyes roll white. Before she can sleep, I take her nose between my thumb and forefinger. "I command thee," I shout, "in the name of the God of Israel, depart from this Jewish body and cling no more!" In Aramaic, I shout a sequence of divine names. And I rip the demon out of her. She shrieks. Blood spurts from her nostrils. Falling forward onto me, she battles for breath. I wipe her face with my sleeve. "You are safe," I whisper. "The demon is gone."

She tries to speak but falls from consciousness.

Father Carlos and I keep vigil with Senhora Faiam and Bento. Gemila's nose has dried. She has been scrubbed with soap and hot water. Her husband has eased her like a newborn baby into their bed. Her pulse comes slow and even, and color has returned to her cheeks. Menachim, her boy, kneels by her side and caresses her hair. The mound of blanket softly breathing at her feet is Belo curled under the covers. Father Carlos sits in his chair praying to himself. When I can face the possibility of another death, I whisper to him, "And Judah?"

He shakes his head and grimaces. "I don't know where he is. When she wakes, we'll talk of where I last saw him." As his eyes close, tears press out and cling to his lashes.

My little brother's disappearance and the demon's words of temptation both haunt me with damp chill. I sit on the floor at the eastern corner of the room, chant Torah as a map that may lead both Gemila and me back to God. After a while, Carlos opens the shutters of a western window. The sky glows with fading light. The sun, disappearing below the horizon, seems to be seeking a permanent hiding place.

It is near midnight when Gemila finally wakes. She sits up, gazes with motherly benevolence at Menachim asleep by her side. She starts as she sees me. "Beri, what are you doing here?" she asks.

"You don't remember?" I ask.

"No. What...what do you mean?"

An eclipse seems to fall over my heart; the demon's knowledge of the murderer's identity must be gone.

Senhora Faiam rushes to the bed. "A dream from the Other Side, dear," she says, caressing Gemila's cheek. "You were having a nightmare and I asked Beri to come to see you."

"Yes," she says, recalling its fringes inside a faraway look. "A dream."

Bento presses his lips into his wife's hands. "It doesn't matter now."

She turns to me, confused. "But you...you were in the dream," she says. "I was being swept away by a river of blood. Like the Nile after Moses touched his... It was cold...so cold." She speaks carefully, as if stepping back into her nightmare. "And you and your uncle were on the shore calling to me. But you were both birds...ibises. And then you were squawking something fierce. Flapping your wings. I was caught in the current, hitting the rocks. And then I, too, was an ibis. I was flying onto the bank, into your arms." She stares off into memory. She shrugs, offers me an apologetic smile. "It's gone. That's all I remember."

"The important thing is that it's over," I say.

Senhora Faiam kisses my hands. "I'll never be able to repay you," she says.

"I have been repaid already," I say. But my words are false, and are returned to me hollow. The cavern of my uncle's death has opened before me again. Every step I take from now on will be a descent. Father Carlos takes my arm. "Come, we must talk of Judah now," he says.

Is he relieved that the girl could not name him as the murderer? "Yes, let us talk," I answer dryly.

Gemila calls my name as we reach the threshold of her doorway. "Beri, I saw one other thing in my dream," she says. "A white creature with a human face. Part vulture, perhaps. But with two mouths, the one below closed tight and fringed by blood. Like the demon Maimon, I think. When you were calling to me from the shore, he was ripping at you and your uncle with his talons. And Berekiah, Maimon had come out of your house, out of the entrance to your store. I was not in a river. I was peering over my wall at Temple Street. Its cobbles were flowing with blood, and I was cursing God for having made it so!"

# Chapter XIV

Carlos and I stand outside Senhora Faiam's house. The recent sins of Lisbon lie dormant for now, veiled by the dark grace of the seventh evening of Passover. Craving human warmth but unwilling to unveil my vulnerability to a man who might have helped murder Uncle, I tug on one of the bell sleeves of his long cassock and say, "Tell me about Judah. I need to know everything."

"He...he was taken. By a group of Old Christians. On Sunday."

"Is there any chance that he's safe...that he's alive?"

"I'd like to think so. But..." The priests brings his palms together into a pose of Christian prayer. "I took him to St. Peter's when the killing started. We hid together below, in the vault. You've been there. Where the relics are. Many New Christians were there. But men came. And they started..." Carlos grimaces, and his voice, having darted between us as if on windblown flame, is extinguished by a gust of horror. He takes my hands, places my fingers over his eyes, inhales as if bathing his soul in the reviving scent of myrtle. He lets my hands drop. "The boy and I slipped out the exit to the court-yard, made our way down to the Tagus," he continues. "Moses Jagos and his family, they joined us. He had the idea to hire a boat to get across to the other side of the river, to Barreiro. He took out gold sovereigns from the lining of his cap. A boatman agreed. But as we were leaving, more Old Christians came. They...they took Judah and the others. I tried to fight. You must believe me. But they threw me in the river. By the time..." He cringes, hugs himself as if he's suddenly frigid.

I shake him. "Just tell me now where they took my brother! Was it to the pyres in the Rossio?!"

"I don't know. Oh God, I...I don't know. At first, toward the Ribeira Palace. I ran after them. I was going to get Judah back no matter what. That boy...that beautiful boy. Berekiah, your beautiful brother... You know the Boatmen's Tavern beyond the Misericordia Church? I found them outside there. Judah saw me. He smiled and stuck his tongue out like he was expecting a present. Can you believe it? What must he have been thinking? I ran up to the Dominican in charge. 'You've taken an Old Christian by mistake,' I told him. I pointed to Judah. 'That boy. He's my ward. He's not a Jew.'

"'God makes no mistakes,' the friar said. He was like Herod, this Old Christian. Swathed in a kind of lunatic power. He ordered Judah stripped. The men laughed at the boy's circumcised sex. But he wasn't crying. He looked like your uncle. Staring at me from behind a kind of sworn silence, as if to say that everything was going as planned. Master Abraham and Judah... I don't understand." Carlos gasps, turns away toward a memory which clenches his breathing.

"Then you know about Uncle. How?!"

"Cinfa told me, of course. Before I joined you in Senhora Faiam's house. She told me about Master Abraham, mentioned what you were doing." He draws near to me, whispers conspiratorially: "They violated me, Berekiah. They were drunk. I was held down to the rocks at the river's edge while they... It was their laughter I couldn't take. When I was able to stand, I rushed to the Rossio. But Judah, he was nowhere to be found."

"Why didn't you come sooner to tell us?"

"I was frightened. I was hurt. My bones ached with the wine smell of them...the smoke. I ran for sanctuary in the Carmelite monastery. Berekiah, I'm not a courageous man. Look at these robes, these idols..." He lifts from his chest his crucifix, rips at it till the clasp breaks. "Look at this traitorous wood that burns into me!" His straining, clawed hands separate the Nazarene from the cross with a snap. Jesus, contorted and stiff, drops as a crippled Jew to the cobbles. Animal grunts rise from Carlos' gut, and he hurls the denuded cross against the whitewashed wall of my house. Becalmed, panting, he surveys the roofs above us, the black mirror of river below. "On Monday," he whispers, "I tried to find him. I even slipped into the lion's den of São Domingos. Berekiah, for the first time in nine years, I wasn't afraid of Christians. Maybe that's what Judah felt. But how? A little boy can't feel such things. I even thought that perhaps he'd simply walk right back here. That somehow..."

Hope is strange; it defies all odds. As Carlos continued speaking, I began thinking: *Then it is still not certain that Judah is dead. Somewhere he is hiding in a protected corner.* I ask Carlos, "Why should I believe what you've told me?"

"What are you talking about?" he asks.

"Have you proof of where you were these past days?"

"You mean you suspect me?!"

"I suspect everyone until the Messiah comes," I say.

He sighs as if ceding to a truth he had long refused to admit. "You can ask the Carmelite nuns."

I decide to test him by pointing the blame toward Simon. I say, "A silk thread was found under Uncle's thumbnail. Black silk...like a filament from one of Simon's gloves."

"Simon? You mean...?"

"Yes. Why not him?"

"Dear Berekiah, I think so much death has got you reading from left to right. Simon loved your uncle. He would never have raised a hand against him."

"But they might have had a bitter argument in the threshing group," I observe.

The priest waves my suggestion away. "An argument over Talmud and Torah may carry one along a path of burning words but will never lead to blood. You should know that by now."

Carlos has passed this little test. But what if he suspects that I know the thread was planted, wouldn't he then react in just this way? "And have you told my mother about Judah?" I ask.

"Yes. She's quiet for now. Cinfa's with her. When the girl whispered to me that you were battling an *ibbur* at Senhora Faiam's house, I thought you might need some help." Carlos bows his head. "Berekiah, you know who's dead?"

An absurd laugh comes from me. "Carlos, you never cease to amaze me. Who *isn't* dead might be easier to answer just now!"

"Dom João Mascarenhas," he says.

I nod. "Yes, of course." Dom João ran the port and customs house for the King, was the Court Jew who ransomed Reza from Limoeiro Prison with gold the previous Sunday. The Old Christians always resented the idea of a New Christian growing wealthy from taxes on their merchandise, and he was the most hated of our compatriots. "How did it happen?" I ask.

"How? Like everyone else. A mob came to his house. Ripped the gates down. He escaped across the rooftops of Little Jerusalem. Imagine, fleeing like a common Jew. Made it to..."

"Carlos, I can't believe you don't get it!" I shout. "To them, we've all got horns and tails. Every last one of us. No matter whether we drop gold leaf into our soup or only egg yolk!"

A prayer for Dom João's soul unites our voices. "Enough religious duty," I say. "Questions... First, do you know the identity of those who helped Uncle smuggle Hebrew books from Portugal?"

Carlos shakes his head.

"Have you no suspicions?" I ask.

"None. Unless it was one of the other threshers. Master Abraham said it was better for no one to know. In case we were caught."

"Then that leaves Diego...Simon and Samson are dead. Did Uncle say..."

"Dead?!" Carlos interrupts. "But you just said that you suspected Simon!"

"No, they're dead. I was...was testing you."

"Berekiah, I need to know the truth. Are my brothers in kabbalah dead or alive? Tell me now!"

"Simon's landlord said he was dragged away by the mob and turned to ash. Samson's father-in-law told me that he saw him captured by the mob."

Father Carlos' shoulders sag. He reaches up to rub his eyes. I ask, "Did Uncle say anything to you about Haman...or mention anything strange about Diego?"

"Not Diego, too?!" he replies. "You believe that he could have been involved in..."

"Uncle was killed with a *shohet's* blade. By someone who knew the location of our trap door and *genizah*. It could have only been a thresher. Or one of Uncle's secret smugglers, assuming that they, too, had been entrusted with my master's secrets."

"And what's this about Haman?" the priest asks.

"Uncle's last Haggadah was stolen. I believe he had modeled the face of Haman upon the smuggler who was betraying him...or whom he suspected of betrayal."

"He made no mention of it to me," Carlos says.

"Did he speak ill of anyone of late?"

"No, no one."

"Had Diego been fully inducted into the threshing group?" I ask.

"You mean, did he know of the existence of the *genizah*?"

"Yes, and the secret passage from our cellar to the *micvah*."

"You found out! How? Or did you already know of it?"

"It would take too long to explain, Carlos. Another death led me to it. Just tell me if Diego knew about it," I plead.

"Not that I know of," he replies.

"And the *genizah*?"

"No. Master Abraham made it quite clear we were not to discuss such matters with him for the time being."

Then it was nigh impossible that Diego had held the *shohet's* blade. And so, if Father Carlos were telling the truth, all the threshers were innocent. The murderer could only be one or more of Uncle's secret smugglers. I ask, "Did you use the secret passageway often?"

"Hardly ever," the priest replies.

"Good," I comment.

"Why, 'good?'"

"That might explain why the killer didn't know beforehand that he couldn't make it through. The tunnel thins. I could barely make it. Anyone larger... So he must have rushed back into the cellar and when he heard me calling from upstairs, hid in the *genizah*. Then, when I went to the courtyard for nails with which to seal the trap door shut, he crept upstairs and left the house through our store—Gemila saw him on Temple Street, cursed the Lord and thereby opened herself up to the invasion of an *ibbur*. The killer must have had a demonic appearance. 'White Maimon of the Two Mouths,' she called him. He probably had a very light complexion. Might have been cowled. Or maybe he wore a concealing hat whose chin strap looked like another mouth to her." I take the priest's shoulder. "Carlos, I must check my uncle's correspondence to see if he named his smugglers. And there's a drawing I want to show you. Of a boy who tried to sell the stolen Haggadah. But we need more light."

I'm about to continue up the street toward our gate, but Father Carlos grabs my arm. "So who do you suppose might have had the courage to smuggle books with your uncle?"

"Don't know. But we probably know him. Maybe they even feigned dislike."

With those words, a perverse thought comes to me. Who was it, aside from King Manuel and certain Christian clerics, whom Uncle despised most in this world? Dear old Rabbi Losa! But what if that antagonism was a show? With his burgeoning business as an official out-fitter of the clergy, Losa travelled anywhere he wanted, would have been able to shepherd Hebrew manuscripts to safety. I ask the priest, "Did Uncle ever mention Rabbi Losa in the threshing meetings?"

"Only rarely. And usually with contempt."

"Carlos, would you come with me to Losa's house, now? The correspondence can wait a little longer. For some perverse reason I cannot fathom, the rabbi always liked you. And I very much need to talk with him."

"He likes me because I'm as frightened as he is," Carlos observes. "We occasionally enjoy trembling together."

As the priest and I head off to the rabbi's house, he asks in a cowering voice, "So do you forgive me?"

"Forgive you?" I ask.

"For not protecting Judah. I need to know."

"Of course I forgive you. You are as much a victim as... Look, Carlos, I'm not sure if I'm Jewish anymore, but I'm no Christian Inquisitor either."

"Not Jewish?! Berekiah, you have to believe in *something!*"

"Oh, do I? Do I really?!"

"Of course."

I stop walking. Deep into my belly and up through my chest I inhale the night scents from the thick wilderness surrounding this pitiful set-tlement called Lisbon. I say, "Breathe in that darkness, Carlos. Something new is out there between the odor of shit and smoke and forest. A new landscape is forming, a secular countryside that will give us sanctuary from the burning shores of religion. We've only gotten a whiff of it so far. But it's coming. And nothing the Old Christians can do can keep it from giving us refuge."

Carlos answers with a preacherly, skeptical voice: "Pray tell me, dear Berekiah, what will this new landscape have as a foundation if not religion?"

"I haven't got a clue, Carlos. The landscape hasn't condensed yet. There'll be mystics and skeptics, of that I have no doubt. But neither priests nor friars, nor deacons nor bishops nor Popes will find a home there. If they take one step on our land, we'll throw them right out on their heads. And no didactic rabbis, either. The minute you unfurl your scroll of commandments, we'll slit your throat!"

"You should beg for God's forgiveness for that," Carlos warns me.

"Go sing it to the goats! I'm through begging! My God grants neither forgiveness nor punishment."

"*Ein Sof?*" the priest asks, referencing the kabbalistic concept of an unknowable God without any recognizable attributes. When I nod, he adds: "There's little comfort in a God beyond everything."

"Ah, comfort... For that, my dear friend, I want a wife to lie with at night and children to hug, not God. You can keep the Lord written on the pages of the Old and New Testaments for yourself. I'll take the one who's unwritten."

Carlos shakes his head as if to consign me to a world he'll never understand. We've reached Rabbi Losa's house. I wait around the corner. In response to the priest's knocks, Losa's teenage daughter Esther-Maria opens an upstairs shutter, brushes tangled hair from weary eyes.

"Sorry to wake you. Your father home?" Carlos asks.

"Out," she answers.

"Where?"

"Don't know."

"Will you tell him that I want to talk with him? I'll be at Pedro Zarco's house or St. Peter's. Tell him to come as soon as he can. Even if he has to wake us. And tell him that we mean him no harm."

She nods. The priest and I trudge back home, sit in the courtyard. Guilt at our being left alive pervades us both like a morbid melody. I slip inside for an oil lamp, bring it back out, unscroll my drawing of the lad who tried to sell Uncle's last Haggadah to Senhora Tamara. Shining a circle of light upon the sketch, I ask, "Have you seen him before?"

Carlos holds the drawing right up to his face. "No," he replies. As I take my drawing back, he asks in a hopeful voice, "May I stay here till morning? I can't be alone."

"We've got no other choice. You mustn't go near your apartment or

St. Peter's. A henchman, a blond Northerner, has been sent by the murderer to kill Diego. He may be after you, too."

"Me?!" The priest starts and his lazy eyes open as if he's swallowed poison. "Then maybe that explains..." He takes from his cape a square of vellum with tufts of yard sewn at the corners like *tzitzit*. It looks like a child's toy. "Read," he says, holding it out to me.

A crude figure of a man is outlined with miniature Hebrew lettering, each character no bigger than an ant. The language used is a curious mixture of Hebrew and Portuguese, and the words are from the book of Job: *She abandons her eggs to the ground, letting them be kept warm by the sand. She forgets that a foot may crush them, or a wild beast trample on them.*

"When did you get this?" I ask.

"Last Friday. I found it slipped under the door of my apartment. At first, I thought it was from your uncle. I thought he was trying to scare me so he could get the book he wanted from me." Carlos smiles as he adds, "Then, I thought that it might have been left by you."

I roll my eyes. "And now that your mind has come home to roost after its errant voyage?"

"Now I don't know. But if someone killed your uncle and now wants to kill me... Maybe this talisman is from him. Maybe the book I have has to do with your uncle's death! Maybe it's more valuable than we think."

"Can you get it for me?"

"No. It's in my apartment. And the Northerner... Beri, it was my last page of Judaism. I held it back because I had to. Your uncle was asking me to retain nothing of what I was."

"It's all right, Carlos. But do have any idea why it would be so valuable?"

He shakes his head, says, "There are other copies extant. It's hardly unique."

"Are there notes in the margins?"

"Nothing. Perhaps whoever was smuggling books with your uncle decided he simply wanted it for himself, didn't want it to leave the country."

"That doesn't seem plausible. After shepherding a hundred or more valuable works across the border, there's no logical reason why the smuggler would suddenly turn against Uncle simply because of your manuscript. Not only that, but there were several precious manuscripts

in the *genizah* which the killer passed up to take Uncle's Haggadah."
I hold up the talisman for inspection, see that the word sand, *areia,*
is spelled incorrectly. "This has been done in haste, probably in secret,"
I observe. "By someone without a complete eduction in Torah. And
without formal training as a scribe. Although the ink is very good.
An amateur scribe who has access to the best, I'd say. Right handed, of
course, because of the slope of the characters. As for the yarn..." I sniff
at it, run the plies between my fingers. "Rather old, I'd say. Smells of
cedar. Kept in a trunk, perhaps. If we want to know more, we'll need
Farid's help. Perhaps even the ink has a characteristic smell." I look to
Carlos. "The creator of this talisman was someone who wants to scare
you. But if he wanted to kill you, he wouldn't have bothered sending
such a warning. May I hold on to it?"

He nods. "Just keep it away from me." He leans his head back suddenly and yawns. "Sometimes I think that I could sleep for a century or
two," he says.

I say, "Look Carlos, you can take my bed. Grab an extra blanket
from the chest."

"The courtyard's fine."

"Your suffering won't bring anyone back."

"Beri, I need to see the sky, the stars. Let me sit here. I'll sleep
when God grants me grace."

With a futile shrug, I wish him sound sleep. On my way to the cellar, I spot my mother standing in her bedroom, a shadow keeping vigil
over Farid. I go to her, find her hugging to her chest a vellum talisman
in the shape of a *magreifah,* a mythical ten-holed flute. We look at each
other across a landscape beyond speech. With common purpose we
shift our gaze to Farid. He breathes freely now, as if re-entering our
world. Has an exchange been made? Farid for Judah? Is that why
Mother will not take her eyes from him?

I whisper to her, "Thank you for giving him your bed and for watching over him."

She takes my hand, squeezes it. The scent of henbane clings to her.
In a drowsy voice, she says, "If only he were one of us."

"It no longer matters," I say.

"You're wrong, Berekiah. It matters more than ever."

We seem representatives of different races. I kiss her neck, shuffle
down into the cellar. But there is little in Uncle's correspondence to give

me hope. Only two letters hold promise, both from the same person. The first is dated the Third of Shevat of this year and written in Arabic. Uncle must have received it just prior to his death. It is signed in florid script in the shape of a menorah. As best I can make out—for the elder generation of kabbalists love to confound the casual reader—the correspondent's name is *Tu Bisvat*. Of course, this is just a pseudonym, *Tu Bisvat* being the name of a Jewish holiday which our mystics associate with the tree of life and certain reparations performed here and in God's Upper Realms.

Unfortunately, my Arabic is woefully inadequate for the correspondent's florid style. There is no doubt, however, that the author makes at least one reference to a *safira* which Uncle was sending to him.

The second letter dates from almost exactly a year ago, is also in Arabic. I can decipher nothing that makes any sense. If I were forced to make a translation, I'd have said that Uncle was negotiating to buy *a tile decorating the center of a sunset.*

I will need Farid's help to remove the serpentine vines of Arabic code from both letters.

Before I close the *genizah,* I examine all the correspondence once again, this time to compare the writing with Carlos' talisman. There are none which match.

Upstairs, I find Farid snoring away. His forehead no longer burns. Although tempted, I do not wake him; it is the first sound sleep he's had in days. I sit in the kitchen to wait for him to stir, the letters from *Tu Bisvat* safely in my pouch. Onto the smoldering embers of our fire I toss pinches of cinnamon. A shower of red-glowing sparkles pricks at the air like shooting stars. I realize that I'm filthy with dust and grime, but my moist stench is comforting. It is as if it is a Jewish smell, as if I have agreed to make a permanent home in grief, as if revenge—once I find Uncle's killer—will intensify this musky scent and render it divine.

I awake early Friday morning at the kitchen table to the smell of brackish seawater—great hides of salted codfish are soaking in a cauldron of water by my head. Roosters cry the dawn. Cinfa and Father Carlos are preparing verbena tea.

It is the seventh day of Passover, and the final evening of the holiday will descend tonight. The fear that time is running out for me to catch the killer shakes me fully awake.

Cinfa fixes my gaze with a cheerful face. "Mother says a person can live like a king on just codfish and eggs," she observes. Her imploring eyes seek to have me confirm her fantasy happiness.

But I am weighted by a sense of entrapment. The house is a prison; Cinfa and Father Carlos unlikely prophets of survival. Jumping up, I ask, "Rabbi Losa hasn't come, has he?"

"Not yet," the priest answers.

"And Farid?"

"Still snoring."

"He's slept enough! I've got to wake him." As I start away, Cinfa rushes to me and presses warm into my chest. "Please don't go out again! Something terrible is going to happen to you today, I know it!"

I should be moved, but I only want the girl away from me. I walk her back to the hearth. "Nothing is going to happen," I whisper. "I promise you that I will never again let an Old Christian hurt me."

I can see in her hollow expression that the thick layer of disbelief which protected her from grief has been stripped away. I hold her hand while I lead her and Father Carlos in morning prayers. Afterward, the priest says, "I'm going back to São Domingos to make some more inquiries after Judah."

"Give it up, Carlos," I advise. "If he's still alive, we'll find him. They're not going to tell you anything. He's just another bit of Jewish smoke to them."

"No, I must go."

"But it's not safe. The Northerner may be out looking for you."

"He'll expect me at home. I'll slip out the store entrance to Temple Street and walk down by the river. Nothing will happen." Carlos nods at me as if he needs my approval.

It seems that courage has finally blessed the priest. "Very well," I nod.

He bows, then shuffles away.

Alone with Cinfa, I say, "Give me a moment with Farid, then I'll come back to you."

Her face reddens and bloats. She stares at me ready to burst into tears. I reach for her, but she breaks away from me and runs out through the kitchen door.

Farid is still asleep, but color has animated his face. The skin of his arms and legs is supple, warm. Mother's talismans dangle over him like crazy confirmations of his health. Knowing that the angels have backed away, a grateful fullness rises as moisture to my eyes, propels me to the window to offer thanks to God. Belo, ears pointing, stares out over the wall of Senhora Faiam's house, his one front leg propping him up firmly. *Blessed are men and women, children and dogs,* I think. *With so much beauty in the world, does the existence of a personal God really matter so much? Can't we be satisfied with what we've got?* When I look down, I discover Carlos' Nazarene, broken from his cross, still lying in the street. The figure and I share questions aimed at an impenetrable future. Farid wakes, taps the bed frame twice to get my attention. "Have you heard from Samir?" he signals.

"Nothing. I'm sorry. Just a second..." I retrieve his father's sandals from my room, kneel by my friend's side and offer them to him. I gesture, "I didn't think it right to show you these before, while you were so... The man at the mosque said that your father left so quickly after the riot started that he forgot them."

When Farid grips the sandals, his eyes shut tight. His thumbs trace the outline of the straps, and he sniffs at the leather. Scenting Samir, his lips curl out, his face seems to peel open. The tendons on his neck strain up toward the judgment of God's wrath. He begins to moan. I lock both hands with him and attempt to pull him free with the strength of my love.

Slowly, Farid's waves of grief subside to a silent flow. When he leans up on one elbow and wipes his eyes with his sheet, I gesture a simple, "I'm sorry."

He nods and blows his nose on his shirt sleeve.

I sit by his side, signal, "You had dysentery. With everything else, I almost missed the diagnosis. I think it was that rice you bought when we were walking back to Lisbon on Monday."

He sweeps his hand across his lips to thank me, then unfurls it in the air to praise the generosity of Allah. His movements are sure, woven by recaptured faith. Envy for his belief in a beneficent God tugs me to my feet.

"What day is it?" he asks.

"Friday."

"Already approaching the Sabbath." He shakes his head and takes a deep breath as if summoning his body's long-dormant resources. "What more have you found out about Uncle's murder?"

I explain, then show him my drawing of the ragamuffin who tried to sell Uncle's Haggadah, then hand him the letters from *Tu Bisvat.*

"Now we have something," he signals as he glances over the first letter, and he translates the important information it contains with rhythmic ease: "I have waited to write to you, Master Abraham, in the hopes that more *safira* would be arriving. But as there has been nothing of late, I am beginning to wonder. Has something happened to our Zerubbabel? Or perhaps you are ill. Please send me news. I begin to worry."

There is a moment when the miniature world of a manuscript becomes real, when the contours of a prophet's hands or twinkle in a heroine's eyes glow again inside the eternal present that is Torah. A similar sentiment of time's cessation captures me now, turns my vision inside. A path unfurls before me. It leads from Lisbon across Spain and Italy toward the Orient. Uncle walks along it, and he is carrying his beloved manuscripts, smiling with the joy of the gift-giver.

These images descend to me because this letter seems to make it clear that the path of my master's smuggled books led to Constantinople. And that his accomplice in the Turkish capital, *Tu Bisvat,* had not received scheduled shipments, was worried that something had befallen Uncle. This news must have alerted him to the possibility that he was being betrayed by one or more of his couriers. Probably, my master kept this information to himself until he could be sure of the criminal's identity. And in the meantime, he went to see Dom Miguel Ribeiro to try to recruit a new accomplice who could carry manuscripts across Portugal's borders with relative ease. When the nobleman refused to participate, Uncle wrote to Samson Tijolo, who, because of his wine business, might also have been able to obtain permission to travel abroad.

As for Zerubbabel, he was a character in the Book of Ezra, of course. It was under his leadership that Solomon's Temple was rebuilt during the reign of King Darius of Persia.

But who was he in this context? A coded name for the man who delivered Uncle's smuggled manuscripts to Constantinople?

In the second letter from *Tu Bisvat,* the author makes reference to the *zulecha,* tile, that he is willing to buy for Uncle in Constantinople. "I don't understand," I tell Farid.

He signals, "In this context, I think it is a veiled reference to a building block for a home. Your uncle may have been negotiating to buy a house on the European side of the Bosporus—the *sunset* side of Constantinople."

# Chapter XV

To Farid, I signal, "So Uncle was planning all along to move, was waiting for the negotiations to be completed before telling us about Constantinople. Byzantium, imagine... A Moslem land. If only he'd shared this information with me. I'm sure we could have all worked harder to raise the money. But perhaps he feared being caught and then compromising..."

The cascade of my surprised signalling is halted by Aunt Esther calling to me from the kitchen. "My God, her soul has returned to her body!" I whisper.

He reads my lips, gestures urgently, "Go to her! She may need you to pull her all the way back to our world!"

As I run in, I see that my aunt is not alone. She holds Cinfa in front of her like a human shield. An old man stands next to her. He is gaunt and tall, very pale, with spiky white hair and furry, caterpillar eyebrows. A man constructed from snow, it seems. Esther's eyes follow me gravely. "You may remember Afonso Verdinho," she says. "He was in Uncle's threshing group."

*O Sinistro*, the man from the left side, we used to call him with a certain ambivalent affection. It was a double entendre taken from the Italian language referencing Dom Afonso's left-handedness and grim otherworldliness. Uncle liked him as a curiosity, used to say that he read the Torah as if it were fixed in fish glue—a consequence of the uncompromising asceticism he picked up while studying with Sufis in Persia. So where has it all gone? Now that I know his identity, he appears even older and more wilted, as if he has been starved and stretched in a lightless chamber. Yellowing sweat stains show under the arms of his crumpled white shirt. A shabby black cloak lined with frayed blue silk hangs over his arm. As our eyes meet, his lips twist uncomfortably. Neither of us makes a move toward greeting.

"You remember him, don't you?" Esther prompts. "You were but a boy when..."

"I remember him," I answer curtly. A sense of imminent disaster fixes me as if in crystal.

"Berekiah, I'm going to stay with Afonso for a while," she continues, speaking slowly and gently. "He rode here when word about the riot reached Tomar. He's rented rooms at Senhor Duarte's inn by Reza's house. We'll be there. Please tell your mother. I don't want to wake her. But if she needs me, she can come for me."

"I don't understand," I say.

My aunt reaches to her temples, rubs them as if trying to center scattering thoughts. Cinfa twists to gaze up at her, then bolts out of the house. Esther calls after her in vain.

Afonso's expression becomes one of gentle compassion as he whispers to Esther in Persian. His protective arm circles her shoulders. He hugs her to him. To me, he says in a dry voice, "Just give your aunt some time. Try to understand that the journey is far more complex than you once thought."

He leads Esther into the courtyard. Huddling together, they disappear through the gate. Jealousy, thick and hot as pitch, sluices through my chest; cruel is the knowledge that a virtual stranger could revive my aunt when I could do nothing.

And that she would abandon her family at this time—it seems impossible!

Dom Afonso...does his presence change everything? Could he have been involved in Uncle's murder, in smuggling his books? But he moved from Lisbon prior to the forced conversion, long before my master and my father dug the *genizah*.

An absurd disappointment buries itself in my gut, is linked to the knowledge that life is not a book, does not hold margin notes explaining difficult events. If it were, Dom Afonso would have remained seated in front of his fireplace in Tomar. His arrival only serves to complicate what is already out of my control.

I hear my uncle say: *dearest Berekiah, life presents us with many*

*paths leading nowhere, doors opening upon sheer drops, staircases ris-*
*ing to locked gates.* And I remember that he used to tell me that all life
is a pilgrimage to the Sabbath. *Even if it is,* I think, *then nearly all of us*
*take the most circuitous routes trying to get there.*

I plod back to Farid. "People are very odd creatures," I comment.
"Why? What happened?"
When I explain, he signals, "You don't know, do you?"
"Know what?" I ask.
"They were lovers long ago. Samir told me."
"Are you crazy, Afonso and..."
"It all ended years ago. It means nothing."

His words are too simple to understand. The floor grows moist,
slides away like sluicing floodwaters. Farid's gesturing hands anchor me
in a spinning world.

Could Esther have been involved in Uncle's murder after all? Maybe
in passing she divulged to Dom Afonso the existence of our *genizah.* He
could have acted on his own out of continuing passion for her.

Farid senses my thoughts, signals, "A house of cards on a slanted
table in a sandstorm."

"Not if she didn't know about Dom Afonso's plans. Perhaps he hid
his scheming from her. Even now, she doesn't suspect that the man giving her solace is her husband's murderer!"

"But from *Tu Bisvat's* letter, we know that one of Uncle's smugglers
was very likely to have been involved. Unless you can believe that
Afonso was one of them...that he was Zerubbabel."

Farid and I sit in an expanding silence for quite some time; I am
still awe-struck by Esther's departure. My friend signals to me from
time to time, but I pay no attention until he grabs my arm. "Someone
with a strange walk has entered the house," he gestures. "I can feel the
vibrations."

A man calls my name suddenly from the kitchen. I rush in. The
"dead" thresher and fabric importer Simon Eanes stands in the doorway, leaning heavily on his crutches, his time-worn mantle of charcoal
velvet draped over his shoulders. He hasn't shaved or bathed, and a
large scab centers his forehead like a wounded eye. Cinfa is with him,
is hugging him like an abandoned child. As he caresses his gloved hand
across her hair, he offers me a nod of solidarity. "Berekiah, I heard
about Master Abraham," he says.

Involuntarily, I look at his foot to make sure that it is human. "You're not dead," I observe.

He shakes his head and smiles, a crazy smile, too wide, as if his lips have been pulled apart by a puppeteer working invisible strings.

The power of shared survival tethers us together, and I step toward him. But his gloves! The one covering his right hand is ripped across its back. Could the silk thread found under Uncle's thumbnail really have been.... Wary, I hold myself back. He fixes another caricature of a grin on his face.

"Are you okay?" I ask. "What happened? Your landlord said...."

"Just fine," he nods. "I told him to tell anyone enquiring after me that I was dead. It seemed safer at the time. Then I fled Lisbon. I've only just gotten back."

*Dearest God,* I think, *will Judah, too, return from the dead? Or is that too much to hope for?*

Simon accepts the stale matzah I offer with gracious bows. "Uncle is not the only thresher who died," I say. "Samson, too."

"I know. He had just visited my store. I told him to stay, to hide with me. But he wanted to get back to Rana and their baby. He was grabbed not fifty paces from the doorway...hadn't a chance with those Christian rioters everywhere."

My body seems very distant. I want to try to trick him, but all that emerges from my mouth is the truth. "Diego and Father Carlos made it. And now, Afonso Verdinho is back in Lisbon."

Simon nods, grins fleetingly as if he hasn't heard me and is being polite. We sit opposite each other. Cinfa mumbles to herself about chores to do so that I'll think she has not been listening to our conversation. My irritated look forces her to skip off into the courtyard.

A taut smile opens on Simon's face, seems painted by a talentless illuminator. I ask, "Is something amusing?"

"No."

I point to his forehead. "You're injured. Were you hit by someone?"

Simon reaches up to the scab, tells me how he tripped over a tumbrel while hiding in a feather-trimmer's workshop, laughs while showing more lesions on his knee. Then he tells a silly anecdote about a dog peeing on a false leg he once tried, grins and blinks, grins some more. His eyes dart nervously around the room when silence finally overtakes speech.

In his grief he has decided to become court jester to a tyrant God.

"We're out of wine," I tell him. "But would you like some brandy? We have some incense from Goa left that might..."

"No, no. I'm fine."

Farid shuffles in, lowers himself next to me. He responds to Simon's smile with an awkward, probing tilt to his head. When it goes unanswered, my friend signals to me, "He's like a starving jasmine blooming madly before it dies."

More to dispel his false cheer than anything else, I tell Simon of my mother and Aunt Esther and the disappearances of Judah and Samir. He nods as if he's heard my stories before. To test his reactions, I say, "I found a rosary bead near Uncle's body. It is my belief that Father Carlos murdered my uncle."

"Carlos, but what possible reason could he have for killing Master Abraham?" he asks.

"They argued over a manuscript that the priest wouldn't give to Uncle," I reply.

Simon smiles as if he's humoring me, steps his fingers like a spider across the table.

"Well, what do you say?" I ask angrily.

"What do you want me to say? I think it's absurd. But if it's what you want to believe, then who am I to dispel your illusions? I'm through trying to find the truth. Illusions are fine. We should all be blessed with a garden of flowering lies—it's much easier to live that way."

Cinfa steps back inside. She huddles under Farid's arm.

"You shouldn't listen to me," Simon suddenly sighs. "I'm an old fool who no longer has any courage. But for Master Abraham's sake I will try to face the truth, if you like. Now tell me, you believe he was murdered by someone who knew him...a New Christian?" His questioning eyes seem almost hopeful, as if death by a Jew's hand is preferable to Uncle having been murdered by a follower of the Nazarene.

"It's very likely," I answer. As I explain about the *shohet's* blade and our stolen minerals, Simon bites his lip. He glances suggestively at Cinfa until his meaning becomes obvious. I ask the girl to fetch some salvaged fruit from the store for our guest.

"I understand," she seethes. "But he was my uncle too!" She glares at me. "I'll get fruit to help Farid get well. But not because you asked me!"

When I reach out to her, she twists away and runs out.

"I don't know what to do with her," I confess. "One minute she's frightened for me, the next..."

"Time will take care of it," Simon smiles.

"You sound like Dom Afonso Verdinho."

"Yes, when did he return?"

"Just rode in," I say. "Curious isn't it?"

"What do you mean? You think that he, too, might have been..."

"It's possible."

"Tell me more about Master Abraham's departure from the Lower Realms."

In tones that race one step ahead of emotion, I describe to Simon how I found Uncle and the girl, the positions of their bodies, slits on their necks. In response, he grins, but his lips quiver. A battle is being waged for his emotions. Interrupting me suddenly, he says in a pressing tone, "And was there nothing else out of the ordinary on your uncle's body?"

My heart beats a code spelling out the words, *um fio de seda,* a silken thread, but I simply say, "Such as...?"

Simon shrugs as if to disclaim his coming words. *"Semente branca,"* he whispers, using the kabbalist's term, "white seed," for semen.

"How did...?" My question is blocked by his upraised hand.

"In Seville, a member of the Jewish community informed on me. I never found out who it was. The Inquisitors don't tell the prisoners, of course. I recanted, but they locked me away anyway. Those black marks on your uncle's neck—they were bruises. I've seen them before. From hanging or garroting or..." He looks down as his smile fails. He wipes at his eyes with his shirt sleeve. "The semen emerges as a bodily reaction to pressure on the neck and windpipe," he continues. "Not in everyone. But it happens. I have a theory that as God approaches to rescue the righteous victim, joy mounts. There is an orgasm. Perhaps even God has an orgasm at that very moment. Your uncle might have known. In any case, the victim faces the Creator as ecstasy ascends to meet pain. As a Master of the Names of God, your uncle would, of course, have reached a very powerful orgasm almost immediately."

"You're saying he was hanged first. But there was no rope, no..."

"Or garroted, even strangled. With a rope or hands. And..."

"It was with a rosary," I interrupt. "I didn't lie about the bead I found."

"And then your *shohet* slit his throat," Simon continues. "Out of habit, perhaps. Or to be certain. One can never be too sure with a kabbalist of such magnitude. There are ways..."

Farid signals, "It would have to be someone he'd allow to get close enough to harm him. Zerubbabel...whoever he is, must have come."

Wanting to keep secret my knowledge that one of Uncle's smugglers may have been involved in his murder, I refrain from translating the last sentence for Simon. He laughs in a single exhale. "A man like me, Farid means."

Simon's fawnlike hesitation has disappeared completely to make way for this new personality of his.

"Yes," I say. "Like you."

"Berekiah, I'm not going to defend myself. Your uncle ransomed me from Christian death. I would sooner have killed myself than..."

"And yet we found something that may belong to you," I say.

"What?"

"Give me one of your gloves and I'll tell you."

He shrugs as if ceding to pointlessness, peels the ripped one free and hands it to me. I reach into my pouch and extract the thread. It is a match; the same black silk, not a shade of difference. "It was caught on one of Uncle's fingernails. It's yours."

After Simon has examined the thread, he pushes up on the table to stand, gives me a sympathetic look. "It may be the same—I'm no expert. But it could have been obtained from my shop, from most any of the silk stores in Little Jerusalem. But of course, you're wondering just how my glove was ripped."

To my nod, he responds in a poetic voice, "When running on one leg, one has a tendency to fall. When falling on stone, one will rip silk. A wonderful material, this fabric of worms, but they who spin it for cocoons do not foresee the idiocy of men."

He reaches for his crutches, inserts their leather pads under his arms. My shame at persecuting a man loved by my master mixes with a perverse desire to continue my assault until I have driven every last possibility of happiness from his soul. I say, "Simon, it's a time of masks. And I don't really know what's under yours. Just like you don't know what's under mine. For all I know, the man you truly are is patting himself on the back for having fooled me."

He hops in order to adjust his crutches. "My old mask was burned long ago in the pyre that consumed my wife. My new one...I don't even know what it looks like." He slips on his glove with an air of resignation. "Maybe I did have a terrible fight with your uncle when no one was looking. That's what would be assumed by an Inquisitor. But is that what you've become? A Jewish mystic turned Inquisitor?!" A bitter laugh rises from his gut. "You wouldn't be the first, would you? Everything is possible in Spain and Portugal. God bless these lands of miracles."

Is Simon's the cynical defense of the world-weary or the sham of a killer? I ask, "Do you know who was smuggling books with Uncle?" When he shakes his head, I say, "Have you no suspicions?"

"None. I've become skilled at not thinking certain thoughts. In fact, not thinking is a special talent one develops in Castile and Andalusia. Go there someday and you will see how valued it is in the good citizens of those hateful provinces."

I unscroll for him the drawing of the boy who tried to sell Senhora Tamara my master's last Haggadah. "Ever see him?"

"Not that I know of," he replies.

"And *Tu Bisvat?*"

"What about it?"

"Not 'it.' There's a man in Constantinople who uses that pen name...who was receiving Uncle's smuggled manuscripts."

Simon shakes his head, says, "There must be a hundred kabbalists in Constantinople. This *Tu Bisvat* could be any of them. Master Abraham told us not to concern ourselves with these other activities of his. We respected his wishes. Just as you did, dear Berekiah."

As he shows me his pitiful grin once again, the desire to slap him burns in my chest. "And Haman?" I ask gruffly.

"What of him?"

"Did Uncle tell you whose face was given to Haman in his last Haggadah?"

Simon shakes his head and walks with his crutches to the door. He turns to me with his hand shading his eyes. The jester has disappeared; he has the vacant look of a man whose hopes have been dashed. He whispers in an urgent voice, "Berekiah, I came to tell you something. A Spanish nobleman staying at the Estaus Palace is asking around town for Hebrew books, illuminated manuscripts in particular. The Sabbath before your Uncle's death, I was approached about selling some. I don't know where he got my name. He would not tell me. Beware of all of us if you like. But beware of him in particular. It may be tempting to sell your uncle's books to raise some money for bribes to escape Portugal. But I don't trust this man."

"And his name?"

"He calls himself a count, the Count of Almira—but I suspect it's all a lie."

After I explain to Simon and Farid that this is none other than the man who took Diego to the hospital after he was stoned, they both insist on coming with me to talk with him. We walk in silence, and slowly, so that Simon can keep pace on his crutches. All that remains now from the killing are the knowing eyes of the Christians; suspicious, as if marking territory, they inform us that we are not like them. As if we didn't know that already. Then they begin their whispers and jerk their glances away from us as if we were the living dead. As if we didn't know that, too.

In the slanting morning shade of the cathedral's twin bell towers, Farid signals to me that he's certain a man is tracking us. "Since we left the house," he gestures. "And he's a Northerner. But don't turn just yet."

We pick up our pace as we descend past the Magdalena Church into Little Jerusalem. Here, we do not walk so much as navigate past the drying cakes of shit hurled by Christians into the streets. Along the cobbles, brown lines zigzag and fade, bloody trails left by Jewish bodies dragged to the pyre. Flies swirl about, poke into our nostrils, feed from our eyes. My thoughts remain with the Northerner tracking us, however. An invisible cord seems to tie us together, to be tugging me back by my shoulders. By the old schoolhouse, I glance behind. Our stalker is striding past pushcarts of dried fish. He's the blond giant whom I saw waiting outside Diego's apartment, I'm sure of it.

Is he White Maimon of the Two Mouths because of his pale complexion?

I take Simon's arm, tell him about our Northern shadow. "He must be after me," I observe. "Something I may know about Uncle...about the plot to kill him. You must separate from me."

Simon offers an accepting smile; he will fight fate no longer. But Farid signals, "Wouldn't it be better to confront him? Three against one."

I nod toward Simon's crutches. "Bad idea. Alone, I'll be able to lose him in the alleys of Little Jerusalem. He's not from here. He won't know what he's doing. I'll meet you both at the Estaus Palace. Wait for me."

They each nod their agreement and continue up toward the Rossio. I turn back for our spy so that I'm sure he can see me, then cut down past the lace-trimming stores toward what used to be the Jewish hospital. In a single jump, I nestle out of view into the limestone doorframe of the Inn of the Two Brothers. From here I will slip down the side alley back into the Rua da Ferraria, Blacksmith's Street.

As I press back into the doorway, several cream-white butterflies flutter in falling angles down onto fresh horse droppings.

The Northerner suddenly stands in the intersection ahead. He removes his hat as he gazes after me. He has high, prominent cheek bones and treacherous eyes. He runs a hand through the front locks of his oily hair, replaces his hat. But his first step is wrong; he marches away from me toward Farid and Simon.

My mistake twists cold inside my gut. I creep forward with the silence of a cat. Yet this Northerner looks over his shoulder directly at me, as if gifted with the powers of a sorcerer. He stares at me with determined eyes, then begins to run. I race after him. His hat falls away. A glimmer of light slips into his fist as he pulls something from his cloak. Farid, too, has sensed danger. A hundred paces up the street, he is motioning in crazy waves toward Simon. They rush through Little Jerusalem's Northern Gate, through the shade cut by the cupola of the Church of São Nicolau. Simon's bobbing gait is awkward, hopeless. "Simon, run!" I scream. But it is impossible. He turns, drops a crutch. I see it as if through a honey-textured time: his face opening as the Northerner plunges into him; his last support flying away, his body crashing into a wall. Farid kneels over him, and the cape of the blond assassin whips behind as he flies ahead.

# Chapter XVI

Simon is unable to speak. Or maybe it's no longer necessary. He lays in Farid's arms and says goodbye to the world with his eyes.

A stiletto with a blackwood handle inserted between his ribs is separating his body from his soul. To Farid, I signal, "Another who will not live to see tonight's Sabbath."

Simon's gloved left hand grasps the handle of the knife. "Take it away," he moans. Farid pulls it free. Like wine bursting from a spigot, blood spurts onto us. A sigh releases from the old thresher. "Thank you," he whispers.

Farid holds up the blade as he nestles his arm under Simon's head as a cushion. "Pointed," he signals.

I nod my understanding; a *shohet's* blade is traditionally square-tipped; this weapon comes to a ferocious point.

"I'm sorry for suspecting you," I whisper in Hebrew to Simon. "I must have..."

He nods as if it isn't necessary to give voice to my regrets, drops his delicate hand to my arm. He is looking across the sky and mouthing prayers. I recognize names of God, then those of his lost family. "Graça" is sculpted by his lips.

Simon's fingers caress my arm as if to offer comfort. At the moment his soul departs, a gurgling issues from his chest and there is a quiver through his hands like a flutter of wings. I brush his eyelids closed.

Surely it is a sin for a man such as I to regard himself as a prophet, even for an instant. Yet I put my lips to Simon's, my eyes to his eyes, my hands to his hands. I fall upon him like Elisha upon the Shunammite's dead child. Then, inserting my thumb and forefinger into his mouth, I pry him open to my breath. I fill him with life from my life seven times. A pain on my shoulder descends in waves as my bellows empties into him. Farid is pulling me away. His eyes connote displeasure. Yet he kisses my forehead. "No more," he signals.

When I look at Simon, there is a flowing movement like an angel's caress across his hair. "You see!" I say aloud.

"He's dead," Farid replies with sure gestures. "He will wake no more." He hugs me to him. The beats of his heart swell around me. His warmth encloses me in the darkness behind my eyelids.

We wait together. I cry for a time. Then Simon's death dries in my thoughts, shows me the present of Lisbon. A crowd closes in on us, all curiosity and speculation, for Christians are fascinated by nothing so much as the sight of a Jew's misfortune. I gaze down the street, signal to Farid that I'll be away only a moment. I retrieve the Northerner's hat. A shirtless boy with Judah's innocent eyes hands it to me.

Back with Farid, I signal, "I'm going to see which way he ran. Can you brave these Philistines alone?"

He nods his agreement. As if spun from a frigid top, I race away. At the opening of Rossio Square, I stop, paralyzed by the twisting conflux of men and woman, carriages and horses. The ridiculous life of the square has hidden him.

An old barber in a tattered doublet calls out in a lazy Algarvian voice, "Senhor, you're lookin' a little scruffy. How 'bout a shave and a haircut. Got hands so swift they could steal the black from a bat."

"A Northerner, blond, have you seen him?!" I demand.

"Perhaps the drought will end with the new month," he replies. He has the cheery disregard of the deaf, grips my hand and tries to lead me toward his chair. I break away. His wife is having her tufted scalp picked free of lice by a young girl. She points a hooked finger up toward the northern edge of the square. "Went that way," she indicates.

I ask shopkeepers there about him in vain until a carpet peddler with a jumpy, effusive manner, points to the left of the São Domingos Church.

I race down the dirt road which we used to call the Rua da Bruxa— Witch's Street—after the cat-eyed old hag there who used to repair a woman's virginity for a price. A red-haired water seller playing cards by himself under an awning has seen the Northerner. "That way!" he shouts, pointing east. I enter the Moorish Quarter, continue racing ahead until the blue and white townhouses give way to wooden shacks. Where the street ends, granite steps lead up like a pleated ribbon toward the great limestone cross that marks the lower edge of the Convento da Graça. Two hundred feet up the scorched and worn hillside is the stone crown of towers and battlements that is the convent itself. I've reached an impasse.

Ragged waifs with dirty, devious faces, more like dwarfs than children, are kicking around a stuffed leather ball by the stairs ahead. High above, on the crest of the hillside, a tiny nun, the runt of her religious litter, screeches at them in a Galician accent. "Shoo! Get away, you little rats! You're going to burn in hell before you can beg God's forgiveness!"

Apparently, the objective of the boys' game is to unceremoniously score direct hits into her beloved limestone cross.

When he notices my presence, a weedy boy with pale-green eyes yells at her in a prideful voice,"*Vai-te foder, vaca!*, fuck off, cow!"

The kids laugh. The nun keeps shrieking: "Your sins will lead you to marriage with the Devil's whores! And your children will all be born eyeless and deaf, with horned tails. Then you will..."

It appears to be a memorized litany, how she responds to this torture every day. Perhaps it is her penance.

I grab the ball when it bounces down the hill my way.

"Hey, give that back!" the kids yell. Their faces are full and furious with irritation.

"Just tell me if you've seen a foreigner," I reply.

"Ain't nothing but foreigners around here. Give us back the fucking ball!"

"A man with blond hair down to his shoulders. A cape with..."

One points a stubby, dirty finger. "Went up the hill like a spider," he says.

I drop-kick the ball toward the cross. A near miss. The kids cheer, then chase screaming after it as it rolls back down the scree.

At the top of the hill, out of breath, I face the flying buttresses of the Convento da Graça as if at the Gates of Mystery. On the other side of the street blooms a marketplace. I ask tripesellers and sievemakers, combmakers and birdcageweavers, even a family of Castilian hunchbacks making a pilgrimage to Santiago, but no one has seen him.

As a last resort, I dare to approach the screeching nun. She has one brown tooth that sticks like a rotten dagger into her bottom lip, eyelids like prunes, a scabbed nose. She pauses in her litany long enough to speak in a tone of wisdom offered, "Search for God, not Northerners."

When I repeat what one of the waifs told her to do, she shrieks like a Brazilian parrot.

Back in Little Jerusalem, I discuss with Farid where to take Simon's body. Unfortunately, we have no clear idea where his house is. Based on his occasional descriptions of views over the Tagus, we've always assumed that he lived on the escarpment crowned by the Church of Santa Catarina outside the western gates of the city. So we borrow a wheelbarrow from Senhora Martins, a friend of my aunt, and begin to trundle the body through the afternoon sun.

Do people stare as we go? I don't know; an inner world of questions and regrets gives me sanctuary. Farid leads us. All I feel is the drudgery of climbing uphill, a vague, distasteful sense of heat and sweat, sun and dust. I only awake to the jarring white angles of Lisbon when we hear Simon's name called. To the east, the bell tower of the Santa Catarina church is arrowing into the blue sky. A stocky woman with a dull face, wearing a white headscarf, runs to us shrieking. She stares in horror at the blood on Simon's clothing. She kneels vomiting. An old man tells me that she is the older sister of Simon's common-law wife. He points to a sagging townhouse. "They live on the second floor."

My mood of disbelief deepens and seems to lower me from the scene. Simon's lover is thin and olive-skinned, possesses a natural, precise elegance as she invites us in, is strikingly strong in profile for such a young woman. She has intelligent eyes, wears a loose-fitting rose-colored tunic. There is an understated regality about her which reminds me of Reza. But almost a girl she is. "This is Graça, Simon's wife," the sister says.

Graça runs to the window to see Simon when I tell her of his fate. Her hands grip the sill. Her howls come animal in their intensity, as if she is calling for her missing cub in a language of the gut. She hugs her belly, and I realize in an instant of sinking despair that she is pregnant. When her first waves of horror have subsided, I say, "Yours was the last name sculpted by his lips."

We descend to the street. People back away. She falls to her knees and caresses Simon's face, soothes him with talk of Christ and their child to be. I realize then what should have been obvious; she is an Old

Christian.

With a desperate, protective force, Graça is suddenly tugged by her sister toward Farid and me. "Tell us every detail of Simon's death!" she demands.

I explain in a voice belonging to another; Berekiah has fled deep inside the armor of my body.

Graça is unable to speak. Her mouth drops open, and her eyes show a hollow despair. The sister asks with clenched fists, "Where do we get justice?"

I shake my head. "When I find this Northerner, I will let you know."

Farid and I are covered in Simon's blood. Kind neighbors help us wash, give us new shirts and pouches, feed us cheese and wine. Too weak to protest, we accept their offerings. Sluggish from drink, wavering in our walk, we slip down into central Lisbon as if leaving behind a Biblical landscape.

After we've returned our wheelbarrow, we wander through Little Jerusalem like ghosts. In front of the dyer's workshop where our Jewish courthouse used to be, I begin to spell "Abraham" in Hebrew with my steps. Then, "Judah." Farid becomes restless after a time. He stops, faces east like a weather vane. "Let's go home," he signals.

I turn to the west to follow the sun's descent over this accursed city. Tonight, a week from the onset of Passover, we should be escorting the Zohar into the dawn with our recitations. But we no longer have a copy of the sacred text. And even if we did... "No, not home!" I shout in my wine-scented voice. I trudge on until we are standing over Simon's bloodstain on the cobbles of Little Jerusalem. "A short time ago, this brown crust was in his body," I signal to Farid. He shakes his head as if this is obvious. But I simply can't believe it, and I recall the day in reverse—as if reading a text from the wrong direction. Simon's warning about the Count of Almira is spoken to me as if accompanied by a cadence played by Moorish tambourines.

Farid says with his hands, "Let's get back to the Alfama. We've got to somehow find Diego...warn him that the Northerner will surely kill him if he finds him."

"No, Diego won't go near his home, and we won't be able to locate him. We're going to the Estaus Palace." When he shakes his head, I take his arm. "I need you with me. No protests."

As Farid and I enter the Rossio, ash and wood flakes from the pyres in which the Jews were burnt blow around us. At first, it seems that this is the only vestige remaining from the mountain of Christian sin, and I think: *Our murdered compatriots now reside only in our memories.*

Farid notices, however, that this is not quite true. "Look down," he signals, and he points with his foot toward a seam in the cobbles. Human teeth. There must be thousands scattered in the square, trapped in cracks and edges. I look up and notice that women and children are kneeling everywhere, picking up these remains as if it were harvest time. Undoubtedly, they will save them as talismans against the plague.

Ahead of us, at the northeast rim of the square, a regiment of royal footsoldiers has cordoned off the Church of São Domingos by forming a semi-circle in front of its entrance. Behind them is a row of cavaliers, perhaps twenty in all.

"A compromise must have been struck by the governor with the Dominican hierarchy to let them into Lisbon," Farid signals to me.

"When all the killing is over, the Crown sends in troops," I reply. "Very comforting to know that he supports us so courageously, no?"

As we walk on, I see townspeople standing in poses of respect who only a day or two before would have called for King Manuel's head. *This passivity is deeply embedded in the souls of the Portuguese Christians,* I think. *No revolt will ever succeed here.*

A crafty-eyed old woman looking to make conversation as people do in the face of regal authority, stops us, says, "Two of the Dominican friars have been arrested. Isn't it terrible?"

I raise my middle finger over her and chant, "May your wicked soul wander the Lower Realms forever!"

When she shows disdain for me with her Christian eyes, I spit at her feet. We rush on. At the front gate to the Estaus Palace, two burly crossbowmen stand flanking a dandified doorman in a feathered cap. Beyond the gate's metalwork, in the shade of an orange grove, rest three carriages. One of them, painted white with gold, is the vehicle I remember from the day of Diego's injury.

"The Count of Almira will see me," I tell the doorman. "Pray inform him that Pedro Zarco has arrived."

"Have you correspondence to this effect?" he asks, his face twisting as if he's had a whiff of something rotten.

I realize then that we look like peasants who've come from a day of labor in the fields. "I bear no letter, but he will see me." As he sizes me up, I hold the Northerner's amethyst hat to my chest and feign the supercilious posture of a gentleman farmer bored with ill-bred servants. I turn to Farid, grumble in my best Castilian accent about a coming banquet for a fictitious friend named Diaz; Castilians irritate but impress the Portuguese, particularly when they can afford servants. My effort seems forced, but out of the corner of my eye, I can see the doorman passing along my message to a footman inside the gate.

We wait under the monstrous sun of Lisbon, watching slippery lizards streaking through cracks in the cobbles. With longing, Farid gazes east along the rooftops of the Moorish Quarter.

"After we're done here, we'll ask again at the blacksmith's workshop for Samir," I signal. "Maybe we can find someone who knows something."

A footman with only one hand shuffles up to me. "I will escort Senhor Zarco to the Count's rooms," he says.

"Come," I say to Farid, and together we pass through the gate.

Inside the palace, the scents are of must and amber. We march down a hallway floored with mosaics imitating Persian carpets. The walls are whitewashed, and every three paces give way to concave alcoves. Centering each alcove is pedestal hoisting aloft a great blue ewer brimming with pink and white rosebuds.

Above us, the vaulted ceilings are painted with gold and white arabesques as a background to carefully executed figures of magpies, hoopoes, nightingales and other common birds. I have no idea what the footman makes of our florid hand movements as Farid and I identify the local names of the various kinds; his eyes betray only a passing interest.

A gnarled tree occupies an immense wire cage at the end of the hallway. Upon reaching it, we discover that finches from Portuguese India and Africa have nested in it, are darting around like arrows of yellow and orange and black. I point to the mess of white droppings they leave in an attempt to spoil the beauty of such a display. Understanding my intention and finding it hopeless, Farid simply gestures in reply, "Even a king may understand something of beauty."

"If he did, then he would not keep them caged," I say.

"For a king, freedom and beauty can never mix!" my friend answers back wisely.

The Count's rooms are on the second floor. The waiting chamber for his apartments is parqueted in a chessboard pattern. A table of rose-colored marble centers the room, is surrounded by four chairs embroidered with the King's armored spheres. We are invited to sit, but on the wall to the right of the entrance hangs a disturbing triptych which grabs our attention. It depicts a bearded, prostrated saint begging in a ruined city peopled by rat-headed priests and all manner of sphinxes. With a wry smile, Farid signals, "Someone who knows Lisbon well."

The door to the inner chambers suddenly opens. "Ah, I see you like our little painting," the Count says to me in Castilian. He purses his lips as if awaiting an important reply. His beaked nose and thick black hair give him the wily, clever profile of an ascetic, a deceitfully youthful air as well.

"I don't know yet whether it pleases me or not," I answer. "But the artist has talent."

"I like a man who doesn't make his mind up too soon. Less likely to get swindled, no?"

"I've no intention of bartering for it," I say.

He laughs with good humor. There is no hint that he recognizes me from our previous encounter. He leans into the main panel of the triptych after dismissing the footman with the slightest of nods. "Frightful what saints have to put up with," he says. "Not worth it, I should think. It's by a Lowlander named Bosch. King Manuel received it as a gift. But he hates it and hangs it here for me when I'm in Lisbon." He smacks his lips. "We always enjoy the King's leftovers."

He gestures for Farid and me to enter his sitting room like an elder inviting youths toward wisdom. The two emerald rings crowning the index and middle fingers of his right hand suddenly seem dyed by holy light.

Inside, the girl from his carriage stands by a shuttered window at the far wall, her right arm behind her back. She wears a long gown of cream-colored silk which rises to a lace partlet and ruffled collar. A violet wimple draws her hair back into a cone ringed with silver filigree. Her face is pale and gentle, curiously girlish, centered by inquisitive eyes. Spurred perhaps by my stare of fond solidarity, she shows her hidden arm. It is short, stubby, reaches only to her waist. A quiver in her tiny fingers as she grips her pearls marks her anxious hesitation, but the longer I gaze upon her, the more solid becomes her expression of tenderness. I sense that she would like to caress the tips of her fingers across my lips.

"My daughter, Joanna," the Count says.

With a mixture of gratitude and sexual desire, I think: *praised be God for not making her his wife.* I bow and offer my name. I extend my hand toward Farid and introduce him. "He is deaf and cannot speak. He will read your lips." Farid bows with the deep Islamic grace he has inherited from Samir. It is intended to remind us that we are representatives of Allah and must meet together with a seriousness equal to our origins.

"I'm overjoyed you've come," the Count says. "You've saved me a trip out to that pestilent Alfama. Let's make ourselves comfortable, no?" He takes the elbow of his daughter's left arm and leads her across the room as if about to dance. Farid and I slip uncomfortably down into gold and scarlet brocade chairs around a table of marble marquetry. A pewter tray holds a rose-colored ceramic carafe and four silver goblets. Joanna pours us wine. The Count studies us with insistent eyes. The two of us seem awkward, hesitant, like sea gulls on land. Farid signals, "The sooner we leave, the better."

"I assume that when you gesture like that you are talking together," the Count remarks. He twists his body to the side as the skeptical often do, stares at me above his nose with a mixture of curiosity and superiority.

"We grew up together and developed a language," I explain.

"A language of the hands. And for obvious reasons," he says, nodding toward Joanna, "I am fascinated by hands. Tell me, do you spell every word?"

"A few. But most words have signs."

"And when you spell, is it in Portuguese or Hebrew?"

The Count smiles cagily at my silence. A grin from a man who likes to pose and prosecute, to confuse his victims before... He laughs suddenly and claps his hands. "Watch," he says. He leans forward and lays an invisible object onto the table, picks corners apart as if unfolding a piece of expensive material. Bowing his head and mouthing some words, he blankets his head and shoulders with an invisible shawl. Facing east, he chants the opening of Jewish evening prayers in a faint whisper. As his words fade, he turns with a gentle expression requesting patience. He says in whispered Castilian, "From our century forward, acting will be a good profession for Jews to study. I predict that we will be the best, in all countries, in all languages, until the Messiah comes, when we will take no more roles." He smiles through pursed lips and nods as if seconding his own theory, straightens up and swirls his invisible shawl into the air like a magician. "No matter how lucrative those roles may be. So forgive my little play. An actor without an audience is nothing, and I must use all my opportunities." He nods at me, then Farid. "I do indeed remember you both from the street. And your uncle of blessed memory, almost caught by the King's guards in his phylacteries." He leans across the table to take my hand. "It's pointless hiding when amongst your own," he observes.

I slip out of his cold and sweaty touch. "Then you *are* New Christians?" I ask.

"Yes," Joanna answers.

"And a little bit 'no,'" adds the Count with an apologetic shrug.

Has the girl spoken because she senses that I do not trust her father? Sensing my weakness for her, Farid signals, "Do not put your faith in *either* of them."

I lay my hand on Farid's arm as reassurance. To the Count, I say, "You'll have to speak more plainly with me."

"Simple really," the Count says. "We *are* and *aren't* New Christians. We have delightful little cards of pardon from King Ferdinand. Blessed be He who creates a stain and removes it. And he's also conferred upon me a sweet little title, of course. How did I get this delicious bit of powerful nothing? Marriage, my young man. Remember that when it comes time to plant your seed. Joanna's mother of blessed memory sprouted from the branches of a very important family tree." He nods toward his daughter and holds up a finger as if the truth must be told. "Very important, but very broke. So money is also how I became a count. Don't look at me as if that's to be belittled. No, senhor. No, indeed! I'm no different from the King of Castile himself. All nobles are fakes. Look below their finery and you'll find a jealous peasant thrilled to nestle between the legs of his maidservant. And they're always overspending. Don't ever forget that! They never learn. It's one of the ways you know that they're not Jewish. If they do learn anything, then our dwarf-minded Dominican friars exclaim, 'Aha! A Jew!' and turn them to smoke. So make a lot of money and buy what you want, and never learn a thing, and you, too, may become a count!" He moistens his lips with a sip of wine. "What business is it you're in, anyway?"

"Father..." Joanna says. "I'm sure that's not necessary."

"Of course, you my dear would think so. Everything but love to a young woman is unnecessary."

Farid signals, "That passes for wit in Castile. I think we're supposed to smile admiringly."

The Count turns to me with raised, questioning eyebrows. "I asked what business you are in, Senhor Zarco."

"My family owns a fruit store. But I really..."

"Oh, please!" he exclaims, flapping his hand at me in protest. "Don't talk to me of family! Family ties are the curse of Spain and Portugal. You must walk away...no *run away* from them, dear boy!"

I look at Farid for his opinion on what to reply. He sighs and signals, "He's trying to confuse us for some reason."

"You're right," I observe, standing.

"'You're right' what?" the Count asks, dumbfounded.

"Just tell us why you wanted to buy manuscripts from Simon Eanes," I say.

"I just told you, my son! *Doubloons, maravedis, cruzados, reis....* Tell me your heartbeat doesn't quicken just a little when you hear the glorious names of money! Like the names of God, they are. Only not the least bit secret. Blessed be He who creates the obvious." He leans toward me, whispers, "Maybe I shouldn't go into it, but... Your uncle knew it. Look, dear boy, I buy the manuscripts here for a pittance. You poor people are just dying to get rid of them. And then I sell them for a fortune in Alexandria, Salonika, Constantinople, Venice—even Pope Julius, blessed be the stone foundations of the Church, is interested. There's no end to the profits to be made. Now I know that you've got a few delicious poems hidden away. So why not sell? Then you can leave this hell. I'll even help you. I've got connections in shipping. Down in Faro, there's a..."

How does this pilfering, silken weasel know that Uncle was keeping Hebrew manuscripts? I ask Joanna, "Is this true? Is it all for gold?"

She fixes my eyes with a grave expression and nods affirmatively.

So this monied vulgarian is implying that Uncle was smuggling the works of Abulafia and Moses de Leon for mere gold! As if such works of kabbalah even had a price in the Lower Realms!

"The time has come for direct talk," I tell the Count, as if it's an order. "Did you have my uncle killed?!"

He leans back, offended, but catches himself and gestures for peace between us. "Of course not. I don't..."

"But if what you say is true, then you undoubtedly considered him a competitor. You might have tried to..." Rage surges as words fail.

"Then you won't sell me anything?" he asks. "Not even a Haggadah? A Book of Esther? A single..."

"Father, please," Joanna begs.

"Nothing!" I say. "And if I find that you killed my uncle, I promise I'll cut your throat!"

The Count smiles. "How very thrilling to be threatened! I expect it's good for adding a little color to my complexion, no?"

"You sicken me," I say. My neck burns as I turn and march to the door. Footsteps run from behind. Joanna's tiny hand presses into my wrist and she whispers, "You must find the noblewoman my father calls, 'Queen Esther!' But beware of her!"

# Chapter XVII

Up close, the scent of Joanna's hair was like an invisible extension of my own desires. She squeezed my hand once, then dashed away. From the back of the room, I heard a slap. "This is serious!" her father growled. "What did you tell him?!"

I turned to her, but her eyes flashed a warning for me to leave. Outside the gates of the palace, breathing in the golden light of sunset, I gesture her words to Farid. He signals, "Every name adds a page to our book of mystery."

"Yes. And we've got to check Uncle's personal Haggadah to see which page. Now I'm beginning to understand. Zerubbabel has got to be there. Queen Esther, too. And when I find them, I believe that they will have the faces of the smugglers."

"Something else you should know," Farid gestures. "This Count, he is the same man as the Isaac who wanted to sell you a Hebrew manuscript."

"What?!"

"They are one and the same, Isaac of Ronda and the Count of Almira."

"How do you know?"

"I know. The eyes for one thing. They can't change. And some of his gestures. Surely you noticed Isaac of Ronda's elegant hands. He's a good actor, as he says. He must be able to change his voice or you would have known. And he has an excellent disguise. But it's not perfect. And underneath his scents, there is one that will not go away. Oil of cloves."

"His blessed toothache!" I gesture. When Farid nods, I signal, "But why would he want to sell a manuscript one moment, then buy Uncle's books the next?"

"We do not have enough verses to know the rhyme scheme."

"Farid, come...we've got to get home to check Uncle's old Haggadah!"

"I need to stay," his hands answer, and he requests forgiveness by bowing his head. "Now that I'm well, I must search for my father. I'll meet you as soon as I can."

His fingertips brush against my forearm, petal-soft. I remember how the angels had him clothed in white and hear Uncle say, "Do not abandon the living for the dead." Yet I am unable to prevent myself from signaling, "I need you to help me. We're so close now."

"Beri, please don't be selfish," he gestures.

"Selfish?! Uncle is dead! What do you want me to do? What do all of you want me to do?!"

"I don't want you to do anything but let me search for Samir! So go from me!"

Farid's gestures cut the air between us. Yet out of guilt and fear, I follow behind him to his friends' homes in the neighborhood. "I'll go as fast as I can," he says.

But his effort to placate me only spills acid onto my rage.

We search with silence wedged between us. The only clue to Samir's whereabouts comes from a toothless fishhook maker who lives across the street from the old confiscated mosque. In an Arabic which fuses all consonants, she says that she saw Samir praying atop his blue prayer rug on the hillside below the castle. Had he stopped for a moment in his race home to beg Allah to spare his son? She points a scarred red finger, withered almost to the bone, to where he had been. Dusty weeds and a withered marigold mark the spot. Farid straddles them and gazes across the rooftops of Little Jerusalem and central Lisbon to the Tagus.

"It's too wide," he gestures.

"What?" I ask.

"The river. One should be able to see to the other side. As in Tavira or Coimbra. Even Porto. Here, we have no intimacy. We cannot hug this city. The width of the river makes us feel like we're all just visiting. That we're all expendable. It's the city's curse."

"We'll keep looking till we find more clues," I say. My cushioned

words belie the impatience twisting my gut; Uncle is dead and he babbles on about embracing rivers.

Farid's black eyes target me with a passive light that hides his rage.
I realize that we have both put on masks again. For each other. For the
first time in many years. Even so, despite all the frustration hidden
under my burning cheeks, there descends to me the calming assurance
that our connection can never be broken. Then, and during many days
since, I have often thought that my life would have been much simpler
had I been able to find physical fulfillment in his arms.

We rush home encased in our separate thoughts. The possibility
that the Count of Almira has turned us both to marionettes turns the
city into a ragged backdrop of gray scenery. Was Joanna's whisper, too,
just a part of a puppeteer's plot?

By the entrance to our store, Farid marches away from me toward
his house without even signalling goodbye.

Mother and Cinfa are arranging fruit at the back of our store.
Miraculously, the doors to Temple Street are back on the hinges and
have been painted deep blue. I'm about to ask about them when
Mother says in a burdened tone, "We've been waiting. Are you ready to
say prayers?"

Her hair is disheveled, her eyes drowsy. It must be the extract of
henbane. I say, "Give me five minutes."

"Sabbath has waited long enough!" she shouts.

"Two minutes then!"

In the kitchen, Aviboa is asleep on a pillow. Reza is boiling cod in
our copper cauldron. "Brites came," she whispers to me. "I gave her the
soiled sheet you hid in the courtyard."

"Bless you," I say, kissing her cheek. "Did Rabbi Losa stop by, by
any chance?"

"No."

"Who painted the doors to the store and put them back on?"

"Bento. As partial thanks for extracting the *ibbur* from Gemila, he
told me to tell you."

"Good. Listen, stall my mother for a few minutes if you can."

Reza nods. Dashing down into the cellar, I slip the *genizah* key from
our eel bladder and take out Uncle's personal Haggadah. Sitting with it
on my lap, my heart drumming, I page through the illustrations looking
for Zerubbabel. His panel tops the sixth page of illuminations prefacing

the text. In my uncle's rendering, he is a young man with long black hair and zealous eyes. He stands in a posture of righteous pride before King Darius, who has the optimistic, outward-looking face of Prince Henry the Navigator. Both men stand in front of the limestone tower of the Almond Farm. In his right hand, Zerubbabel carries a scrolled Torah, the essence of truth. In the left is the golden Hebrew letter Hé, a symbol of the divine woman, Binah. Two emerald rings shine from the index and middle fingers of his right hand.

These gemstones gift me with Zerubbabel's true identity; men's faces age, emeralds do not. Zerubbabel is none other than the Count of Almira.

"The sun's chariot is about to pass beyond the horizon," Reza calls down. "You're making the Sabbath bride wait for her betrothal. And it is the last evening of Passover. Come up now!"

"Let her wed without me!" I shout up.

"Stop being so stubborn!"

"Reza, you know the prayers. You've got a voice. Do it yourself!"

"What serpent has eaten your sense, Berekiah Zarco? You know I can't conduct services."

"Then have Mother," I say. "Just leave me be. Please."

"We need a man, you idiot!"

It is blasphemous, but I shout, "The Sabbath bride needs only a voice, not a penis! Get Cinfa to lead you if you're afraid."

Reza slams the trap door to the cellar. We have peace.

I page through the panels of the Haggadah searching for Queen Esther. Her regal face confronts me from the bottom of the very next page. Her identity makes my heart race; Esther, the Jewish Queen who kept her religion a secret and who later saved her people from the wrath of the evil courtier Haman, is none other than Dona Meneses! Here, she is depicted carrying the Torah to Mordecai, her adopted father. Partially concealed beneath her arm is a manuscript, probably the Bahir—the Book of Light—since Uncle has gifted it with a brilliant nimbus. The face of Mordecai is someone I've never seen. But he wears a Byzantine cross, a Jewish prayer shawl and a blue aba fringed with green arabesques. Is it a reference to a man of the Eastern Church? A Jewish friend in a Moorish kingdom? A dervish from Turkey? "Someone who reconciles all of the Holy Land's religions," I hear my uncle say. To myself I whisper, "Or a man who wears all three masks."

*Perhaps,* I think, *he is Tu Bisvat.*

These findings extract thought from me for a time. Then I realize that for so important a discovery, I must have the confirmation of Farid's falcon eyes. As I poke my head form the trap door into the kitchen, Reza says, "So, Berekiah Zarco, you've come to your senses after all!"

I rush past her, ducking my eyes from the Sabbath ceremony. Farid is in his bedroom. On his knees, facing Mecca, his eyes closed, he sways forward toward the ground like a palm leaf bending in a breeze. When his back raises up, a furrowing in his brow indicates that he knows I'm with him. Yet his eyes do not open. He lowers himself again. Anger stiffens me when he refuses to acknowledge my presence with a hand signal. The word *betrayal* engraves itself in my mind. With my heel, I tap thrice, then once, then four more times. He sits up. Passive eyes open. I signal, "Please, I need your clear vision."

He stands, his face elongated into a dry expression of feigned disinterest. Gliding like a ghost, he follows me into my house. Reza says in a gentle voice, "Will you join us now?"

I neither look nor answer. We slip into the cellar.

Farid takes one look at Zerubbabel and signals, "It's the Count of Almira." As for Queen Esther, he isn't so sure until I point out the choker of emeralds and sapphires which she always wears around her neck. "Yes, that's her," he gestures.

Swallowing hard, I think, *an alchemy unanticipated by Uncle turned the love of these friends to fear. Then to hate and finally murder.* For who could be more fearful than New Christians? Who more hateful than Portuguese and Spanish nobles? Who, then, better to betray Uncle than aristocratic former Jews helping him smuggle Hebrew books: Zerubbabel and Queen Esther!

Had something recently gone wrong between them? *Tu Bisvat* wrote that a *safira* sent by my master had not reached him. Maybe Dona Meneses had begun diverting profits intended for the purchase of new manuscripts. Or perhaps Uncle's uncompromising judgments had begun to constrict Zerubbabel's business dealings. Had he begun selling books elsewhere?

The villainous Haman, then, would be portrayed in Uncle's newest Haggadah—the one stolen from our *genizah*—by the Count of Almira as an old man. His was the face my master had been looking for, the one he had told me he'd finally found just before Passover dinner.

And yet, if the Count was guilty, if he had wanted to silence Simon and the other threshing group members who might have known his identity, then why did he agree to take Diego to the hospital? To Farid, I signal, "We need to find the missing Haggadah as proof that the Count had Uncle murdered or killed him himself."

"How?" he gestures.

"We'll have to trap Dona Meneses and the Count somehow. They must have it."

"Berekiah!" Reza calls suddenly. "You have a visitor...Father Carlos."

Is this a trick designed by my mother to get me upstairs? "Send him down!" I call.

"Who is it?" Farid signals.

"The priest," I answer.

I slip the Haggadah into its hiding place, lock the lid, then drop the *genizah* key into the eel bladder.

Father Carlos feels his way down the stairs. Sweat beads on his forehead and his breathing comes greedily, as if he's been running.

"Judah?" I ask.

"Nothing." He comes to me, takes my hands. In a quivering voice he says, "You must help me!"

"Is it the Northerner? Is he after you?!"

"No, no...not that. But dearest God. I was talking to the Dominicans... They must have summoned a demon to kill me. Berekiah, I've realized something—evil is jealous. The Devil wants to destroy what is most good. And your uncle had benevolent powers that healed both the Lower and Upper Realms. If the Devil had wanted... I think he and the Dominicans are sending demons after us all. White Maimon. Gemila did see him! She was right!"

In his frantic eyes, I can see that the madness of Lisbon has finally overwhelmed the priest. "Carlos, please stop! I have no time for metaphorical speech."

"Then look at this!" he shouts.

He takes out yet another talisman. Upon a square of polished vellum minute Hebrew letters form two poorly sketched concentric circles spelling out quotations from Proverbs: The outer circle reads, *Violence is meat and drink for the treacherous;* the inner, *The embers of the wicked will be extinguished.*

"I found it in the lining of my cape!" Father Carlos shouts. "In my cape! How do you explain that?! How?!"

"Shush!" I say. I take out from my pouch the talisman he gave me the other day. The writing on this new talisman is in the same precise script in some places and in others far less assured, as if executed by someone weakened by disease or too much wine.

When I hand it to Farid, he sniffs at it, then licks. "It looks like your ink," he signals.

"My ink?!" The solution then descends to me and forces a groan from my gut. I've been avoiding the obvious answer. "Carlos, these scribblings have nothing to do with Uncle's death," I say. I turn the vellum in my hands, confirm from its texture the identity of the artist responsible. "Come," I tell the priest.

He and Farid follow me upstairs. Mother is saying prayers in a fragile voice. She stops to glance at me with resigned, heavy eyes. Reza infuses the silence with her glare of righteous disapproval, an expression which Cinfa copies. We rush to my mother's bedroom. In the secret panel above her door frame, I find the talismans she's been working on. The micrographic writing is the same.

"I don't understand," Father Carlos says.

"She must have overheard your argument with Uncle. She thought she could help. Judgment clouded by worry and grief produces such monstrosities. This last one she must have slipped into your cloak while you were sleeping last night. She's been taking extract of henbane, cannot write as carefully as normal—nor think with any rigor. I'm sorry. I'm sure she meant no harm. Only to get the book by Solomon Ibn Gabirol which Uncle wanted so badly. In her state, she may even think these talismans will bring her brother back. Two mysteries had woven together. We thought they were one and the same."

If I had listened to my own words closely, then the mistake I was about to make would not have been made.

Farid, Father Carlos and I go to the store where my family cannot hear us to discuss how we should proceed. After I tell the priest of the identities given Zerubbabel and Queen Esther in Uncle's personal Haggadah, Farid signals with certain gestures, "We go back to the Estaus Palace and confront the Count of Almira again, force an admission of guilt from him."

When I translate for the priest, he says, "And if our Count should refuse?"

Farid lifts out from his pouch the most fearsome dagger from his collection, six inches of deathly sharp iron curved like a sickle. He swivels it menacingly under the priest's nose. "The Count won't refuse!" he signals. "And why? Because an actor needs his voice. I shall place the tip against his Adam's apple and core it with a single twist unless he answers us truthfully."

The priest leans back and pushes Farid's hand away. To me, he says, "I don't know what he just said, but I don't like it. Dona Meneses... She's more likely to admit the truth."

"Why, because she's a woman?" I reply scornfully. "If she's a secret Jew needing to protect her identity, then she'd have no hesitation ordering her henchmen to chop off our heads!"

"Joanna, the Count's daughter," Farid signals. "She will help us."

"If we can get to her."

As I translate for Carlos, a knock comes from my mother's entrance to Temple Street. We rush in, and I open the door to find a round-faced little boy with bulging eyes. He takes a note from his pouch, extends it toward me. "Message," he says. When I take it from him, he runs off. The note reads:

"Berekiah, meet me on the King's Road to Sintra, just before Benfica. I will be waiting by the twin water mills rising beyond the ruined Visigothic church. Come alone. Tell not a soul. And come right away. I found out something you need to know about Master Abraham's death."

The note is signed in Diego's slashing script.

Father Carlos takes it from me. After he reads it, he says, "Don't go, dear boy. It's still too risky to travel around Lisbon alone."

The obligation to warn Diego about the smugglers and inform him of their identities weighs on my chest. Perhaps, too, what he has discovered will help me trap Queen Esther and Zerubbabel. "No, I'll go," I say. "It's night, and there's little else I can do for now." Turning to Farid, I take his shoulder and spell an apology for my earlier selfishness. I add, "I've no intention of going alone, if you'll gift me with your presence."

His eyes close and he offers me a bow of agreement.

We leave before my family's supplications become wailings and curses, before Cinfa can fix me fully inside her abandoned eyes.

Farid pauses at home to slip on his father's sandals.

Friday night deepens with a fierce wind from the east, from accursed Spain. On the road to Sintra, beyond the exposed arches of the Visigothic church, we head down a foot-trodden path toward the abandoned water mills. Their forms are wild and spidery in the moonlight. Five leagues off, Sintra Mountain rises from the horizon like a fallen cloud pointing upward toward an answer beyond reach. Farid sniffs rabbit-like at the air, surveys the landscape. A white hawk circles overhead, ghost-riding currents of air, a creature free of land, beyond history. "Is the attraction of birds that they presage our liberation from this world?" I signal to my friend.

"Perhaps that they both share our journey and escape it," he gestures. He sniffs around once again. "Deer have passed recently," he signals. With pensive, cautious movements, he indicates, "And something else." After a few more steps, he squats, runs his fingers across a streak his deaf-man's eyes have spotted in the dirt. "Men," he signals. He points to an impression my vision cannot perceive. "One walking with boots. Heavy, with stomping footsteps."

"Maybe Diego," I say.

"Two other men, as well. A small one who creeps. The other hesitant, turning constantly to face around."

"Now *that's* Diego," I smile. "The others are probably his bodyguards."

We rush on. A barrel-like shape on the path before the mills takes on angular contours, shifts suddenly. A fallen man condenses in the silver moonlight. Long-haired and broad-shouldered, he drags himself forward like a caterpillar, his right leg apparently wounded and trailing mercilessly behind. His grunts carve agony in the wind-sounds of night.

"The Northerner who emptied Simon from his shell!" Farid signals with a flurry of gestures.

From up close, the dull, thick features of his face are unmistakable. "Yes."

We stand above him like towers. He is enormous, bulky, like a bull turned human. He lifts himself to his knees. We step back. Our daggers center our fists. A patch of dark wetness soaks into his thigh.

"You killed my friend," I say. "Why?"

He answers in a foreign tongue which I don't understand.

"English, French, Dutch...?" I ask.

"*Flamenco,*" he answers in rough Castilian. "*De Bruges.*"

Has he had training as a *shohet* amongst the northern, Ashkenazi Jews? I point to him and ask, "*Nuevo Cristiano?*"

He laughs in a single exhale. "*Viejo,*" he replies. He points to himself, whispers, "*Muy Viejo Cristiano,* very Old Christian."

"Why did you kill Simon?" To his indecipherable shrug, I hold my foot and ankle to my rear to imitate the stump of a leg. "*Porqué él?*"

A laugh bursts, becomes a cough. His eyes close and he tilts his head to indicate that it was inevitable.

"Dona Meneses?" I ask. "Do you know her?"

He smiles and nods. As I turn to catch a signal of Farid's, the Fleming leaps for me. His oxen weight topples me. I strike out, but his callused hands grip my throat. My knife buries deep into the welcome of his shoulder. I am screaming for Farid. Fighting. But he is too strong. The vise of his grip tightens. My chest heaves. An exploding cough trapped in my throat wells tears in my eyes. And yet I see him clearly. As if a scarab trapped in amber: bulging eyes, reflective cheeks, a mouth grimacing with hate.

I learn that there is a moment when death is accepted as inevitable. My hands loosen from around his wrists. Neither anger nor fear possesses me. Only distance. As if I am standing behind myself and turning to walk away. As if Uncle is calling to me from across the Rua de São Pedro: "Berekiah, hearken unto me! I'm right here waiting..."

A cringing pain. Constriction like rope burning my throat. Spurts of salty liquid from the Fleming's mouth. I have been tugged back to my body. My stinging eyes, my lips, are soaked with blood. His hands, like gates parting, drop away. Weight is pushed from me. Farid's face descends. He grips me with one hand; the other gestures my name.

Gulping for air, I spot Farid's dagger buried at the back of the Fleming's neck. "I'm okay," I signal.

"I killed him," he gestures. This time, there is no hesitation in Farid's hand: fingers thrust out, fisted, then twisted palm-down as if to snap a branch from its mother limb.

Farid digs our knives from the assassin's flesh, wipes them against his pants. Except to express my thanks, we do not gesture; what is there to say? We trudge on to the mills instead. A man lies face-up on the pathway, by the base of the nearest one, blank fish-eyes fixed on the quarter moon high in the sky. His neck is still warm with eclipsed life. When I squat to look more closely, a face I know forms: that of the bodyguard Diego brought to my house.

I whisper a prayer that Diego, too, hasn't been summoned to God.

"Do you hear anything?" Farid signals. "I sense movement close by."

"No."

Suddenly, out steps Diego from behind the mill wheel. He wears a thick, fur-lined cape which descends to his ankles. Even in the pale light, I can see his face is beaded with sweat.

"You're safe," I say. "Why didn't you..."

"Berekiah, they're...they're trying to kill everyone in the threshing group!" he moans. "All of us. There's no safety anywhere. We...we must..."

"Calm down. We killed the Northerner back along the pathway."

Diego grabs my shoulders. "That won't end it. They got your uncle and Samson and Simon—and now they tried for me! Don't you see, the whole threshing group... All of us!"

I place my hands against his chest. "Don't worry. We know their identities now. It's Dona Meneses. She and the Count of Almira are behind all this. They must think that the members of the threshing group know their identities and can compromise them to the Royal authorities."

"Dona Meneses?! It's impossible! She would never..."

"She was smuggling books with Uncle," I say.

"But she's a noblewoman!"

"So much the better for getting Hebrew manuscripts safely out of Portugal, don't you think?"

Diego stares off into the night as if his response may lie somewhere along the dark horizon. Turning back to me, he says, "I don't know. I just never thought..." He stares at his dead bodyguard. "Fernando wounded the Northerner in the leg, but the blond bastard was too skillful with his knife. Oh God! I mustn't go back to Lisbon."

"So you intend to wait here the rest of your life?"

"I won't let them get me! When they drip the boiling oil on you, it's as if your skin is being peeled open with a rusty blade. You pray that your life will end. You'll do anything. I won't let it happen again. Ever. You hear me! Never again!"

I suddenly recall the thick line of scar across his chest which I saw when he collapsed on the street. "They gave you the *pinga*?" I ask.

He replies, "In Seville there was a specialist who could draw pictures across your body with burning oil and ash he rubbed in the scars. Onto the chest of a girl of nineteen whose crime was to use clean sheets on Friday, he dripped an entire Passion scene. She simply would not die. Her breasts became the hills of Jerusalem, her navel the heart of Christ. It was too much to..."

"Diego, listen. They could just as easily send someone after you. Wherever you go. You'll be safer in town. With people you know."

"Not my house," he intones with dread. The wind tousles his silver hair, and I realize he no longer wears his turban; we are becoming less obviously Jewish by the day. "They know to look there. And when they realize that the assassin sent to kill me is dead, they'll send someone else."

"I meant that you'll stay with us," I say.

Diego gazes down, considering. I can see that he has already agreed. So I ask, "Why did you want me out here in the first place?"

"Berekiah, I remembered something important...that Dom Miguel Ribeiro, the nobleman for whom Esther scripted a book of Psalms, had an argument with your uncle a week ago." He takes my hand, continues in a whisper, "Your master mentioned it in passing in our threshing group. I made some inquiries, learned that Dom Miguel was staying in a stables not far from here. On the outskirts of Benfica. I intended my bodyguard to go with you. To surprise him at night. But now, I'm not..." His words fade as he looks around.

"Diego, I know all about the argument. Miguel and Uncle fought over his refusal to accept his true past, his Judaism. I was told about it by..."

"Not that! It was the book...the Book of Psalms Esther wrote for him. He didn't want to pay the price they'd agreed upon. Apparently, he threatened to tell the authorities that your aunt and uncle were concealing Hebrew manuscripts if they didn't gift him with it. Now I think that maybe he was involved with Dona Meneses. There must be a connection there somewhere."

"No, no. Uncle sent him a note asking him to become a smuggler," I say.

Farid has had trouble reading Diego's lips in the dark. When I translate into signs, he gestures back, "But Miguel Ribeiro is rich. He could afford to pay for Esther's work. And he spared your life when you went to see him. He could've killed you with impunity."

"What's he telling you?!" Diego demands.

"That it makes no sense."

The thresher laughs in a single ironic exhale and grips my hand tightly. "Has anything over the past week made any sense? Let me tell you something, my boy. The Lower Realms aren't ruled by any logic which you're likely to find scripted in the kabbalah."

Diego steps across the Northerner's body. He spits on his head and kicks it. Then on he trudges, sweating like a beast of burden. In his erudite voice, he soliloquizes about leaving for Rhodes and Constantinople on a boat scheduled to depart from Faro in one week. He will begin his journey south from Lisbon tomorrow evening. "And Constantinople is such a lovely town," he says. "Not like Lisbon at all. It even rains. Big beautiful drops. Like pearls. Good for kabbalists, too. It's where Asia meets Europe, where two become one like your uncle used to say. Remember when he..."

The dust and night and Diego's rambling voice intertwine like rope around my thoughts. Vultures spiral overhead, trail us back to Lisbon. When we pause inside the city's gates at the *Chafariz da Esperança*, Fountain of Hope, I douse my face and hair. I wonder what the hidden connection between Miguel Ribeiro and the smugglers might be. I stare at Diego through the dripping water. He's combing the new beard which already covers his cheeks and chin. "Neatness is a holy duty," he reminds me.

Perhaps so. But what defines his inner being? Is he the Wandering Jew in person, a terrified being somehow less than human, ready for the next migration to yet another hostile land? Is that what we've all become, characters defined by Christian mythology?

As we reach my house, little Didi Molcho comes running to us from our gate. He shouts, "I've found him, Beri! I've found him!"

"Who?"

"Rabbi Losa!"

"Where is he?!" I demand.

"In the *micvah*. Murça Benjamin is being married."

"What....now? It was to be tomorrow. It must be long after midnight. And it's still the Sabbath!"

He whispers, "To fool the Christians, the wedding has been changed to tonight."

We walk together to the courtyard. Father Carlos comes out to meet us. He, Didi, Diego, Farid and I stand by the stump of our felled lemon tree. I say, "I must confront Rabbi Losa, make sure he's got nothing to do with this. I'll be back soon."

Everyone begins to raise their voices against me. "It's too dangerous for Jews to meet together in ritual," Diego concludes, speaking for all of them. "What if the Christians find you?!"

My distrust of Losa is so complete that I cannot resist the urge to confront him. "Even so," I say, "I must go. Besides, there is nothing we can do about Queen Esther and Zerubbabel in the night. At dawn, I will begin to draw them out of hiding."

I leave my friends for the *micvah* and Murça Benjamin's marriage ceremony. As a childless widow, she has been obliged by the law of Levirite marriage to wed her late husband's elder brother now that he has chosen to take her as his bride.

A weedy man whose face is hidden in a cowl guards the bathhouse door. "May I go in?" I ask. "I'm a friend of Murça's."

"Hurry."

The stairs are lit by wall torches. A small gallery of witnesses draped in cloaks of fluttering shadow and light is assembled in the central chamber, men in front, women behind. But as I descend, I notice that something is amiss. Rabbi Losa sits at the center of a tribunal of five judges. He starts as if burned when he spots me. His wicked eyes show cold dread. Rage presses into my groin, hot and demanding.

And yet, what is happening? Murça stands opposite her brother-in-law, Efraim. Her hair has been gathered up under a burlap headscarf. Her face is drawn, hopeless, and her hands are trembling. A black ceramic plate rests on the ground between them. The *halizah!* Oh God, when will Thy mercy ever reach us? After the riot against the Jews, Efraim must have reneged on his agreement to marry. We are well along in the ceremony that will free him from this duty. As for Murça, she, too, will be liberated. But into what future? With little dowry and half the Jewish youths of Lisbon gone to ash, her chances of finding the happiness she deserves are slim.

Efraim announces his refusal to marry Murça in a judgmental voice. In quivering, hesitant syllables, Murça replies in Hebrew, *"Me'en yeba-*

*mi lehakim leahiv shem beyisrael lo aba yabmi,*" then repeats her words in Portuguese so all may understand: "My husband's brother has refused to establish a name in Israel for his brother and does not wish to marry me in the Levirite marriage." A sigh comes from deep in her gut as she finishes.

"Do you understand what she said?" Rabbi Losa asks Efraim.

"Yes."

The judges rise. Murça trudges toward Efraim, crouches, and with her right hand alone begins to undo the leather sandal straps circled three times around his right calf. Her agonized breaths scrape the air. When the laces finally dangle free, she raises his foot and slips off his shoe. Lifting herself up, she reaches back for leverage and throws the sandal to the ground between Efraim and the judges.

Rabbi Sabah nudges Losa and whispers in his ear; the traitorous lout has forgotten his place in the ceremony because of his fear of me. In a rushed voice, he says to Efraim, "Take a look at the spittle which is coming out of her mouth until it reaches the ground."

Murça trembles, manages with great effort to lean over and spit into the black plate to symbolically humiliate her brother-in-law for refusing to give her children.

Defiant, Efraim retrieves his sandal and hands it to Rabbi Losa as if serving a summons. All five judges intone in unison: "May it be God's will that the daughters of Israel will never come to need the *halizah* or the Levirite marriage."

The ceremony over, Murça melts to the floor. As the women rush to her, Losa breaks for the stairs. *All rabbis know how to kill like a shohet!* I think. *He was the one blackmailing Uncle's smugglers. That is why God meant for me to attend this halizah!*

I push past the men of the gallery, rush up after him. Outside, I spot him lumbering toward his house. In a moment, I have reached him. My hands form fists around the silk of his collar. When I shove him against the wall of Samir's house, I say, "A great scholar and rabbi of rabbis like you should not be in such a hurry to leave."

He pushes back at me. "Let me pass, you little catamite."

"You mistake me for Farid, a lover of men whose name you are unequal even to pronounce."

"Would you beat me right in the street in front of everyone?" He looks around to force me to consider the small crowd that has gathered.

"I might," I say. "I care not what the others think of me. But I will be fair. I will not kill you for your crimes against your people, only if I find you murdered my uncle."

"Murdered your uncle? Me?!"

"Is that so astounding? You betrayed him! You dare deny it? You took out your *shohet's* blade and slit his throat!"

"I do indeed deny it. Of course, we disliked each other. But there is a Red Sea between hate and murder. And I have not crossed it."

"Where were you the Sunday of the riot?" I demand.

"In my home praying. One of my daughters is ill."

"To God or to the Devil?"

"May a wild boar press its tongue into..."

I knock his head against the whitewashed wall. He shrieks, groans. "And witnesses?!" I ask.

"Both my daughters were there with me!"

"All day?"

"Yes."

"Then why did the Dominicans spare you?"

He shouts, "I work for the Church now, you fool!"

"Are your daughters at home?"

"Don't you dare..."

A week of little sleep and food is beginning to take its toll on my reasoning and balance. I tug the terrified rabbi down the Rua de São Pedro toward his house. A retreating part of me realizes that I have let my desperation get the better of me. Am I afraid to see the truth, to string all the clues together into an easily understood verse? They are all safely placed in my Torah memory: White Maimon of the Two Mouths; Diego's stoning; the *shohet's* slashing cut across my uncle's neck; the letters from *Tu Bisvat*. If they were citations from Torah or kabbalah, I could weave them together into a sensible commentary, an answer. Am I simply afraid to end the journey toward vengeance and pass through the final Gate of Emptiness beyond my master's death?

# Chapter XVIII

According to kabbalah, honey has one-sixtieth the sweetness of manna; dream one-sixtieth the power of prophesy; the Sabbath one-sixtieth the glory of the world to come.

And the sleep of sickness, what is its fraction of death?

Rachel, Rabbi Losa's youngest daughter, lies under a woolen blanket, on her side, the back of her hand curled like a flipper over her forehead as if she is seeking protection from an ogre. Her eyes are closed, but every few seconds she shudders, seeming to cast away an inner damp. Esther-Maria, her older sister, sits vigil at the end of the bed with the worry-reddened eyes of failing resolve. A chaplet threads through her fingers. She nods up at me as those beyond speech do, acknowledging kinship yet distance.

I consider the failure of the child's body as if aligned to Efraim's denial of Murça. The broken promises of betrayal seem to be the binding glue that seals all our lives together.

"How long has she been like this?" I ask.

"Since last Friday," Esther-Maria replies. "But at first it wasn't so bad."

"And was your father with her all day Sunday?"

"This is preposterous!" Losa bellows. "Asking my own..."

Esther-Maria raises her hand to quiet her father. "Yes," she whispers. "All day and night."

She stands, presses her fists into an ache in her lower back. I say, "I'm asking because my uncle, he was..."

She nods. "We've all heard. You don't need to explain. Look, when the Old Christians came, we stayed here and hid. Father said we'd be spared, but how can killers be trusted? Until...was it Tuesday? I can't seem to recall days very well."

I turn to Rabbi Losa. "Then why didn't you let me in when I came for you before? Or stop by my house? And just now in the *micvah*, when you..."

"Are you delirious?! You were kicking down my door. I had a sick child here. Everyone knows you wish to avenge your uncle. And now, if you... Wait..." Losa marches across the room, unhooks a tarnished mirror from the wall and carries it to me. "Look!" he demands. "Wouldn't you run from this?"

In the faded silver, by the dim candlelight, a drawn and debased figure with lichenous stubble on his cheeks sprouts wild and filthy hair.

"You're right," I admit. "I'm quite a sight." I take out from my pouch my drawing of the waif who tried to sell Uncle's Haggadah. "Do either of you recognize this boy?"

Esther-Maria studies him as she leans into the aureole circling the candle flame. "No," she says. She hands it to her father. He shakes his head.

To the rabbi, I say, "Then you never helped my uncle smuggling Hebrew books?" When he shakes his head, I add, "You must swear it on the Torah."

As he swears, Rachel wheezes in her sleep like a torn bellows. "May I touch her?" I ask.

Losa nods. The pulse in her wrist races. Her forehead burns, but curiously, she does not sweat. "What other symptoms does she have?" I ask.

"She cannot eat," Esther-Maria says. "And she bleeds from her bowels when she..." The girl leans toward me, and her expectant eyes show that my interest has unintentionally offered her hope.

"It's either dysentery or the Spanish rash," I say. "Spread by the foul air and muck." Passages from Avicenna trail across the pages of my Torah memory. "Boxwood tea with vervain, and plenty of it," I say. "She needs liquid to sweat out her tumors. And give her enemas of arsenic diluted with pomegranate juice and water. Not too much of the poison, though. A few drops at the most." Losa peers at me over the tip of his flattened, owlish nose with a look that could make even a prophet itch. And yet, after all that's happened, his pose strikes me as humorous rather than insolent. "Save your foolish looks for Sabbath services," I tell him.

"No more such services," he says sadly. "Never again."

"Just as well," I sneer.

"What would you know?!" he shouts. "What did you give up but your Jewish name?! Did you take a vow never to set foot in a synagogue again if the Lord would save our community? Did you give up what you held dearest? What would you know of sacrifice?! You were an eleven-year-old boy. Yes, I remember you clinging to your father. And you remember me racing to the baptism font. Did you ever ask why? Did your uncle? Can you understand that it was to prevent more of us from dying or killing our children. I'd made a pact with our Lord—save the Jews of Lisbon and I will convert. Was it wrong? Who can say? Can you?! Can your uncle?!"

Losa wipes spittle from his mouth with his sleeve, glares at me with years of rage burning red on his cheeks.

Esther-Maria comes to him. Caressing his shoulder, she whispers, "Calm yourself, Father."

"My uncle is dead and cannot say anything," I answer in a calm dry voice which belies my anger. "And if I were a more faithful kabbalist than I am, perhaps I wouldn't judge you. Maybe you did betray us for a higher loyalty. Or maybe that's what you've told yourself so you can go on living. Anyway, your motives don't matter to me anymore. It's your actions which counted so many years ago, that count now. I am learning that for men like you and me, our acts are more important than our words, than all our secret pacts and whispered prayers. For Uncle, I think it was different. His chanting summoned angels into this world. For men of wonders like that..." My words fade; Rabbi Losa, bloated with fury, has turned away. Talk seems pointless. I brush Esther-Maria's shoulder to fix her attention. "Keep Rachel washed with rosewater boiled with vervain and egg yolk. And for God's sake, change these foul sheets. Or better still, burn them!" I hold my hand over her head and bless her.

"Will my sister die?" she asks.

"Only He can say," her father intones. His pious look upward toward the Christian heaven is meant to remind me of the sacrifice he claims to have made.

"Probably she will," I answer with the callous tone of a challenge; at this point, affirmations of the existence of a cloud-dwelling God guarding over us seem cruel and absurd. Yet for Esther-Maria, for myself, I add, "But if you do as I say, she has a chance."

The girl nods her thanks. Rabbi Losa pulls in his chin as he's always done in my presence and suffers my bow of goodbye with disdain. I amble home looking at the jagged constellations quilting the sky, knowing at long last that he, and all the self-righteous rabbis the world over, have lost their power over me. Forever. That, too, has been the journey this Passover.

Whenever you think you've recognized the true form of a verse from Torah, it has a way of shedding its clothes to reveal inner layers. So, too, the events of everyday life.

Diego, Father Carlos and Farid meet me in the kitchen with a letter from Solomon Eli, the *mohel* with whom we discovered the secret entrance from our home to the bathhouse. "Berekiah Zarco" is scribbled on coarse, badly made linen paper whose surface is pressed with an arc.

"While you were gone, we got some bad news," Diego says. "Solomon the *mohel* was found hanging by his *tallis* from the rafters of his home. Suicide. Farid, Carlos and I went there. He left this note for you."

"But he'd survived!" I shout. My words fall hollow between us. What, after all, is the endurance of the body compared to the decay of a grieving soul? "The note's not sealed," I observe. "And he wrote my given name, Berekiah. He never called me that. I was 'Shaalat Chalom.'"

"It was the way it was handed to us," Carlos shrugs.

"By whom?"

"His sister, Lena," Diego answers. "Apparently, she found the body, and while going through his things, she found the note."

Master Solomon's words to me are written in a hurried, childlike script, framed inside a circular impression pressed into the paper:

"Does one's training as a *mohel* make one callous to the pain of the flesh? I did it. That is proof of something. My body is slack. The New World will never feel my footsteps. Too many discoveries in this century. It is good for some things to remain hidden. I informed on New Christians. On Reza, too. I had to, really. The threat of *pinga* is a burning shadow, and the body is a terrible coward when clothed in darkness. A single drop of oil sends it racing toward screams that curl from the bowels like shedding snakes and... Master Abraham swore that he would have me judged at a Jewish Tribunal. That he would find a way to see me punished. We argued that Sunday morning. Fear. He must have smelled it on me. He said, 'You carry a knife, and yet you are ter- rified.' He smiled as if to welcome me to his home. 'Your iron blade will anneal me to God and maybe even serve a higher purpose, but the girl is not yet ready. Solomon, leave her be and I will come to you like a bride.' But a girl breathes Inquisitional fires as well as a man. To be like Adam...if only I could. I didn't intend to take his life. Or that of the girl. I cannot ask your forgiveness or the forgiveness of Esther and Mira, but when I am gone, please say a *kaddish* for me so that I may leave the Lower Worlds. Will there be peace for such a man as I? A blessing for you, Solomon."

"What's it say?!" Diego demands as I read.

My lips are sealed together by the jagged confession and its flaws. The suicide explains the book he left for me as a gift. But why the sud- den doubt of the profession he loved? Why no mention of his wife? Was there no clarity to his final moment?

Is this, then, a forgery scripted by Zerubbabel and Queen Esther? Do they suspect that I am walking within their shadows?

"How long had he been dead when his sister found him?" I signal to Farid.

"She said she found him this morning. But the note only just now. She hadn't the strength to go through his possessions any sooner."

"What are you two signalling about?" Carlos demands. "And what's it say, damn you?!"

After I read Solomon's words aloud, Farid takes the note from me and sniffs at it, licks its edge. "Very cheap quality," he says.

"As a *mohel*, Solomon was very skillful with knives," Carlos observes.

"It might explain things," Diego adds. "We certainly never sus- pected he was working with Master Abraham. That's just the way they both would have wanted it."

He's right. And yet, could Gemila have mistaken a balding, olive- skinned finch of a man for White Maimon of the Two Mouths? And for what reason would he have hired a Northerner to kill Simon and Diego?

"You have opened another gate," I hear Uncle tell me. "Now, Berekiah, fill your lungs with the breath of the Lower Realms and jump through before it has a chance to bang closed."

I take the letter back from Farid. My pounding feet lead me to the cellar so that I can meditate upon its script. "Alone," I whisper, and Farid lets my hand slide from his.

Downstairs, I take Uncle's topaz signet ring from the storage cabinet and slip it onto my right index finger. I sit on our prayer mat above his bloodstains. After opening the doors of my mind with patterned breathing exercises, I transpose the scripted letters of Solomon's note using the monotone of chant. When his words lift from the paper and twist like a juggler's rings in the air, they shed their meaning as unnecessary weight. My arms and legs grow light with grace.

Imagine looking upon a cuneiform tablet. When the knots of mind are untied, Hebrew becomes that foreign. The letters reveal themselves as dismembered shapes; music without melody; animals unnamed by Adam. The solidity of the world grows translucent and finally opens.

Through the largest God-given space—the one of emptiness beyond thought—words with the certainty of prayer come to me: *This must be the script of Uncle's killer; it is his confession, not Solomon's. He left it in the mohel's house after his suicide. For his sister or someone else to find and bring to me...to tempt me away from his trail.*

*Perhaps he even killed poor Solomon to advance his plans in some way!*

I sit alone, exhausted; the effort to summon insight has been costly for my weakened body. My hands are weighted as if by lead. *Rest till dawn,* I think to myself. In response, my eyelids close. My uncle speaks to me. "Sleep," he says, his voice plaintive, seductive. "You need to slumber in silence if you are to complete the journey."

"No, not now," I answer aloud. Opening my eyes, I think: *I must check Solomon's apartment, talk to his sister. Then go back to the Estaus Palace. I must try to speak to Joanna, the Count's daughter.*

"As defiant as ever," Uncle replies. I close my eyes to see his smile. "You must give way to dream," he continues. "The desert of Lisbon has passed beneath your feet. You are indeed close. Rest your head upon my lap. Use your dreams to ask a question."

"Is that not a sin?" I ask. "One must not question the dead, the prophets say."

"One may always speak with God. It is within his ocean that this single drop now resides. Simply take the ribbon with both our names scripted in gold from your wrist and place it over your eyes. Then sleep."

I obey my master. And a dream does indeed descend.

I am enfolded by a warmth akin to homecoming. My master is standing above me, framed by the tiles of the cellar wall, his prayer shawl draped over his head and shoulders.

"I do not believe that Dom Miguel Ribeiro or any Northern henchman in the pay of your secret smugglers would have planted a silk thread on your thumbnail or killed like a *shohet*," I say. "So who else is involved? Who did Queen Esther send to murder you?"

"You already know who separated my body from my soul," he replies with a cagey smile. "The question is 'where' and 'when' you shall realize it."

"As usual, Uncle, you want to make me work for an answer. Very well. Where and when shall I learn his name?"

As the white wing of his robe unfurls, a breeze scented with myrtle blows over us. The ceiling thins and fades. Walls drop away. The sky opens, is washed pink and violet at the western horizon. We sit together below the tower of the Almond Farm.

"Why here?" I ask. "Why at sundown?"

Uncle shows me his piercing look meant to indicate that I must listen closely. He raises his hand of blessing over me and says, "The map of a town is in a blind beggar's feet."

Golden light shines through the eyelets of windows at the northern rim of the cellar ceiling. It is Saturday morning. The eighth and last day of Passover. I sit up and gaze back at my dream as if upon a departing guest. Opening the *genizah*, I search in vain for handwriting that matches that of Solomon's bogus note. Then, just to be sure of my reasoning, I page through Uncle's personal Haggadah. Solomon the *mohel* was not given a Biblical cognate. In all likelihood, he could not have been involved in smuggling books with Zerubbabel and Queen Esther.

Upstairs, Reza is building a fire in the hearth, Aviboa in her arms, balanced on her hip. A plump orange marigold is pinned in the girl's hair. Diego and Carlos sit across from each other at the kitchen table sipping steaming barley water from ceramic cups.

Reza is the first to turn to me. Her eyes betray the grudge she carries for my not leading Sabbath services the night before.

"You've slept," Carlos says. "That is good."

We exchange blessings. "Where's Farid?" I ask.

"At home, saying prayers," Diego replies.

I make for the door to the courtyard.

"Where do you think you're going?" Father Carlos demands.

"Out," I reply.

"You're going to Solomon the *mohel's* apartment, aren't you?" Reza asks bitterly. Before I can tell her my true destination, she says, "Can't you just let it be? He's dead. We have our vengeance. So now we must find a way to move on, to care for the family we still have. That's what your master would want. And believe me, Berekiah Zarco, there's a boatload of chores for you to do should you ever want to rejoin the living!"

Reza stares at me as if I'd better give her the response she wants.

"My path is not yours," I tell her. "If I don't proceed on my own now, I'll never be able to rejoin you later." The destination she has chosen for me serves as a convenient lie, however, so I add, "Besides, I'm only going there to pay my respects. Even a murderer deserves our prayers."

Diego stands and says, "I'll be leaving this evening for Faro and the boat to Constantinople. Perhaps we should say our goodbyes."

"I'll be back soon. No time for farewells just yet."

Farid is praying in his front room when I enter his house. When he spots me, he lifts straight up as if reeled in by the hands of Allah.

# Chapter XIX

As Farid and I spire up the hillside of mottled scrub toward the towers of the Graça Convent and morning sun of Lisbon, the dwarf nun with the single saber-tooth who guards the sanctuary's limestone cross swivels around to glare at us.

Dona Meneses' mansion is perched on the dirt road which rims the northern slope of the hill. A stone fortress adapted from an abandoned Romanesque battlement, its only modern exuberance is a marble balcony supported by four flying buttresses braced into the exposed limestone of the hillside below. I have come here twice before, both times to deliver silk dresses my mother had been commissioned to sew. As we walk to the gated entrance to the side of the house, a garden of towering Moroccan cedars offers us shade. From here, we can see the edge of the balcony at the back. A gaunt man in a plumed blue beret stands at the far end. He holds a red glass goblet, is conversing leisurely with someone I can't see from this angle. As he turns to his left to note something in the distance, I recognize him: the Count of Almira.

Zerubbabel and Queen Esther have come together.

At the gate, a blond guard in the characteristic amethyst hat of Dona Meneses' henchmen takes my message inside the house. As we slip away, Farid signals, "Maybe she gets a discount for ordering those northern monsters in bulk."

I would like to laugh, if only to confirm that I am still the young man I was, but I no longer seem to possess the ability. As we pass the saturnine nun still standing guard at the convent, my heart seems to leap from my chest. I think: *If my life were to end here, what would it have meant?*

There is no time to consider a reply. We run-slide-run down the hill. Lisbon's insanely tangled streets welcome us with anonymity.

Back at home, I take from the *genizah* two priceless philosophic treatises by Abraham Abulafia, "The Life of the Future World" and "The Treasury of the Hidden Eden." Both are gifted with margin notes in the master's own hand.

"What are you doing?" Diego asks from the stairs. He and Father Carlos stand on the steps giving me motherly looks of worry.

"I understand now what Uncle wants me to do. If Dona Meneses is seeking to purchase Hebrew manuscripts through the Count of Almira, she will have them. But for a very high price. I want my master's last Haggadah. It's the proof I need."

The priest says, "But you told us that you believed Solomon was responsible for..."

"Who cares what I said!" I interrupt. "Do you believe everything you hear?!"

He frowns as if he's smelled something rotten.

Diego asks, "An exchange? Master Abraham's books for the Haggadah?"

"Exactly."

"You've got your uncle's guile," Father Carlos tells me, his tone wary. "Can't argue with that. But maybe you're a bit *too* clever."

"You're tempting the Devil, you know," Diego counsels.

"You two are beginning to sound alike," I observe. "I think fear makes all Jews say the same things. And it's getting tiresome. Anyway, I'm not tempting any devil. Dona Meneses is just a frightened Jew like the rest of us."

"A Jew?!" Diego exclaims. "She's no Jew!"

"She portrays Queen Esther in Uncle's personal Haggadah...is depicted bringing the Torah to Mordecai."

"That's no proof!" he scoffs.

"It is for me!"

With the voice of a learned elder, Diego says, "Even if you're right, she's no Jew. She's a New Christian. The gap grows wider between the two each day." When I roll my eyes, he adds, "In any event, a knife knows no religion. And her bodyguards have very sharp ones in their possession. We have all found that out from close range of late."

"So what do you want me to say? I know all that."

The priest steps to the bottom of the stairs and approaches me. With supplicating eyes, he says, "Berekiah, now that you have neither your father nor your uncle..."

"Save it, Carlos! I don't want your protection."

He gives me the burdened sigh I've heard all my life meaning that I'm too obstinate for my own good. I slip the manuscripts into the leather day pack Uncle used to take on his spiritual outings to Sintra Mountain.

Diego comes to me. "So where will you confront her?" he questions.

"At the Almond Farm," I reply.

"Why there?"

"It's where my uncle said to go."

Father Carlos gasps. As I pass him, he grabs my arm. "Master Abraham appeared to you?" When I nod, he asks in a hushed voice, "And you spoke with him?"

"I asked God a dream question and Uncle appeared to me."

"What...what did he say?"

"That the last gate would be crossed at the tower on the Almond Farm."

Diego says, "Berekiah, if you're right, then Dona Meneses and the Count of Almira had Master Abraham and Simon killed. You shouldn't go. I'll get your mother. I can see you won't listen to us."

"Stop! Don't bring her here! Simon wasn't prepared. And neither, apparently, was my uncle. They didn't know how dangerous she really was. I do."

He continues to protest in a voice ascending toward hysteria. I raise my hand to call for silence. "If you tell my mother, she'll just start sewing some more of her hideous talismans. Leave her in the store. We should say goodbye now. You may be gone by the time I return."

Diego and I hug, but it is impossible for my emotions to reach toward his tears; there is a callous deadness in me linked to revenge. "May you find those pearls of rain you want from the skies over Constantinople," I say. I smile as best I can. "And don't forget those treatises you wanted from Senhora Tamara. You won't be able to get them just anywhere. If you need some money..." I reach into my pouch and hand him Senhora Rosamonte's aquamarine ring.

He takes it from me. "Berekiah, I don't know what..."

"Say nothing. All will be well for you in Turkey."

"I will miss the wonders of Portugal. And the good Jews of Lisbon most of all." He blesses his hand over me. "May you and your family find the peace you so long have deserved."

As Farid and I walk to the Almond Farm, the amber grasses and blossoming trees of Portugal seem to connote separation. We Jews are scattering again, and these mulberry and lavender bushes, poppies and magpies will not hear their Hebrew names for centuries to come, perhaps never again. Maybe it is even a good thing for them.

The scores of graves on the farm remain free of weeds because of the drought. Wooden markers scribbled in Portuguese sprout like hands reaching toward life. We enter the tower and ascend the spiral staircase. Round and round we climb, into the belfry, empty now except for a patchwork of bird droppings. We gaze out at the carpets of golden barley and plowed earth separated by rims of cork trees, their twisted, noble trunks stripped to a vulnerable red.

And we wait.

The sunset which marks the end of Passover rises with reflections of the great topaz-colored palm leaves which canopy Eden.

A few minutes later, just as I requested in my note, Dona Meneses' coach approaches, stops at the property line of the farm. Alone, she strolls toward us through the old grove of almond trees, a scarlet parasol over her head. Yet she holds no manuscript in her hand. Farid signals, "The time has come." He places his dagger in the waistband of his pants. Trying to remain calm, I lift up my pack weighted with Abulafia's manuscripts. We descend from the belfry, Uncle's hand guiding me at a leisurely pace wholly out of step with my nervous breathing.

On the ground floor, Farid and I stand amidst the stone rubble and await the noblewoman.

Dona Meneses does not disappoint. She steps confidently across the threshold of the tower and acknowledges me with a stiff nod, the kind of regal gesture she shows her drivers to ready them for departure. Her face, though not unpleasant to look at, seems too round and small, perhaps because her brown tresses have been drawn tightly back and wrapped inside a tall black cone tasseled with yellow ribbon. Her flowing silken jupe bears vertical stripes of royal blue and brilliant green, is puffed fashionably at her belly to give the impression of pregnancy.

Staring at her as I never have before, I have the impression that she is terrified of aging; her flaring eyebrows and long lashes are thickly penciled, black as midnight, and an unsightly pinkish powder pales her olive complexion. Her lips are pursed to indicate impatience, are the red of rubies. She closes her parasol suddenly, fingers her choker of emerald and sapphire beads with exquisite reserve. She targets her gaze at Farid. Turning back to me, she assumes a kind of false and urgent sympathy. "I came as you asked," she says. "So would you be kind enough to please tell me what it is..."

"Why haven't you brought my uncle's Haggadah?" I demand.

"Rude, you are," she says, as if that's a proper answer to my question.

"Where is it?" I repeat.

"I don't know." She raises her eyebrows as if puzzled by my concern. "But you can rest assured that I haven't got it."

"That's impossible," I say.

"But it's true," she replies. "Tell me, have you told anyone about me, about..."

"Don't worry, we will trail no spies to your door. As far as the world outside knows, you are as Old Christian as the Castilian Inquisition itself."

"Would you tell me how you found out?" she asks. "Your mother, perhaps?"

"Does she know?!"

"Ah, so dear Mira kept her word and didn't tell you." She caresses her fingers down from her chin across her neck with noticeable relief.

"No, she said nothing." As I speak, insight comes with a jolt. "The basket of fruit with which you always left our house," I say. "The books were always hidden below. She knew."

"Once, Attar's 'Conference of the Birds' got stained by grapes. Your uncle was furious." Dona Meneses shows me a false, practiced smile. Seeing I won't reciprocate, she asks in an arrogant voice, "So how *did* you find out about me?"

"You're illuminated in my uncle's personal Haggadah as Queen Esther. There could be no doubt of your religious origins. And in his depiction, you are shown not merely bringing a Torah to Mordecai, but also concealing a copy of the Bahir below your arm."

She fingers her necklace and proffers a deferential bow. "Clever.

My compliments. But I must say that your uncle took far too many chances in his work."

"Is that why you killed him?" I ask.

She starts. "Killed him? Me?!"

"Your surprise is as false as those crystals around your neck."

"These *gemstones* happen to be worth more than both your lives," she points out.

"These days, that means they are worth almost nothing, dear lady."

"I can see you are much like your uncle."

"But not as naïve," I reply. "I know who you are and what you've done."

"Do you?" She tilts her head and grins, as if amazed by the tricks of a dog. "Tell me what you *think* you know!"

"I'll tell you nothing." I take out the manuscripts from my pack. "I've come to offer you these for my uncle's last illuminated Haggadah. I know you have it. And these are worth far more. Both have annotations in the hand of Master Abraham Abulafia himself, blessed be his name."

"If you're sure I've killed your uncle then why haven't you already tried to take my life?"

"Your death would not bring him back," I say.

"Logic matters not to revenge. Your hesitation must mean that you're not absolutely sure about my guilt." She nods up at me as if to receive my assent.

"I want his Haggadah!" I shout. "And you won't leave here unless I get it!"

Disregarding my threat, she asks in a calm voice, "Why here? Why the Almond Farm?"

"It was also illuminated by Uncle, in the same panel with Zerubbabel. When I dreamt of it, he told me that I would cross the last gate of this mystery here. Now where's..."

"*He* told you that? Master Abraham?" She traces her fingers along the taut tendons of her neck. She is as nervous as I am.

"Yes, I spoke with my uncle," I reply.

"When?" she asks urgently.

"That's of no concern to you. You are simply here to..."

"Did you know that it was here that we sealed our fate together?" she interrupts in a voice which seems to come from her gut, from fear.

"Four winters ago, on the thirteenth of Adar, the day before Purim. We were to symbolically re-enact the ancient victory of the Hebrew people over the Syrian army which took place on that day." She stares inside herself at memory. "Your uncle insisted that I meet him here at the Almond Farm to set up our smuggling network."

"Why here?" I demand.

"You know the story of Aaron Poejo and his..."

"Yes," I interrupt.

"And his vision...?" she asks.

"The blond savages with iron masks over their mouths who would come to sack Lisbon."

"Iron masks to prevent communication," she says, as if offering a citation of wisdom. "Blonds because they are Christians. You should understand. You were Master Abraham's chosen one. Imagine it as scripture."

"Yes. It was a vision that the Christians would one day take our words from us, our books."

"And it was here, your uncle said, that we would plan their downfall."

The answer to a riddle which Uncle posed to me just before his last Sabbath sprouts inside me. He had asked, *What lives for centuries but can still die before its own birth?*

*A book*, I now realize; it is born anew in each of us when we read it. And it can die in the Inquisitional flames as surely as any of us.

Dona Meneses peers at me over her nose. "You know, if you hadn't asked to meet me here, I might have had you killed, as well. But there is something about this place..."

"Where's the Haggadah?!" I ask her with renewed fervor.

"I haven't got it. Berekiah, let me..."

"I do not grant you permission to speak my true name! Use my Christian one!"

"As you like. Pedro, I was working with your uncle. For more than three years now. Tell me, do you remember Senhora Belmira?" she asks.

"The Jewish woman beaten to death by the Madre de Deus Fountain a few months ago."

"Yes. Have you wondered why she was killed?"

"There are Old Christian men in Lisbon who will do anything to a..."

"No! It was my driver. Remember him? The swarthy one I used to have. Not one of these new Flemings I've got."

"Your driver killed her?" I ask.

"Yes. A note had been sent to me. A blackmail note. I was to start handing over the Hebrew manuscripts your uncle was entrusting to me or the blackmailer would reveal my Jewish past. Not a very good position for me to be in. And not just for me, but for members of my family, as well. I was to leave a first manuscript in a hiding place by the Madre de Deus Fountain. So I did. Or rather, my driver did. He hid and waited. A woman came for it at nightfall. Senhora Belmira. My driver took her, tried to find out who had sent her. But she would not talk. Nothing he did... I'm afraid he got carried away in his loyalty to me. A boorish man. I've sent him back to his family in Toledo. Castilians are born murderers. Never hire them except for bullfights."

"Did you tell my uncle?" I ask.

"I told no one," she replies.

"You didn't trust him?"

"In my position, I can't afford trust. For all I knew, *he* was the one who had betrayed me."

"My uncle never betrayed anyone!"

"No, perhaps he never did. But in such a dilemma... Pedro, trust is something that few of us can afford these days. It can be too...too costly."

Her face suddenly elongates toward the sadness of regret. She takes a step toward me, but I raise my hand to keep her away. I feel as if she is tainted with a dangerous kindness.

"I began to have him watched, your family, as well." Dona Meneses' words fade as she takes a deep breath. "In any case, I received another note after Senhora Belmira was killed. This time, the blackmailer wrote that if I tried to find out about him, my secrets would be revealed to the Church and to King Manuel himself. He had proof, he said, of my Jewish background. So I began leaving manuscripts for him which your uncle had entrusted to me."

"Do you still have the notes?" I ask.

She nods cagily. "You want to know if we can trace the man from his writing. I thought of that. His notes have always been scribbled, written as if in someone's left hand. Or by a child perhaps. But I came up with a plan. I have an old friend from childhood. Someone beyond doubt who was helping us smuggle books across the Spanish border. You know him as..."

"The Count of Almira," I interrupt.

"Yes. He came..."

"And Isaac of Ronda," I add.

She purses her lips and gives me an astonished look. "So you figured that out, too."

"Farid did," I reply.

"How?"

Farid points to his eyes and nose.

She bows towards him. "My compliments. So I devised that the Count would come to Lisbon in order to offer books for sale in one guise, buy them in another. We hoped to flush out this blackmailer one way or another. To be neat and clean about it. I know that he, this blackmailer, tried to sell your uncle's Haggadah to Senhora Tamara. A mistake on his part. He must have panicked right after the riot. Unfortunately, the Senhora scared his messenger away without making him talk. It was then that the blackmailer realized his error and became more cautious. In any event, I know that he has to be someone who was in—or had been in—Master Abraham's threshing group. Only they were entrusted with the secret of his smuggling books. He told me so when we made our agreement. I began having them all watched. The Count himself was following one of them, that old misfit Diego, when he was attacked by Old Christian boys that Friday before everything in Lisbon began unraveling. One of the Count's drivers saved him. And then came Sunday...the pyres. After that, with everyone calling for Jewish blood, I couldn't afford to wait any longer. My instincts told me it was Simon Eanes, the fabric importer. So I had him...'relaxed.'"

She speaks as if the order to kill came naturally to her, uses the accursed terminology of the Inquisition; since no ecclesiastic person is supposed to shed blood directly, those condemned by the Church in Spain are handed over or "relaxed" to civil authorities for burning. "I had hoped that my troubles were over, but I got another blackmail note," she continues. She takes another step toward me, implores me to suspend judgment with a fragile look in her eyes. "I was to hand over more books by the Madre de Deus Fountain just yesterday. But I didn't."

"So then you tried for Diego," I say.

"Yes, God forgive me, I did!" Her hands have formed fists. "What would you do?!"

"Me, I wouldn't kill anyone because I haven't the courage to admit who I am!"

"Very honorable. When the Inquisition swoops down upon Portugal and you feel its talons around your neck, we shall see if you still feel that way."

"Will you try for Diego again?"

"Yes. And Father Carlos, as well. I cannot risk... They will be located soon. And my men have their orders. I can wait no longer. I have no choice."

Farid points at her choker and signals with angry, chopping gestures, "Too many emeralds at stake, no doubt!"

When I translate his condemnation of her, she shouts, "You're heartless!" She curls her fingers around her necklace and tears at it. Beads scatter on the floor. "Take it!" she says, offering what's left of the string of jewels to me, then Farid. "It's not about money. It's my life! It's all our lives!" A grimace of anguish crosses her face. The slap I feel is her necklace thrown against my cheek.

The three of us stand silently in the room like prisoners who dare not escape into language out of guilt and shame. I close my eyes and follow my breathing. Farid takes my hand and names a suspect with the shape of his fingers. "Yes," I signal back. "It could still be him." As I turn, however, a magic moment occurs; the marble-white ring of skin that was always hidden below Dona Meneses' necklace confirms another stunning possibility.

"There are only two people left who could have murdered my uncle," I say. "Give me until morning before you have anyone else killed."

"Too long!"

"Until midnight then. You are killing innocent men!"

Dona Meneses nods her agreement, glares over her nose at Farid and me like a defiant princess scanning men who have violated her. She lifts the train of her dress and sweeps it behind, turns and marches out the door.

# Chapter XX

Farmlands give way to the wooden shacks and dungheaps of the city's outer districts as Farid and I race back to Lisbon.

At the Senhor Duarte's Inn of the Sacred Body, we approach the manager. A tiny man with wisps of hair combed forward into bangs, he sits ladling soup into a toothless mouth. His cheeks open and compress like a stretched bellows.

We stand over him. "When did Dom Afonso Verdinho arrive?" I demand.

He squints up at me and sticks a chunk of soggy millet bread into his mouth. "Who's asking?"

"Pedro Zarco. Dom Afonso is with my aunt. When did he come?"

Each chomp squashes his face and closes his eyes. "I'll have to check my books," he says. His cracked lips drip soup. "And as you gentlemen can see, I'm eating."

I reach into my pouch for Senhora Rosamonte's ring, then remember with a curse that I'd given it to Diego. Farid catches my desperate look with a smile. He takes out one of Dona Meneses' emeralds and hands it to the man, then furtively slips several more gemstones into my pouch.

Shaping the words, "Bless you," against Farid's arm, I say to the innkeeper, "The gem is yours if you tell me when Dom Afonso Verdinho arrived."

His tongue slips snake-like between his lips. With a ribald nod up toward me, he scrapes the bead against his ceramic bowl. A curl of glaze lifts away from a dot-sized impurity jutting from the emerald.

His eyes shine. "She's a beauty," he observes with a greedy smile.

"I ask you now, when did he come?!"

"Wednesday." He holds the stone up to the light of his candle.

"This past Wednesday, after the riot, or the one before?"

"This past one."

"You're absolutely positive?!" I demand.

He tucks the bead into the inner curl of his lower lip as if it's a cardamon seed. "See those men over there?" he questions, pointing to some merchants eating at a dining table.

"Yes."

Between slurps of soup, he says, "The one with a beard deals in sugar but stinks like rotten cabbage. Arrived yesterday sweatin' like a priest in heat. He likes big-busted women without teeth. The clean-shaven one is from Evora, is here to buy copperware. Arrived today. He likes *carne preta*, black meat, if you know what I mean." He squints at me. "Nothin' goes on here I don't know about. Your man arrived Wednesday, lookin' and smellin' worse than his horse."

"What room is he in?"

"Upstairs." He points to an open door at the back of the dining room. "To the left. Last door on the right."

Aunt Esther answers my knock with a gasp. "Berekiah! Is everything all..."

I push past her. Afonso sits on an unmade bed in his long underwear. His feet are shriveled and coarse, like unearthed mandrake roots. "Ever hear of Simon the fabric importer?" I ask him.

"A friend of your uncle's. Esther wrote to me about..."

"So she wrote to you." I bow toward her. "You've been using your gifts well, dearest aunt."

Her face becomes hard and cold. "Your judgment is noted," she says. "Now get out!"

"Did you ever meet him?" I ask Afonso.

"What's this about?" he questions, his face all shock and puzzlement.

"Just answer my question!"

Esther pushes against me as Afonso answers, "I honestly don't remember. I may have."

Without warning, my aunt slaps my face. As I grab her wrist, Afonso jumps up. "Leave her alone!" he shouts.

Farid steps between Esther and me, removes my hand. He glares at me, signals, "Don't you dare touch her again," then leads her to the bed.

She sits and rubs at her wrist. Her eyes are glassy, and her back is bent forward as if she's weighed down by a locket bearing her grief. Such is my rage, however, that her figure cannot elicit from me even the ash of the burning solidarity I once felt for her. To Afonso, I say, "So you wouldn't know if he has any disabilities? That he has crutches, wears black silk gloves to..."

Farid signals that I talk too much and suddenly tosses a few of Dona Meneses' emeralds and sapphires toward Afonso. The old thresher thrusts a hand out and catches one. "What's this...?!" he demands, showing it to me.

Farid grips my shoulder. "Forget about him!" he signals with a cutting motion. "Not only wasn't he in town, but look at which hand he used!"

"The left!" I signal back.

"And the slope of the cut across your uncle's neck, it was..."

Each step in our flight back to my house seems to fix the last of the missing verses of a long-lost poem into place. White Maimon of the Two Mouths! Of course, Gemila was right! In her hysteria, who else would she form out of a hooded killer with scars on his face and blood on his hands? Everything fit: the timing of Uncle's discovery of Haman's persona; the blackmailer's choice of Senhora Belmira as a go-between; even the murderer's own words about never being tortured again.

And the date on which the blackmailer demanded that Dona Meneses turn over the latest manuscripts to be smuggled from Portugal—that, too, implicated only one suspect.

The garments of mystery drop away one by one until a single face stares at me.

In our courtyard, a donkey with raw saddle sores is tossing flies away with his tail. From the inner window in my bedroom, I see that Cinfa, Reza and my mother are standing in the store with my cousin Meir from Tavira. "Beri!" he cries. He rushes to me open-armed.

"Not now!" I say, raising my hands to keep him away. "Mother, where's Diego and Father Carlos?"

"Why?"

"Must you ask questions! Where are they?!"

"The priest has gone back again to the Church of São Domingos. Diego is in the cellar. He went downstairs to say evening prayers. What do you..."

Cinfa interrupts, "No, Diego came upstairs while we were in here. Just a few minutes ago. You weren't looking, Mother."

"Let's go!" Farid signals.

"Wait, I think I know why he went to the cellar. And what we discover there may help us cross the last gate."

I unhook one of the lamps hanging from the crossbeam above the table. After sliding away our Persian carpet, Farid rips open the trap door. I take out my knife, descend. But the darkness gives up only emptiness. The *genizah* is closed. *Neatness is a holy duty*, I think. It was the murderer himself who reminded me that. With the key from the eel bladder, Farid opens the lid. I shine my light into the hiding place. All of Uncle's manuscripts are gone! Even our pouch of coins.

We rush up the stairs and head through the courtyard to the Rua de São Pedro. Farid's fingers play against my shoulder blade. "Do you know where he was leaving from?" he gestures.

I shake my head. "But I think I know where he's gone. He wouldn't dare try to leave Portugal with Hebrew books. If he were caught— *pinga*. He must..."

"Berekiah!"

António Escaravelho, the New Christian beggar, is slumped in his usual spot across the street, calling to me.

"Have you seen anyone come from my house—out the courtyard gate?" I shout.

He nods and points down the street toward the Cathedral. "Set off that way just a little while ago."

Farid grabs my arm, signals, "So where's he gone?"

"To *trade* them. With what he stole and the ring I gave him, he could get anything he wanted. He could even buy the volumes of Plato he wanted."

Soft candlelight frames the shutters of Senhora Tamara's bookstore. "Blessed be He who opens the Gate of Vengeance," I whisper as the door handle turns in my hand. Farid comes panting to my side. I caress the wood open. We step inside.

Diego.

Surprise crosses his face for only a moment. He stands over the desk at the back of the room, wary, an owl's impenetrable silence concealing his thoughts. The books stolen from our *genizah* are piled by his feet. Senhora Tamara is seated on a stool, her hands linked in her lap. She speaks, but I do not hear. Behind her stands a wiry African slave with large, dull features and the imploded cheeks of a starving man. Confusion and fear crease his sweaty brow.

I fix the scene in my Torah memory.

Diego and I continue to stare at each other across a ritual space of flame-like heat and clarity. Senhora Tamara stands. Her mouth moves. The shadows on Diego's white robes tremble as he straightens up. My legs tense as if preparing me for flight. My heartbeat swells toward a grace akin to sexual power. Beneath his beard, I imagine the scar on his marble-white chin, red, lined with vertical stitches, a second mouth of betrayal and murder. "White Maimon of the Two Mouths," I whisper.

He slips a knife from his cloak, long, squared at the end; a *shohet's* blade. The slave takes a stiletto from his pouch. In his other hand, he clutches a cane ending in a serpent's head.

Senhora Tamara's words penetrate my nervous rage for the first time: "Berekiah, what's wrong?" She steps toward me.

"Leave!" I order her. My glaring eyes remain fixed on Diego.

She comes to Farid, presses desperate hands to his chest. "What's wrong, my boy? Tell me!"

"He killed Uncle," I say.

"Diego?!" She whips around to him. "Is this true?!"

He opens his hands palm up in a peacemaking gesture. "Of course I didn't," he replies.

I reach for the Senhora and tug her toward the door. "Go!" I shout.

She stands firm. Still keeping my eyes focused on Diego, I pull the door open. She resists my prodding, caresses my chin. "But dear boy, Diego said you had given him permission to trade the books...that your mother was too frightened to keep Hebrew books in her house."

"In the name of God, leave!" I say.

"What will you do?!" she demands.

I signal to Farid, "Stay here." I tug Senhora Tamara fighting and shrieking through the door.

Outside, she shouts at me in a voice entreating further explanation.

But a caped giant standing across the street in the shadow of a moonlit burlap awning draws my attention; he wears a wide-brimmed amethyst hat. "God bless Queen Esther," I whisper to myself.

The man and I talk in racing tones. He accepts my offering, thanks me in halting Castilian.

I rush into the bookstore again, lock the door behind me. Diego proffers an acknowledging bow and says, "There you are, Berekiah! I was just telling Farid here how surprised and pleased I am that Dona Meneses let you both live. But I'm never sure that he understands a thing I say."

"Farid understood more than you the day he was born," I remark.

A twinkle of humor is reflected in his eyes. "So condescending you always are. But really, who would expect her to show mercy now? Must be her Jewish blood coming to the fore."

"Why did you kill Uncle?" I ask.

"Why? You mean you haven't guessed that, too? You seem to have found out everything else. Too clever, you are, just like dear Carlos is always saying. Seville... Think of Seville."

"What about it?"

The door handle jiggles. Senhora Tamara begins knocking and calling for me.

"She won't give up," Diego says with a smile.

"None of us will," I reply.

"She must like you. We all do really. In spite of yourself. It's why I tried so hard to talk you out of continuing your troublesome search." When I frown, he says, "So where was I... Yes, Seville. It was there, of course. An accident. Your uncle had seen me. Too volatile, he was, all passion and energy. When you're like that, you create accidents. He was there to free Simon from the Inquisition. At my home, he pushed past my servants at the wrong moment carrying his ransom of lapis lazuli. The Bishop's legal assistant and I were discussing my...my salary. For informing on Simon and the others. Of course, I turned my back to your uncle immediately, left the room without another word. But he had a good Torah memory. Not as good as yours, but quite out of the ordinary."

"You went clean-shaven in those days," I observe.

"Yes. You figured that out too, did you? The beard was for Lisbon. A mask for every city is essential these days, don't you think?"

"Then you're not even a Levite?"

"No, I am. The lie does not have that many layers. But you were right. We don't all have beards. Even in orthodox Andalusia. No, I know you've never been. And now, if you're not careful, you'll never get a chance to go. And there's so much to see. The Alhambra, the great mosque of Cordoba. There are jewels in the walls there that..."

Farid brushes his hand along my spine. "You take the slave and I will take Diego. It will be a pleasure to end his life."

"Wait," I gesture back. To Diego, I ask, "Why did you inform on Simon and the others to the Inquisition?"

"So naïve you are." He grits his teeth and closes his fist. "When the Church surrounds you, squeezes you, you do what you are told. Anything you're told!" He smiles. His hand unfurls. "You Portuguese Jews have had a life of milk and honey—you wouldn't know."

"More smoke than milk and honey of late."

"That was just a small bonfire," he notes. "Wait a few years and things will really light up. Then you'll do what you're told or..." He pulls open his cloak, unties his shirt. The line of scar on his chest reflects the glare of candlelight. "...Or you'll pay with your flesh. I told you of the pictures they sear into your skin. My landscape had just begun. Can you see the horizon? If you come closer, you can make out the gates of Jerusalem." He closes his shirt. "This mortal body we have is weak. You'll find pain most disagreeable."

"After your beard was shaved last week, Uncle recognized you as the informer he'd seen in Seville," I say. "In the hospital, that discussion you had....my master's whirling gestures... It's why you were so desperate to have the beard kept, why you didn't like us visiting you."

"Another accident. Life is full of them. One gets used to it after a while. Though I expect that chance still bothers you. Your uncle didn't understand it either. Many things were beyond him. He wasn't a man of compassion. To have compassion, you must be like other men and he..."

"How dare you!" I shout.

"One who has lost his family can dare most anything!" he replies. "Why, look at you! Vengeance from a kabbalist? What would Uncle say?"

"He'd say that you lost your central core of soul long ago, that returning you to the Other Side was a *mitzvah*. Metatron will record your murder as a righteous deed."

"A convenient self-deception," he says.

"Deceptive conveniences are your specialty," I note.

He holds up his knife and proffers a bow. "My specialty is meat and fowl."

"You should have stuck to it."

"I didn't have a choice," he sighs. "Life tugs you. Like a tide. You can fight the ocean only so long. But you're too young to..."

"You discovered the girl, Teresa, in our cellar, when you went to see Uncle, didn't you?"

"He'd already pulled her to safety. He'd been bathing. The secret door to the bathhouse was open a crack so he could listen for anyone else needing help. I'd been coming to see him when the riot reached the Alfama. I'd put on a big wooden cross to protect myself, even blessed a few murderers along the way. Amazing what people will bless one another to do." He crosses himself and rolls his eyes. "As a pious Christian, I slipped inside your house."

"And so you killed him."

"Not so fast. You make everything sound easy. Life isn't Torah. You can't read the verses at top speed and reread them when you don't quite grasp what they mean. He wasn't reasonable. He said he'd have me judged by a Jewish council for informing on Simon all those years ago, that he'd find some way to see me punished. I knew your uncle well. He would have discovered some way to make my life hell. Even when I told him that I'd informed on Reza and her in-laws, that if he didn't desist I would do it again, he refused to listen. I thought it would convince him. I was silly to think that your uncle would behave like a normal father. And if he had ever told Dona Meneses that I had been the one black-mailing her, that I knew that she was Jewish, my life wouldn't have been worth the price of a turnip! Only his swearing on the Torah to keep our secret would have saved his life. And he refused."

"So you were responsible for Reza's imprisonment, as well."

"Whatever the situation demands. One must be flexible...change one's form according to circumstance. A beard and sumptuous clothes for Lisbon... In Constantinople, I may even become a Moslem. It's the same God, after all. Right Farid?"

As Farid signals something obscene in Diego's direction, I think: *A courier who cannot recognize his own face. Uncle meant Diego, the Wandering Jew, a courier not of books or merchandise, but his own soul.* I say, "And so what you wrote in Solomon's fake confession was true...applied to my uncle."

"Yes. The *mohel's* suicide was convenient. When I heard, I went there, paid a little ragamuffin to buy some paper from a witch who shreds linen, then left the note for Solomon's sister to find. Most people are so easily fooled."

"You told Uncle you'd spare the girl if he gave up his life?"

"Yes. He spoke of sacrifice. It meant a lot to him. I think he expected to die. 'For a greater good and higher purpose,' he said. He had strange ways of reasoning, don't you think? I told him, 'I could kill you without batting an eyelash.' And he answered, "And I could die without batting one either!' Imagine that! And imagine, at this late date, wanting to assemble a Jewish council! He never realized that it's the Christian year of fifteen and six, not the Hebrew year of fifty-two sixty-six. And dear Berekiah, it's time to reset your own clock before it's too late. Accept the Christian calendar before time runs out for you."

"You didn't go to see Uncle just to argue with him. You planted that silk thread of Simon's. You must have known beforehand that you were going to kill him."

"One must have a back-up plan. You can't begrudge me prudence."

"Prudence? You even wanted to kill me and Farid! That's why you sent the note for me to meet you by the water mills."

"Another good improvisation ruined by Dona Meneses and her henchmen."

"And you stole Uncle's Haggadah. Our lapis lazuli and gold leaf. Like a common thief!"

"Why not? Are you above such desires? I think not. And manuscripts. Yes, that was, after all, how this started. So it seemed..."

"But how did you find out about them? Simon and Carlos said you hadn't yet learned of the *genizah.*"

"Even a kabbalist makes mistakes, dear boy. Our friends were simply wrong. Your uncle approached me in secret, explained all about his smuggling activities, told me that he would be getting some valuable manuscripts and would need my vigilance in making sure his smugglers did their work—in particular, he was having doubts about Dona Meneses. He felt that she was growing weary of the risks she was taking. Your uncle feared betrayal. I began tracking her, learning her methods. I found out about Zerubbabel, how he took the manuscripts across the border to Cadiz. Master Abraham didn't want anyone to know that he'd told me about the *genizah* and his smuggling activities so that I would attract no special attention."

"He trusted you," I say.

"I'm afraid he did. A mistake. In our age, no one merits trust. Remember that if you remember nothing else."

"He should have asked me. If only he'd..."

"You still don't understand, do you?" Diego asks.

"Understand what, you bastard?"

"He couldn't risk your life. You were to be his heir, carry forward his plans for healing the Upper and Lower Realms...the greatest kabbalist Lisbon had ever seen! You don't risk such a man's life by getting him involved with smugglers. As it stands now, you'll probably be the last kabbalist of Lisbon." Diego shrugs and offers me a weak smile, as if accepting an inevitable truth. "No books, no kabbalists, no Jews. A shame, but such is life."

*Amazing,* I think, *that this murderer could understand so clearly what was hidden from me. Was I afraid of the responsibility? Or of being the last of my kind?* I ask Diego, "Why didn't you take all the books from the genizah when you killed him?"

"I was looking at the manuscripts, evaluating them, taking my time. I wasn't worried, knew that with the riot raging and my knowledge of the secret passageway to the bathhouse that I was safe. Then I came upon Master Abraham's last Haggadah. Beautiful work. I leafed through it and found my image as Haman, tore it out, of course, put the whole book in my pouch for safekeeping. To see my face in his illuminations, it was a shock... I was suddenly panicked. Silly, I suppose. I was about to go through the secret door when you began calling for your family from above. I started to go through, but I'm afraid that with my girth I couldn't make it. I turned back, entered the cellar again, closed the door after me. Just before..."

"Why didn't you just hide behind the secret door, in the passageway?"

"I'd never been through before. I worried that if I closed the door, some secret latch would fall and I'd be entombed there. Not a very nice fate that would be! So just before you came down, I managed to curl myself into the genizah and shut the lid. Thank goodness for all the banging you were making. By the time you came downstairs, I was safe in my nest. Though I was worried that you could hear my heartbeat, that I might have to kill you as well. But I was fairly confident that you'd be fooled at first, that you'd think Old Christians had done it. When you went upstairs, I emerged, locked the lid and put the key back in the eel bladder. I slipped out through your store to Temple Street. I didn't think anyone had seen me. But that Gemila... It's lucky for her she's such a hysterical cow with her hallucinated demons or I'd have had to..."

"Senhora Belmira? Why her?"

"Miriam? She was in love with me. Don't look surprised. I'm quite a nice man to those who... Remember the hours we spent sketching birds together? Anyway, it was safer that way. If she were caught, she'd have preferred death rather than give up my name. And she did. Women are stronger than men in that way. I learned that in the dungeons of Seville. They'll see their feet melted and still won't sell the Moses in their hearts to the Christians."

"The boy who went to sell Uncle's Haggadah to Senhora Tamara? Who was he?"

"I'm afraid that was my mistake. I got nervous. I have my frailties, as I've already admitted. As for the his identity, some things should remain a mystery, don't you think? His name is Isaac. He's a good, sweet child. It is all I'll tell you."

"The note that fell from your turban? Was it really about the Count of Almira or this Isaac?"

"Another mystery I will not solve for you. Sorry."

"So, now that you've got your Plato...?"

"I'll be leaving tonight as I said. By carriage to Faro. You can forget all about me."

"I won't let you leave," I note.

"You have no choice." Diego taps the edge of his knife against his slave's shoulder. "My new bodyguard is skinny but desperate," he says. "He wouldn't want to return to his old master. Put a bit in his mouth. Beat and fucked him senseless. They say he even knows spells. A regular black kabbalist if you ask me. From one of our lost tribes perhaps. You'd better just back outside and let us go. Or you'll end up with your soul separated from your body just like Master Abraham."

"And a curtain of blood across my neck. I'll never forget what you did to him!"

"Poetic words. Yours or Farid's?"

Diego picks up two leather-bound volumes from the desk. He motions the slave before him. The African crouches, holds his knife and cane out in front of his chest, slides forward.

Farid signals against my back, "You take the slave and..."

"No." I toss my knife to the floor, twist around, grip Farid's upraised arm.

He tugs against me, signals, "What do you think you're doing?!"

"Go now!" I shout to Diego. "I cannot hold him long!"

I wrap my arms around Farid, pin him back to a wall of books. Though he still grips his dagger, I know he'll never use it against me. As he struggles to break free, I shout again, "Leave, demon, before I change my mind!"

I press against Farid with the terrible strength of my vengeance. The slave and Diego rush past. "You've chosen wisely," the murderer hisses.

My eyes close tight as if to shut out sin as the bolt on the door clicks open. The night air, sharp and chill, blows against us. "Fly back to hell, Diego!" I whisper to myself.

"Berekiah!" Farid's voice comes garbled, honked, but clear as prayer. At the same time, his fist catches my shoulder and opens its old ache. With a sweeping kick, I manage to take his feet from under him.

The door slams closed. We are alone. A warm and bitter pleasure rises into my chest.

Farid jumps up, glares at me. I open my hands in a gesture of peace, take his shoulders. "You spoke!" I signal with a smile; it seems a crowning miracle atop all this debased horror, a sign from the Lord, perhaps, that I have chosen Diego's fate correctly.

With whirling gestures, Farid says, "Because you were letting him get away. It's all for nothing now. Nothing. Unless we can..."

"Don't worry," I signal. "Diego was wrong. Some men can be trusted. You shall see."

Outside, Senhora Tamara stands trembling in her bare feet and nightgown. As Farid wraps his arm around her, I spot Diego running down Goldsmith's Street behind his slave toward the Rua Nova d'El Rei. The moon lights him as a stealthy animal, a night creature fleeing hunters. To myself, I whisper words from Jeremiah: "He shall dwell among the rocks in the scorched wilderness, in a salt land where no man can live."

"But he's getting away!" Senhora Tamara moans. She gives me an imploring stare.

Her words etch a line of burning doubt across my gut. I start walking, then sprint ahead as if in search of Uncle.

A dark shadow suddenly crosses from the right. It trails Diego for a few moments, shows a hatted profile, swings closer. A glint of metal. An arm raised. When it falls, Diego melts to the cobbles. A sound like the knocking of Simon's gloved fist on our door is carried to me by the dry wind. It is unable to reach the gates of my compassion.

Farid, who has been running behind me, holds out a hand as I slow to a walk. He signals, "Who was..."

"One of Dona Meneses' killers," I answer. "He was waiting for Diego. He had orders not to strike until midnight just like we asked." I take out a few of the sapphire and emerald beads left from Dona Meneses' necklace. "But I changed the timing."

"You paid for him to kill Diego?!"

"He would have anyway. But I couldn't risk the wait. May God forgive me."

I cup the noblewoman's beads in my hand. "It only took one to convince him to kill Diego right away," I say. "A Jew's life, a man's life, costs almost nothing."

Approaching Diego on wary feet, we find him clutching his volumes of Plato. A line of blood runs from the corner of his mouth toward a speckled lizard asleep inside a crack in the cobbles. In his pouch is the vellum plate of Haman.

Inside a timeless silence, we watch the body as if we are facing an empty Torah ark that will never be filled. When I awake to myself, I step into the light of a candelabrum centering a nearby window and study Uncle's drawing. Yes, Haman is Diego. There is no mistake.

A shiver snakes up my spine as I consider that Uncle's last act of artistic creation was to illuminate the face of his own killer.

In the panel, Diego-Haman is a stooped and vulturine figure with an unmistakable line of scar across his chin. He is pictured whispering in King Ahasuerus' ear of his desire to exterminate the Jews. In his left, claw-like hand, he clutches a shimmering portion of the ten thousand talents of silver which he has promised to give to the royal treasury in exchange for approval to carry out his monstrous plan. In his right hand, at the same moment, he is receiving the royal signet ring from the King, a sign of permission granted.

The deal has been made.

Queen Esther is not pictured in the panel. But her step-father, Mordecai, is there. He stands humbly in the corner, in the sackcloth of mourning with which he clothed himself upon hearing of the decree for his people's destruction. His pose is one of pride, however, and his expression is wily, almost humorous. Undoubtedly because he holds in front of his chest the noose with which Haman will later be hanged. A spark of emerald passion in his eyes convinces me that Mordecai is modeled on Uncle himself.

Farid squeezes my arm, points to the drawing and signals, "It's you."

"What is?"

"The man in the corner. The one with the noose. Mordecai."

The pounding of my heart comes wild and forlorn. Could Farid be right? It doesn't seem possible that Uncle could illuminate me as the savior of the Jews. And the Mordecai pictured is simply too old.

My hands clutch the vellum. Tears come to my eyes when I consider that he may have gifted me with the guise of a Jewish hero.

So many questions I should have asked him will never be answered.

My glance is drawn into the sky by a moonlit sea gull crossing the night. Mosquitoes buzz at my ears as if seeking entry to my thoughts. My Hebrew prayer for Diego's peace, for the world's peace, comes edged with the texture of Uncle's hand squeezing hard at the back of my neck, then dropping away. His movement toward forever absence is so immediate that I gasp and turn around. My eyes survey the empty street until they reach the moist emerald light of two candles guarding over me from the highest window on the block.

# BOOK THREE

## Chapter XXI

In the vacant world beyond Diego's death, I slept for days on end. Behind the locked doors and sealed windows of my bedroom, inside a stifling atmosphere scented with my own rot. I got up from my bed again only when a vision of Joanna, the Count's daughter, descended like a silk veil across my face. Her eyes shimmered with the reflective grace of pearls, and she whispered to me in a language beyond understanding. Summoned into the night, my feet took me along the lumbering walls of Lisbon until a destination became obvious. I found myself howling up at what I hoped was her window at the Estaus Palace.

A dwarf with tufted hair opened his shutters. "I'll have you castrated if you don't stop your cock crows!" he cried.

"I'm searching for Dona Joanna, the Count of Almira's daughter," I explained.

"Not here!" he frowned. His shutters banged closed.

The putrid stench of dungheaps stalked me all the way home. Craving the void of *Ein Sof,* I sought refuge in my bed once again. Days of wavering edges followed, of mossy light and dark, until Joanna's voice pierced through my walls as if atop a winged prayer. When she entered my room, she was dressed in black. I was lying under my blankets.

"I cannot stay long," she said. Her eyes were glassy, as if tears might gush in them at any moment. "Have you been ill?" she asked in a hesitant voice.

"Yes," I said, sitting up. "I suppose so. Where have you been? I came looking for you."

"Here, in Lisbon, but I dared not come before now."

"I have never wanted a woman as much as I want you now," I confessed. "It's as if only you can heal me...or save me."

She sat at the edge of my bed and pressed the delicacy of her tiny, deformed hand to my lips. I was about to beg her to stay with me forever, but she shook her head as if I must not profane the silence between us. She began to unlace her dress. I was already naked. When she lay down beside me and opened her arms, I buried myself in her.

Walled inside her warmth, defended by the softness of her body, a tautness akin to prison rope snapped inside me and I was crying in a voice from so deep in me that it seemed to rip at my bowels. Joanna whispered, "I cannot stay. I am betrothed to another. Do not wait for me. I leave Lisbon tomorrow. Forgive me and forget me."

When the balm of her fingertips dropped from my cheek, she said again, "Do not wait for me. Do not withhold your love from the next one..."

In my hand, she left behind her pearl necklace.

When loved ones depart forever, all that remains is the light from their eyes trapped in their jewelry. Beyond memory, it is the only souvenir we ever keep.

Madness: if it doesn't swallow you whole, it may one day loosen its jaws from around your neck. Yet something—or someone—must help tug you free.

When I emerged in the morning, empty of Joanna, Farid read what had happened in my eyes. He dragged me to the Maidenhead Inn. For several months, I lived there, inside the warmth of Lisbon's temptresses, waiting no longer, clawing and thrusting my way into their life in order to retrieve my own. Farid paid, though from where he got the money I do not know. Maybe he sold some of Dona Meneses' sapphire and emerald beads; there were only three left when we finally bid goodbye to the Judiaria Pequena.

The miracle, of course, is that none of the diseases of brothels erupted inside me. Perhaps it takes a heart willing to suffer love to know such illnesses.

When I wasn't nestling inside a woman or squeezing the liquid arc of a wineskin into my mouth, I walked. Once as far as the amber hills above Mafra. Along the scorched dirt roads, I stopped to recite to myself each of the five books of the Torah: Genesis before the temple of Mount Abraham near Belas; Exodus under the bridge of a fallen pine tree beyond Montelavar; Leviticus over a Roman mosaic in Odrinhas; Numbers while balancing on a limb of a carob tree in front of the Visigothic church of Igreja Nova; and Deuteronomy over a honeycomb gifted me by an Old Christian girl just inside the gates of Linhó. The rhythm of walking is good for prayer, I discovered. Sleep, as well. The stars welcomed me at night without protest or judgment. Arrows of woodpeckers hurtling from tree to tree awoke me in the mornings. For a fortnight, I was safe beyond the confines of Lisbon.

Gradually, an energy akin to the rushed expectancy of chant began to surge in me, and I found it possible to work in our store during the day. Cinfa guarded me with fierce allegiance. She even lay beside me in my bed at night, looking up at me without criticism when I left for the ladies of the Inn in the wee hours of morning.

Reza and my mother fought their moralistic battles against me in silence, their condemning eyes as locked as prison gates. As for the world beyond my borders...

A flotilla of warships entered Lisbon's port on Monday, April the twenty seventh, and secured the city for the Crown. No justice was really attempted, of course. King Manuel, our *melekh hasid,* good and gracious king, spoke of the pogrom as "certain negligences." More to entertain the burghers and peasants than anything else, dear departed Manuel, may his name and his shadow be erased, ordered forty Old Christian rioters picked at random by his royal judge, João de Paiva. Before a crowd of several thousand basking in the sun-filled bleachers of the Rossio, the prisoners were garroted and burned.

Does charring Old Christian flesh smell any different than that of a Jew? I admit that I could tell no difference. "Ah, but if you'd been at the Rossio..." more than one New Christian told me with a caustic smile on his face.

As for the ecclesiastics of the São Domingos Church and Convent, King Manuel ordered the good friars dispersed throughout his kingdom at the end of May. Have no fear for their broken hearts and nostalgic members, however; they were back in their mistresses' arms in Lisbon by the end of October thanks to the intercession of Pope Julius II, may his name and its shadow be erased as well. Except for two of their number, I should add. Frei João Moucho and Frei Bernáldez, the two men who exhorted the rabble to mass murder that fateful afternoon before the São Domingos Church. Arrested and taken to Evora, they languished there for a time in the municipal dungeon. In October, when few people remembered anymore what they'd done, they were garroted and turned to ash.

It finally rained again on May the ninth.

But little of this do I remember. The first of March, fifteen and seven, is the only date that takes on hard edges for me. (Yes, for a time I learned to think within the Nazarene calendar. I take it as a symptom of my madness. May I forever cast out the Christian from within me!)

That morning, little Didi Molcho pulled me from our store as if toward treasure. "Run!" he shouted. We raced toward the voice of a crier on the steps of the São Miguel Church. He was reading a vellum decree from King Manuel: "Henceforth, New Christians will be allowed to leave my kingdom, and there shall be no..."

Hope for another landscape pulled my head into the sun. I breathed into swelling lungs for the first time since the death of Diego.

A barber shaved my beard while his daughter de-loused me. In her tiny hands, her comb digging my scalp, I began to consider for the first time how I'd paid for Diego's murder. Should I have felt the claws of sin in my chest? I didn't. And I don't now. Maybe that makes me a man bereft of a higher soul. I don't care. I look not in mirrors, and something in my face seems to elicit discretion from kabbalists who might be able to see a terrible absence in my aura.

And yet, another sin I committed long ago does sometimes trouble me—even penetrates my prayers. That young nobleman whom I pushed from a roof in the Moorish Quarter. Did he survive? I doubt it. Occasionally, in dream, I see him staring up at me from the bottom of a putrid well.

Mother and I gave all of Uncle's books to Dona Meneses. She got away with her murder of Simon, of course. Not only was I not in any position to cast stones at her, but I knew that any accusations I made would have dire consequences for me and my family. Guarded by her retinue of blond Flemings, she continued to live her charmed Old Christian life above her marble balcony in the Graça. From what I hear, she died four years ago, in the spring of fifteen twenty-six, of an infection caused by an idiot bleeder with slippery fingers.

After seeing my uncle in a dream, Father Carlos also asked Dona Meneses to smuggle to safety his part-Hebrew, part-Arabic copy of

Solomon Ibn Gabirol's *Mekor Hayim,* the Fountain of Life. As far as I know, it is now in Salonika.

Will any of our books survive the centuries, or will Uncle's fight have been in vain?

With all the New Christians leaving Portugal, houses could only fetch a fraction of their real value. Rather than sell for a pittance, we offered our home to Brites, our laundress; she lived in a slum beyond St. Catharine's Gate that wasn't fit for a person of her spiritual grace.

She stamped her feet when we told her and said, "I can't accept it!"

"You must," Aunt Esther insisted.

"No!"

"Then on loan," I suggested. "If Reza ever wants it back, she'll come for it."

Tears gushed in her eyes. The deal was sealed with hugs. She ended up spending the rest of her life there.

A few weeks later, just before leaving Portugal, while on a delivery of fruit to a store in the Bairro Alto, I spotted the boy in my drawing who had tried to sell Senhora Tamara my uncle's Haggadah. He had a naturally kind face, closely cropped black hair. "What's your name?" I asked him.

"Diego," he replied.

I whispered, "My Jewish name is Berekiah Zarco. I need to know what they call you in the holy language."

"Isaac Belmira Gonçalves," he said.

"A man named Diego Gonçalves adopted you, didn't he?"

His eyes opened wide with surprise. "Yes. How did you know?"

"I knew him well."

In a local inn, over steaming cinnamon bread and wine diluted with water, we talked of his adoptive father's love of birds and ancient manuscripts. The boy lived with Senhora Belmira's sister. He was shy, but a quick passion trembled his lips when he spoke of battle. He was going to be a crusader. I will never understand how it is that the young are so eager to die. Before we parted, I kissed his forehead and blessed him silently.

Rabbi Losa, the willing convert and enemy of my Uncle's, still lives in his house just below the São Miguel Church. He bowed and groveled his way into the Bishop of Lisbon's heart and has even become one of his advisors in ecclesiastic law. Both his daughters are grown and married, living together in Santarém, I'm told.

Father Carlos decided to stay in Portugal as well. "May God make me either a good Christian or a better actor," he said when I last saw him, twenty-three years ago. His words reminded me, of course, of Zerubbabel, Isaac of Ronda, the Count of Almira. I have heard nothing of his fate. Maybe his real name was something else entirely. Maybe he wasn't even Castilian or New Christian. Perhaps Joanna wasn't even his daughter.

Of course, I have heard nothing from her. Yet, on occasion, even today, she still descends into my dreams. The bitterness is gone from her lips, however, and I ceased forcing comparisons with my wife years ago. Even a Torah memory melts with tears.

Neither have I had news from Helena, the girl to whom I was betrothed so many years ago and with whom I lost my virginity. It is better that way.

In May of fifteen and seven, as we were making plans for departure, a merchant in scarlet and white robes came to our house with a letter from the New Christian beggar, António Escaravelho. Just after the riot against us, long before King Manuel's decree allowed New Christians to leave Portugal, he was able to secure his exit permit to visit his beloved Pope Julius.

"Do you know if he's doing well in Rome?" I asked the courier.

"Rome, what are you talking about?! He's in Jerusalem. Already got himself a silversmith shop in the old Jewish Quarter."

I ripped open the letter's wax seal: "Dearest Berekiah, I told you and Master Abraham that you should plan to come with me. This old donkey wasn't so crazy after all, was he? Fuck Pope Julius. I spit on the whole Italian peninsula. May a plague of venomous serpents descend on Rome and bite all its Christian residents in their fat asses. You will always be welcome with me. Next year in Jerusalem."

Not next year, but perhaps soon. After all, we have moved closer. And I'm not getting any younger. If I'm ever going to go...

In July of fifteen and seven, Farid took a boat to Constantinople, carrying the address of Tu Bisvat and what money we could spare. Mother, Cinfa, Esther, Afonso Verdinho and I followed him in August, our ship setting sail from Belem on the nineteenth of Av. To our surprise, a ramshackle two-story house in the small Jewish quarter was waiting for us; with help from Tu Bisvat, whose true name I am not at liberty to mention, Uncle had been able to make a small down payment on some property.

Roseta remained behind with Reza; she was pregnant with her first child—Reza, not Roseta, that is—and moved with her husband and Aviboa up to a farm near Belmonte in the mountains in northeast Portugal. I haven't seen them since the dock at Belem. They have three surviving sons, Mordecai, Judah and Berekiah, and a daughter, Mira. Aviboa is married to a farmer of chestnuts and wine. She lives nearby, has two surviving children. She never did grow a thumbnail or receive news of her parents.

We pray that the fire of the Inquisition will pass over their valley when it spreads into Portugal from Castile. I fear that it is now only a matter of months. So little time for peace we have in this world.

Judah. When I could get his trousers and shirts away from my mother, I buried them on the Almond Farm, by Uncle's grave. We said a *kaddish* to ensure that his soul was set free from the Lower Realms.

Twenty-four years have passed since his disappearance and yet, he's still just a whisper away. Only three years ago, I believed I recognized his moonstone eyes in a man in Portuguese merchant's garb sunning his face in the garden below the southeast minaret of the Hagia Sophia mosque. My heart boomed as if shot from a cannon. Dizziness swayed me. I thought: *It's all a mistake. He's alive, been raised by Old Christians. And he'll explain now where he's been.* I crept to him and said, "Is it you, Judah?" At his confusion, I took his arm. "Don't you recognize me? It's Berekiah. Your brother!"

He patted me on the back as if I were a drunken old fool. "Better get home to your wife before she comes looking for you," he advised. He laughed at me.

Such is what the younger generation make of sorrow.

Samir, Farid's father, was never heard from again.

I remember Rabbi Verga telling me in our courtyard that we must remember the dead and how they lost their lives. His words make me smile; are there really persons who can forget?

It turns out that Samson Tijolo, who crossed out all of the names of God in his Old Testament, was right about Jews not being able to speak a future tense in Portugal. Had Uncle lived, could he have done anything about that? There are certain powers which great kabbalists have, and perhaps if he had concentrated...

Or is that all a lie? So much of my faith flowed away with my master's blood.

Rana, Samson's wife and my old neighborhood friend, still lives on her farm outside Lisbon. Miguel, her son, apprenticed to a silversmith. Late at night, behind locked shutters, he makes Torah pointers and other holy objects, I'm told.

Our neighbor, Senhora Faiam, died in fifteen-twelve. Gemila and her family are living in their old house as secret Jews. Their dog, Belo, died without ever finding the bone for his missing leg, of course. Some vestiges of life can never be recovered. Although that doesn't stop us from searching.

I think often of the lemon tree growing above Senhora Rosamonte's hand. So nice it would be to be tossed some of her fruit.

How does Uncle's almond tree grow? His death still carves deep furrows inside me in the early morning, when the dew sits on my forehead and my resistance is lowered. Lately, I've realized that I'm like a tree whose main limbs were cut with a *shohet's* knife. From the scars, I succeeded in branching out as best I could. I flowered even. Many times. But the tree is just not the same as it would have been. How much more upright I would have grown had he...

Forty-four years have watched me pass. I am an old man, with children of my own. Yet how dearly I would love to be fixed in Uncle's emerald eyes, to feel the protective wing of his white robe unfurl around me. To kiss his lips. Never will it be. Not even were I to chant the Zohar every night for an entire year.

Murça Benjamin persevered after her wish to fulfill the obligation of Levirite marriage was refused. She married a wealthy New Christian barrel maker from Porto—a good man, she wrote to me—and works as a translator for merchants in São João da Foz.

Manuel Monchique, whose wife, Teresa, died alongside Uncle, emigrated to Amsterdam and is one of the directors of a banking institution there. I hear that he has developed an interest in sea voyages and has even traveled to Brazil, where he has made lovely sketches of the native butterflies. He no longer lugs around a sword.

So maybe one can find one's way home in another country.

Before we left Lisbon, my mother was kind enough to sew a new aba for Attar, the man who lent me his clothing as I fled through the Moorish Quarter on that fateful Sunday of Jewish death. He welcomed me with a hug. Before I left his home, I'd eaten an entire chicken bathed in prunes and lemon. We locked hands to pray in silence, then recited suras from the Koran together.

Isaac Ibn Farraj, the ascetic who rescued his friend's head from the pyre in the Rossio, ended up in Valona and is a successful scribe. I met him by accident once in Rhodes after it was taken by the Turks, and he looked as if he hadn't eaten a thing since he'd left Lisbon. Goat ribbed, he was. With a beard like a white fungus. Apparently he'd learned a thing or two about the new fruits arriving from the New World, because he kept repeating to me, "Beware of tomatoes!"

Dom Miguel Ribeiro, the nobleman who learned of his Jewish origins from Uncle, still lives in Lisbon as a secret Jew. He lost an eye in a hunting accident shortly after we left. I suppose that he simply could not give up one last Old Christian vice.

Oh, a curious thing happened to Didi Molcho. He rose through the ranks of the Portuguese court system to become a royal secretary. Then, as he recounts it, there appeared before King João, King Manuel's heir, a swarthy little Jew with glowing eyes akin to my uncle's claiming to be a representative from the lost tribe of Reuben in the desert wilds of Arabia. His called himself David Reubini, and he came to Portugal hoping to gain troops for a plan to win back Jerusalem from the Turks. Although King João soured of him, Didi was captivated. He embraced Judaism once again and circumcised himself. His study of the kabbalah brought on visions ending in prophecy.

Using his Jewish name of Solomon, Didi journeyed to Italy to preach, and the accuracy of his predictions earned him fame amongst Christians and Jews alike. In May of fifteen twenty-nine, after exchanging correspondence, I received him in my home in Constantinople and, over the next six months, helped him learn Abulafia's techniques for untying the knots of mind. His book of sermons, based partly on our studies together, was published in Salonika that same year. He's back in Rome now, following his visions, and has even gained Pope Clement's favor. I fear for his life, however. Popes are envious of men with true faith and as devious as famished ferrets. And Didi, God bless him, has had his earthly vision clouded by higher landscapes.

Farid lives just down the street from us, has had his poetry published with success here in Constantinople. His lover of seventeen years is a blacksmith named Shamsi who plays the oud and sings with the voice of a rustic flute. He's an outgoing, humorous man with lean muscles and eyelashes like black rose petals. Not gifted with the dimensions of a Basque, of course, but he seems to keep Farid satisfied. Years ago, they adopted two orphan boys, Samir and Rumi. They were always good, if somewhat rough, playmates for my girl, Zuleikha, and boy, Ari.

We all eat together every night. It is a great comfort to me to be able to converse with Farid with my hands. Sometimes, when memory assaults me and I haven't the will to hear my words...

When we were last in Lisbon together, all those years ago, I asked Farid, "Will God be waiting for us in Constantinople, you think? He's disappeared without a trace from Lisbon."

His hands twirled up and around, quoting Uncle: "You must knock upon yourself as upon a door. It is there where you will find Him if He still exists for you."

I have waited for a reply to my rapping these many years. Apparently, one must play the ever-willing woodpecker to this hard-of-hearing God, and I simply haven't the beak.

So maybe I have found that secular landscape I predicted so many years ago. The one toward which I sense the world is moving, with neither rabbis nor priests, populated only by mystics and non-believers. Which one of these groups will finally win the throne of my heart, I cannot say.

My daughter, Zuli, is eighteen now, wants to be a scribe like Aunt Esther. But I see more of Reza in her. Naturally aristocratic, with passionate eyes that dance when she talks. And when she's angry, she intimidates me with the lambent glare she used to practice in looking glasses.

Ari, who is sixteen, has a strong build, my wife's curly black hair, Uncle's intelligent and penetrating eyes. He has studied to be an illuminator and could make a fine artist one day. But he's dreamed of sailing off to adventure in the New World since he was a child.

"A Jewish manuscript illuminator in the jungles of Brazil would be like a matzah on the moon," I've always told him.

The other day, he came up with this reply: "But some of the Indians there are circumcised. Tu Bisvat says they're Jews."

Sounds a little like me as a young man, no? I wonder what Uncle would make of him. I suppose that if he really wants to go to Brazil, maybe he should become a *mohel*.

The loss of Judah and Uncle condemned my mother to a life on the margins of emotion. She began sewing garments for the Turkish aristocracy in Constantinople and took impeccable care of the fruit store we opened here, but shied away from all gestures of approach. Conversation, even with Aunt Esther, came to her with difficulty. In the early morning, I caught her several times standing vigil over my bed with the inhuman stoicism of a sculpted goddess on a ship's prow. Whenever I needed to voyage far from home, she would pat my hand, then turn quickly away, as if it were already too late to hope for my return. Prayers and chants only made her anxious. Henbane helped some. She died during Passover almost eight years ago.

As for Aunt Esther, she and I reconciled years ago, right after Diego's death, in fact. Why should I have kept a grudge against her and Afonso Verdinho? Had I the right to deny her whatever companionship the world could still give her? Just before we left for Constantinople, he rode into the Little Jewish Quarter bearing a gold engagement ring. Just like a cavalier in some Arabian legend. They were married when we reached Turkish shores.

So, as my own life should prove, love is not always limited to a single object. And I've no doubt that Aunt Esther loved Uncle and would have given up her life for his. Once, while she was bathing, I opened the lid of her silver locket and found several of Uncle's long gray hairs. I stole a single strand and ate it.

Esther's a very old lady now, nearing seventy. But her work as a scribe in Hebrew, Arabic, Persian, Castilian and Portuguese continues to be without equal. She and I recently completed a copy of "The Conference of the Birds" for Sultan Suleiman the Magnificent, may God bless him each and every day. No notes or drawings were left to me from my birdwatching expeditions back in the hills beyond Lisbon, but my Torah memory is still complete enough to gift me with the curve of a crane's beak and the tone of an owl's gorget.

The peacocks I included were of Uncle's design. I like to think that he would be proud of our artistry.

Cinfa. Life has not been easy for her. No sooner was she gifted with a baby girl named Mira six years ago than did she become a widow. Her husband was an eye doctor from Alexandria. A lean and soft-skinned man, with the kindly look of someone who always forgives.

And yet, we soon learned that he drank anise seed aqua vitae like a Greek sailor. And that he didn't like that I educated his wife in Torah and Talmud. None of this was evident before their marriage. I'd quite forgotten about masks after leaving Lisbon.

When Cinfa was seven months pregnant, he beat her with a cane across the face. "Your sister corrected my Sabbath prayers," he told me after I'd seen the tender blue and yellow bruises puffing from her eyes and cheeks. His tone implied: *I had to do it.*

"As well she should have, you lout!" I replied. "The Sabbath is more important than your skinny pride!"

He apologized because of my spiritual standing as an eccentric but learned kabbalist in the community, but I saw in his defiant eyes that he was hardly repentant. I'm not much of a fighter and resorted to trickery. While I blessed my hand over his head in feigned forgiveness, I kicked him so hard in the balls that he writhed on the ground for a good five minutes. I screamed, "And if you ever do it again...!"

When I explained what I'd done to Aunt Esther, she said, "That's about as practical as the kabbalah ever gets! Good work!"

But maybe I shouldn't have tempted him with my warning. The brute repeated his evil deed the next day.

Farid then accompanied me to their home. He held his dagger to the eye doctor's chin and had me translate his signalling: "Ever touch her again with any intention other than love and I'll cut your eyeballs out!"

Later, Farid told me, "Always threaten a man with something he knows the value of."

It seemed like good advice. But brutes don't change without God's grace. In her eighth month, the Egyptian doctor kicked Cinfa down the stairs of their home. Broke her right leg and her collar bone. Cinfa had the baby while splayed on the ground. Her screams alerted Zuli and the neighbors. We would have lost little Mira except for their quick work.

I searched for the evil doctor with Farid. Couldn't find him anywhere. A month later, he turned up dead outside a nearby brothel. Apparently, he got a little fresh with a prized Yemenite girl. As Aunt Esther observed, "Not much risk in beating a Jewish wife. But raise a hand to a high-priced Moslem whore and you won't last too long."

Leci, my wife, is gifted with that ironic way of thinking as well. Didn't start out that way, though. She's the daughter of a shoemaker who became our first friend here in Constantinople. When I met her, she had long, henna-tinted black-red hair, green eyes of restricted longing that always seemed afraid to ask a secret question. Lips sealed to silence. Maybe it was the death of her mother when she was just five.

Frightened she was when I met her, spiritually shivering. And yet, she had the sexual sleekness of a wet cat. When she moved, she seemed to drag the ground and air with her.

I came to her one evening when her father was out of town. Appeared in silhouette in her doorway. She'd been reading. After sharing a look connoting secret adventure, she lay her book on her chest and blew out her candle. Without words, I lifted away my shirt and stepped out of my pants.

When our desires rose beyond the explorations of our mouths and hands, she climbed on top. Bracing herself as if before an altar, she sheathed herself down upon me.

Can the perfect fit of a couple's sexual organs be symbolic of a spiritual correspondence?

As she gyrated her wet warmth over me, I pictured my old friend Rana Tijolo suckling her baby, Miguel. I buried my head deep in the warmth of Leci's breasts and thought: *Here is the woman I will give myself to.*

And so it has been. More than my manuscripts, more than my studies of kabbalah, I consider my life's accomplishment what I have given her and my children. It hasn't always been good, or even enough, but I have offered what I've had without any mask.

Which leads me to the reason I have taken up my reed pen once again and told you our story.

As I said at the beginning of our tale, I had a visitor just yesterday, around midday: Lourenço Paiva, the son of our old laundress and friend, Brites. Before his mother's death, she had asked him to come and offer me back ownership of our old house at the corner of the Rua de São Pedro and Rua da Sinagoga, to see if I wanted to return home.

With our old house keys biting into my closed fist, I turned away into a vision of Portugal: Cork trees and poppies. Roseta and her collar of cherries. Mordecai and my father. Lisbon's houses of white and blue. Rossio Square. The mirror of river beyond our old synagogue. The sweet scent of the oleander bushes in our courtyard. Judah and Uncle. The graves on the Almond Farm.

Then, a vision opened inside me, one in which my master tossed me Portuguese letters knotted into a chain which read: *as nossas andorinhas ainda estão nas mãos do faraó*—our swallows are still abandoned to

Pharaoh. As my gaze passed over these words of New Christian code a second time, they lifted into the air, then broke with a tinkling sound.

When I came to, my chest was pounding a verse that said: *I have a chance to go home.*

And that's when isolated events in my Torah memory suddenly linked together into a reading of the past which I believe my uncle had counted on me to make so many years ago.

I reached for my wine carafe and grabbed the vellum ribbon on which Aunt Esther had written my name and Uncle's—the ribbon which he gave me just before his death, when he promised to come to my aid no matter what the circumstances. Alone in my prayer room, I remembered the terrible verses from Genesis about the sacrifice of Isaac which my master made me recite to Judah that fateful Passover... He had explained to us that in order to achieve the highest of goals, the self had to be extinguished. He had meant *his* self.

Before his death, in our cellar, Uncle had posed questions to me about my willingness to leave Portugal. He spoke of his grave fears that my mother and Reza would never be willing to depart. These fears betray his motivation; he was implying that only the most terrible tragedy could sever my mother and Reza—his only living child—from Portugal.

Even the words of my uncle's which were quoted by Diego in the bogus suicide note he wrote for Solomon the *mohel* make reference to an occult reason for his death: "Your iron blade will anneal me to God and maybe even serve a higher purpose."

What higher purpose could his death have served? What was my master thinking?

Over the last twenty-four hours, I have let my speculations mingle with my questions till they formed a knotted pattern which refused to release me. So I took down my ink well from its shelf and got out the manuscript which I had originally written in the Christian year of fifteen and seven and which—with a few minor alterations—has now become what I refer to as Book One. And that's when I began to complete our story for you.

*Mesirat nefesh,* the willingness to risk everything for a goal that will effect reparations in the Lower and Upper Realms. Only now do I believe that I understand how such unspoken courage lit Uncle's emerald eyes, moved his hands to bless the world.

"I swear to protect you from the dangers which dance along the way," he had pledged to me when I was but eight. Yes, he had lived up to his words. For here I was, safe, in Constantinople!

What I am trying to say, fitfully, hesitantly, because of my own failing strength and the effect of too much Anatolian wine, is that Uncle sacrificed himself. In part, probably, to try to save the girl, Teresa, who was murdered alongside him. But more importantly, I believe that he let himself be killed *for the generations to come.* To force my mother and Reza—our entire family—to leave Portugal. To enable our family tree to take root securely in another land. A land with soil willing to accept Jews without masks.

Not that I'm theorizing that my uncle willed Diego down into his cellar or brought him there through practical kabbalah. No. But perhaps Uncle suspected that he'd receive a visit. Whatever the case, there came a moment—maybe only when Diego descended the cellar stairs—when my master began to understand the *true* meaning of the riot against us, when he saw the possibilities which would spring from his death at the hands of a murderer. For better or for worse, he concluded that our family, our people, had reached a terrible impasse, and that only his violent death would compel us to break through.

Is this theory insanity? Maybe so. Maybe only God knew that my uncle was going to be sacrificed that Passover.

And yet there is more evidence to support my theory, a bit of proof which may convince you that what I say is at least possible.

Years ago, Farid claimed that the drawing of Mordecai in Uncle's last Haggadah was modeled on my face, that I was cast as the savior of the Jews from the Book of Esther. I didn't think it possible; Mordecai appeared far too old in the drawing.

I reasoned, too, that even if Uncle *had* modeled this hero's face upon my own, it was because he had had a mystical inkling that I would later take revenge on his Haman—Diego.

In examining this illuminated panel yesterday, however, I discovered something astounding. Mordecai looks very much as I do now, twenty-four years after Uncle drew him. We share the same closely cropped graying hair, the same weary eyes—both of us survivors, but witnesses to tragedy as well.

You see, Uncle had so discerning an eye that he was able to paint what I would look like nearly a quarter of a century into the future.

So only now do I begin to accept that my master had gifted me with a greater purpose, had divined that I, like this ancient Jewish hero, would one day fight to save our people.

And I am convinced that this is the reason why—in the vision I had yesterday—my uncle called me "Mordecai." He wasn't using my older brother's name, as I originally thought, but that of the Biblical saviour of our people.

Yet how had he intended for me to rescue them—I, Berekiah Zarco, a man who no longer even believes in a personal God?

Your hands are touching the answer; I suspect that Uncle sensed that only the nightmare of his death would compel me to write this very book which you are now reading. That only his violent departure from the Lower Realms would make me see that our future in Europe was finished. That only the most terrible tragedy could convince me to beg all the Jews—every last one of us, whether New Christian or not—to move to where we will be safe from the Inquisition and whatever other horrors the Christian kings will one day dream up for us.

For if there is one thing we can say about the European monarchs it is that they have no shortage of dreams about the Jews. We haunt them in their spiritual darkness.

If you don't admit that there is even a small chance that these speculations are a valid reading of his actions, then I wish you well in your loneliness; it is clear you have never known anyone with my uncle's spiritual strength, with causeless, unconditional love for you, who would sacrifice himself for your survival.

Or perhaps it would be more appropriate for me to pity my own talents as a writer; my tale has not succeeded in convincing you that Master Abraham Zarco was real. I apologize. But now I tell you, and you must find the courage to believe: there exist men and women with such passionate resolve that they will willingly give up their lives for generations of children whom they will never even meet.

So I was wrong all those years ago when I told my old friend Rana Tijolo that Uncle still believed Jews could speak in the future tense in Portugal. He knew then that there was only the past for us in Iberia and in all the Christian lands of Europe. Can you believe it was mere whimsy that made him plan for us to move to a *Moslem* land, to Turkey?

No accidents, no coincidences. Is it possible?

So far, I have only dared to tell Farid of my theories, and in reply he signalled, "But don't you think Uncle could have done more for the Jewish people alive than dead?"

A good question. Events may have moved too quickly for my master to control them. And as I say, he may have only understood his purpose in a flash of insight, just as Diego tossed a rosary around his neck.

I believe that he trusted that God could make better use of him dead than alive.

In any event, I have no answer except the faith which burns in my gut. But even if my theory is dreadfully wrong, I still dare not put my pen down or tear up these pages. I cannot bet the survival of the Jews on the righteousness of European Kings who have shown time and again that they bear no sense of justice. Because even if I'm wrong, even if I am reading from left to right, even if my master was so exhausted from his vigil for Reza that he could not lift his hands to fight Diego, can you be sure that the Christians won't one day come for you, for all of us? That traitors like Diego won't help them?

And so, we finally come to Diego and to what the *true* meaning of his betrayal might be. This I have asked myself many times, of course.

The key to my interpretation of his actions resides in the kabbalistic definition of evil—*good which has departed from its rightful place.*

I believe that Diego was a man who could have flourished amongst his own people. In living with Old Christians, however, in having to struggle against the terror which their Church and Inquisition inspired in him, he turned to evil.

And so I believe that there will be many others like Diego who will conspire against us unless we move from Europe. That, too, is part of the meaning of Uncle's death.

As for my hesitation to speak of this... Not surprisingly, part of me would like to dismiss my words as rubbish. For if my faith points toward the truth, then I have failed my uncle miserably. Twenty-three years ago, I allowed my cousin, Reza, to remain behind in Portugal. May Uncle forgive me. For if he is right, if my reading of the verses of the past is correct, then her family is doomed.

That is why I must take the blessed keys dear Lourenço has given me and re-enter Portugal's gates. This manuscript is the weapon which I will carry with me. May its words string together to form the noose that will hang Haman.

Farid says he will accompany me, that I will need his protection.

Perhaps he is right. Together, we will fetch Reza and her family and bring them back to Constantinople.

May all the New Christians and Jews accompany us.

And may my children and wife understand my reasons for leaving.

The first thin light of dawn has just pierced my window shutters, and my wrist aches. It is time for me to reach into my ink well for the last few strokes of my pen. Let the angels behind my words press understanding into my soul and yours.

As I said at the very beginning, this is a story of warning. You who read these words, whether Jew or New Christian, Sephardi or Ashkenazi, if the borders of Europe still enclose you, then you are in grave danger. The Inquisition will spread, and very soon our Bleeding Mirror will run with blood as it never has before. That is why Uncle appeared to me now. The killing is only just beginning. You can be assured, the European kings and their hateful bishops will never stop dreaming of us. They will never allow you and your children to live. Never! Sooner or later, in this century or five centuries hence, they will come for you or your descendents. No village, no matter how remote, will be safe. No aristocrat or foreign army will come to protect you. This is the meaning I make of Uncle's death. So take off your mask. Face Constantinople and Jerusalem. And start walking.

Cast out Christian Europe from your heart and never look back!

Blessed are all of God's self-portraits.

Berekiah Zarco, Constantinople
The Seventh of Av, 5290

# Glossary

**Adar**  The sixth month of the Hebrew lunar calendar, generally coinciding with part of February and part of March.

**Anusim**  Hebrew word for Jews forced to convert to Christianity.

**Asmodeus**  The king of the Jewish demons.

**Av**  The eleventh month of the Hebrew lunar calendar, generally coinciding with part of July and part of August.

**Ba'al Shem**  In kabbalistic texts, a title applied to mystics who possess secret knowledge of the holy names of God and who can make magical use of such knowledge.

**Bahir**  The Book of Light. An influential kabbalistic text discovered in Provence in the 12th century.

**Challah**  A jewish egg bread.

**Chametz**  Food which Jews are forbidden to eat during Passover, especially leavened bread.

**Chazan**  The leader of prayers and chief singer of the liturgy in a synagogue.

**Ein Sof**  The hidden God which cannot be perceived, described or in any way approached. The existence and nature of such a God can only be deduced from its emanations or attributes in our world.

**Elohim**  One of the names of God.

**Genizah**  A depository for sacred books.

**Golem**  A creature, usually in human form, created by magical means through the use of holy names, particularly the Tetragrammaton.

**Haggadah**  The text containing both the story of the Exodus and the ritual of the ceremonial meal which is eaten in celebration of Passover. Jewish manuscript illuminators from Iberia and other parts of Europe frequently illustrated Haggadahs with Biblical scenes.

**Halizah**  Biblically prescribed ceremony performed when a man refuses to marry his brother's childless widow.

**Haman**  A Persian courtier who plotted to massacre the Jews (from the Book of Esther).

**Hanukkah**  A Jewish festival held in the winter which celebrates the victory of the Maccabees, a Jewish tribe, over the Syrians in 165 B.C.

**Heshvan**  The second month of the Hebrew lunar calendar, generally coinciding with part of October and part of November.

**Haroset**  A mixture of chopped fruits, nuts and spices eaten on Passover and representing the mortar used by Hebrew slaves in building for the Egyptian Pharaoh.

**Ibbur**  An evil spirit or wandering soul of a deceased person that enters the body of a living person and controls his or her behavior.

**Kaddish**  The prayer for the dead which is recited by mourners.

**Kislev**  The third month of the Hebrew calendar, generally coinciding with part of November and part of December.

**Kosher**  Fit for human consumption, according to Jewish dietary laws.

**Lez**  A mischievous Jewish demon or poltergeist.

**Levite**  A person belonging to the religious caste of priests descended from Levi, son of Jacob.

**Lilith**  In Jewish legends, a female demon who strangles children and seduces men. She is sometimes regarded as the queen of all that is evil.

**Magen David**  A six-pointed star used as a symbol of Judaism.

**Maimon**  A powerful Jewish demon.

**Matzah**  Unleavened bread baked by the Israelites during the Exodus from Egypt and eaten during the holiday of Passover. The only ingredients are flour and water.

**Menorah**  A candelabrum generally having seven or nine branches which is lit during the fesitval of Hanukkah.

**Metatron**  The heavenly angel who records good deeds.

**Mezuzah**  A small case containing a piece of parchment upon which is written the particular Jewish prayer which begins "Hear O Israel." This case is affixed to the doorpost of a Jew's home and was sometimes regarded as offering protection against the attacks of demons.

**Micvah**  Ritual bath in which women immerse themselves following menstruation. It is also used by men for purposes of ritual purification.

**Mitzvah**  A divine commandment. There are 613 such commandments in the Torah. It can also mean any good deed.

**Mohel**  A person trained to perform ritual circumcisions. Jewish male children are generally circumcised on the eighth day after birth.

**Mordecai**  Jewish courtier who thwarted Haman's plan to massacre the Persian Jews (from the Book of Esther).

**Neshamah**  The divine spark of God in man; the soul.

**Nezah** Divine endurance.

**Nisan** The seventh month of the Hebrew lunar calendar, generally coinciding with part of March and part of April.

**Passover** The Jewish festival commemorating the escape of the Hebrew people from bondage in Egypt, traditionally celebrated for eight days in the spring.

**Purim** A Jewish holiday which celebrates the downfall of Haman's plan to massacre the Persian Jews.

**Rahamim** Divine compassion.

**Rosh Hashanah** The Jewish New Year.

**Samael** The name of Satan in Judaism.

**Seder** The traditional ceremonial meal eaten on the first and sometimes second nights of Passover. (Christ's Last Supper was a Jewish seder.)

**Sefer** Hebrew for "book."

**Sefirot** The ten aspects or manifestations of God, sometimes represented as divine lights and often associated with the Cosmic Tree, the names of God and various parts of the human body.

**Sitra Ahra** The kabbalistic term for the domain of evil emanations and demonic powers (The Other Side).

**Shefa** A divine influx or moment of divine presence.

**Shevat** The fifth month of the Hebrew lunar calendar, generally coinciding with part of January and part of February.

**Shofar** A ram's horn blown to produce a trumpet sound during certain Jewish rituals.

**Shohet** A Jewish butcher specially trained in the techniques governing the slaughter of animals.

**Tallis** A rectangular prayer shawl.

**Talmud** An ancient compilation of Jewish Oral Law which includes rabbinical commentaries.

**Tefillin** Phylacteries.

**Tishri** The first month of the Hebrew calendar, generally coinciding with part of September and part of October.

**Torah** The Pentateuch or first five books of the Old Testament. In a broader sense, it can refer to the complete Old Testament or even all of Jewish teaching.

**Tref** Food unfit for human consumption and which must be discarded according to Jewish dietary laws.

**Tzitzit** The fringes which dangle from the four corners of a Jewish prayer shawl.

**Tu Bisvat** A Jewish holiday connected with the Tree of Life and the eating of fruit associated with the land of Israel.

**Yom Kippur**  The holiest Jewish holiday, on which Jews fast to atone for their
sins.

**Zedek**  Divine Justice.

**Zohar**  The Book of Splendor. The most influential book of kabbalistic mysticism, written in Guadalajara, Spain, between 1280 CE and 1286 CE, by
the Jewish mystic Moses de Leon.